VIAL OF TEARS

CRISTIN BISHARA

HOLIDAY HOUSE • NEW YORK

Library of Congress Cataloging-in-Publication Data

Names: Bishara, Cristin, author.
Title: Vial of tears / Cristin Bishara.
Description: First edition. | New York : Holiday House, [2021] | Audience:
Ages 14 up. | Audience: Grades 10–12. | Summary: When Samira receives a
strange vase with some ancient coins, she and her sister Rima are pulled
into Baalbek, a Phoenician underworld where they are caught up in the
struggle between deities, shapeshifters, and ghouls—and Eshmun, who
wants his obol, his burial coin, back.
Identifiers: LCCN 2021014704 | ISBN 9780823446414 (hardcover)
ISBN 9780823450343 (ebook)
Subjects: LCSH: Phoenician antiquities—Juvenile fiction.
Sisters—Juvenile fiction. | Shapeshifting—Juvenile fiction.
Monsters—Juvenile fiction. | Magic—Juvenile fiction. | CYAC:
Phoenician antiquities—Fiction. | Sisters—Fiction.
Shapeshifting—Fiction. | Monsters—Fiction. | Magic—Fiction. | LCGFT:
Fantasy fiction.
Classification: LCC PZ7.B5239 Vi 2021 | DDC [Fic]—dc23
LC record available at https://lccn.loc.gov/2021014704

ISBN: 978-0-8234-4641-4 (hardcover)

For my family,
always close
no matter how far.

Paradise is there, behind that door, in the next room; but
    I have lost the key.
        Perhaps I have only mislaid it.

—Kahlil Gibran, from *Sand and Foam*

PROLOGUE
Karm El Mohr, Syria (modern-day Lebanon), 1903

On the night his mother disappeared, the boy had tiptoed to her room to ask for a glass of water.

The moon shone through the windows, casting a glowing walkway across the floor. The air was fragrant with blossoming orange trees. He would tell her that he couldn't sleep, that lately his dreams had been strange. Had hers been, too?

It was an uncertain time. The Turks had been coming without warning. They galloped through the village taking whatever they wanted—livestock, clothing, jewelry, young men for their army. In his dreams, they rode dragons instead of horses.

He nudged her bedroom door open. Father was not yet home; he was drinking *arak* and playing backgammon next door at Aami Hanna's.

Mother stood in the center of the bedroom in her nightgown. Her hair was down, long tangles of black. In her arms she cradled a jug—the one she'd found yesterday while exploring the mountain caves. Over the years, she'd come home with other treasures: a metal spear, the jawbone of a lion, a clay seal, glass beads. Truly, though, she told her son, the most precious thing she found was a bit of solitude.

"Mother," he whispered. Was she asleep with her eyes open? Behind her, the moonlight glistened on a spiderweb, a hexagon of silken threads. *"Shoo saar? Shoo aam b'seer?" What happened? What is happening?*

She tilted her head as if she'd heard something beyond his voice. Perhaps it was an animal; wolves sometimes stalked the village at night. He, too, listened so intently that, for a moment, he thought he could hear the spider plucking its legs along the web, perfecting its trap.

He noticed she held something—small and round—between her fingers. "What do you have, *immi*?" he asked.

And then he saw something strange spreading before his mother's bare feet: a dark pool, black smoke bubbling up from its center.

Fire!

He tried to scream, but he could hardly breathe. Instead he stumbled backward, bumping into the half-open door, his heart pounding against his ribs. Why was there no burning odor, no heat from the smoke? The air was cold.

"Get back, Mother!" he managed to whisper desperately, shivering.

But she seemed oddly calm—trancelike—as she stood near the cusp of the widening pool, which began to swirl like a pot of soup stirred by an unseen ladle. The boy knew he should cry for help or pull her back, but now he himself was unable to turn away, unable to move.

What was it? What was in there?

What was at the bottom?

Long fingers, tendrils of smoke, beckoned him forward with a shushing noise like a mother soothing a child. Mesmerized, horrified, he stepped closer.

Something was materializing and rising up out of the churning pool. Some*one*.

A man.

"Give it to me," the man hissed, shadowed in smoke.

His face was hidden by a beard, his cloak trimmed with fur. He spoke in a foreign tongue, with ancient words—but the boy understood. It was the language of his long-lost ancestors. It was in his blood.

But give *what*? Perhaps he wanted the jug?

The man glanced at the boy before grabbing his mother by the wrist. Her face collapsed into an expression of pain. The jug fell with a thud.

"Let her go!" the boy begged, frozen.

"Mine," the man said.

"She is *not* yours!"

His mother's eyes snapped into focus. She finally looked at her son—finally saw him standing there—and her face dimmed with terror.

"Go," she croaked. The ghostly man pulled her toward the pool, which was now a yawning black mouth consuming half of the room.

"You cannot take her!" the boy cried.

"*Habibi.*" His mother's voice was nothing more than a thick moan. "*Bhebak aatool.*"

He reached out to her, the tips of his fingers grazing her nightgown. His balance wavered at the edge of the spiraling chasm.

With a grunt of determination, she pushed the boy away with more strength than he'd known she had, sending him across the room. He landed on his back, hitting his head on the doorframe. Helplessly, he watched as the man wrapped his cloak around his mother, enveloping all but her pale face. Outside, a cloud slid over the moon, turning the light ashen. His mother and the stranger stepped into the bubbling black vortex, which narrowed.

And disappeared.

A final sigh of smoke lingered briefly before it went out like a forgotten campfire.

All was quiet. The bedroom floor was as solid as ever.

But his mother was gone.

He whimpered and pulled himself across the room, lying flat across the spot where she'd been just moments ago. Under his cheek, the floor grew cold and wet with tears. Surely this was only another nightmare—his worst yet—but he could not wake himself up.

I love you, she'd said. *Forever.*

He picked up the jug and held it to his chest; he rocked back and forth and called for her. Outside the window, an owl responded with a forlorn *who-who.*

When he finally stumbled next door, frantic and babbling, his father stubbed out his cigarette and cursed. "The Turks!" he cried. He stood and knocked over the backgammon board, scattering pieces everywhere like a fistful of lost coins. "They kidnapped her!"

He tore through the village, his angry shouts waking children from their sleep. A few men mounted horses and went chasing shadows into the night, ready to slit the throats of her captors. Other than a pack of hyenas, they found nothing.

Secretly, no one held out hope. She was too beautiful. She had surely been taken as a bride. After a month, the village priest stopped praying for her return. After a year, no one spoke of it.

"Bayye," the boy would say to his father, tugging on his pants in their grove of walnut trees. "It was not the Turks."

He had told and retold his story, but the more he recounted what had truly happened, the less people listened. They patted his head, crossed themselves, and changed the subject.

"There is no such thing as a genie!" his father said finally. "Now

stop your talk, once and for all. People are beginning to think you are *akhwet.*"

But the boy knew what he had seen. He kept the jug hidden and close. He rubbed it every night, making the same unfulfilled wish—*Please bring my mother home*—until he was an old man ready to die.

1

"No, no, no." Sam swore under her breath. "Go away."

She pressed her eyes shut, as if that would make their landlord's car disappear.

But his ancient Mercedes was still rasping along behind her, its belly low to the ground, slinking like an animal. Sam dipped her head and picked up the pace. Her shoes were tucked under her arm, and the gravel road bit into her bare feet. As she reached the mailbox, she heard the car sputter to a stop, and there was the snap of the driver's door.

"What's the rush?" Mr. Koplow called, laughing as he trailed her up the cracked cement driveway.

Sam stopped and steeled herself before turning to face his empty smile and icy blue eyes. His pants hung low underneath his belly; his thinning hair was combed straight back.

"It's not the first yet," Sam said, even though she knew they still owed last month's rent.

Mr. Koplow tipped his chin toward the trailer. "Your mother here?"

"She went to get milk."

"Milk," Mr. Koplow repeated.

"And toilet paper," Sam said, adding to the lie.

"Right. So she'll be back soon," Mr. Koplow suggested, reaching

into his shirt pocket for a pack of cigarettes. He pulled one out, crooked, and pressed it between his lips.

Sam glanced up at the sky, where the sun was inching its way down. "Sorry, but I really need to get to the lake." She raised her hand. *Goodbye.*

Mr. Koplow didn't move. He let out a curl of smoke. "She wants me to fix the back stoop. I need to take a look, see what happened."

"Nothing happened. It's rotten."

At her feet was an oil stain from her mother's leaking car, and behind her there was yet another dent in the carport. She knew Mr. Koplow was keeping tabs; they would never get their security deposit back when the time came.

He squinted at her dirty feet, at her chipped green toenail polish. His eyes climbed higher, lingering on her purse, then the stack of bracelets up her arm. "How much did those cost?" he asked as his phone rang.

Three dollars. That was how much she'd paid for her bracelets. Clearance table, plus her employee discount.

"Yeah, this is Alan. Slow down, slow down," Mr. Koplow said into his cell, his voice rising. "What's leaking? The toilet on the *second* floor?" He pointed his cigarette at Sam. "I'll be back."

A moment later, his car engine sputtered and caught, and Sam watched as he vanished down the gravel road, a wall of dust rising behind him.

With a sigh, she turned to face the lopsided trailer with its mildew-stained siding and ripped welcome mat. Mr. Koplow had once told Mom that it wasn't the Taj Mahal and she was no princess, so what did she expect?

Whatever it was, it was home. It was the place of rushed Monday mornings and the smell of Mom's perfume. It was where Rima

had fallen against the coffee table and gotten the scar on her shoulder, where Dad had taught Sam how to cast a net from the top of the picnic table, pretending the backyard was teeming with baitfish. It was the place Dad would come home to, when he finally came home. He could fold his clothes and put them away. His grape soda would take up the top shelf of the fridge. He'd get *Outside* magazine delivered again. He'd pick up right where he left off.

"See you soon," he'd said the day he was deployed, ruffling Sam's hair. "Take care of your mom and baby sister while I'm gone."

"Yes, sir," she'd said.

Then he'd stooped down and put his hands on her shoulders. His military boots—which always smelled like motor oil—were tightly laced under his flight suit. His hands were so big. Invincible. He could survive anything.

"Promise me," he said, his blond eyebrows drawn together. The air had been laced with the sweetness of spring flowers and grass and new leaves, just like today. "Promise me you'll look out for them until I get back."

"I will, sir," Sam had repeated, an uneasy knot in her stomach. "I'll try to, Dad."

"Try hard, kiddo. I love you." That was the last thing he'd said to her.

She could almost feel Dad's hands on her shoulders now as she jiggled the house key into the rusty lock. Another broken thing that needed to be replaced.

Behind her, brakes squealed and then sighed. She spun around to look. Was it Mr. Koplow again, or Mom finally home, or someone Mom owed money, or a favor?

It was a hulking UPS truck. A man in a brown uniform hopped down with a box in his hands.

"It's probably for Mrs. Jarvis," Sam said to the deliveryman as she finally jerked the door open. She pointed down the street at a lawn cluttered with gnomes and metallic balls on pedestals. "QVC addict."

"Nope," he said, reading the box. "This is for Samira Clark. That you?"

"It's just Sam," she said. "Nobody calls me Samira."

"Whoever sent this package does. I'll need a photo ID for this one."

Sam pulled her wallet from her purse and handed over her driver's license.

"Wow, your hair," the deliveryman said as he glanced back and forth between her face and her license. She was sixteen in the photo, almost two years ago. At the time she'd had shoulder-length hair bleached to a brassy shade of blond. Now her black hair hung down to her waist.

"That's me," Sam assured him.

He held the electronic clipboard out for her. "Initial here. And put the date right there at the bottom."

The date. It was Friday. Mom had been gone since Monday. That made four nights. Too long. If she didn't hear from her by tomorrow, she'd have to call the police.

"Hello?"

"Yeah, sorry," Sam said, scribbling her signature. "Stressful day, that's all. Couldn't remember the date for a second."

He smiled, took back the board, and handed her the package and her driver's license. "Hang in there."

"Thanks," she said, though he was already jogging back to his truck.

Sam stepped inside, looking at the box. It was lighter than she expected, and it smelled like spices and tobacco. Postage stickers

were everywhere, and on the right-hand corner LIBANPOST, BEIRUT was stamped within a rectangle of bright blue ink. The sender had meticulously written *The United States of America* under Sam's zip code, and the return address had been perfectly penned, as though a ruler had been held underneath each line. *Karm El Mohr*, it said, which Sam recognized as the name of her mother's hometown in Lebanon, a little village in the mountains.

Curiosity tugged at her, but it was getting late. She had to hurry to the lake, or there would be nothing at all for dinner.

"Rima?" Sam called into the house. Their tiny kitchen table, too small for three people, teetered when Sam set the package on top. She tucked her driver's license away and tossed her purse and shoes into the corner.

"Hello?" she called one more time before peeking into her mother's bedroom. There was always the slim chance she could be back, and asleep.

But nothing had changed since the last time Sam looked. Mom's bed was unmade, her floral comforter tangled. The curtains were drawn. On a chair, nestled between two throw pillows, a teddy bear stared at Sam with vacant eyes. MY VALENTINE was stitched across its heart-shaped belly. Sam stared back. Though she'd never asked, she was sure it was a gift from Dad—it had been around a lot longer than any of Mom's boyfriends.

She closed her mother's door and went to her own room, where she changed into jeans, a fishing shirt with a dozen little pockets for supplies, and sneakers. Her old Girl Scout sash—loaded with badges for archery, horseback riding, cookie sales—had fallen from its thumbtacks again. She pressed it back into the wall and then tossed a makeup bag and a jacket onto Rima's upper bunk, which was already piled high with dirty clothes, schoolwork, and at least twenty jars of

nail polish. There was only enough space in their windowless room for one dresser, and there was no closet, so the floor was cluttered with semiorganized piles. Picking through them, Sam found everything she needed, making a mental checklist as she went: fishing rod; Dad's Swiss Army knife in case she needed to cut a line; a cooler. Back in the kitchen she grabbed an ice pack from the freezer and, finally, moldy cheese for bait.

"Go, go, go," she urged herself.

The winter had been so long and gray. She'd missed Glen Lake's waters—turquoise blue and crystal clear, a reassurance that not everything in the world was dark and muddy underneath. No matter how many times she pulled her boat out onto the lake, her heart still swelled, as if those Caribbean-looking waters were a gift just for her, and that unexpected beauty was all she needed to carry on.

Her hand was on the door, but at the last moment she glanced back at the UPS package on the table. If Mom came home while she was fishing, she would open the package herself, even though it was addressed to Sam.

What could be inside?

The only person they knew from Lebanon was Mom's grandfather, Jiddo Naameh. Packages from him came very rarely, and they were always for Mom, never Sam. She'd never even met her great-grandfather, had only seen him in a handful of yellowed pictures that hung on the walls of Mom's bedroom. He looked old in those photos, and they were all taken before Sam was born.

It would only take a second to open the package. She took her hand off the doorknob, set her fishing gear down, and found a pair of scissors in the kitchen junk drawer.

Judging by the weight and size of the box, there might be a book

or two inside. In the past, he'd sent calendars, tourist guides, poetry written in Arabic, and books with glossy photos of Roman and Phoenician ruins. Sometimes he'd include bars of olive oil soap, jars of pomegranate molasses, and cans of sesame seed paste.

Sam slit the tape along the edges of the box and pulled the cardboard flaps up. A white envelope sat on top of the packing material, addressed to her.

She ran her finger across the handwriting, then slid her thumb under the envelope's flap and pulled it open. Inside was a piece of folded paper, so thin it was translucent. She unfolded it, eager to read, but the entire note was indecipherable to her: It was written in Arabic, in bright purple ink, the color of peacock feathers.

She dug into the box again, half convinced that only pillows of bubble wrap filled the rest of it, but her fingers hit something solid. The hairs on the back of her neck stood up as she pulled out a fat, pear-shaped object enshrouded in newspaper. Setting it on the table, she began unpeeling the sheets, layer after layer, her fingertips turning black from the newsprint.

Finally, the last square of paper fell to the floor. Sam stood staring at a piece of dull clay pottery.

Its narrow neck was flanked by two circular handles, hardly big enough to fit her fingers through. Simple, symmetrical lines crisscrossed its belly. It had a look of homemade imperfection; maybe Jiddo had made it himself.

The letter surely explained it. She refolded it and tucked it back inside the envelope, glancing at the clock on the microwave. She'd already wasted a solid ten minutes of fishing time. She had to hide everything and get out on the water.

"Go," she told herself again, pushing away from the table. It wobbled, and the jug shuddered off the edge.

"No!" she cried.

For a moment, the jug seemed suspended in air, simply waiting to be caught—and then it hit the linoleum floor with a hollow, sickening sound.

Sam let out a groan as she knelt to examine the damage. It had split in half; she tried to fit it back together like two puzzle pieces, but there was a thin seam between them. *Just like my life,* she thought. Split apart and then precariously put back together. You only noticed the cracks when you got close enough.

And that was when she saw the coins.

There were seven, crusted to the dirty bottom of the jug. She tipped it upside down over the table, shook, and the coins spilled out.

Sam blinked.

Treasure.

Time and dirt had turned a few of them black. Others were only slightly tarnished, stamped with images of pine trees and ships, sea castles and owls, spears crossed to make an X. PIASTRES, one of them said; another had a perfect hole drilled through its middle, flanked by two small lions.

Sweat trickled down her temples. Her mind raced. What if Mom came home right this second? She had already pawned every last item of worth in their possession. She would take the coins without a second thought.

There was one more, she noticed: stuck to the bottom, caked with a mud-hardened residue, so camouflaged with the dark pottery she almost missed it. She tipped the jug piece again and shook, hard, but it wouldn't come loose. When she tried with a fingernail, her nail bent and snapped, and the coin stayed put.

"Super," she said, sucking on her finger to take the sting away.

Letter-like shapes arced along the top edge of the coin. They might have been words, but they were written in an alphabet she didn't recognize. Even though she couldn't read Arabic, she knew its familiar curves and dots. This was something altogether different.

Sam glanced at the clock again.

She needed to go—but instead she pulled Dad's Swiss Army knife from one of her shirt pockets. His initials were engraved on its bright red side: B.C.C. She gave the knife a quick kiss like she always did before she used it, knowing her father's fingerprints were still there underneath her own.

Carefully, she worked the tip of the smallest blade under the coin, until it finally sprang out onto the table.

For some reason, she hesitated to touch it. It seemed different than the other coins. Older, thicker. It made her heart beat faster. These coins could change everything for them. This one could really be worth something.

She picked the coin up, and the moment her fingers met the metal, her hand turned icy cold. She bit the inside of her mouth and winced, tasting blood.

A presence filled the room. She was suddenly sure she was being watched.

"Who's there?" she asked, spinning to look.

Something pulled on her, pushed her. The room turned dark, as if

the electricity had failed and a storm cloud had rolled right inside the house. There was the distant sound of a flute, and then a whispering voice. Raspy and urgent.

You have what is mine!

The language was foreign, but somehow she understood.

Give it to me!

The pull on her intensified, a fierce current sweeping her out into deep waters. It felt as though her feet were no longer on the floor, that the worn gray linoleum beneath her had become fluid. The storm cloud swirled and widened into a funnel in the floor, a pit of smoke. Her hand had frozen shut, fingers curled tightly around the coin. But with a determined shriek, she threw it down.

The strange storm stopped as suddenly as it had started.

The light returned to the room. The linoleum was as chipped and ordinary as always. She stood panting for air, staring at the coin where it had landed.

Sam rubbed her throbbing hand, her heart pounding with such ferocity she had to lie down. She made her way to the couch and collapsed, listening.

All was silent, other than her own frantic breathing. There was no hypnotic flute, no voice. Her stomach turned over with something that felt like motion sickness, as if she'd just stepped off a spinning carnival ride and still couldn't find her footing.

Outside the window, a dog barked, and Mrs. Jarvis yelled. "Get over here! Peanut!" She called the dog's name over and over again. "Peanut! Peanut! There you are!"

Sam counted to one hundred and then stood.

Warily, she went back to the kitchen and stared at the coin. She was afraid to touch it, but she couldn't just leave it there.

After pacing the house, searching for an idea, she went to Rima's

collection of beauty supplies, a pink plastic cabinet with four drawers. She yanked open the drawer labeled EYES and dug through a rainbow of shadows, liners, and tubes of mascara until she found the tweezers.

Metal meeting metal made a dull *ting* as she tapped the coin. Carefully, she slid the tweezers around it and clamped down. All good. Nothing happened. As Dad would say, *No holes in the boat.*

She let out a little laugh of relief. She had almost expected it to spring to life like a coiled snake.

Back in the kitchen, she slipped the coin into a large Ziploc bag, along with the other seven coins and the two halves of the broken jug. The back door squeaked behind her as she headed outside, down the rotting stoop and into the yard. The gardening tools were already laid out, right next to the plants she'd bought last week. After setting down the bag, she thrust the big metal shovel into the ground, thinking how her mother accused her of burying everything—her emotions, herself—in school and work.

She would get some answers tomorrow. At the library or on the internet, there would be information about old coins. She would find someone—other than Mom—to translate Jiddo's letter. In the meantime, this was the best hiding place for the things he had sent her.

An hour later, she had a decent-sized hole in the backyard, deep enough. After burying the bag, Sam looked back up at their sagging trailer.

Maybe it wasn't lopsided after all. Maybe it was her.

2

A door slammed with a gunshot *bang* and Sam sat up.

She was surprised to find herself back on the couch; a rogue metal spring dug through the thin cushions and jabbed at her thigh. Across the room, their hazy TV was on mute, and a woman silently urged her to *act now and buy an Immortal Youth skincare system in three easy payments.*

Sam had a dim recollection of putting on her nightshirt, of trying to stay awake until Rima came home. She'd never made it to the lake. Morning sunlight streamed into the room, illuminating the dusty air.

"Rima?" she called, her voice hoarse.

She cleared her throat and stood, rolling her neck until it cracked. Her fingers ached where she'd touched the coin.

The coin.

She sucked in a breath as the whole thing came flooding back to her.

The remote shook in her hand as she clicked off the TV. She must have fallen asleep watching some crazy movie, that's all it was. Her imagination on overload. She tossed the remote onto the couch and went to the kitchen for a drink, but with a start she remembered the smoky pit in the floor, exactly where she stood now. She skittered away from the spot and tried to laugh at herself.

There was no way that had happened.

And yet she was completely sure it did.

Heart thumping, she poured herself a glass of water from the sink and drank it in one long gulp. She grabbed Jiddo's letter from the table and backed away from the kitchen, feeling like it was set with snares.

"Rima?" she called again.

She padded cautiously to their bedroom. Her sister's clothes were flung across the floor, making a trail to the bed, where she snored quietly on the top bunk, murmuring in her sleep, her arm slung over the railing. Sam felt a surge of relief before catching a whiff of vape and beer. And barf.

"Soccer practice," Sam mumbled under her breath. There were brambles in Rima's hair. "Yeah, right."

She slid Jiddo's letter underneath her own pillow, and then crossed the tiny hallway to open her mother's bedroom door.

She was back. Finally.

Her duffel bag was on the bed, its contents spilling out, and among the jumbled clothes was the picture she always took with her, no matter where she went. Her wedding photo, framed in silver. Dad in a suit and tie, so serious. Mom in her white gown.

"Mom?" Sam called, walking quickly through the small house, searching.

Her mother's voice answered, muffled and distant. "Out here!"

Through the kitchen window, Sam could see her waving from the backyard. Sam waved back.

Still in her bare feet and nightshirt, she threw open the patio door and ran out across the weeds and dirt. Above her, the sky was a happy pastel blue, like some sort of candy drink. The cold air took her by surprise, though. Yesterday had been summer-like, but now her breath spilled out ahead of her as she rushed toward her mother.

"You're home!" Sam said.

"Hey, gorgeous," Mom said, smiling up at her.

Mom was the one who was gorgeous. Her black hair shone almost blue in the sunlight, and her skin glowed with olive undertones. She was on her knees with a rusty gardening spade and polka-dotted gloves; the potted vegetables Sam had bought the week before were beside her, an investment that would literally grow all summer. A five-dollar plant gave them vegetables for months.

"Stand up so I can hug you," Sam said, her teeth chattering against the cold.

She nervously scanned the grass, looking for the rock that marked the place where she'd buried everything. Exactly where she'd put it was a blur; she'd been in such a state of shock and panic, and had worked until after dark.

"Yes. I could use a hug." Mom pulled off her dirty gardening gloves and stood, dusting her knees. "And a week of sleep."

Sam wrapped her arms around her mother's waist and kissed her cheek. She seemed thinner than ever; Sam's arms could practically go twice around her tiny waist. "Where've you been?" she asked, sneaking in one more peck on the other cheek before her mother pulled away.

"Getting stuff to plant your garden," Mom said, dodging the real question.

Sam looked down at the dozen or so plants she had already bought, plus a few bags of black soil Mom must have just brought home. A fat bumblebee floated past, investigating the new plants.

"Thanks," Sam said.

"Tomatoes need phosphorus." Mom pointed her gardening spade at a bag of fertilizer. She read the planting instructions aloud. "'Roma tomato. Pear- or plum-shaped. Plant in full sun in rows thirty-six inches apart.'"

"Yeah, I was kind of waiting for the weather to warm up," Sam said. "For good."

She'd covered the plants the previous week because it had dipped into the thirties overnight. The old sheet she'd used to protect them was strewn across the ground now, streaked with mud. Underneath a corner of the striped fabric, a rock—*the* rock she'd used to mark the spot—peeked out.

"I got some stakes and twine," Mom said, "and a green pepper plant." She bumped her hip against Sam's. "You're shivering. Go get dressed. You'll catch a cold out here."

"The entire garden is supposed to go over there," Sam said, pointing to the opposite corner of the yard. "All these plants need sun."

"*You* need sun," Mom said. "Look how pale you are. Go inside and get a warm drink."

"Come with me," Sam said, but Mom put her gardening gloves back on and squinted at the tag from the green pepper plant. Sam studied the rim of bone under the collar of her mother's shirt. So thin.

"Where were you?" Sam asked quietly. "I was going to call the police today."

Mom dropped the tag she was holding. "Do not do that." All the cheer that had been in her voice moments ago was gone. "Never ever do that."

"I know, but..."

"You're not eighteen yet. They'll put you in a foster home. And Rima somewhere else, in a different one." She cast a gloved finger in one direction and then in another. Opposite ends of the world.

"Why was Mr. Koplow here yesterday?" Sam pressed. "How many months behind are we? He said he was here about the stoop, but it's more than that, right?"

Mom sighed and raked her fingers through her hair, sending a stripe of dirt through her bangs. "The credit card company won't increase our limit." She shook her head. "I had to get new brake pads

for the car. Then your wisdom teeth came out, and that wasn't completely covered. I bought soccer cleats for Rima, plus her summer registration fees. Things add up."

"Why didn't you tell me?" Sam looked over her shoulder toward the house, wondering if Rima was awake yet. She didn't need to hear another argument. Especially not the same old argument. "I could have put in some extra hours at the jewelry store."

She held back the rest: *I don't like how Mr. Koplow looks at you. I don't want you owing him anything.*

Mom considered the hole she'd just dug. "Do you think that's deep enough?"

"How much did you spend on all this gardening stuff?" Sam asked. "Maybe we can return a couple things."

"Well," Mom said, a smile tugging at her lips. "I wanted to save the surprise, but since you're asking..."

From the front pockets of her jeans, she pulled out two thick wads of cash. And then, while Sam stood frozen with disbelief, she sprinkled the bills all over the ground. Like she was planting seeds for money trees.

"*What?* What did you do?" Sam asked. Possibilities—all of them bad—swirled through her mind. "Where did you get all this? Is it real?"

There were tens and twenties...even fifties. The wind picked up and Sam dropped to her knees to gather the money before it blew away.

"I won at the casino." Mom laughed. She sounded proud of herself. "I won big."

"You were *gambling* all week?" Sam held the money tight in her fists, fighting back the torrent of angry words that swelled inside

her. Mom had been playing slots at the casino again? *That* was where she was?

But the money. The money! It was more than Sam made in a month. Maybe even more than their check from the Marines.

"Karma, baby!" Mom said. "Mercury retrograde ended last week, so the timing was good." She looked up at the sky. "I wonder if there's a lunar eclipse in Pisces right now. I should check on that."

"The stars were aligned," Sam said.

"Yes," Mom said, ignoring Sam's sarcasm. "And today, we're going to Lowe's to buy a washer and dryer. No more trips to the laundromat." She dipped her hand into her shirt pocket and found a pair of sunglasses, then slid them on and smiled, posing. "Like them?"

"Yeah. They're great, Mom." Sam sighed, reluctantly handing the money back. "Really great."

"We'll get Alan off our backs, buy some new clothes," Mom continued, "and go out for steaks tonight. Let's go see a movie, too." She cleared her throat. "What? I see your wheels turning."

"I just...We have a lot of bills to pay, obviously. Those should come first. And that other thing...remember?" But clearly Mom had forgotten. "The entrepreneurship certificate program. The small-business classes I've been saving for."

Mom swatted her words away. "You haven't even graduated high school yet. Enjoy the last few weeks of senior year. Enjoy the summer."

"But—"

"Your dad took a few college classes, you know, before he enlisted. And what did they get him? Nothing." Her eyes lit up. "We should spend the money on a prom dress for you!"

"No! That's a total waste. I'm just going with my friends anyway," Sam said. "I'll wear Rima's blue dress."

"That dress won't fit you. Come on, you could be the belle of the ball," Mom said, fanning the bills. She twisted her mouth when Sam shook her head. "You are no fun." She shoved the cash back into her pockets. "You're so serious all the time, so practical. You weren't always like this. I worry about you."

"I worry about *you*," Sam countered, keeping her voice in check. "Next time please leave a note. That's all I'm asking, so I know where you are. I called all your normal jobs. I was starting to think you were dead."

"Dead!" Mom said. "That's dramatic."

"'Dear Sam, I'll see you Saturday morning. Here's how you can reach me if you need to. Have a good week. Love, Mom.'"

"A note," Mom repeated. "That would've been thoughtful. But then you might have come searching for me."

And she didn't want to be found.

Sam gave her mother a look. They'd had this standoff so many times, and getting angry only made things worse. Mom was home, with money to spare, so Sam tamped down her frustration and pasted on a smile.

"I'm glad you're home," she said, picking up the shovel and ducking underneath the branches of the only tree in their yard. Its trunk wore a hundred scars where she and Dad had thrown knives into it. Sam could almost see herself taking aim, see the ghost of her ten-year-old self, of Dad standing by chewing on a toothpick. *It's all in the wrist,* he would coach, but more often than not she missed the tree altogether and the knife would land in the grass.

Mom pushed her new sunglasses onto the top of her head. They were Ray-Bans, and they weren't knock-offs. The wad of gambling money would be gone by next week.

"Yep," Sam mumbled, deciding for certain that she needed to

keep the jug and coins a secret. With a grunt, she jammed the shovel into the ground. She'd worn blisters across her palms last night from digging, and now they flared up again. That part, at least, had really happened—burying the Ziploc bag. Her mind flashed to the smoky mist and the man's voice, which now felt so dreamlike and impossible.

"Are you okay?" Mom asked. "You really do look sick."

"The last time I ate was yesterday at lunch."

"Inside," she said, putting an arm around Sam. "You're freezing! I bought bagels. I was just waiting for Rima to wake up."

"I'll go play reveille in her ear," Sam said, but when they turned to walk back to the house, she saw that Rima was standing at the door with a cup of coffee. She lifted a hand toward Mom as if she'd been gone five minutes rather than five days. No big deal. Totally normal.

Mom kissed Rima's forehead before she could duck away. "How's my baby?" she asked. "Good?"

"How was the party last night?" Sam asked, following Rima into the kitchen. Her hair was in a messy knot, her face oily with yesterday's makeup. "I mean, soccer practice?"

Rima shot her a look. *Shut up*, she mouthed silently.

"Mom won some money at the casino," Sam added, opening the refrigerator and handing Rima a tub of cream cheese. Mom had bought caramel-flavored, the best, and probably without a coupon. Sam chose a cinnamon bagel from the open box on the kitchen table. "We're going shopping today."

"After I nap," Mom said, stifling a yawn. In the kitchen's fluorescent light, the skin under her eyes looked purple. She'd probably gambled all night and slept in her car during the day. "It's hard work winning cold, hard cash."

"How much?" Rima asked, trailing Mom into her room. "What'd you play? Slots or blackjack?"

Sam swallowed the last bite of her bagel. She showered and dressed, stacking a few bracelets over her wrist and slipping on her old sneakers. The lake was calling to her, but she had econ homework, an entire business plan due on Friday. Plus, if she went to the library, she could search for clues about the coins.

She tucked Jiddo's letter into her pocket and walked through the house. When she looked inside Mom's room, she found her already asleep, her cheek pressed crookedly against her half-unpacked duffel bag.

The back door was ajar, and Rima was singing somewhere.

And then Sam heard a noise that made her spine stiffen: the *chink* of a shovel hitting rock.

Panicked, Sam pressed her fingertips against the window. Rima was on her knees in the yard. She was digging.

Sam threw open the back door. "What are you doing?" she asked, her voice cracking as she sprinted toward her sister.

"Mom told me to move all the plants to this one spot." Rima had the Ziploc bag in her hands, the pieces of the broken jug showing through. The hose was running, creating a thin river of mud around Rima's bare feet. "But check this out," she said. "I found this."

"Don't open it," Sam warned. She was breathless from running.

"But there's a bunch of coins in here." Rima pointed through the clear bag. "They look old."

"Give it to me," Sam said, thrusting her hand out.

"Finders keepers," Rima replied, pulling the bag toward her chest.

"You don't understand," Sam said. "Jiddo sent that to me. It's mine."

"Huh?" Rima made a face. *"Jiddo?"*

Sam nodded.

"So why is it out here?"

"Because," Sam said. "I needed to hide it for now." She put her hand out again, but instead Rima opened the bag and pulled the two chunks of pottery out. Three or four coins fell to the ground. "You're going to lose something!"

"Is it from Lebanon?" Rima let out a low whistle. "This stuff looks ancient."

"One of the coins is..." Sam's voice trailed off. She wanted to say "magical" or "cursed," but that seemed ridiculous in the broad daylight of their backyard. Birds chirped, and the clouds were ribbons across the blue sky.

Rima picked up the coins and set them in the palm of her hand. "Do you think they're worth something?" She smiled and her eyes lit up with excitement. Her enthusiasm was contagious, and Sam felt herself smile back.

"We have to research everything first," she said. "Don't tell Mom, okay? She'll just take them to the pawnshop. I need to go to a museum or find a guidebook or something, so we can sell them for the right price."

"Yeah," Rima said. "That makes sense."

"They might not be worth anything," Sam cautioned. "And they were from Jiddo, so part of me thinks we should just keep them anyway. Maybe they're family heirlooms. I thought I'd glue the jug back together, at least."

Rima nodded. She took the last few coins from the bottom of the bag and placed them alongside the others in her cupped hand. Her posture turned rigid. "C-cold," she gasped.

It was happening again.

A small patch of soil seemed to turn loose at Rima's knees.

"Drop them," Sam cried. "Hurry!"

She grabbed Rima's wrist and shook until the coins fell to the

ground. Sam knelt over them, guarding them, counting them: five, six... There were supposed to be eight. The seventh coin was nestled next to Mom's gardening gloves. Where was the last one?

"D'you hear that?" Rima asked, her words slurred. She looked around the yard. "A flute." Smoke rose from the twisting earth.

"Are you still holding one?" Sam demanded, horrified. She dragged Rima back, away from where the ground was moving, turning, becoming a dark spiral that widened and reached toward their toes. "Drop it! *Drop it!*"

Rima's eyes, so full of life a moment earlier, were glazed over.

"Look at me." Sam snapped her fingers in front of Rima's face, but she was somewhere far away. "Listen to me. Let go of the coin!" She shook her by the shoulders.

Rima slumped into her arms, but her fingers held the coin like a vise.

Sam peeled them back, one by one, and plucked the coin from her sister's palm. She pinched it between two fingertips, and the mesmerizing, eerie music of the flute filled her head once again. The inky fog rushed to embrace her, twisting, pulling, shushing her. Sam felt her voice trapped in her throat. The world was unfurling.

It's going to take us.

"Mine," a man's voice said.

Sam turned to look. There was no one in the yard—other than wide-eyed Rima—but now there was the smell of incense burning. Her fingers refused to open. The coin's icy poison was spreading, making her entire arm brittle.

"My obol."

The man's voice was closer... and then Sam saw him.

Bearded and cloaked and made of the dark clouds that spun across the yard. His breath spilled from his mouth in cold currents.

He lunged with dizzying swiftness, his hands going to Rima. *I have the coin,* Sam wanted to say. *Leave her alone!*

Rima cried out as the ghost gripped her by the wrist and yanked her away. He looked at Sam, his face full of fury. His eyes were golden, but his pupils were all wrong. One of them was the shape of a keyhole.

Stop! Sam silently screamed over the sound of the flute, a drumbeat also rising. She desperately crawled after Rima, her fingers finding a belt loop in her sister's jeans. They were at the cusp of the dark, revolving funnel.

With a last, desperate effort, Sam flicked the coin away. Over her shoulder, she caught a glimpse of it flipping through the air, as if someone had tossed it to call heads or tails. It landed in the black soil of their garden, behind them.

No. Above them.

It was too late. The three of them were sinking down, down, down; the backyard had become something like a raised stage they'd fallen from.

Sam closed her eyes and spun.

3

I rolled off, she decided.

It's okay. I rolled off.

That's all.

She'd fallen asleep on Rima's top bunk and slipped over the railing. She'd hit her head when she landed on the floor. She was dizzy, but fine. She just needed a minute to breathe. There was the smell of food; Mom must have gone to get pizza for lunch.

Everything was fine.

"Rima?" Sam whispered, opening her eyes and squinting.

Her neck was stiff, and her fingertips ached as if they'd been stung by bees. One of her shoes lay on its side nearby, and she put it back on with trembling hands. Slowly, her foggy vision cleared.

And she saw that everything was *not* fine.

There was no carpet underneath her; the floor was the right shade of gray, but it was stone. This was not her bedroom. Not home.

Around her, hidden in dark cubbies, statues of round-bellied women squatted as if giving birth. Rectangular columns created a maze of passageways. She looked up and found there was no roof, just a dusky sky, a smudge of blue and purple. Music carried faintly on the air.

There was nothing familiar about this place. Not one single thing.

Sam stood up and gulped down a whimper, remembering.

The funnel.

The ghost.

Desperate, she turned in circles, taking jagged breaths.

"Rima," she whispered, terror pounding its way through her. She realized she was panting, hyperventilating, so she sat back down on the hard floor, her head spinning. *Is this a dream?*

"Where am I?" she murmured.

She put her fingers to her lips. Her voice—the words—sounded strange. They *felt* strange.

Waves of fear threatened to wash her back under and into unconsciousness. But she fought it. She had to figure out what had happened. Slowly, she forced herself to her feet. Forced herself to walk.

She had to find Rima.

On either side of her, the walls were inlaid with hundreds of little colored tiles—mosaics. There was a woman wearing a feathered headdress, staring at her with orange, glassy eyes. A sailboat overflowing with fish. A golden sun. A field of flowers. A man with a beard surrounded by half-naked women.

Sam took a slow, long breath through her nose and let it out through her mouth, hoping the dream would dissipate. But the longer she looked, the more intensely real it all became.

"Rima? Are you here?" she called tentatively. And then she clapped a shaking hand over her mouth, her tongue turning dry with fear.

Now she knew why the words felt so different in her mouth. Whatever language she'd just spoken wasn't English.

What is wrong *with me?*

She was afraid to speak again. It was probably best to be quiet anyway.

She tiptoed through the corridors, the music growing louder. It

was the flutelike instrument she'd heard both times she'd touched the ancient coin. Women sang in high voices that warbled with sharp notes.

The smell of sweet tobacco smoke, laced with incense, filled the air. She had reached an enclosed courtyard, where the small fires of candles and clay lamps made a constellation of light across the floor.

Sam hid behind a column and gaped at the scene before her. A crowd of young women mingled, all holding drinks, all with hair cascading down to their waists. Some were costumed with robes and soft-looking hats; others were all but naked, wearing sheer wraps around their waists. A table of food towered nearby. A circle of girls drank from a large jug and then passed it along. It seemed to be some sort of party.

She scanned the crowd, looking for Rima, but then the music turned rhythmic and someone howled a high-pitched *ka-la-la-la-la!*

Others joined in until the air was filled with it, echoing like a war cry. A line of women linked hands and started to dance, each raising a knee and then stamping the ground in unison. It made a percussive sound, and Sam saw that they wore little tambourine cymbals around their ankles. Someone chanted strange sayings over the music, lines of poetry or prayers.

"Bi`urpāti, šitiyī bikâsī ḫurāṣi, maḥmūdu ḫurāṣi."
In the clouds, drink from cups of gold, the choicest of gold.

"I'm dreaming, I'm dreaming, I'm dreaming," Sam repeated under her breath, still trying to convince herself. And then she blurted in her new language, *"In the name of the gods!"*

A peacock had brushed past her feet, startling her. She stumbled into the wall, her bracelets clattering against the stone; the bird peered up at her as it sashayed away, its display of feathers trailing behind it like a wedding veil.

Sam's vision began to darken at the edges. She squatted, putting her head between her knees, willing herself to stay conscious.

Stand up straight, Dad would say. *Get your shit together.*

But instead she pulled her shoulders in, making herself small behind another rectangular stone column, glad the corridors were dimly lit. She breathed in deeply. Exhaled. Then dared to peek around the column to watch the party once again. No one had seemed to hear her.

At the front of the dance line was the only man in the room. He stood with his hairy chest thrust forward proudly, and he wore an elephant-hide mask with tusks, sandals that roped up his muscular calves, and tight leather gloves pulled up to his elbows. All eyes were on him.

The music, the singing, and especially the rhythmic dancing were mesmerizing. The drumbeat penetrated her; her hand throbbed in time, aching down to the bone where she'd held the coin between her fingers. She rubbed it and moved soundlessly away from the party, keeping herself hidden as she went.

Soon she found another courtyard with a vacant swimming pool, its waters glimmering in the fading sunlight. She wondered if the party would move to the pool later, after dark; it seemed like it had been prepared for visitors. Around the rim, small tables were set with vases of flowers, and on the ground lavish blankets had been spread. In the corners of the yard, statues of stone animals held pots full of blossoms in their mouths; Sam could smell the small white blooms of jasmine from where she stood.

"Rima!" she whispered, but there was no reply.

Long wooden tables were filled with food. Bowls brimmed with bright green pistachios. Pomegranates were broken open, their shiny seeds spilling out like dark gemstones. There were figs, dates, lemons;

eggs so large she couldn't imagine what had laid them; fat grapes were strewn all over the tables like little party balloons. It all smelled good—spicy and sweet.

There was something that looked like the baklava Mom made every Christmas Eve. It was sliced into diamond shapes, and Sam reached out to take one.

"*Šlama 'lekh,*" a velvety voice said, and Sam jumped.

She pulled her hand back from the food and turned to find a young woman standing there, smiling with brilliant white teeth.

The woman wore a sheer dress cut in a low V all the way to her belly button, which was pierced with a golden hoop. On her head was a soft hat, dyed a dramatic shade of purple. Her skin was an odd color—gray—and she nearly blended in with the stone walls. Even her long silky hair was gray.

"*Šlama 'lekh,*" Sam choked. Somehow, she understood that the greeting was layered with meaning: *hello* and *peace to you.* She wondered how long the woman had been silently watching her before she'd chosen to be seen.

"Welcome to Melqart's temple," she said, spreading her arms wide. She was exquisitely beautiful, despite her gray skin. Her eyelashes were so long they looked like feathers.

"Wh-where...?" Sam stammered. "Who are you?"

"I could ask the same question."

"What language are you speaking?" Sam pressed. "Why can I understand you? Why can I speak it, too?" She could feel the vowels rolling in her throat.

"Such very odd questions," the woman said. "Is this some sort of trickery?"

"No," Sam said. "I am...I am simply..." It took her a moment to decide what she was. "Lost."

The woman's kohl-blackened eyes swept over Sam, coming to rest on her bracelet set. "Pretty baubles," she said. She herself wore a gold pendant around her neck in the shape of a crescent moon—or maybe the hull of a boat?—dotted with blue stones.

"Who *are* you?" Sam asked again.

"The question is who are *you*?" the gray woman asked. "A spy from Gadir? A messenger from Ugarit?"

"Ugarit...?"

"Judging by your fine kid leather, you have come from afar." Her eyes were on Sam's scuffed shoes. "Such unusual workmanship."

"Afar? I come from..." Sam faltered, feeling like she was paging through a thick dictionary, the paper stiff. There was no word for it. "...Michigan," she finally finished in English.

The woman furrowed her brow with a look of incomprehension. She tilted her head.

"Glen Arbor," Sam said in English, and then switched languages again. "Arbor," she repeated.

"Do you tend trees?"

"No...I...," Sam started. She let her voice run out, almost certain her next question would be useless, but she tried anyway. "Do you have a...cell phone?"

"Such a perplexing dialect," the woman mused. "Some of your words are like empty vessels. They hold no meaning." She assessed Sam again from head to toe. "I shall let my master know you are here."

"I'm not here to see anyone," Sam said quickly. By *master*, she must have meant the man with the mask, the one who seemed to be the center of the party.

The woman's eyes were round pools of amber. They darkened with what Sam read as curiosity laced with distrust. The feeling was mutual.

"My name is Zayin," she said finally.

"I'm Sam."

"A pleasure." Zayin stepped closer, but instead of offering a handshake, she took a lock of Sam's hair and spooled it through her fingers. "Would you like to swim?"

The nearby pool suddenly contained two other women, their clothes abandoned at the edge. Between the dark water and the dusky light, Sam could only discern flashes of bare skin.

"No, thank you." She backed away from Zayin and flipped her hair over her shoulder, out of reach.

"But of course you will stay awhile."

"I... I don't know. I should go."

"You must be hungry after your long journey." Zayin retrieved a platter of food from a table and pressed it toward Sam. "Perhaps you have traveled through the mountains?"

"Not mountains." Sam mentally leafed through words again. "A storm," she tried. "A tornado," she added in English.

"You endured a storm?" Zayin asked, her eyes on Sam's. "In the name of Ba'al Saphon, this cannot be."

"It wasn't a storm. Not exactly." *Ba'al... who?*

Zayin pushed the food under Sam's nose, insistent. Sam chose a slice of fruit that might have been lemon, but the juice that ran across her fingers smelled more like liquor.

Zayin set the platter down on a table and circled the pool, lighting a row of small lamps along the perimeter. The firelight flickered across the water and caught silvery highlights in her hair.

"You may give me whatever you have brought," she said, "if you are afraid to approach King Melqart. Or are you here to offer yourself to him?"

"What? No," Sam said. *Offer?* She looked back toward the other

room, where the man had commanded the party. "Why would I...? Who would want to...?" She swallowed. She hardly knew how to frame her questions; confusion dragged her in a thousand directions. She wanted to turn and run, but to where?

"Why are you here, then? What are you? You do not strike me as *ḥayuta.*"

Ḥayuta? Why would she take Sam for an *animal?* Sam hesitated. "A ghost brought me. A man."

"Who?"

"I don't know," Sam said, putting the lemon down on a nearby table—it was definitely more alcohol than fruit. "He's tall, with a dark cloak trimmed with fur. He has a short, curly beard. Strange golden eyes."

The women in the pool went quiet. The sound of the drum and flute in the other courtyard was the only thing that filled the silence. Zayin approached Sam and gripped her by the arm.

"Strange eyes," she repeated, squeezing Sam a little too tightly. "In what way?"

"His pupils," Sam said, pulling away. "One of them looks like a keyhole."

"Eshmun," a woman in the pool whispered.

"You came here with Eshmun?" Zayin asked eagerly, looking around Sam as if he might be with her.

"We...we were separated." Sam got the uneasy feeling she was telling Zayin too much. "I don't know where he is."

Zayin considered this for a moment, and then a smile bloomed across her face.

"And now you are safe here with us," she said emphatically, suggesting that being with Eshmun was the opposite of safe. The music and laughter from the other courtyard grew louder. The women in the

pool were joined by three others whose lithe bodies and elegant eye makeup made them look feline.

"Safe here?" Sam's eyes went to the array of food on the long wooden tables. There were bright green olives, the color of springtime leaves. There was bread. She could smell meat cooking. Her stomach growled.

"You will stay," Zayin declared, following Sam's eyes. "You will dine with us. I will prepare a bed for you."

"No," Sam said, "I wouldn't be able to sleep anyway." She glanced up at the sky. She had to find Rima before dark. "You haven't seen another girl like me, have you?"

"Another?" Zayin blinked, fanning her feather-like eyelashes against her cheekbones.

"I really think I should go." Zayin was getting answers from Sam, but not giving any in return. Sam swallowed down the lump of desperation that had lodged itself in her throat. "I'm leaving now. Thanks."

"But where will you go?" Zayin asked, tucking a gray lock behind an ear. Underneath her shining hair, she had huge, oblong lobes that were paper-thin and pierced with dozens of gold studs.

"Home," Sam said, looking for a doorway that might lead out.

"But you said you were lost," Zayin continued. "Eat and rest, and then you can continue your journey with a full stomach and a clear mind. You are quite a long walk from the nearest harbor. If you came with Eshmun, your ship must be in Sidon."

"I didn't come by ship," Sam said. *Sidon:* another strange name. She rubbed her head. "I fell. I...fell..." She bit her lip, trying to find the right way to describe it. "I blacked out," she said in English.

Zayin softened her voice into a soothing tone of sympathy. "You are distraught. Disoriented."

"Yes." Sam glanced at the women in the pool, and then down the dark corridors leading off the courtyard. "Where is the exit?"

Zayin didn't answer her question. Instead she asked another of her own. "Tell me, my dear, why did Eshmun bring you here?"

"To reclaim his property," a man's voice called out.

It was him. *The ghost.*

He was suddenly in the courtyard with them, his face taut with anger, his powerful arms crossed over his chest. His golden eyes went straight to Sam.

Her stomach lurched. "No," she choked. An electric current of fear crackled through her, and again her hand pulsed with a dull ache where she'd held the coin.

Zayin clapped her hands, her eyes flashing wildly. "My dearest Eshmun," she cooed. She held out her arms as if to embrace him, yet neither of them moved closer to the other. "How our paths are destined to cross time and again."

"We meet only because of wrong turns," he said without a moment's pause. Sam took small steps sideways, edging toward a doorway.

"Oh, Eshmun," Zayin said coyly. "How you cast your blame in the wrong direction. The sun is behind you. That is your own shadow you see."

"There is no sun here," Eshmun said.

They were locked in an unfriendly standoff, both of them calculating. Zayin's face shifted between a forced smile and a sneer; Eshmun seemed to be waiting for her to make the next move. More women had come into the courtyard, and they were all staring at Eshmun.

Everyone seemed to have forgotten Sam. She seized the opportunity and silently made her way toward a hallway, hiding herself behind one column, and then the next.

Zayin asked loudly, "We all want to know: Who is the beautiful young woman?"

With that, Sam turned to flee and ran right into one of the feline women from the pool. She purred at Sam, dripping wet, and pushed her back toward Zayin, who put an arm around her.

Zayin stroked Sam's cheek with the backs of her fingers. "So pretty. So unusual." Her stone-studded rings were rough against Sam's skin.

"She is mine," Eshmun said. He advanced with a few swift steps and clamped down on Sam's arm. She expected an icy grip, but his hands were surprisingly warm. He wasn't made of smoke. He was *real*. Solid. He yanked her against his side, out of Zayin's reach.

"Let me go," Sam hissed.

"Give me my obol," he growled low into her ear.

"Why not stay?" Zayin asked him. "The party has just begun. We have all your favorite dishes, Eshmun. Food, drink, and"—she swept her hand toward the women in the pool—"otherwise."

The women cast their eyes upward at him, emerald and narrow at the edges. Water trickled down their faces, and one of them seductively licked the drops from her lips.

"Once again," he said bitterly, "you mistake me for my father."

For one brief second, Zayin looked wounded—and then she recovered. "What are you doing in Baalbek?" She raised an eyebrow and turned sideways, tipping her chin toward her shoulder. "Did you miss me?"

"No," he said curtly.

"Not even a taste?" Zayin asked, plucking a large, glistening grape from a nearby platter. She slid it across her lips before opening her mouth to take a small bite. She stepped forward and held it out to Eshmun for him to finish.

Sam turned away, feeling as though she was witnessing something far too personal. She twisted her arm, trying to loosen Eshmun's grip.

"In the name of the gods," he said, "we decline your generous offer."

"There is only one god here," Zayin snapped, as if she were correcting an ill-mannered child. Then she let out an apologetic laugh and smiled, taking the rest of the grape into her mouth. "Unless I am to calculate your diluted blood?"

"Insolence," he said, raising his voice angrily.

Zayin pointed at Sam and then Eshmun, back and forth. "Do tell me. How are you two acquainted?"

"She is my servant," Eshmun snapped.

Sam nearly choked. His *servant*?

"Are you?" Zayin asked Sam.

She opened her mouth to respond, but Eshmun spoke first. "She wandered off like an errant dog," he said, which made the women in the pool snicker.

"What?" Sam gasped.

"Pumāk ṣkur," he told Sam sternly. *Shut your mouth.* He dipped his head in farewell, never averting his eyes from Zayin's; there was a clear look of warning on his face. He spun on his heels and dragged Sam along.

"Let go of me!" she hissed. But he held on tight while Zayin's taunting voice echoed after them. *"Rḥaṭēn!"* she cried gleefully. *Run!*

Sam tripped along beside Eshmun as he navigated the labyrinth of passageways as if he knew them by heart. They hurried through a great entrance flanked by bronze columns, and suddenly they were outside, where a coterie of statues—women armed with bows and arrows, or pregnant with sun-shaped stomachs—watched with hard eyes. The sounds of the party faded behind them as they descended an immense white marble staircase.

"You're hurting me," Sam said. Her bracelets bit into her skin

where he held her by the wrist. They'd started down a narrow road, a city sprawling dark around them. "I'm not going anywhere with you!"

"I demand my obol," he snarled, finally releasing her. "The coin."

"Where is my sister?" she countered. His eyes swept over her body and the front pockets of her pants; she pulled them inside out. "See? No coin."

"It is under your tongue," he said. He reached for her face, but she dodged his hands.

"What are you doing? There's nothing in my *mouth*." She glared at him. "Just tell me where Rima is!"

"Quiet, fool," he hissed. "You do not understand the danger you are in." He glanced back toward the temple, as if worried someone might be following.

Sam tried to stay steady on her feet. But this man—this place—those women. She felt like she was in the funnel again, the earth spinning underneath her; fear was sending her in nauseating circles.

"Come," he demanded, hooking a finger at her.

She shook her head. Tried to clear her thoughts, to form some kind of plan. "I'm going back to Zayin," she said. "She offered a bed."

"Not for sleeping."

She felt her cheeks turn hot. One look at Eshmun and she realized this should have been obvious to her. "Fine. Then I'll go it alone."

But now that she was outside, she knew beyond a doubt that there was absolutely nothing familiar about her surroundings. There were no signs, no recognizable landmarks, and the city around them was made of crude rectangular buildings and uneven walls of rock. The roads were unpaved and riddled with potholes. Even the trees looked wrong.

In the distance, a range of rocky mountains brimmed along the horizon. Sleeping Bear Dunes—made of sand—were the highest points back home.

This wasn't home.

"At the moment I am your preferable option," Eshmun said. "Unless you would like to ask these ladies for help?"

He motioned to a group of women sauntering down the road, tipping back dark flasks and wiping their mouths on their sleeves. Eshmun pulled Sam against a tree to hide. He put a finger to his lips. The women passed, dragging an animal carcass behind them—something with antlers—and leaving a shiny trail of blood along the road. Sam caught a glimpse of the women's teeth: long and canine.

"Where am I?" she asked Eshmun, after the women had disappeared down the road. "What is this place?" she whispered shakily.

"The city of Baalbek."

"Baalbek," she repeated.

Zayin had said the same thing. Sam was sure she had heard the city's name before—had seen it written somewhere, maybe. Almost, *almost,* she could conjure the memory: words penned in blue ink on the back of an old photo.

Eshmun took her by the wrist again, forcing her down the road and deeper into the tangle of buildings. His pace was merciless—until he stopped suddenly for a black shape gliding across their way, floating listlessly above the ground. It seemed to be made of dark strands of gauze, pieced together into the patchwork form of a man.

As it passed a lantern hanging from a post, Sam realized she could see through it. It looked at her with black holes for eyes, nothing in them at all. Two empty wells.

"Do not look into the eyes of the dead," Eshmun warned. "They will use you for a taste of life."

She violently jerked away and clamped a hand over her mouth, stumbling. Even as her heart pounded in her chest, she somehow knew that this creature had none of its own. It was a shell.

"Dead," she finally managed to croak. "That thing was…?"

"*Ruḥā,*" he finished for her. "A spirit, a breath, the wind. Have you never seen one on Earth, or in your dreams?"

"No." She stared at him. A lantern's flames glowed just behind him, but no light passed through his body. "I thought I had. But you're not dead, are you?"

"I am not dead," he said, curling his upper lip. "Though I should be."

An icy finger of dread traced Sam's spine. She shivered while Eshmun spread his arms wide.

"Do you want to know where you are?" he asked. "Truly?"

She nodded hesitantly, now terrified of having the answer she'd demanded.

"This is the underworld," he said darkly. "Welcome."

4

*T*he *underworld.* Sam let out an incredulous laugh. "You mean we're in hell?"

"No," he said. "*Gihannā* is yet another realm, one you should hope never to see."

"But..." She paused, afraid to ask. "Am *I* dead?"

She desperately held her hands out in front of her. The blisters from digging the hole in her backyard were still fresh. She felt her pulse pounding. Blood was flowing. She was breathing.

And so was Eshmun. His nostrils flared as he glanced over his shoulder. "You soon will be dead," he said, "if you continue to bleat like a lost lamb."

"Are we being followed?" she asked as he took her wrist again and hurried them urgently between buildings.

"Possibly."

"I'm not going with you," she said, looking around for another route, another option.

"If you wander these streets alone, you will find yourself wishing for death."

"Tell me how to get home," she demanded. "Where is my sister?"

So many questions welled up inside her, one wave of them crashing after another. She felt sick with confusion. *Why is Zayin's skin gray? Where is Sidon? Who is Melqart? Why does everything here look so incredibly old?*

"I need *something* to make sense," she said. "Anything! Tell me—"

"Silence," he hissed.

"You brought me here. I deserve answers from you. Why—" she started, but Eshmun put a hand across her mouth and pulled her away from the road once more. Her spine met with the side of a stone building, and she opened her mouth to bite his palm.

But a moment later, a woman hurried past. At first glance, Sam thought she was belly dancing, the way she undulated.

But then she saw what she truly was.

From the waist up, she was beautiful and human—but her lower half tapered into the form of a snake.

The snake-woman paused a moment, stretching up to lick the air; she was so close that Sam could see her narrowed eyes. She'd clearly caught the scent of something, and whipped off around a corner, her iridescent scales glinting as she slithered. Sam squeezed her eyes shut and tried not to scream.

Is she looking for us? Why?

"Come," Eshmun whispered, pulling her into a narrow alley. "Hurry."

Dazed, Sam followed him down the rough road lit by hanging lanterns. As a donkey cart clacked toward them, Eshmun swept Sam behind him, enveloping her in his cloak. She held her breath as the cart clattered by, and saw that it was full of clay bowls and jugs—just like the one from Jiddo.

Mom would have woken up from her nap by now. She would have gone outside to find the broken jug and the hose running. If she'd looked closely enough, she would have seen coins scattered in the mud. Sam could almost hear her calling for her daughters. *Where did you two disappear to?* She would search the house for a note, because unlike Mom, Sam would have left one. She would check the driveway for the car.

"This way," Eshmun said sternly as soon as the road was empty.

She shook her head, untangling herself from his cloak. "Why should I trust you." It was an accusation, not a question.

"You should not."

"Then I'm going to look for my sister," Sam said. "She could be in terrible danger. I need to find her! I can't just—"

"My uncle is on the prowl," Eshmun said, punctuating each word, "as are his servants. My father will also want to know who you are. And that is only the beginning."

Sam opened her mouth to argue, to ask more questions, but then felt a shadow—something dark and cold—pass just behind her. Turning, she found another lifeless *ruḥā* with holes for eyes.

Quivering, she followed Eshmun, doubting every step.

Her shirt snagged on the walls of the buildings they skirted: They were rough and unpainted, crumbling at the corners, nothing more than dried mud. Every once in a while, she heard voices—people talking inside.

"Maha ta'ruǯanna?" What do you want? "The goat? What can you trade for it?"

A child laughed and a stern voice followed. *"Al tappulā!" Climb down!*

By now they had navigated an intricate web of alleyways, so tight in some places they had to turn sideways to angle through. Finally, they reached what seemed to be Eshmun's destination: a square building with a wooden door and a large, clawed pawprint marking its wall.

Eshmun knocked quietly in a series of rhythmic taps.

Hardly a second later, a small window near the top of the door opened. Black, beady eyes peered out, and the smell of tobacco smoke and firewood followed. The window snapped shut, and then the entire wooden door swung open with a creak.

A huge man stood just inside the threshold. There was no telling where his beard ended and his chest hair began: Black curls spilled out from underneath his clothes and sprouted wildly from his head, thick and long. His arms were so hairy, Sam couldn't see the skin underneath. He smelled as awful as he looked.

For a moment, he seemed overjoyed to see Eshmun. But then his attention went to Sam, and his eyes widened as his smile vanished.

"My lord, what is this?" he asked gruffly, towering over her.

Sam turned on her heels to flee, but Eshmun stood directly behind her, so she met with his hard chest and stumbled backward—right into the beastly man who'd opened the door.

"Fool," Eshmun said to her. "Where do you think you will go?"

The hulking man grabbed Sam by the shoulder and pulled her into the dimly lit house. She tripped against a small table, sending a plate and knife to the floor with a crash; bones and a fish head fell on her shoes, the fish's vacant eye staring up at her. She turned, but the beastlike man had already slammed the door shut behind her, locking it with a black metal bar.

"What in Ba'alat Gebal's name is this?" the man asked Eshmun, staring unabashedly at Sam. The only places he wasn't covered in hair were his cheeks and forehead, where his olive skin was creased like a road map that had been folded and unfolded far too many times.

"Teth, old friend. You don't say hello?" Eshmun asked with a wry grin.

The man seemed to snap to. He laughed and pulled Eshmun into a tight grip; Sam almost thought she heard Eshmun wheeze from the embrace.

"My lord," he said. "It is an honor to see you." His deep voice carried like thunder through the small house. It shook Sam's nerves.

"And you as well." Eshmun slapped the man's shoulders affectionately. "It has been too long."

Teth's one-room house had only a few pieces of carved wooden furniture: a chair, the table Sam had disturbed, and a bed topped with a thin mattress. Pine needles poked out of its seams and were scattered all over the floor, giving the dwelling the feeling of a woodland cave. Small flames crackled in the soot-stained fireplace, sending as much smoke into the house as up the chimney.

"But what are you doing in Baalbek?" Teth asked, echoing Zayin's question. "What business do you have with Melqart? And..." He paused to sniff at Sam's hair. "What is this?"

Sam recoiled. "I'm not a *what*."

"You will not believe what has come to pass," Eshmun said, ignoring Sam's comment.

Teth studied Sam more carefully, his eyes lingering on her bracelets and her shoes. He then intently turned to Eshmun once more. "I believe you always."

"Brother," Eshmun said. He put his hands to his chest as if the words wouldn't come unless he steadied his heart first. "You know— of all people, you know—that I lost my final shreds of faith a century ago."

"You must tell me everything," Teth said, his lips pulled back so that his teeth showed, too many for his mouth. He was rapt. Sam had no idea what they were talking about, but it was clearly important— and judging by the way Teth had stared, it might have something to do with her.

"We have taken every route on foot and by sea," Eshmun said. "We have spoken with every tribe, fought and formed allegiances."

"You found the gateway," Teth gasped, looking as though he

might cry. "You discovered the *tar'ā*!" He lurched for the chairback as if to steady himself from falling. "Where?"

"No," Eshmun said, holding up his hands.

"You will lead the stranded to paradise, to *Ĭmayyà*!" Teth sat down heavily on the chair, the legs creaking beneath him. He smacked his stomach as if he'd just devoured a satisfying meal. "I knew this day would come," he said, shaking a thick finger at the ceiling. "The prophecy has been fulfilled!"

Gateway, paradise, prophecy. Sam's mind spun. She clenched her teeth, still trying to gauge whether any of this was even real.

"Listen," Eshmun said. "You misunderstand."

"I misunderstand? Then what?" Teth asked, leaning forward. "Tell me! Did you not find the way?"

"There *was* a rift," Eshmun said, "but this girl slipped through the veil from Earth, not from *Ĭmayyà*." He curled his fingers into an angry fist. "She has my obol."

"Your...your *burial coin*?" Teth sputtered.

"I *had* a coin," Sam corrected. "But it was my great-grandfather's, not yours."

"Silence!" Eshmun said. "You have no right to speak." He pointed an accusatory finger at her. "She took it in her hand, and thereby I was summoned to claim it. Awakened by her touch, its power called to me." Eshmun took a step toward her. "Now give it to me, thief."

Sam backed toward the door. Her eyes went to the dinner knife on the floor, then to the shattered clay plate. A large shard with a pointed end.

"I dropped it," she said. "It's not here."

"*Daggálá*," Eshmun hissed. *Liar.*

Anger swelled inside her. "I'm telling the truth!"

"The other girl has it, then?"

The other girl. "You mean my sister," Sam said. "Tell me where she is. You brought us here—you must know!"

Teth threw his hands in the air. "There is another?" he asked, incredulous.

"Yes," Sam said. Rima was out there somewhere among the ghouls and half-humans. She might have hit her head when she fell from the funnel; she could be blacked out in the streets or in the temple—anything could have happened to her. "And I need to find her."

"We will," Eshmun said coldly. "If you do not have the coin, then she does. I will find her." He scowled. "Do you understand its power and worth? A golden coin forged by a god, infused with blood and magic?"

"No." *Blood and magic?* "I don't understand."

"It is *priceless*," he seethed. "May the gods forbid, but if I do not reclaim it, it could be melted and sullied, reforged for dark deeds. Many would die to possess it. Gods would go to war for it."

Whatever its value, Rima didn't have the coin either, Sam was certain. Sam had flicked it back into the garden before they were sucked down into the funnel. "I don't care about your coin. We just need to get home."

Teth studied her curiously. "Where is home?"

"Glen Arbor, Michigan," Sam said—in English, the only way she could. "Wilderness Cove Trailer Park."

"What is she saying?" Teth scratched at his beard and looked at Eshmun with wonder. "Which route did you take to find her, my lord? You went through the Strait, did you not?"

"No. This has nothing to do with navigating ships, my friend."

"We fell." Sam's voice wavered, and she looked at Eshmun. "Everything sort of...unraveled."

Teth squinted and shook his head. "I do not know this place—what

did you call it? Michigan." He pronounced it all wrong, like it was two words: *Mish Again*.

"We have other problems," Eshmun said grimly. "She arrived in Melqart's temple. She was seen there by some of his...attendants."

Teth let out a short growl. "Zayin?"

Eshmun nodded tersely.

"Then she has told the king by now."

Eshmun sneered. *"King.* My father is but a lazy squatter in the home of Ba'alat Gebal. While she searches to the east for the passageway, for the *tar'ā*, he eats her food and sleeps with her servants. He should be in his *own* city-state of Tyre, not in Baalbek." A taut line of muscle twitched along Eshmun's jaw. "He has likely sent his least-friendly *ḫayuta* after us already. He will pursue the girl, he will—"

Teth let out a small laugh. "He is likely too intoxicated to act so quickly." He bent down to clean the mess off the floor, putting the fish bones and broken plate into a basket and slipping the knife into his pocket. "And what of your uncle? No one knows what evil he brews, but the god of death is most certainly setting traps. You should be in Sidon with your men."

Sam pressed her hands to her cheeks. *Eshmun's uncle is someone called the god of death?*

"I need water," she said. "Please."

She looked around the room for a sink, but there was nothing at all that seemed to bring water into the house. No shower, no toilet, no dishwasher. She also realized there was nothing electrical. The house was devoid of light fixtures. There were no clocks.

Eshmun nodded to Teth, who then opened a back door Sam hadn't noticed, one hardly big enough for his barrel-like body. He

disappeared outside for a minute, and then squeezed back through with an opaque, heavy glass.

Hesitantly, she tasted the liquid it held. It had an earthy flavor.

"It is only water," Teth assured her.

She took another sip. Teth offered her a bowl of walnuts, but her stomach was already full of fear and dread, and she pushed the bowl away. She glanced at the door, but based on what she'd seen of Baalbek, it might very well lead into a walled yard, a dead end—no escape there.

"You said there was another," Teth said to Eshmun. He helped himself to a handful of the walnuts, crushing them in his fist. The shells made a popping noise, and Sam winced. "Where?"

"I do not know for certain," Eshmun said, bringing his eyebrows together. "The three of us were separated. I believe she has been taken by the Wanderers."

"Taken?" Sam blurted.

"Possible, yes," Teth agreed. "A caravan is passing through."

"Before I found this one"—Eshmun flicked his eyes toward Sam—"I caught news of it in the streets: gossip that they found a girl, strangely dressed and lost."

"What will they do with her?" Sam cried. "How do you know it was my sister they were talking about?"

Eshmun ignored her questions. He tipped his chin at Sam, but spoke to Teth. "I cannot travel with her in these odd garments. She will attract undue attention."

"She is to come with us?" Teth asked, making a face.

"Us?" Eshmun asked in return.

"I am with you," Teth said, "as always."

Eshmun held up a hand. "Friend, I only came here to find Meem.

She is to thoroughly search this girl on my behalf." He looked around the small house. "Is Meem in the courtyard?"

"S-search me?" Sam repeated with a stutter of panic. "No one needs to search me."

"You only came here for Meem," Teth repeated. Sam shielded her face with a hand as he let out a heavy breath, a potent mix of garlicky fish and liquor. From inside his shirt, he pulled out a leather necklace with a large pendant: It was a red clay face with a beard made of a half dozen snail shells pressed together.

It was unmistakably Eshmun.

"Teth. Old friend," Eshmun said gently. "I do not wish to set my troubles upon your shoulders."

"By the order of Rabā, my Meem has left this home." Teth's eyes dropped to the floor. "I am coming with you, my lord. I would once again serve as one of your guardsmen in Sidon. I have no reason to stay here. Meem has...we are no longer..."

"You don't need to search me," Sam repeated. Between the hazy smoke of the fireplace, the rank smell of Teth, and her suffocating fear, she thought she might faint again.

Get your shit together. Get your shit together, Sam.

"I will call for my Meem," Teth said, "if you wish."

Eshmun turned his full attention back to Sam, his keyhole pupil flaring. "Yes," he said. "I do."

Teth hesitated and then dipped his head. He slipped out the front door and was gone.

The house was silent, other than the quiet snap of flames. Sam swallowed.

Eshmun coldly assessed her, his eyes lingering on her pockets and collar, and finally her hands, which she'd pulled into fists. Ready for a fight. He took a step toward her, and then another, until she was

backed against the smoldering fireplace. Teth, she realized, had left the front door unlocked.

With a grunt, she shoved Eshmun aside and lunged for the door handle, the metal ring. She pulled with all her weight, the thick door opening a crack. Eshmun grabbed at her, and she thrust an elbow into his stomach, but he caught her arm and twisted it until she faced him. Crying out, she kicked him, but he hardly flinched, forcing her backward against the door.

"Give me your hands," Eshmun said.

"I don't have your stupid coin," she said, panting. She unfurled her fists to show him they were empty; the blisters from digging were all she had in her palms. Furious, she slapped him hard across the cheek, a fresh wave of pain flaring through her hand. "Let me out of here. You have no right to hold me prisoner."

"Tell me," he said coolly. "What is this?" He took her left hand and held it upright, pushing her bracelets toward her elbow and pointing to a thin white line across her wrist. A scar.

"Nothing," she said. "I cut myself cleaning a fish."

"And how you recoil," he said, smiling ruefully, "when I call you untruthful."

"You know nothing about me," she spat, edging sideways.

She bolted for the back door, but her calves met the frame of the bed and she toppled onto the mattress. The smell of pine—dry and pungent—wafted up from the bedding. Eshmun leaned over her, arms folded, staring at her with his strange keyhole pupil.

Sam steeled herself, ready to kick or scratch, but he stood back and crossed the room, assessing her again from a distance. She took a jagged breath; her shirt had turned wet under her arms. Shakily, she stood and smoothed out her clothes, brushing pine needles from her pants.

In front of the fireplace sat a set of utensils she hadn't noticed before; the fork looked more like a two-pronged skewer. Fork to the eye. All it would take was one decisive stab. Sam's heartbeat thrummed in her temples. She took a step toward the fork, and then it was too late.

The front door swung open and Teth huffed back inside. He wiped his hand across his brow and closed the door, locking it once more.

"Where is Meem?" Eshmun asked.

Teth stepped aside. "Right here," he said.

She was behind him, but so small—especially compared to Teth— that Sam hadn't seen her. Perhaps only four feet tall, Meem had a sharp nose, high cheekbones, and eyes too big for her face. Teth put a hand out, as if to smooth the wild hair on top of her head, but she looked at him pointedly, halting him. He let out another cloud of sour breath and backed away, glancing at the floor.

"Meem," Eshmun said. "Let me see your face."

At the sight of Eshmun, who had been standing in the dark corner on the opposite side of the house, Meem startled and dipped nearly to the ground. "My lord," she said in a trembling whisper. She would not meet his eyes—she kept her focus on the wall behind him instead.

"I hope you are well," he said. His cheek was red where Sam had slapped him, and she smiled inwardly at her small victory. He wasn't invincible.

"I am well," Meem said, turning toward Teth, as if he were the one who had asked the question. "In my parents' home, I am...where I belong."

Teth grumbled under his breath.

"We must soon be on our way," Eshmun said. "And so we must make haste. You know your task?"

She nodded quickly several times in a row, a nervous birdlike pecking motion. "Teth has told me what I am to do." She held a brown sack, tied at the top, and Sam wondered what was inside. Tools for searching her? Did they mean to tie her down? Was the sack to go over her head?

"We will wait in the courtyard," Eshmun announced. He clapped a hand on Teth's massive back.

"My lord," Teth said. "Give me a moment. There was a disturbance as we walked here. Something is afoot."

Eshmun's expression turned a shade darker. He nodded. "Go then. Be quick."

He bolted the lock behind Teth, then turned to face Sam. "Do not attempt to flee again," he warned, moving toward the back door. "There is nowhere for you to go." He took two steps backward and plucked the fork from the hearth.

The moment the rear door was closed, Meem began circling Sam, assessing her from all directions.

"Why would you keep the coin from Eshmun?" she asked.

"I'm not," Sam said, twisting to look over her shoulder.

Meem shoved her hands into Sam's back pockets, digging to the bottoms. Sam squirmed, tamping down the urge to put an elbow into Meem's chest.

"What is this?" She slid Jiddo's letter out. Sam had forgotten it was there.

"I can't read it," Sam said. "I don't know what it says."

Meem unfolded the paper and made a face. "It says nothing. These are only lines and dots. There are no meaningful shapes here."

"Yes, there are," Sam said, gritting her teeth. "It's just in a different language."

"An encoded message."

"It's Arabic, that's all."

Meem set the letter aside and dipped her probing fingers into Sam's front pockets this time.

"You want to go home?" Meem asked, bobbing around her a second time. Her wild hair tickled Sam's neck like a plume of feathers; Sam grimaced and scratched at her skin. "Do you not?"

"I need to find someone first." Sam glanced once more at the lock on the front door. With every passing minute, her worry grew sharper and deeper, sinking itself into her bones. *Rima.*

"Might this someone have the coin?" Meem's round eyes never seemed to blink. "Or—if you have the coin, then you would be wise to hide the coin," she reasoned, circling, "so that Eshmun would want to find your someone, who might have the coin, if you do not. If you gave him the coin now, he would have little incentive to look for this someone. So you keep it from him."

"Is that what he thinks?" Sam said, twisting left and right to follow Meem, feeling like she was being spun into a knot of bewilderment.

"That is what *I* think," Meem said, stopping to face Sam. Her eyes were owl-like, Sam decided. Luminous, yet predatory. Perhaps she was not so harmless, despite her diminutive size.

Meem cocked her head. She took a step closer, examining the buttons on Sam's shirt.

Sam knew she could only stall for so long before her clothes would have to come off. *But what are ḥayuta? Why do she and Teth call Eshmun my lord?* A hundred more questions needed to be answered. She looked around Teth's home with its primitive furnishings. "What year is this?" she asked, bending down to slip off her sneakers.

"Year?" Meem repeated.

"How long ago are we?" Sam tried. She tapped her wrist. "You know, where are we in time?"

"Time abandoned us after the horrible siege of Tyre." Meem held Sam's shoes in her hands with a certain kind of awe. She studied them intently, turning them over to look at the soles. "Ever since our ancestors fled here to the underworld."

Baalbek, Sidon, Tyre. Something finally clicked. Sam put the city names together.

"I'm in Lebanon," she said with disbelief. "But...but why is everything so ancient? This must be..." Her mind flashed to the books on Mom's shelf in her bedroom. Mostly romance novels, along with crystal and tarot reference guides, and the few books Jiddo had sent over the years. "...Phoenicia? The coin brought me to its own time and place."

"The coin brought you to its rightful owner," Meem said. "You may give it to me now." There was lust in her voice as she held a small hand out in front of her, cupping the air. "To have a coin forged by the great Chusor..."

"Someone named Chusor makes these coins? So he can make another one," Sam reasoned. "Couldn't Eshmun ask him...or her?"

"Teth said you fell," Meem said, then pursed her lips to a point.

"Yes."

"And were your senses knocked from your head? Such questions! Chusor was a deity. He was an artisan. And he is gone," Meem said, sounding indignant. "He crafted obols from gold and the feathers of angels, first turned to ashes over a sacred fire that was never allowed to die. Also, of course, a royal peacock's feather, and a drop of Chusor's own blood. But Eshmun's obol went beyond even this, because he is the son of Melqart and a Tyrian princess. His coin also contained a drop of his *mother's* blood. Royal blood. Ancient and powerful blood."

"But why does he think I want it?" Sam pressed. "What I would do with it?'

"Melt it. Sell it in small increments, each worth a fortune," Meem said, the word *fortune* lingering on her lips. "The buyers would consume their share, eating it to attain godlike powers. Some would wear it as royal jewelry. Others might reforge it with hellfire and add the scales of crocodilians, in hopes of summoning the damned from hell to command them." She watched Sam closely. "An obol is meant to take its owner to paradise, but there are countless tales of a sacred coin's *repurposed* power. It has been a long time since there was an obol in this world. Many would like nothing better than to find out if those alchemical tales are true, or merely legend. There are even gods who would covet this."

"And you?" Sam asked. Something glinted in Meem's spiky hair, she noticed now: a tiara. Golden, studded with green stones. "Would you wear it as jewelry? Are you a princess like Eshmun's mother?"

"I am of the noble class," Meem said. "My grandfather aspires to match me with a royal."

Sam gauged the tone in Meem's voice, the fire in her eyes. She sounded bitter. "Weren't you with Teth?"

"He is not suitable," Meem said. "If he had more wealth, perhaps. If only—"

A series of rhythmic knocks at the front door interrupted. Meem slid a chair in front of the door to climb up and peer out through the small square window. "What have you there?" she asked.

Before an answer came, she snapped the window closed, climbed down, and unbolted the metal lock. The front door creaked opened and Teth ducked back inside, barely dodging the low lintel. His huge hairy body and its pungent smell once again filled the house.

And again, he was hiding someone behind him.

5

Rima tripped across the small room, knocking Sam against the wall with the desperate force of her embrace. Sam clutched her fiercely. "Rima!" she cried with relief.

"Are we dreaming?" Rima asked shakily into Sam's ear, after pulling a wad of gray fabric from her mouth and dropping it to the floor.

"I hope so," Sam replied. She couldn't remember the last time they'd hugged like this. Rima still smelled like home, a mixture of coffee and the crisp air in their backyard. She pressed her nose into Rima's hair. "I'm so, so happy to see you." Gently, she pushed her sister away so she could look her over, holding her by both shoulders. "What happened to you?" There were a few scratches on Rima's neck, but otherwise she seemed unscathed. "Are you okay?"

"Um," Rima said, letting out a pained laugh. Tears had run lines down her cheeks, streaking what was left of her makeup. "Let's review. First I did the barfy tornado ride. Then a bunch of stranger-dangers grabbed me and tossed me in a cart. They were taking me somewhere to *sell* me. Then three of them got in a huge argument, like trying to *kill* each other, and the cart tipped over and I ran. And then Bigfoot here grabbed me, shoved a nasty sock in my mouth, and tossed me over his shoulder." She cast a reproachful look at Teth.

"You would be wise to resist speaking in strange tongues," he said, squinting at Rima.

"I do not care for your language," Rima said to him, forming her words slowly, as if she had to think about them first. She turned to Sam and made a face, and in that instant, Rima was five years old again, the kid sister pushing her plate away at dinner. "Can you speak it, too?"

Sam nodded, and Rima switched back to English. "Half the words sound like you're trying to cough up a phlegm-ball." She shook her head. "What is happening to us?"

"Search her as well," Teth grumbled, and then exited through the small back door into the courtyard to join Eshmun outside. Sam could hear him through the mud-brick wall—the triumph in his voice as he told Eshmun what he'd caught wandering through the streets.

"Do you think we died and went to hell?" Rima asked Sam. "I stole lipstick from Walmart and this is what I get for it? I mean, really? Okay, and there was also the Ecstasy that one time, and maybe what I did with Jake in the bathroom at school—"

"We're not dead," Sam said. "And Jake? What?"

"Remove your clothing." Meem interrupted, extending a small, bony hand. "You must give all of it to me. It is what Eshmun has ordered."

"Who ordered what?" Rima asked. The lilt in her voice had vanished; she sniffled and hugged herself, her knuckles turning white. "Are you sure we're not dead, Sam? I saw ghosts out there, I swear."

"Now." Meem waved an arm toward the back door. Outside, Teth's voice rose and fell, penetrating the house's thin barrier of dried mud. *Barter*, he boomed. *Prophecy*. "Unless you would like one of the men to help?" Meem cupped a hand to her mouth, ready to call them.

"No!" Sam said.

"What is going on right now?" Rima asked, her eyes flashing with fear.

"We're going to be strip-searched. We're going to prove to them that we don't have the coin," Sam said, trying to sound calm, "and then we're going to find our way out of here."

Rima drew her eyebrows together. "You have got to be kidding."

"It'll be okay," Sam said, but her fingers fumbled over each button of her shirt. She had to peel it off, it was so damp with sweat.

"If you say so?" Rima gave her a fearful look and retreated to the bed to sit on the edge of the mattress, her back turned.

"We're just going to get it over with," Sam said, handing the shirt to Meem, "and then they'll let us go."

"No more talking," Meem commanded sharply.

Sam unzipped her pants, her hands doing one thing and her mind telling her to do another. Meem's throat looked so fragile. Sam could choke her. She glanced at Rima, who had pulled her knees to her chest, hugging herself into a ball. Sam didn't think she would be able to stand the sight of Meem touching her little sister's bare skin. She felt sick to her stomach.

"It would be unwise of you to fight me," Meem said, as if she could read Sam's mind. "Did you make this?" She peered at the shirt's stitches, turning it inside out. "The method and the fabric confound me."

"I don't sew," Sam said, handing Meem her pants. It felt like a gesture of surrender. Rima glanced over her shoulder and quickly turned back to face the wall.

Meem held the pants to her nose for a moment, and then pulled them inside out as well. "You have an unnamable odor," she said, studying the zipper with a look of consternation.

"Juicy Couture," Sam said. A disconcerting Christmas gift from Mr. Koplow to Mom, which she hadn't wanted, so Sam ended up with it.

Meem furrowed her brow. She tugged on the zipper, making it slide up and down with childlike fascination. Her tiny mouth twitched with glee. She tugged the zipper up one more time and finally tossed the pants onto the floor. Glancing at the back door, she lowered her voice, speaking so quietly that Sam could hardly hear her. "Are you his lover?" she asked.

"No!" Sam said with such force that Meem took a step back.

"Then you are truly strangers to each other?" she asked. "Who are you?"

Sam countered with a question of her own. "Did Eshmun ask you to interrogate us?"

"No," Meem said, a note of disappointment in her voice. "He did not." She snapped her small fingers at Sam. "Give me the breast cloth next."

Sam shook her head. "You can see that I'm not hiding anything."

Rima's hunched shoulders shook. She looked like a miserable kid who'd forgotten her winter jacket. Sam wanted to hug her again. She wanted to get them out of Teth's house.

"I cannot," said Meem.

"I promise you," Sam said. She shivered, too, even though she felt like she was suffocating. The fire still snapped within the fireplace. Outside, Teth talked in urgent tones.

"Undress."

With hands shaky and uncooperative, Sam unhooked her bra and slid it off. It was warm with her body heat. She handed it to Meem, who held it like an untrustworthy animal. She squeezed it and stretched it in every direction, trying to rip the elastic straps apart without success. Finally, she pulled a long knife from underneath her tunic.

She had been armed all along. Of course she had. If Sam had

actually been able to summon the courage to grab her by the neck, she might have ended up with a knife in her stomach.

"Don't cut it," Sam said, her arms folded across her chest. "I'd like to put it back on."

But Meem sliced into the padding anyway and proceeded to pull the entire bra into pieces. Eshmun's voice filtered through the door, and Sam felt a hot edge of hatred cut through her. *Search them thoroughly,* he had said.

Rima spoke to the wall. "You sure about this?" she asked in English. "We could...you know? It's two against one right now."

"We can't," Sam answered. Meem held the long knife firmly in her hand. "She's got a weapon."

"Get dressed," Meem said abruptly.

Sam narrowed her eyes, not sure she'd heard correctly. "What?"

Meem untied the sack she had brought and emptied the contents: a folded white garment, and a pile of brown clothes that could have been mistaken for dirty rags.

"You're done?" Sam asked warily. "But I thought—"

Meem halted her with a hand in the air. "You have been searched," she said pointedly, giving Sam the white clothing.

Sam slipped the gown over her head, hurrying before Meem changed her mind, or before the men walked back inside. Although it was sleeveless, the dress was modestly cut with a V-neck that showed only a hint of cleavage. The fabric along the neckline was dyed a pale shade of purple, and thick golden threads weaved their way along the bottom hem, which hit just above the knees.

"This?" Sam asked, holding a long piece of fur. *A scarf?* she thought. *A boa?*

"The belt."

Sam glanced at the pile of dingy brown clothes, and Meem

followed her eyes. "That will not fit you," she said. "You are...fuller than Teth described, and shorter. It will do for her, though." She tipped her head toward Rima.

Though the white dress was thin, Sam was relieved to be covered again. Meem gave her a pair of brown leather sandals, plain and flat, with a ring to hold her big toe in place and a strap across the center.

"I want my own shoes," Sam said. Only hours ago, she'd thought of them as worn out and old, but now she saw them as broken-in and comfortable. She could run in them, if she had to.

Meem laughed. "Your shoes are an oddity. You cannot wear them without attracting attention. If you are to blend in here, you will also need to cut your hair." Meem assessed Sam's grown-out bangs. "I do not have an appropriate hat for you, either."

"I'm dressed, Rima," Sam said.

She put a hand on her sister's back and took her spot on the bed; the process was repeated behind her back, and a few minutes later, she turned to find Rima dressed in a drab brown dress. She was tugging at it, trying to pull it down to cover her knees.

"This thing itches," Rima said. "And it smells like ass."

"What are you conspiring?" Meem asked angrily. "Stop speaking in your foreign tongue."

"She only said that her dress has a bad odor," Sam said.

"Teth told me there was but one of you," Meem said, frowning. "You are lucky I brought a second garment."

"Yeah," Rima said. "Super lucky. I should run out and buy a lottery ticket while I'm enjoying such a charmed state." She twisted her shapeless and stained dress again. "You can get us back home," she said to Sam, her voice turning desperate. "Right? Mom's probably worried."

Sam nodded. "Don't cry."

Outside, Teth barked something, an expression of wonder. Now Eshmun's voice could be heard: a steady stream of murmurs, as if he were giving instructions or making a list. The tenor suggested their conversation was coming to an end.

Meem's eyes were on hers. She leaned in toward Sam's ear.

"I believe you," she said, lowering her voice. "You do not have the coin—not at the moment. And I believe that you are here for a reason. A reason bigger than any of us know. You are not of this world, are you?" She leaned in farther. "If we are to meet again, I would like you to look kindly upon me. I have done you a favor."

"I see," Sam said. "So now we owe you one." She studied the girl's face. "What do you want?"

"I do not know yet," Meem said, her small lips curling into a smile. "Time will tell." Then she called out to the men, and a moment later the back door swung open with a creak.

Teth came through first, and when he took in Sam's new appearance, he made an unhappy noise. Eshmun stopped short, too, with a flustered double take.

Rima leaped sideways into Sam, her terror palpable. "It's the guy from our backyard!"

"It's okay," Sam said, trying to calm her, taking her hand.

Eshmun glanced at Rima and then continued to stare unabashedly at Sam.

"Do you find them acceptable?" Meem asked.

"No," Teth said at the same time Eshmun said, "Yes." Both of them sounded a bit too emphatic.

Teth turned toward Rima in her sad brown dress. "She will have to play the attendant of the other," he said. "And what is this malady?" He squinted at Sam's green toenails.

"It's nothing. It's paint."

"It's Jungle Canopy," Rima murmured shakily. The name of the polish shade.

Eshmun took a step toward Sam, his eyes on her set of bracelets. Meem had never asked her to remove them. Another favor. "What did you find?" he asked Meem.

"Only this," she said, handing Eshmun the letter from Jiddo.

"No obol?" he asked, his voice laced with anger.

Meem swiveled her head back and forth.

Eshmun's face shifted; his jaw clenched. He stared into the fireplace and the flames licking upward. The moment lengthened.

Teth finally spoke. "What do you have there, my lord?" he asked, motioning to the paper Eshmun held in his hand.

Eshmun unfolded the letter and studied it silently. "It is an odd but familiar script...and this is not papyrus." He ran his fingers over the thin paper. "What does it say?"

"I don't know," Sam said, and the moment the words left her lips, she knew Eshmun would think she was lying. He scowled at her. "I'm telling you the truth. I need someone to translate it for me."

Eshmun looked again at the letter, his eyes flicking between the script and Sam's face. Finally he folded it and tucked it inside his robes, mumbling to himself.

"What is it?" Teth asked him quietly, but Eshmun shook him off with a troubled look. "You were meticulous in your search, Meem?"

She bobbed her head—nodding over and over again—and then shook herself like a bird. She seemed, quite literally, ruffled. She was a terrible liar.

"Be well," Eshmun said to her. "And tell no one we were here." He gathered up Sam's and Rima's clothes and gave them to her. "Burn them."

"No!" Sam said. "You can't do that."

"All of it," Eshmun said. "Into ashes." He handed Meem a small fur bag that bulged at the bottom—apparently payment for her work. "Give my regards to your parents, and to your grandfather."

"Thank you," she said with a deep bow. "I am always, in all manner of ways, at your service." Teth ushered her to the door, where she almost imperceptibly brushed a hand against his, before ducking away and flitting out of the house.

As soon as the door was shut and bolted once more, Eshmun turned to Teth. "Gather the supplies. We leave for Sidon."

"My sister and I are staying here," Sam said firmly. "You know we don't have your coin. We've been searched. You don't need us anymore. This is where the funnel dropped us, so the way back must be nearby."

"Yeah. Let's go," Rima said, taking a brave step toward the door. Teth blocked the way. She looked up at his hairy face. "Move it, Sasquatch. Or I'll scream."

Teth didn't move.

"Do not speak," Eshmun said, "with your foreign words. Do not call for help." He paused, then tipped his head toward a thought. "Or perhaps you should. Yes. We shall sit back and see who comes for you." Rima slowly turned to face him, her lower lip trembling. "I am certain your former captors would enjoy a reunion," he added.

"Leave her alone," Sam said.

Eshmun pulled a thin blanket from the bed and tossed it at Teth. "Bind and gag them."

"You can't do this," Sam said, angling herself to guard Rima.

Teth was silent as he ripped the blanket into long strips. He moved behind Sam and gripped her—struggling was useless—mumbling in her ear as he tied her wrists behind her back, too tight.

"*Tyābutā*," he said. *Shame. Regret.*

Sam wasn't sure if he was feeling uneasy with his task, or if the remorse should be her own. Apparently, she was a *thief*, after all. She kicked at him uselessly while he threaded the gag across her mouth, the taste of the fabric rife with body odor. Teth then pushed Sam and Rima into opposite corners of the house while he and Eshmun discussed what they needed to pack, which route to take, weighing one weapon against another. Teth tested the blade of a knife against a fingertip, drawing a drop of blood.

"I'm sorry, Rima," Sam choked unintelligibly through her gag. Now they faced a journey even deeper into this strange world.

Sam looked up at Eshmun, who was deliberating between two vials of liquid. He corked one and placed it inside his bag. Something dark welled inside her. If he hurt Rima, she would kill him.

She would drive something sharp straight through his keyhole pupil. She would not hesitate.

6

The outline of Baalbek and its temple had long faded behind them.

Sam worked her jaw back and forth, forcing the gag in her mouth to stretch. The taste was nauseating, but she licked the strip of cloth anyway, turning it damp and limp. Her new sandals—too small—bit into her toes. Rima walked ahead of her, her hands ruthlessly bound, and Sam could see where the fabric had cut sores into her skin.

She felt a burn behind her eyes. Rage.

"Think of the prophecy," Teth said as he huffed alongside them. They marched through a valley on a worn dirt road, among fields of crops, blue in the twilight. "What if these girls are here to help you fulfill it?"

"*Lā,*" Eshmun said. "My obol has come for me. I am on my way to *ʾmayyà* to be with my family. This world is not for me, not any longer."

"Of course, my lord," Teth said. His eyebrows dripped with sweat, and he wiped it away with his sleeve, a rough, dull fabric like burlap. "It will be a great *marzeḥ*—a glorious reunion—when you are in heaven with your mother and cousins and friends once again." He paused, as if weighing his choice of words, then spoke haltingly. "I am certain, my lord, that you have thoroughly considered the prophecy in light of...others, and their own desires."

"Yes, of course," Eshmun said tersely. "My uncle's machinations

are always at the forefront of my imagination. And my nightmares." He waved them forward, his cloak snapping in the wind. "Hurry."

Patches of lavender lined the path they followed, and the air was tinged with the scent of the flowers. They were the same shade of purple as the sash Eshmun wore, slung low around his waist. He wore high leather boots that fit tight against his calves, and in them he stalked noiselessly ahead.

With every step they took, Sam felt more and more defeated. With his knives, Eshmun could kill them at any moment. Teth could crush their bones like walnut shells.

"The clothing Meem gave the eldest is too fine," Teth called ahead to Eshmun as he struggled to keep pace. "No servant of yours would wear a white linen dress and a rabbit belt. With a clasp made of gold, no less!"

Rima glanced over her shoulder, and Sam caught the look of hopelessness on her face. They locked eyes and exchanged a wordless moment of solidarity, and then Rima faced forward again, her shoulders slumped, though Sam could see that she was still working her wrists against the fabric ties.

"She could appear to be a relation of yours, dressed so richly," Teth continued. Sam could hear his labored breath as he fell farther behind. "How will you explain her in Sidon? Any woman you bring will be noticed."

Sam wrenched her jaw back and forth, and finally, the gag slid over her lower lip and onto her chin. Her pulse roared.

A moment later, to her delight, Rima had managed to wriggle free of her hand bindings. Warily, she looked back at Sam; Sam in turn glanced at Teth, but he hadn't noticed.

"Of course, by the time we reach the sea, her dress will no longer be white. It will be caked with filth." He cupped his hands over

his mouth. "Friend or foe, cousin or confidante," he boomed, "you will need to decide before we reach Sidon!"

What was waiting for them in Sidon? How far away was it?

Keep your hands behind your back, Sam mouthed, frantically stretching the fabric around her own wrists, twisting and pulling.

Rima nodded.

"The golden threading in her dress suggests royalty," Teth called after Eshmun. "Is that what you intend to claim her as?" And then suddenly, he announced, "She will be your concubine! Your favorite, and that is why she wears these fineries!"

Sam's face went hot. *Concubine*. Rima turned with wide eyes.

Eshmun halted on the path and faced them, his arms at his sides, his hands in fists. Nearby, a river rumbled without pause like a perpetual roll of thunder. Above, the sky was navy blue and streaked with clouds.

With a start, Sam realized it was still dusk. It had been dusk for hours and hours—for as long as they'd been there—with no sign of the moon or stars.

It sent a chill down her spine. This place was wrong... in so many ways. They had to get out.

"You go left and I'll go right," she whispered to Rima.

They would have to stay off the road, or they might run into whoever was following them—the snake-woman, or whomever Eshmun's father had sent. Though she hadn't started running yet, Sam's heart pounded furiously.

"If we get separated," she hissed, shedding the bindings from her wrists, "I'll meet you on the steps of the temple."

"What?" Rima asked. She scrunched her face into a questioning look. "Right now?"

"Yes. *Go!*"

Rima pivoted and broke into a sprint. Rima's soccer legs carried her fast, but Sam's sandal straps gouged her with every stride.

Teth swiped at them as they bolted around him, dodging his meaty fingers by inches. Eshmun bellowed behind them.

"Above!" he shouted. "Above!"

Above? That wasn't the word Sam had anticipated. She looked up.

Something was there. At first she thought it was a small airplane, but then its wings flapped.

It flew in circles, surveying the land below. A bird? A deafening shriek ripped the air in half; Sam pressed her ears closed, her eyes watering from the sound. The creature shot downward, and Sam could see that its body was covered in scales rather than feathers, and its talons were black daggers. It had mottled, toadlike skin, wide-set eyes perched high atop its head, and the nostrils and teeth of a crocodile.

It was a monster.

She wheezed an unintelligible warning at Rima—too far ahead. They were both out in the open, completely vulnerable.

Rima threw her hands over her head and screamed, running toward a thick and sprawling tree for cover. But in one quick swoop, the beast was upon her. Its talons gripped her by the shoulders, digging into her flesh, snatching her up. Her dress instantly turned red.

"No!" Sam screamed, struggling after her.

Then the thing turned and flapped back toward Sam. Its enormous wings were strangely quiet, hitting the air with silent strokes. Hovering above her, it assessed. Taunted.

"Help me, Sam," Rima gasped. Her face was white with terror. She dangled like a captured rabbit.

There was a growl behind Sam and then Teth was at her side, aiming a long knife. He flicked his wrist, and the weapon sank into the thing's cheek.

It shrieked and dipped, and Teth plucked up a boulder from the earth and hurled it. The rock clipped the beast's wing and it wavered downward. Closer. Sam put every ounce of strength into leaping for Rima. Her fingertips grazed the soles of her sister's sandals, but she fell to the ground empty-handed, tasting dirt in her mouth.

Above her, Rima had gone limp, her eyes closed.

With a throat-shredding scream, Sam pulled herself to her feet, snatched a bronze-handled knife from Teth's belt, and hurled it at the flying monster. She was suddenly ten years old again, throwing knives at the tree in the backyard while Dad stood by chewing on his toothpick. The trunk full of scars. The knife would miss. It always did.

But this time she'd aimed perfectly. It sailed straight for the beast's throat—

—until another one of Teth's rocks struck its face, and the monster spun sideways.

"No!" Sam screamed with despair as the knife uselessly sailed through empty air.

Suddenly, Eshmun was at her side. He pulled a jeweled knife from his belt, and, with a quick nod, handed it to her.

Without hesitation, she flung it. *Hard.*

And this time, it slid into the thing's left eye.

Sam gasped at her success. But the beast's cries shattered the dusky sky, its high-pitched screeching like glass in her eardrums—the pain was excruciating. She sank to the ground and covered her ears, watching through tears.

The monster flapped its wings crookedly. Rima fell from its talons.

There was a long, gaping silence, and then there was the blunt sound of Rima hitting the rocky ground with a bone-breaking crunch.

"Oh God," Sam choked. "No, no, no."

She rushed to where Rima had fallen, then fell to her knees and desperately cradled her sister. A thin trail of blood spilled from Rima's mouth; Sam wiped it away with her thumb, streaking it across Rima's chin. She looked up to catch the last glimpse of the monster disappearing, heading toward Baalbek, screaming as it went.

"Please don't be dead," she sobbed into Rima's ear. "Wake up. *Please*, Rima."

Teth shook his fist at the sky. "It...it...no, it cannot be! A *tannîyn*!"

"Silence!" Eshmun roared. "Do not speak its name!"

"What could it be doing here?" Teth spat. "What is it looking for?"

"Them," Eshmun said, nodding at Sam and Rima. "It will soon double back, and it will be angry."

"Mom," Rima moaned.

Sam gently pushed her hair away from her face. "I'm here. It's Sam."

Teth looked down at the two of them. "In the name of Ba'alat Gebal," he murmured, pressing a hand to his heart. "First a funnel from another realm, and now a..." He dropped his voice to a whisper. "A *tannîyn*. What will the heavens bring next?"

"That beast has nothing to do with the heavens. It was birthed at hell's doorstep," Eshmun said darkly. "We must rethink our route. Let us cross the river as soon as possible—it will not be able to follow us into the mountains." He knelt next to Sam and Rima.

"Get away," Sam said hoarsely, her throat sore from screaming at the *tannîyn*. If Rima died here, in this world, Sam would never forgive herself. "This is all your fault." She pulled her sister closer. Her dress was soaked with blood at the shoulders.

Eshmun leaned into her face, his teeth bared. "How dare you? You, who took my burial obol? My sacred coin should be in my

possession as we speak. Your sister hangs on the verge of death because of your theft."

"Because *you* brought us into this world!" She smacked his chest and shoved. "If you lay a finger on her..." She hunched over Rima, shielding her. Anger like boiling poison burned her from the inside out. "I'll kill you. I swear it."

Teth let out a grunt of laughter. "She is a feisty one!"

Eshmun let his eyes linger on Sam's face. "Hold her back."

"What are you doing?" Sam cried as Teth took her by the arms. Eshmun pressed his hands against Rima's wounded shoulders; Sam tried to lunge at him, but couldn't. "Stop!"

Eshmun's voice dropped into a chantlike cadence, quiet and reverent. He was listing strange names, or maybe places. *Is he reciting some sort of prayer for the dying?* Sam twisted to try to free herself. She kicked Teth's shins, but they were stones of muscle and bone.

Eshmun held his fingertips to his eyes and then gently stroked Rima's forehead. Finally he stood aside, and the moment Teth released Sam, she fell at her sister's side. She was sure Rima was dead.

"I love you," she sobbed. "I love you so much."

But Rima stirred. Sam's heart ascended with such velocity she felt like she might faint.

Her sister's eyelids fluttered open. Her breath came out in spasms. Her hazel eyes, wet with tears, darted back and forth.

"Rima!" Sam cried. "Thank God!" She hugged her tightly, tears still streaming down her face. "What did he do to you?"

Sam pulled Rima's stained dress open to look at the skin where the *tannîyn*'s talons had cut her so deeply. There was nothing there. Not a scratch. Even the old scar from when Rima had fallen against the coffee table was gone. "I...I don't understand. He...healed you?"

Rima shrugged, her eyebrows furrowed. She seemed to take

inventory of herself, rolling her shoulders, flexing her fingers. "Mostly," she winced.

"What *are* you?" Sam asked Eshmun. "How did you do that?"

"He is Eshmun," Teth said solemnly. "Sole offspring of Melqart and a Tyrian princess, Nuhrā, a great healer. Her father was a healer before her, and her grandmother before that. Eshmun bears the gift of his ancestors."

For one fleeting moment, Sam thought to thank him. Rima was alive and breathing—she couldn't help but feel a sense of awe. Eshmun had powers.

But then she felt her jaw tighten, her fury plunging deep. He had bound them and dragged them across the valley. He had brought them here. He had put them in danger.

"Come on, stand up," she told Rima, rising and offering her hand.

"She is unable to walk," Eshmun said. He glared at Sam. "Or *run.*"

"It's my ankle." Rima grimaced. "I think it's broken. From when the monster thing dropped me." She slumped backward, lying flat on the ground. "I just...I feel like I need to sleep."

Sam felt her throat tighten. The cold realization hit: Eshmun had not healed Rima completely. He'd saved her life, had taken away her mortal wounds.

But he'd purposefully left her a little broken.

He gave Sam one last look of warning before scooping Rima up into his arms. "Come," he commanded, leaving Sam no choice but to follow.

7

"Make haste, child," Teth said to Sam. "Those who follow us will close the distance. The beast will return. And there is always the chance of lions. We must continue."

But Sam didn't need to be told. Eshmun was striding ahead with her sister, Rima's feet hanging on one side and her hair on the other, brushing against his thigh with each step. She scrambled after them.

"Put her down," she demanded. "Fix her ankle."

But Eshmun only walked faster, and eventually, Sam grew tired and fell behind with Teth.

Ahead, the snowy tips of mountain summits glowed white against the twilight sky, and a warren of foothills stretched before them. "Will we stop for the night?" she asked, wondering how they could cross a river and navigate ascending trails in the dark.

"There is no night," Teth said.

"What do you mean?" Sam asked. "It never gets dark?"

Teth gave a curt shake of the head. "May the gods forbid," he said. He unfolded a parcel from his bag and handed Sam a piece of thin bread. She pushed it away, too sick with worry to eat.

"There are lions?" she asked, finally registering what he had said earlier.

"Of course. Why do you think this is called the Lions' River?" He pointed toward the channel of water they'd begun to follow. "This is

where they come to drink." He raised his nose to the wind. "A female was stalking us for a time, but she took a deer instead."

At that, Sam paused, untied her sandals, and tucked them under her arm, picking her way along the damp ground, giving her blisters a reprieve. She could run faster barefoot.

When the river's dark water turned, so did they. It rushed over rocks, muffling Teth's voice. "The river narrows eventually," he shouted, "but we cannot risk following it any longer. We will ford here."

Near the bank, the stony bed shone through the surface, but after a few feet the water turned a deep shade of green and she could no longer see the bottom. A broken branch sped past, bobbed underwater, and resurfaced again much farther downstream. A few boulders rose from the river like knuckles, but there was no bridge, no easy walkway of stones. She wondered what kinds of creatures might be hiding beneath the surface.

Rima was limp in Eshmun's arms, her eyes closed. Sam glanced at one of the knives in Teth's belt, close enough to try for. Eshmun followed her eyes and then set his jaw.

"Go on," he said. "Try."

When I get the chance, she thought.

"My sister is injured and in pain," she said, glaring at him and pointing to the roiling water. "We can't possibly cross here."

Eshmun held Rima out toward her, like an offering—and then pulled her back. "I have your sister," he said grimly. "I am crossing the river. You will cross the river. You have no say. Do you understand?"

Sam nodded, swallowing down her anguish. Baalbek was no longer in sight. There was no way to get Rima away from him. There was the *tannîyn* out there somewhere. There were lions. He was right: she had no say.

Eshmun handed Rima over to Teth, then stripped off his clothes

until only a short tunic covered him from waist to midthigh. He folded his cloak and tied it with his belt into a compact square, then stooped to take off his leather boots. Around his neck hung a necklace on a leather strand: a pendant, a symbol of the sun. He took Rima again and draped her over his shoulder like a spare jacket.

"You will carry Teth's belongings," he instructed.

He snapped his fingers and Teth dutifully dropped to all fours. Eshmun climbed onto his expansive back, straddling him. As soon as he was situated, Teth stalked like an animal toward the river and entered the water without hesitation. He swam swiftly across the current, letting Eshmun and Rima off safely on the opposite bank.

Teth pivoted and swam back to Sam. Once onshore, he shook the water from his hair, turned his back to her, and crouched down. When Sam didn't climb on, he let out a low growl, one that suggested that he would force her if he had to.

She put her sandals inside Teth's bag and slung it over her shoulder. "I can swim," she said curtly, wading out into the water at the river's edge.

With the next step, a rock rolled underneath her and she felt her ankle turn. Even in the shallows, the current challenged her balance, and the water was frigid, already making her legs numb. She realized that Teth's heavy bag—weighted with a frying pan, a wool blanket, and various vials and weapons—would take her straight to the bottom.

"Get on his back!" Eshmun yelled from the opposite bank. He had put Rima down on the rocks. "Now!"

"Damn you!" she said, turning around and climbing back to where Teth was waiting. She gripped the nape of his neck and swung a leg over his back. He smelled like a wet dog. *"Go,"* she said, and he stalked toward the river.

She was certain her head would go under, but despite his size,

Teth was buoyant. He cut effortlessly through the current, while the freezing water turned her legs to lead on either side of him. When they emerged on the opposite shore, Sam crawled and scrambled up the rocky bank, scraping her knees as she went.

Shivering, she went straight to Rima, who was—miraculously—pulling herself to her feet. The color had returned to her cheeks. Her eyes were bright.

Sam felt queasy with relief.

"He fixed it?" she asked, gripping Rima's hand.

Rima nodded, turning to watch Teth as he shook the water from his hair, sending droplets flying. He had a fish in his mouth—a trout—and his canines seemed longer than before, almost extending over his bottom lip. His nose twitched as he took the fish from his mouth and held it in his hands, his dark fingernails like claws curled around the trout's silver body.

"I suppose we cannot eat now," he said, disappointment in his voice.

"No," Eshmun said, scanning the sky. "We cannot."

Teth tucked the fish into his bag while Sam wrung the water from her hair. She looked over her shoulder at the wide and angry river that kept them from running back to Baalbek. It rumbled and churned, spitting over the rocks.

"Shall I bind them again?" Teth asked Eshmun.

"No," Eshmun said, his face and beard still wet. "There is nowhere for them to go." He tipped his chin toward Sam. "Give her the smaller bag you have within yours. Fill it and let her carry it."

From a distance came the sudden and unmistakable sound of the *tannîyn* screeching. Rima let out a terrified gasp.

Wordlessly, they rushed to gather their supplies, then hurried deeper into the rough terrain, threading their way over gritty, rocky

ground and beneath an archway that looked like a rib cage. In its dark recesses, Sam caught a glimpse of black fur, maybe a bat.

The air was still, and the way became steep and stony. With slabs of gray all around them, Sam felt as if she were walking through a tomb. Soon the ground became fractured, making a rough natural staircase, and Sam could feel it in her thighs as they worked their way up and into the mountains. She shifted her bag—it had already burrowed into her shoulder, weighted with the frying pan.

Along the pathway, small, chalky stones lay in piles. She picked one up and scraped an X on the wall to her left.

She knew it was no better than leaving a trail of bread crumbs. But it was all she could think of, the only way she could mark their route when it came time for them to flee again and double back. After all, that was her plan: wait until they had an opportunity, then run and retrace the way to Baalbek. That was where the funnel had brought them.

It had to be the way home. It had to be.

Once, Sam remembered, Dad had lost them at the county fair. Rima was nine and Sam was eleven. They'd eaten caramel-dipped apples while they rode the carousel. When the ride ended, it left them off opposite where Dad had paid for their tickets. They circled the ride three times searching for him, the carousel animals peering down at them with painted eyes. There had been a bear, a tiger, an ostrich, and a zebra rearing and flaring its nostrils. Sam had expected Rima to cry, but she hadn't been afraid. Not one bit. They had a pocketful of tickets and no one to tell them no. Rima made faces through the House of Mirrors and tossed popcorn off the top of the Ferris wheel. They were barely tall enough for the Tilt-a-Whirl, and then they watched a magician make a dove fly out of his hat. *Daddy will find us,* Rima had said lightly, stuffing bright blue cotton candy into her mouth. They

still had five tickets left, so Rima raced off for the bumper cars, and Sam did her best to keep up. *Don't worry, Sam! We're not lost forever!*

Sam shivered in her damp dress. Even in the sunless sky, the snow-capped peaks shone bone white. She hadn't heard the *tannîyn* again. Maybe it had given up on them. Or maybe it would be waiting on the other side of the mountain range.

"They say a giant dropped his dinner plate from one of the summits," Teth said, tipping his chin upward. "We are walking across the broken pieces."

"What's so important in Sidon?" Sam asked. "Why do we need to get there so fast?"

"It is my lord's city-state," he explained with a proud lilt in his voice. "He hastens home, where he reigns—and where his loyal people and his army await."

"What the actual fuck?" Rima asked.

Teth raised a bushy eyebrow at Rima. "Speak the native tongue, child. It is to your benefit to be less conspicuous." He glanced over his shoulder. "Your arrival and the call of my lord's obol are like stones upon water. Ripples will emanate. Unseen creatures will stir. The god of death has felt your presence."

"We'll find our way out of here," Sam reassured Rima. "Don't worry."

When Dad had finally found them that day at the fair, she and Rima had been eating a giant, sugary sno-cone. They were all out of tickets and money, and Sam remembered clutching a little strip of photo booth pictures. In the bottom frame, Rima had her mouth stretched open with her fingers, while still managing to press her nose back. *Where the hell've you two been?* Dad had asked with a laugh. He was grinning from ear to ear, amused by their apparent lack of concern. But Sam remembered the way his hands had been shaking when

he scooped them both up, and how he'd said into their ears, *Don't you ever disappear on me like that again, hear me?*

And then he was the one who disappeared. Missing In Action.

Sam put one foot in front of the other. The mountains grew taller. Dad was still alive. They weren't lost forever. They would find each other again.

The wind whistled, and Sam thought she heard singing—or laughter.

Teth heard it, too. *"Ruḥā,"* he said, touching a finger to his ear. "They are trying to speak to us."

"It is only the wind," Eshmun countered. He had stopped to wait for them. Ahead, they'd have to crawl through a crevice in the rock: The path went directly through a cracked face of limestone.

"Not. Wind," Rima croaked.

Sam saw the shadow first, then felt the movement in the air. Eshmun was right: it wasn't *ruḥā*.

The *tannîyn* hovered above them, its wings silently beating, as quiet as a butterfly.

Its left eye, bloody and sunken where Sam had thrown the knife, was useless. But its right eye was quick and alert: It went from Teth to Eshmun to Rima, and then settled on Sam. She felt her blood turn as cold as the mountain wind. Opening its fanged mouth, the *tannîyn* hissed like a boiling kettle.

"Go!" Sam screamed, shoving Rima past Eshmun toward the crevice. Her heart pounded so hard it felt like it was breaking her, a hammer against glass.

The *tannîyn* tucked its wings against its sides; it landed and balanced in the middle of the pathway. Eshmun and Teth were trapped behind it.

Sam backed up against the limestone face as Rima crawled inside,

screaming for her to hurry. The *tannîyn* stretched its toadlike face, its nostrils flaring inches from Sam's chest. It was smelling her. Tipping its head sideways, it pulled its mottled lips back and grinned.

As if it were considering how best to eat her.

The world turned dark at the edges. Sam closed her eyes and collapsed to her knees as the *tannîyn* snapped its mouth above her, a spray of acid saliva raining down on her shoulders, blistering her skin.

Through the narrow opening, Rima shrieked, *"Come on!"*

Teth roared, and the *tannîyn* suddenly slid backward. Was he *pulling* it? It sank its talons into the rocky path, screeching and gashing the stone.

Sam thrust her head through the crevice, an avalanche of fear threatening…She would faint soon. She crawled forward, her hands bruising on loose rock, but her feet weren't through yet. The *tannîyn* would grab her by the ankles.

Rima hooked her hands under her arms and yanked. Sobbing, Sam kicked forward, and together they got her inside. She curled into herself and looked back.

The *tannîyn's* good eye—reptilian yellow—peered at her from the crevice's cleft, its scaly face pressed against the opening.

Rima screamed. And then so did the *tannîyn,* its pupil a sudden black chasm of surprise.

Its shrieking split the mountains, echoing, ricocheting. Sam felt like its talons were digging inside her ears, piercing her head from one side to the other. Finally its screams stopped, but she could hear it flailing against the limestone, raking and clawing, the sound of its wings beating like a desperate moth against a closed window.

And then there was silence.

Teth was at the opening. "I left a knife in the beast's belly," he explained, drenched in sweat. Grunting, he pulled a slab of rock aside,

making the opening wider. Even so, his hips barely cleared each side as he squeezed through. "My biggest and sharpest blade. I am sorry to see it go," he said as Eshmun followed more gracefully.

"Did you kill it?" Rima whispered desperately. "Is it dead?"

"I believe so," Teth said, huffing to catch his breath. "I watched it fall."

Sam looked down at her trembling hands. She'd crushed the chalky stone she'd been carrying. Fine white paste coated her sweaty palms.

"I thought you said it couldn't follow us into the mountains," Sam said to Eshmun, wiping her hands on her dress. The *tannîyn*'s saliva had burned through the fabric and into her shoulders; they stung horribly.

Teth sat on the ground wiping his brow and taking inventory of his remaining weapons. He reached into his bag, pulled out a jar, uncorked it, and took a long, gulping drink. The smell of black licorice and liquor filled the air.

Eshmun flicked his hand at them dismissively and began walking again.

Sam helped Rima to her feet and nudged her ahead. They left the shelter of the stone for the open air, and soon, the trail dropped away on one side. If she wanted, Sam could reach her toes into the thin air and touch the tips of pine trees. On the other side, the mountain wall was so close that her elbow became scraped with cuts.

They walked in silence for a long time. Teth had fallen so far behind she could no longer see him. After all that liquor he'd gulped down, she didn't know if he could keep his balance at all.

The path narrowed even more, and she stopped.

"Are you kidding me?" she asked. She wiped a hand across her sweaty upper lip. The rocky chasm waited patiently for her to make a mistake with her footing.

Eshmun and Rima were now well ahead of her, out of sight;

perhaps they had not slowed down for this precarious section of trail, but then again, Rima had never been afraid of heights.

Sam took a few shaky steps, one foot directly in front of the other. At this altitude, the air was empty. It was hard to breathe. She could hear a sickening scraping noise, like nails on a chalkboard, and realized it was the sound of her grinding her teeth.

A gust of frigid wind descended from the peaks above, pressing Sam flat against the wall and then pulling her away. She clung to the knobbed surface of the mountainside, her nails breaking against the stone.

I will not fall. I will not fall. I will not fall.

Ahead, she could see the way widening, a small respite—the mountainside curved inward like a cupped hand, and there the footpath broadened. Sam cautiously hurried forward, but just as she reached safer ground, a familiar voice rang out.

"*Šlama 'lekh.*"

Sam startled backward, sending pebbles skittering. "How...how did you get up here?" she asked, her heart pounding in her ears.

Before her stood Zayin, almost hidden against the rocky wall.

"Easily," Zayin said, fluttering her long gray eyelashes. She nodded to a massive hawk above Sam, perched on a hump of stone. It tipped its head sideways at her, eyes narrow, its yellow-and-black beak sharp at the tip.

"Take this and fill it." Zayin offered Sam a vial the size of a salt shaker. She wore a gray tunic now, tied tight at the waist, and her gold pendant had been traded for a necklace of sharp animal teeth. Her legs were sheathed in leather boots, laced tightly up to her thighs.

"Do what?" Sam asked. She pressed herself tighter to the mountainside.

"Fill it," Zayin repeated pleasantly, pressing the vial into Sam's hand. She squeezed her fingers around Sam's, her gray skin warm

and smooth, her beauty radiant, mesmerizing. "Fill it with the tears of Eshmun."

"His *what*?" Sam asked, bewildered. "Why?"

Zayin smiled with her even teeth. "If you do not carry out this task for me," she said, "there will be consequences." She shrugged. "I might take your sister. I might take you as well. You would make interesting additions to Melqart's harem. Or perhaps I would enjoy a fresh female in my own bed." She reached out and twisted a lock of Sam's hair around her supple finger. "I have not yet decided. Maybe I will sell one of you."

Sam swallowed. She pulled her hair away from Zayin, then looked up at the hawk and its beady eyes. "Why can't you get your own tears?"

"Alas, Eshmun's tears are quite difficult to procure. Those I have purchased in Kition's black market are diluted or counterfeits," Zayin said, sighing. "Pure tears are rumored to be hidden in Sidon, but soldiers guard the walls and streets of the city. We have failed at flying in."

The hawk lifted a wing to expose the tip of an arrow lodged in its side. It looked like an old wound, healed over.

"But you," Zayin said, "will walk right into Sidon on the arm of Eshmun." She gave Sam a coy shrug. "Your fate is in your hands. Make haste. I do not care to grow any older waiting." The hawk dropped down from its ledge to the alcove beside her, and she flung a leg over its side, mounting it. "Do not tell Eshmun."

"Why not?" Sam demanded. She reached out and grabbed Zayin by the ankle. "Why shouldn't I tell him, or Teth?"

Zayin's eyes darkened. "You *do* understand, do you not? That he will never let you go?" She yanked her foot out of Sam's grip and kicked her in the chest, knocking her against the mountainside. "Talk of the prophecy has begun to spread across this world like hellfire."

Sam reeled from the blow, dizzied. *What is this* prophecy *everyone*

keeps mentioning? She struggled for a breath to ask a more important question.

"If I get the tears, will you help me?"

Zayin let out a wicked, honey-coated laugh. "No."

Sam swallowed. She could hear Teth approaching from behind.

"You are in no position to haggle," Zayin continued. "I have found you. I know where you are. Others would like to know as well. They would like to meet you. I can fly to them. *All* of them—and make a handsome profit in exchange for what I know. And believe me: they are far worse than Eshmun."

"But I *am* in a position to bargain." Sam regained her breath, steadied her voice. She held up the empty vial. "You said Eshmun's tears are hidden in Sidon."

Zayin narrowed her eyes. "Yes."

"What if I can offer you more than one vial's worth?" Sam asked. "What if I find the rest?"

Zayin grinned, clapping her hands together. "Clever, clever girl." She tipped her head back to laugh, her silken hair cascading around her. "You impress me. In that case, yes, I will help you."

"You'll tell me everything you know about how to leave this world and get back to Earth? You'll tell me where the portal in Baalbek is?"

Zayin winked, pressing her luxuriant eyelashes against her cheek. "Of course. I'll tell you everything I know."

Sam was making a deal with the devil, she knew. The hawk angled its beak toward her.

"I'll do it."

Zayin smiled and gave her a curt nod of agreement. Then she and her mount lifted into the air and were gone.

8

The weight of Zayin's bargain was heavier than the bag of supplies Sam carried. She shifted the deal she'd just made back and forth in her mind, trying to judge what was really inside it.

Why did Zayin want Eshmun's tears? She should have pressed, but she suspected Zayin wouldn't have told her anyway. And how could she possibly fill a vial with them or find where they were hidden in Sidon? Would Zayin actually help her in return? Was she being naïve?

What other choice did she have?

She tucked the vial beneath her fur belt, navigating the narrow path with small, careful steps until she caught up with Eshmun and Rima. They were resting on a bluff, wide and safe; over their heads a precipice jutted out, sheltering them underneath. There was a sea in the distance, a blanket of dark blue. Before the sea, though, there was a forest and what might have been a village, a cluster of buildings.

Sam's entire body ached with fatigue. What she would give for her soft bed at home, or even their thin sofa with its springs poking through.

"Where *are* we?" Rima asked, exhausted.

"In between," Teth said, joining them. "Neither light nor dark. Neither paradise nor hell, *šmayyà* nor *gihannā*. This is the realm of both the living and the dead."

"Drink," Eshmun said, handing Sam a jug.

As she gulped the water down, Teth produced the fish from his bag. "We must eat, too!"

Sam sat next to Rima on the ground, taking her hand and squeezing. "You okay?"

Rima nodded. Her sandals were off, and she rubbed her chafed feet.

"We're going to have to run again," Sam whispered. "To get back to Baalbek."

"Why, though? Does that even make sense?" Rima asked. She glanced toward Eshmun. "He's the one who brought us here. What if we need him to get home?"

Sam let out a troubled breath. She thought of what Zayin had told her. "What if he won't *let* us leave?"

The funnel, the coin, Eshmun and his tears, Zayin, Baalbek. Which led to freedom? Which did they need?

Rima's lower lip trembled. She leaned against Sam, and Sam could practically feel the heaviness of her sister's heart. "It was the cream cheese," Rima said.

"The what?" Sam asked, blinking up at her sister. She'd been taller than Sam for about a year now, though there was no mistaking who was older. Rima still had the face of a child, heart-shaped and tender. She had freckles on her cheeks. "What are you talking about?"

"You know," Rima said, "what we ate for breakfast? When we were home, right before this all happened?"

"The caramel-flavored cream cheese?"

"Yeah, it was bad. We got, like, mad cow disease, or something? Some weird food infection. It's the only thing that makes sense," Rima said, sniffling. She wiped a hand across her nose.

"I think you are totally right," Sam said. She put an arm around Rima's waist.

Teth had retrieved the frying pan from the bag Sam carried. "Forged by Sarepta's best blacksmith," he said, unsheathing a highly polished blade with a handle of bone. Dusting off a flat rock with his hand, he placed the trout on top and began sawing into it.

Sam couldn't help herself. "Stop!" she said, throwing her hands in the air. "You're butchering it." She was hungry, and he would waste half the meat.

Teth considered the fish. "I would prefer to eat it raw and whole," he admitted.

"You think you can do better?" Eshmun asked Sam.

"I know I can."

Teth's eyebrows shot up. He looked for the response from Eshmun, who let the moment hang before answering. "Give her the fish, my friend. You start the fire."

"Hmm," Teth said, his huff of complaint playing out into a low growl. He reluctantly handed over his catch. It was heavy; Sam judged it to be an eight-pounder. "There is no river nearby to catch another," he reminded her.

"I need your knife," she said.

Teth's eyebrows descended just as sharply as they had risen. The wrinkles on his forehead deepened. "I do not think so."

"She knows now not to attempt anything foolish," Eshmun said. "Let us see what she can do."

"We have *seen* what she can do," Teth cautioned.

"Give it to her," Eshmun said, leveling a warning look at Sam.

She held out her hand and Teth placed the knife in her palm, still blistered from digging the hole in her backyard.

The knife was heavy and solid. She'd promised herself. She wouldn't hesitate. Eshmun was a quick lunge away. If she stabbed him, would he cry tears of pain? Could she fill the vial with them?

But no—thanks to the deal she'd struck—one vial wouldn't be enough. Besides, what would Teth do to her, to Rima?

Now was not the time. She would have to wait.

She steadied her hands and tried to concentrate on the fish. Piercing it just behind its head, near the dorsal fin, she made the first diagonal cut.

"You are an expert," Teth admitted. His wild hair was a mane against the dusky sky as he started the fire. It began to crackle, and Sam realized that the smoke would create a beacon, if anything was still following them.

Eshmun must have been thinking the same thing. "Make haste."

"Haste is the best way to cut yourself," she said. "That's what my father always said." Dad had taught her how to scrape scales, pick pin bones out with tweezers, snip off catfish spines. She knew how to get a hook out of her own finger.

"Your father was a fisherman, then?" Teth asked.

She flipped the fish over, sliding the blade against its backbone until she reached the tail. "He was in the military," she said, knowing they wouldn't understand what a lance corporal in the Marines meant.

This produced a sound from Eshmun, a lilt in his voice. Approval. "He died while fighting," he said, more a statement than a question.

"No." Sam hesitated. She glanced at Rima, who was either asleep or feigning it. "He disappeared over an ocean." He was a crew member on a V-22 Osprey on a disaster relief mission. No one knew what had happened to the plane, or anyone on board. It was a mystery.

But he could still come home. He could be serving out some secret mission, or surviving on a remote island, or trapped in a prison. Whenever she saw news of air strikes, she imagined the door of his cell blown off. He'd walk away with a few cuts on his face.

With every passing month, though, and each passing year, a thin

layer of doubt accumulated. She would dust it off and polish her hope like a dutiful housekeeper. If she kept up with it, it never tarnished beyond repair. Not for Dad. Plenty of other things in her life had black lines in the details—no way of buffing those out—but when it came to her father, she was vigilant.

Teth finally spoke. "Blessings upon your father, a warrior who serves with honor."

Sam felt her eyes go damp. She nodded.

Teth turned to speak to Eshmun, and while they had their heads pressed together, she carefully looked back the way they'd come. Through a gap in the mountain walls, she could see the fine line of a river—maybe the one they'd traversed earlier. From this vantage point, it looked like a gash through the belly of the earth. How long would it take them to hike back? Could they even cross it without Teth?

With a start, she realized she was still holding Teth's knife. She had finished with the fish and no one had noticed. She gripped it close against her thigh, and as the men continued talking, she sidestepped toward Rima, pretending to check on her. Nerves blazing, she tucked it inside the bag she'd carried.

She returned to the fire just as Teth uncorked a glass vial. "Oil pressed from olives," he said. He drizzled it into the pan, and when it began to pop, he added the fish fillets she had carved and sprinkled them with coarse sea salt. "Now it is ready to eat."

Sam woke Rima to make sure she had her share of the food. Teth ate noisily, somehow managing to find his mouth through his beard, drinking from a bottle of liquor. As he chewed, a giant moth perched on his head, flexing its wings. He took it onto his finger and set it on his shoulder, whispering to it like it was his pet, until it took flight once again.

"I detest even the thought," Teth said. He stopped eating and

looked at Eshmun with utter seriousness. "I pray it isn't so. But he *must* have a hand in this."

"Without a doubt," Eshmun said. He stabbed at the fire with a branch, the light casting shadows onto his face.

"Who?" Sam asked.

"Môt," Teth replied.

The fire's flames suddenly turned green. Sam skittered backward away from them. "What's happening?" she asked.

"Douse the flames!" Eshmun told Teth. "Quickly!"

Teth growled, piling rocks onto the fire until it was smothered. Small green sparks sizzled along the edges, and Teth stomped them with his feet. "That madman!" he cried. "That plague!"

"What madman?" Sam asked. "What are you talking about?"

"My uncle," Eshmun said, his jaw tight. "God of fire and death."

"He is the rightful ruler of the underworld," Teth added. "He is able to wield his power through fire—use it as a way of seeing. Flames are like windows for him. In this way, he can spy into the corners of the underworld."

"You summoned him to this fire," Eshmun said reprovingly.

Teth looked at Eshmun. "My lord, his name has been mentioned in the company of fire many times. I recall the green flames only once, long ago, when I was a boy."

"He stirs again," Eshmun said. "He is restless."

"What does he want?" Sam asked. If Eshmun was related to Môt, mad ruler of the underworld, then the same plagued blood must run through his veins.

"Devotion," Eshmun said. "The fervor he once enjoyed. Where once he was worshipped, now he is despised."

"He has been simmering since Ba'alat Gebal left him," Teth said, shaking his head. "A god with a broken heart is a dangerous thing.

Though I will never understand why she ever poured her love into him. He simply drank it up and pissed it out."

"They were ill-matched from the start," Eshmun said.

"That is true, my lord," Teth said with a heavy sigh. "One so precious might alight for a moment alongside an ogre, but she will not stay."

Eshmun flashed a sad smile in Teth's direction. "You are no ogre, my friend, and I will speak to Rabā on your behalf."

"My lord," Teth said sadly. "You have my unending gratitude, but it is a matter of wealth. My humble status does nothing to elevate Meem's family name."

"I will pay you handsomely for this journey," Eshmun said. "If my suspicions serve me, your wages will be well earned." He clapped Teth on the back. "I will be the first to dance at your wedding."

At that, Teth grinned, but Sam felt no comfort. With the heat of the fire gone, she shivered. The sounds of the wilderness drifted up to them: a lonely call in the distance, an owl's hooting, the whining of wind. No one suggested walking farther. There would be no nightfall, and somehow that comforted her—at least she wouldn't have to be in this strange world in complete darkness. She and Rima lay down to sleep, but the men sat together, murmuring.

"What will you do with these two?" Teth asked. Even when he whispered, his voice rolled out of him like a low thundercloud. "My lord," he pressed. "Forgive me if my tongue is loose from liquor, but I must speak."

"Then speak."

"You cannot afford to make the same mistake twice. Opportunity is revisiting you, against all odds."

Eshmun said something terse in response. It was one angry word that Sam couldn't make out. There was a stretch of silence, and then Teth tried again. "Perhaps it is *your* child who is meant to—"

"There was no missed opportunity!" Eshmun barked, cutting him off. "Helena had already birthed her one son. I made no mistake."

Sam nestled close to Rima, her mind full of sharp, dangerous questions. They prodded at her harder than the rocks under her hips and spine. She didn't understand what Teth and Eshmun were talking about—all she knew was that there was a god of death named Môt, that Eshmun was a kidnapper, and that Baalbek was increasingly far behind. This place seemed to become more treacherous with every breath. And there was a prophecy...one that she and Rima might have something to do with.

After a while, Teth started snoring, probably too drunk to keep his eyes open, although he was meant to keep watch. In the distance, Sam heard an animal howling—a wolf, maybe. Eshmun had quickly succumbed to sleep, too. His chin dipped into his chest, which rose and fell with his steady breath.

Sam sat up. She counted to one hundred, and with every second she thought of a reason to do it, or not.

Her heart pounded out question after question. *What about the tears? What will Zayin do if she finds me again and I don't have them? Maybe we don't need her to get home. Maybe we should just run.*

But Eshmun would chase them. She was sure of that. And she couldn't let him hurt Rima again.

She pulled the knife from the bag and held it firmly in her hand.

Teth was smiling in his sleep. He let out a small chuckle as she crept toward Eshmun and stooped over him, her shin brushing against the velvety fur of his collar.

She wanted to touch him, to make sure that the knife wouldn't slide right through him, but she knew by now that he wasn't made of smoke. He was muscle and veins, and she could hear his breathing: soft and even, while Sam's heartbeat hammered down to the bone. He

smelled like lemons, and then she remembered that he'd packed two in his satchel. He was talking in his sleep. "Cadmus, brother in arms," he murmured. "Hanno the Navigator. Ithtobaal, eyes purple as plums. Sor, heart of rock..."

She pulled the knife up, ready to strike. Her stomach churned and she tasted acid in her throat, the fish she'd just eaten. There was another howl in the distance. She glanced at Rima and wished she could scoop her up and fly away, the way Zayin had done with her hawk.

You promised yourself. You wouldn't hesitate. It would be like the knife going into the *tannîyn.* Like a knife flicked into a tree. That was all.

But...if she killed Eshmun, she would have to kill Teth, too. Maybe hit him over the head with the frying pan first, then plunge a knife into his chest. The thought made her shake.

Dad would do it, she thought. He would do it to protect them.

Coursing with adrenaline, she thrust the knife toward Eshmun's closed eye.

But she stopped short, a breath away from his skin. Her palms were slick with sweat.

Do it!

Instead she groaned and sat back on her haunches, cursing herself. She couldn't. She would wake up Rima instead. They would run while the men were sleeping.

And then Eshmun's eyelids snapped open. He sat up and snatched her by the wrist.

"No!" she cried. She dropped the knife and held up her other hand in surrender.

His pupil flared red. He stood and forced her up with him, backing her toward the edge of the precipice. "What were you doing?" he growled.

"I...I...thought...," she stuttered. "I heard...howling."

"Lies," he said. "Where is my coin?"

"I don't have it," she said, looking over her shoulder at the drop-off.

"Why do you want to return to Baalbek? Did you hide my obol in the temple?"

"No," she said, and then regretted her honesty. If he thought the coin was there, they might turn back. "I mean yes."

He scowled at her and took another step forward, forcing her to retreat, her heels inches from the edge.

"Stop," she gasped.

And then, with a swift yank, he pulled her back onto the ledge and released her. She stumbled to the ground, her elbows and knees scraping against the rock, her bracelets biting into her wrist.

"Use your eyes," Eshmun said smugly. He raised his hands to the sky and its cloud streaks. "Do you see a way home? Where is the road you traveled? Where is the funnel? It is not here, nor is it waiting for you in Baalbek."

She would be bruised tomorrow, if there was such a thing as *tomorrow* in this godforsaken place. Today, yesterday, forever. It was all one continuous strand. *I hate you. I hate you for bringing me here.*

"I *will* find a way home," she said, her voice turning savage. Angry tears burned her eyes.

He shook his head. "People have come into this world before," he said. "And they will likely come again. But they do not go back."

She pulled herself to her feet and pointed a finger at his chest. "You call yourself a healer?" She let out a bitter laugh. "All you do is break things. I'm sure your mother would be proud of you."

To her surprise, Eshmun's face went pale. "What did you *dare* say to me?" he asked.

Sam thought of the word Teth had used when he bound her hands

in Baalbek. *Tyābutā*, he'd said: *shame, repentance, regret*. At first she thought Teth had meant it for himself, because he felt guilty for tying her hands. Or that he'd meant it for her, that she should feel ashamed for taking Eshmun's coin.

But what if Teth, under his breath, had been aiming the word at Eshmun, for his violence?

Sam took a step closer, her finger still trained on his chest. "Your grandparents, too," she hissed. "All those healers in your family. You're really honoring their legacy."

"Insolence," Eshmun said. "No one speaks to me in this manner." His voice was cold and stern, but his eyes betrayed him. He'd been thrown off-balance. Sam smiled inwardly, knowing that she'd gotten to him. She'd managed to hit a nerve.

"The truth hurts," she said. "Doesn't it?"

She pushed past him, back to the campsite, where Teth was still snoring loudly. But something wasn't right. The air was sour with danger.

She sensed them before she saw them: the feral, doglike women from the streets of Baalbek.

9

S am recognized their stained sleeves, the length of their teeth. The largest, with wiry golden hair and shoulders raised to her ears, snarled. The others snatched Rima from her sleep, clamping hands over her mouth as her eyes sprang open with terror.

The largest lunged at Sam, but Eshmun was there with Teth's knife. Blood misted the air. Yelping, wounded, the attacker dropped to all fours and slunk backward, her copper eyes glinting wild.

"Teth!" Sam screamed. She kicked his side. "Wake up!"

The women dragged Rima—thrashing and kicking—underneath a rock overhang. Then a roar shook pebbles from ledges—and Sam could practically feel the mountains tremble as Teth barreled toward them.

"Release her!" he bellowed.

The wounded woman tipped her head back—her thick, muscular neck raised—and barked an order. Instantly, over the crests of the rocks, three more dog-women appeared. Sam could hear them panting, see the eagerness charged in their eyes.

"How dare you?" Eshmun seethed.

"*You must take the obol,* he commands," one of the women said, thrusting her narrow chin forward. Her ears were high and pointed. "The god of death himself demands it."

Sam helplessly watched Rima struggle. There was no way she could fight all of these women, but maybe she could push one into the dying campfire—maybe she could shove one over the edge.

Before she could gauge her chances, a sinewy arm hooked around her neck. Tightened. She gasped for a breath.

"I will kill you all!" Teth roared, raising himself to his full height. "Release them now!"

"Give us the obol," the women sang in chorus, their voices shrill and cold.

As Sam choked, she locked eyes with Eshmun. Her anger coursed hot. *Your fault,* she thought, as she thrust her elbow backward so hard she could hear something crack—maybe a rib. Her attacker dropped her.

She scrambled away as Teth moved toward Rima and the feral dog-women. He seemed to have grown two feet in each direction. The savage women were cornered, trapped in an alcove, clutching their prey—there would be a bloody fight. But just as Teth should have been upon them, they disappeared, one by one—including Rima—into darkness.

Sam gasped and rushed forward to look at the face of rock they'd vanished into. Was it another trick of this world? Had they vanished by magic?

No. There was a hole—a cave, narrow and dark. She ducked her head and angled inside, but Eshmun caught her by the arm.

"There could be a precipice within."

"I don't care!" she cried. She already felt like she'd fallen and shattered, like there was nothing whole left inside her. "I need to get to my sister!"

"If you perish," Teth said, "you will become *ruḥā.*"

"I have to follow them!" Sam said, wrenching away. She could still smell the women, rancid and sweaty. Her throat throbbed where she'd been choked; it felt like she'd swallowed gravel. She heard Rima's terrified voice, echoing.

"We light a torch." Eshmun motioned to Teth. "Your eyes go first."

Teth nodded. He quickly gathered their supplies and handed Sam her bag to carry.

But inside the cave, Teth was too tall to stand. He crawled, pressed tight against the sides, and Sam followed closely. "Faster," she begged.

But a fork in the cave's pathway made Teth pause. Sam could hear him sniff the air.

"Blood," he said. "This way."

They followed his chosen route: It widened and soon led back outside onto another mountain trail.

"Where did they go?" Sam asked desperately, spinning left and right. Frantic despair tangled inside her.

"I am sorry," Teth lamented, shaking his head. "Meem has told me that my snoring is like a conch shell blaring. I gave us away. I should have been awake and on guard."

"No more *arak*," Eshmun said firmly.

"We have to find them," Sam said, her voice cracking. She felt gutted. Like someone had slapped her down on a cold rock and cut her, straight through to her backbone. "Those women will take Rima to your uncle, won't they? We can track them. There must be footprints...pawprints! And we'll be able to hear them. They howl!"

"No," Teth said regretfully. "There will be an entire pack. More than even I can fight." He turned to Eshmun. "Do we proceed to Sidon, my lord?"

"Listen to me," Sam said. She forced herself to look Eshmun in the eye, willed herself to keep her voice steady. "We wrapped the coin in a piece of cloth," she said, "and tied it to Rima's hair, underneath, at the nape of her neck." She tilted her chin high and pulled her shoulders back. She had to be a convincing *ðaggálá*, a liar. "Rima has it. So we *neeð* to find her."

Teth grunted. Eshmun held Sam's stare for a long minute, but she

didn't waver. She felt like she was holding a weight over her head, her muscles growing weary.

"Chasing after them would ensure capture, or worse. We continue to my walled city-state," Eshmun decided. "It is our only course. Our safety and strength lie in Sidon alone."

"I don't care about safety!" Sam said. "My sister isn't *safe* right now. Where does your uncle live? I need to go there!"

"He was meant to stay in Gadir," Eshmun said. "But he could be anywhere. Everywhere. This is his realm."

Teth bent toward Sam. "This world was set with traps before, but now you must calculate every step. You would do best to follow us willingly." She couldn't tell from his tone if he was threatening or comforting her. "We will likely hear of your sister's fate once we reach Sidon, and from there my lord can order a search. He may return her to you yet."

"May?" Sam asked. She glared at Eshmun. "You *will*."

Her fate. Sam squeezed her eyes shut. She pressed her hands to her head and gripped her hair. *Oh, Rima.*

I'm sorry.

I'm so, so sorry.

What could she do? Teth and Eshmun wouldn't let her follow the savage dog-women; even if she did, she couldn't fight them alone. Was reaching Sidon her only hope now?

Eshmun handed Teth his knife. "You misplaced this," he said. Teth's face went slack. He looked at Sam and then took the knife from Eshmun, sliding it back into its sheath as he stuttered an apology.

For what felt like another day and night, they walked and walked, succumbing to bouts of fitful sleep. The blisters on Sam's feet popped. Tears ran a constant river down her cheeks until, finally, the mountains stood behind them. She dropped her bag and turned to look back. Thousands of feet, slim corridors, and monsters. She'd made it through.

But Rima hadn't.

The white summits glared coldly at her. Sam slung her bag across her shoulder once more. The forest of pine trees awaited.

〰〰〰

"Behold the mighty cedars," Teth said. He spread his arms wide and grinned, sucking in a deep breath. The trees stood close, head to head, like they were comparing battle plans. "The smell of our prosperity."

The forest smelled like Teth's house, his mattress. Pine needles, along with grassy undergrowth, lay thick upon the ground. Sam took off her sandals to walk barefoot. Eshmun showed no sign of slowing his pace.

"I have never seen him so intent," Teth said, struggling to make his stocky legs keep pace.

"Why does he want this obol so badly?" Sam asked. At the very least, she should ask questions. It would distract her from her crippling worry—and knowledge was power. "I still don't understand. What does his coin do?"

"Upon his death, it will take him to *šmayyà*."

Heaven, Sam thought in English. *Sky.*

"But isn't Eshmun...a god?" she asked, not entirely sure.

"My lord is half-god, half-mortal."

"*Can* he die?" Eshmun had called her a fool more than once, and maybe she was, at least in this world. Could she actually have killed Eshmun with Teth's knife? She had so much more to learn.

"Though it takes extraordinary means," Teth said, pausing to pull a branch out of their way, "even the *full* gods can perish. None is truly immortal."

"So *šmayyà* is where Eshmun would go, after death, to be reunited with his dead family and friends."

"Yes," he said.

She studied Teth's expression. His lower teeth worked at his upper lip, and his eyes were glazed with a wistful look.

"You don't want him to leave, do you?" she asked. "You can't go with him when he goes."

"That is correct," Teth said. "The obol is his, and it is his redemption alone, forged with his mother's blood by Chusor. Only *he* can use it to ascend to the highest realm. No one else can use it for that purpose."

"You'll miss him."

Teth nodded. "I might never see him again."

Eshmun was ahead by a hundred yards, and in his dark cloak, he seemed to vanish now and then between the trees. Sam caught sight of his knife, which he'd been holding ever since they entered the forest. He was chanting something as he walked. She could hear his voice drifting back to them.

"What's he saying?" she asked.

"He recalls the names of lost family members and friends, along with one marked trait of each," Teth said. "The color of an aunt's hair or a cousin's particular interest—a memory of some sort."

"Why?"

"Some were friends from all the ages Eshmun has lived through. Others..." Teth took a long breath. "Others he buried with his own hands, victims of the siege."

"What happened?" Sam asked, remembering that Meem had mentioned a siege, too. "There was a war?"

"On Earth, long, long ago. Invaders came from across the sea," Teth said. "Eight hundred warships. Our ancestors were enslaved and slaughtered. Thousands of men impaled and displayed like battle flags along the shoreline. Eshmun himself placed many burial obols after his loved ones died—in that way, he made certain they would go

to paradise, to *šmayyà*. He could not heal them, their injuries beyond repair, and so he is wracked with guilt, you see.

"Eshmun wishes he had stayed to fight on, but he was deceived to leave Earth. His father had stolen his obol, and Eshmun did not know where it was. He followed his father in a rage, and then he could not return. The storm god, Ba'al Saphon, had sealed the boundaries between worlds."

"*Melqart* stole Eshmun's obol," Sam said, understanding.

"And left it on Earth, yes," Teth said. "Some say he lost it in the chaos of war. Others claim he purposefully hid it."

"Why would Eshmun's own father steal his obol?"

Teth shrugged. "If you choose to believe his intentions were pure, Melqart wanted to lure his only son away from the war, for he was sure to perish in his zeal." He patted his thigh. "Here, he could be safe by his father's side."

"And if you believe Melqart's intentions were bad?"

Teth chuckled. "Melqart is the brother of Môt. Like all gods, they are both driven by both power and love. Or driven mad by them. What's more, Melqart and Eshmun have a long history of grievances, as fathers and sons do."

Eshmun's muffled voice, still a steady cadence, carried through the cedars. "Cadmus and Ithtobaal," Sam remembered. "Eshmun was listing names in his sleep."

"Cadmus!" Teth said with a smile. "A dragon-slayer. Yes, Eshmun is always calling to those he has lost along the way."

"I used to do the same," Sam said. "My dad...he's been gone a long time. Captured, maybe. I would call his name over and over again, thinking I could somehow guide him home if I kept the signal going." She'd believed it would work if she performed it with absolute reverence, and maybe under a full moon. If only she could call out to

Rima now, to send her some sort of message. *I'm coming for you. I'll find you, I promise.*

"But I don't understand something," she said. "If Eshmun leaves the underworld, I mean...you'll follow him eventually, won't you?"

"We put our faith in Eshmun, that he might find the *tar'ā* so we may leave upon our deaths. He is the healer of us all, the salve of this world.

"You see, my *ḥayuta* people came to this place long ago—many even before the siege—exiled to the underworld." Teth spread his arms. "I was born here. We have no obols. No way to leave this plane upon death without the opening of the *tar'ā*."

"What?" Sam asked. "Hang on. You're saying that if Eshmun dies and goes to *ʃmayyà*, then he can't do that," she reasoned. "He can't find the gateway for everyone else to get out."

"It is his right."

"He would be abandoning this world," she said, feeling her hackles rise. "He's the only one who can find the *tar'ā* to heaven?"

"Another may *find* it," Teth said, "such as Ba'alat Gebal. Blessings upon her as she searches now to the east. But—as the prophecy tells us—Eshmun is the only one able to *open* the door."

"It's his duty, then," Sam said as they picked their way over mossy rocks and roots, which threaded through the earth like thickened veins.

Teth's shoulders were set hard and square. "His obol calls to him." Devotion rang in his voice. "My lord will claim it, as he should."

Sam let out a curt laugh. "My dad taught me a lot about duty and honoring promises," she said. "Leaving seems like the opposite of honor. He would be abandoning *you*."

"Hmm." Teth growled, and Sam took it as a warning. She'd pushed too far. She wanted to ask *how* Eshmun could be killed, if it took *extraordinary means*, but instead she tried another route. "You said that your ancestors were exiled. Why?"

Teth sighed. He pressed a hand to his heart. "When our people were a mighty civilization on Earth, the *ḥayuta* were known as protean beings who changed into animals. Some dangerous, yes.

"But," he said, lifting a finger, "we were also the birds and the butterflies, the makers of honey and the messengers flying between homes, delivering good dreams and love songs."

She snapped her head up at him, realizing. "You're a...a *bear*, aren't you?"

Teth grinned a toothy smile. "Of course I am," he said. "What did you think I was? A mouse?"

Sam almost laughed, but instead her heart twisted with another realization. "The women who took Rima. They were coyotes?"

"Jackals," Teth said. He reached out and patted her shoulder.

They walked in silence for a while, but Sam could hardly stand the sound of her own thoughts pounding in her temples.

Will they murder Rima? Eat her? No—they have to give her to the god of death. But will they hurt her? Would they torture her to find the obol? Were they coming back for Sam?

A splintered despair cut through her. She clutched her chest and took a deep breath.

"Continue your story," she said desperately, needing to divert her thoughts before they made her so heartsick she'd have to stop walking. "Please."

"Of course," Teth said. "As I was saying, one dark year, our people and the gods alike were blinded by the crimes of a few *ḥayuta*. The atrocities committed by a small group became the reputation of us all. We were slippery, not to be trusted. A man could turn into a beast without warning. A woman could seduce you and then consume you."

"Meem is an owl," she said, "and Zayin is an elephant."

"It is so," Teth said as he looked down at Sam. His eyes were

on her neck, which was probably purple with finger-shaped bruises where the jackals had choked her. When she swallowed, she felt a lump—some small broken piece of herself—throbbing underneath her skin.

"How do you even know the *tar'ā* exists?" Sam asked. "Why do you still believe after Eshmun has searched for so long?"

"As you have seen, there are ways between the worlds," Teth said. "Veils hang between the boundaries. Fissures provide passage."

"Rima and I came through a fissure."

"Yes." He paused to catch his breath and wipe the sweat from his forehead. Sam slowed her pace to stay at his side. "Only *ruḥā* can traverse the boundary—they return to Earth to haunt people's dreams," he said, "or roam the lands where our ancestors once lived."

Sam shifted her heavy bag to the opposite shoulder and looked skyward. *Send me a sign,* Mom always said. She called them love notes from the universe. A perfectly timed green light, a winning lottery scratch-off card. The last seat on the last bus. Finding that long-lost earring, the one she wore on her honeymoon. She'd thought it was gone forever.

"Where is Rima?" she finally asked. "Is she alive? Will I be able to find her?"

"One cannot be sure," Teth said. "Young women do not often fall from the sky. The god of death will be eager to have her. Understand, there are those who would pay a high price for you. Some will think you possess magic powers or secrets. Some will want to own you. Some will suspect you have brought an obol—a coin of Chusor's gold—with you. You might even provide a clue to where a passageway is hidden." He looked down at Sam with pity in his eyes. "You are lucky, at least, to be in the hands of Lord Eshmun."

Lucky? Sam thought ruefully.

The deeper they walked into the forest, the darker it became. With no river to follow, Sam wondered how Eshmun knew his way around one tree and past another. Teth uncorked his bottle of *arak* once more and fell farther behind, and soon she could no longer see Eshmun ahead. She was alone. She stopped and held her breath.

Had Eshmun believed her lie about the obol being hidden in Rima's hair? Would he want to find her? Would he *really* look for her when they reached his city?

Sam pulled her hands into fists and pictured her sister, limp and dangling from the *tannîyn*'s talons, lost to the clutches of jackals. A fresh surge of desperation tore through her like a jagged knife.

There was a crackle. A few feet off, the remains of a campfire glowed in the darkness, its cinders still sizzling with life inside a ring of rocks.

"Hello?" she whispered, surprised, taking a step into the trees toward it, the start of an idea already warming in her mind. "Eshmun?"

She nudged the ashes with a stick and watched a small flame hiss. What had Teth said? *Flames are like windows*. He had said that fire was a way to *spy into the corners of the underworld*.

She looked over her shoulder and wondered how much time she had before Teth caught up. She breathed gently on the orange ashes and then fed the birthing flames more pine needles, which ignited like matches.

"Where are you, Rima?" she asked the fire, which glowed and grew; she fixed her gaze on it, searching. "Rima?" she called, keeping her voice low. "Are you out there?"

The flames fattened and turned over. They spread and multiplied, but the fire was still ordinary, revealing nothing.

"Môt," she said, and in an instant, the flames turned green.

She sat back, startled it had happened so quickly. But, steeling

herself, she leaned in again, peering into the green snaps of light. The smell was nauseating—she pulled a wool blanket out of her bag to shield her nose and mouth.

Her eyes watered as she strained to make out any discernible shapes. Finally, a long, thin face twisted upward. Her heart pounded ferociously. Despite the searing heat of the fire and the fear burning inside her, she leaned in even closer.

"Hello," she choked, trying to track the figure's eyes, which undulated within the flames. His pupils seemed to be liquid, molten.

"Hinnē," the voice replied. *Look!* "I am Môt, god of death, ruler of the underworld, gatekeeper to hell. Why do you summon me?"

"My sister," Sam said. "I want to see her."

"I want to see *you*," said the god's voice, strong, resonating with power. "Are you my queen? I knew you would seek me out. Come closer. Let the blanket drop."

Sam did so, almost without thinking, driven by hope, hypnotized by the flames. She was sweating in her thin dress, and the fire seemed to grow in response.

"Tell me, are you a virgin?" the god's voice asked eagerly.

"What?" Sam asked. She struggled to take a step backward, feeling tethered, weak. The sour tang of regret burned in her throat. "Why?"

"Have you birthed a son?" The voice hissed and snapped.

"No," Sam said. Her heart pounded faster. She'd made a mistake. "I just...I need to see. I want to see where someone is. My sister. Do you have her? Where is Gadir? Where are you?"

"Say my name again," he said. "Say it again and again. I want to see where *you* are. Who you are with. *Speak my name,*" he chanted. *"Call to me, my bride."*

Sam forced herself to look away. Willed herself to step back,

away from the fire. "No," she said, her voice strengthening. "This is all wrong."

"So be it," Môt laughed, and the flames dipped low and fat and wormy, bubbling like a cauldron's brew.

They're maggots, Sam realized with a start. *Maggots.*

She fumbled backward, gasping for breath as the flames crawled over each other, mounds of them, spilling out over the edges of the rocks.

"No!" she cried. She tossed the wool blanket over the fire, trying to smother the flames. But it was already too hot, too alive. It ate the blanket, using it for fuel. The flames writhed their way into the forest's floor of dry pine needles, lighting one after another. And then sparks—no, they were *flies*—swarmed out. Buzzing flies of fire.

Sam fled, screaming back toward the way she'd come. "Teth!" she shrieked. "Fire!"

It spread. The ground raged green, and then it climbed the trees, consuming branches. Sam could feel the searing heat press close against her back.

"Samira." Eshmun's voice cut through the toxic air, and then he was there, grabbing her by the arm. She was startled by her name in his mouth. Had he ever spoken it before? Had he even known it?

"Where's Teth?" she asked.

"Here," Teth said. He lobbed her over his shoulder in one quick swoop, and then they were running, her ribs banging against his shoulder blades. The smoke was as thick and black as night. She coughed and her lungs rattled as the forest was eaten by a death fire, consumed like a rotting corpse.

10

S he awoke in a field of lavender, but all she could smell was soot. It was in her hair, her mouth, her skin, so deep it felt like her bones had been burned.

Eshmun sat nearby. He stared into the distance, his expression blank. She turned to follow his gaze and saw the forest still licking the sky with cursed flames. Teth paced and chanted prayers for his mighty cedar trees.

She pressed her palms against her eyes. What if Rima was in the forest as it burned to ash? She tried to push the thought away. Above the flames, the smoke billowed like a thousand *ruḥā* rising.

"It's my fault," Sam said, coughing out the words.

Eshmun leveled a look at her, his keyhole pupil narrowing. "Your fault?" he asked. His eyes trained on Sam's neck, on the bruises the jackals had left. She put her fingers to her throat where it was most tender, and then he was suddenly upon her. His hands were around her neck, and her eyes went wide with fear.

Maybe her lie had backfired. If Eshmun actually believed that Rima had his coin, maybe he'd decided he didn't need Sam any longer. He would search her dead body just to make sure, and that would be the end of her.

"Samira," he said, surprisingly gently.

"You're...choking me," she gasped.

"Only because you are struggling." He rubbed her throat with his thumbs.

Her eyes were on his chest where his tunic dipped and showed a firm pillow of muscle. Was his heart as strange as his eyes? She stretched her fingers outward and put her hand inside her bag, finding the handle of the frying pan.

"Trust me for a moment," he said.

Warmth spread through her neck. It felt like sunshine, like she'd tipped her head back on a hot summer day under the noon heat. She remembered what it was like to lie on a blanket on the shore of Glen Lake—with her eyes closed, the sun's fiery glow had made everything orange against her eyelids. The color of a blooming flower.

"What are you doing?" she asked, loosening her grip on the pan. She felt weak and flooded with a sweet calmness; her throat tingled like she'd swallowed something smooth and melted. Warm honey.

"Now, Samira," Eshmun said. "Open your eyes."

She blinked, disoriented. "Did I fall asleep?"

The tender bruises on her neck from the jackals' attack were gone. The lump under her jaw had been healed, too—she felt for it with her fingertips and found nothing.

She stopped herself before thanking him. He'd left Rima's ankle broken. He'd nearly pushed Sam over a mountainside. He'd bound them and forced them along like dogs. He was the one who'd brought them to this hellhole in the first place.

"I thought you were going to kill me for starting the fire," she said.

"And what were you trying to see within its flames?" he asked, rubbing his eyes with the sleeve of his cloak as another wave of smoke billowed over them.

"My sister, of course. Or a way out of here." She hesitated. "Your uncle spoke to me. Asked me if I had birthed a son. Why?"

"The prophecy, reimagined," Eshmun said, curling his lip with disgust. "He wants to twist it to suit his own purposes. No—his *delusions*." He stared at Sam, his eyes intense. "Does he know where we are? Did you let him see?"

"I don't think so," she said, her neck still warm, her eyes still heavy from his healing touch. "He wanted me to say his name again. I don't think I opened the window wide enough for either of us to see clearly."

Eshmun nodded. "My uncle's fires are mirages and lies. You must find your truth elsewhere."

Sam sighed. "My mother says I ask too many questions," she said. "And now look what I did. I burned the world down looking for answers."

"No." Eshmun shook his head. "You may have pushed the vessel out to sea, but the tide was coming for it nonetheless. Môt's cruelty is no longer tempered by Ba'alat Gebal. It was only a matter of time before he started to blister and singe this world again."

"I still need to find Rima," she said. She gripped handfuls of lavender, tearing them from the ground. "*We* need to find her."

Eshmun pulled in a breath, and then paused. "I know how you suffer," he finally said.

She ground her teeth. "You don't," she said. "You can't."

"Hyenas," he said. "We were children. One morning, we went to the spring for water too early. It was still dark. I tried to frighten them, striking stones against each other until they sparked. But the hyenas were undeterred. They took her while I watched. My aunt's daughter."

Sam watched Eshmun's face, the intensity in his eyes. Why was he telling her this? To make her waver with sympathy?

"What was her name?"

"Ḥzirān," Eshmun said. "Hair like polished ebony. Born under the summer sun."

"When you find your obol and leave this world, you'll see Ḥzirān

again, won't you?" Sam asked. "In *ǰmayyà*." She tipped her chin upward. "Heaven."

"Yes," he said.

She looked toward the burning forest. The glass vial prodded her hip, still secure beneath her belt. All she could think about was Rima, while Eshmun only thought of himself.

"You're the *only* one who can open the gateway for the *ruḥā*," Sam said. "For the countless souls who are trapped here. But obviously you'd rather see your pretty cousin again instead."

His shoulders straightened; his jaw twitched. "My obol contains Chusor's gold, valued beyond compare. What's more, in the hands of darkness, it could be melted and altered and used for unspeakable things. I must find it."

"*Wāy!*" Teth shouted with anger, still pacing and praying.

Eshmun stood and put a hand on his shoulder to stop him. "Brother. You are wasting your steps and your breath. Come. We continue to Sidon."

"*Hā,*" Teth said, thrusting his hands toward the dying forest. "*Ša`tā mtāt.*"

Behold. The hour has arrived. "What hour?" Sam asked.

"Of Môt's return," Teth said grimly.

Eshmun gave him a curt nod and waved them forward. Silently, they waded through the lavender, a shallow ocean of purple. The smell of the burning forest faded, but it never completely left, following them like a shadow. Sam looked up at the evening clouds, dotted and curved into shapes almost like Arabic. She thought of Jiddo's letter. What did it say? Would she ever know?

Eyes trained on the sky, her foot caught on something. She tripped and stumbled to her knees.

It was the ankle she saw first, swollen and veined.

"Oh!" she cried out, scuttling backward.

There was a man lying on the ground, hidden in the flowers. His kneecaps shone through his skin like small, full moons. His eyes were open but blank. Sam's heart slammed against her chest. Eshmun must have walked right past him. She turned to find Teth, but he was only a silhouette against the horizon.

She looked down again at the dead man. His hair hung in long silver tangles, the odd angles of his limbs like an insect's. A gray horse stood nearby, looking like it didn't know what to do next. It stamped a hoof nervously.

"It's okay, girl," Sam said. "I won't hurt you."

A dark shape hovered nearby. The *ruḥā* of the dead man.

It came closer, floating above the ground. Its garb was a loose weave of emptiness, long strands of a midnight sky. Trembling, Sam stepped back, but the *ruḥā* followed gingerly, as if trying to reassure her, just as Sam had done with the horse.

Eshmun had told her not to look into its eyes, but why? Was he protecting her—or hiding something? What secrets would a ghost know? What could it tell her?

Is my father dead or alive? Is Rima?

How do we get back to Michigan?

She had failed to see anything through Môt's fire, but here was another chance. Risky again, maybe foolish. But as far as she could tell, the *ruḥā* were simply trapped souls. Why should she fear them? For Rima's sake, she had to try every possibility.

She gazed into the spirit's hollow eyes, and felt them instantly catch. Slowly, they reeled her into their cold, strong current.

Feeling dizzy, she turned away, but the raspy voice of the *ruḥā* was already inside her head. It sang to her, a mournful ballad: dry leaves falling from trees, lost children calling, the creak of old bones.

You want to go home.

"Yes," Sam said, her voice quavering. "Do you know the way? Tell me."

Take my hand.

"No." Sam shook her head. "Tell me."

Touch me. Give me a sip of life. In return I will show you a glimpse of the way. The dead never lie. Death is truth, the only thing that is certain. Death never breaks its promises.

"You'll show me," Sam said. "A touch for a glimpse."

With shaking fingers, she reached out and let the *ruḥā*'s cloak of shredded dreams brush against her skin.

Instantly there was the sound of rushing water, and then a chorus of voices, far away. She gripped the *ruḥā* tighter, wanting to listen longer. *Mom? Is that you?* An ache spread through her fingertips, deeper than pain. It was heartache and loss, memory and regret. She pulled away just as Teth caught up, thrusting himself in between.

"Begone!" he growled.

The *ruḥā* lifted away and upward, a dark kite. It seemed to find a crack in the air. It was like a letter slipping into an envelope. It was gone.

"I should not have left you alone again," Teth said, puffing for breath. "You have a penchant for finding trouble. My lord will not be pleased. Are you hurt?"

"I don't think so," she replied, shaking the sting from her fingers. She'd heard her mother's voice, she was sure of it. "Where is it going?"

"Earth," Teth said. "To haunt the living."

"Can it go wherever it wants?" Sam asked. "To anyone?"

"So the legends tell us."

Sam reached up and touched the place where the *ruḥā* had been. There was nothing but empty air.

They found the horse not far off. Sam rode her until the lavender thinned and they picked up a dirt road, following it until they reached a fork. Teth turned right and Eshmun turned left. The horse lifted its hooves in a vertical dance, flicking the ground and deliberating between the two directions.

"My lord?" Teth asked, tugging on his beard.

"Sarepta first," Eshmun answered. "A slight detour. A necessary one."

Teth's eyes brightened. "To consult with Arba`ta`esre?"

Eshmun nodded. "My thoughts have been cleaved, my friend. Perhaps she can divine the future—"

"*Lā*," Sam interrupted. "We're going straight to Sidon. That's where we're supposed to send out a search for Rima." *And where I'm supposed to steal your tears.* She steered the horse right and tapped her heels.

"You will never get through the gate!" Teth called after her. "The guards will turn you away."

She clenched her jaw. Even though her hands were no longer bound, she felt as though she were still leashed to Eshmun. She tugged the mare back toward the men and grudgingly followed once more.

Soon the occasional voice rose above the otherwise quiet landscape, and then Sam smelled food: *laham mishwi*—grilled meat. It transported her home for a moment, and she closed her eyes, wishing it could be true. Dad manning the grill, red peppers blistering—Rima's favorite. Dad's freckled face, Rima's eager smile, the summer sun.

She opened her eyes to what could only be Sarepta. Through stone columns, she could see a sprawling *ɉuqā*, a marketplace, packed with vendors.

There was a squat building, a barn at the edge of the settlement,

where a woman stood next to a sheep in desperate need of shearing. As they approached, Eshmun paused to talk with her; Sam heard her say that she would send her sons to carry the old man's body from the lavender fields to be buried.

"Sweet girl," the woman crooned, patting the gray mare's head and offering her a handful of hay. All the while she stared at Sam, taking her in from her grimy hair to her green toenails.

"Have you seen another girl like me?" Sam asked. "Taller and younger, wearing a brown dress?"

The woman shook her head. "Like you, no," she said.

Eshmun pressed his hand against the small of Sam's back. "The horse stays here for now," he said. "This way."

Soon they were swept up in the current of the marketplace. Young women carried bowls made from enormous seashells, filled with pine nuts, dried fish, and capers. A seller's basket of woven palm fronds was filled with colorful olives. Teth wandered off on his own, his nose twitching furiously, but Sam kept close to Eshmun, bitterly reminding herself that she likely needed him in order to find Rima.

As they walked, Eshmun purchased food: meat wrapped in thin bread, a salad of herbs, a cup of creamy warm milk. He shared them with her, and it was useless trying to hide her hunger; Sam couldn't help but eat too fast and lick her fingers. There was more, too: She sampled a seafood stew, rich with butter. Spiced lamb rolled into lemony grape leaves. Sour white yogurt to dip cubes of meat into. Sesame pastries, still warm.

The streets were lined with tin bowls and clay jugs, wooden cups and ivory figurines. All of it for sale. There were rugs made of wool dyed shades of red and purple. Scarves and sashes that lifted with the light breeze like sails. A woman offering jars of honey. There was a man who mended clothing. Bins of glass beads made a river of

color along the edge of the road. Firewood for sale. Wooden ladders. Grinning clay masks, and statues with tall hats. Garlic sold by the handful.

"Alabaster!" someone called out, holding up a pot brimming with fragrant mint.

All around them, men pulled smoke from their pipes, sending the sweet fragrance of cherries through the air. A few puppies playfully tumbled over each other, a woman with impossibly long legs scolding them to stay close. When the puppies darted off, chasing each other, the woman transformed into a greyhound and streaked after them, barking.

Sam blinked with disbelief, wondering if she'd imagined the whole thing.

Finally they stopped at a blacksmith's shop, full of knives and tools and nails. The man's hands were covered in thick burn scars. He watched Eshmun and Sam with curiosity, struggling not to stare, and finally dipping his head in deference. "My lord," he said to his feet.

"Greetings, Mhaymnā," Eshmun replied. "Please, do not bow to me when your own veins carry the mighty blood of Chusor."

"Ah, but does a single drop of water call itself a river?" Mhaymnā asked. "The relation is so far removed."

"And yet you know that a mere ounce of gold carries more value than a mountain of rock. What are you working on there?"

"Just what you speak of," Mhaymnā said. "Gold melting into its next incarnation. What was once a ring becomes a necklace, which then might become a ring again. It is a cycle. How things change with fire."

"Your fire," Eshmun said, tipping his chin toward the small flames. "Be aware of it, my friend."

Mhaymnā looked stricken. He lowered his voice. "The marketplace is a den of rumors," he murmured. "Is it true, then? There is hellfire in the cedars? The Lord of Death stirs once more?"

Eshmun nodded, a grave look on his face. "My uncle will be brought to reason."

Mhaymnā snuck a glance at Sam, so she stepped forward to speak to him. "*Šlama 'lakh,*" she said. "Sir, have you seen anyone like me recently? A girl about my age?"

"Of this I am certain," he said, bowing. "You have no equal."

"*Yishar,*" Sam said, brushing off another sting of disappointment.

Eshmun wished the blacksmith well, and they continued on through the *šuqā*. The throng bowed and parted for them as they went, though Sam couldn't help but notice the few scattered looks of disdain cast in Eshmun's direction. *Why?*

"A gift of turquoise for Helena?" a jeweler called out, sweeping his arm over his array of goods. Engraved seashells and silver bird earrings. Faience amulets. Clay and glass pendants like the one Teth wore around his neck. Sam stopped: A dozen tiny bearded faces peered up at her, unmistakably Eshmun. Some were detailed enough to show his keyhole pupil. His hair and beard were made of small spiral shells.

"Amethyst, chalcedony, carnelian," the jeweler continued, touching each bin as he went. "Serpentine, quartzite, onyx, lapis lazuli, and jasper. A pin for your cloak, sire, or a gem for your princess." He winked at Sam.

Eshmun declined. Instead, he led Sam on to step inside a roofless shack, where a single chair sat in the center of a simple room. In the corner, a woman was hunched over a whirring contraption, her white hair as shiny and fine as a spiderweb. She pumped a pedal up and down with her foot, which made a stone wheel rotate; a hissing noise filled the room each time she pressed a metal blade against the spinning stone.

A whetstone. She was sharpening something. Were they here to purchase a weapon?

"Hello," Eshmun said, and the woman turned with a start. She took her foot away from the pedal, and the wheel slowed to a stop.

Though the silkiness of her hair suggested youth, her face was ancient. On her forehead, warts peppered her skin. They looked like eyes, dark at the centers.

"Forgive me," she said. "I did not hear you come in." She did a double take, flustered. "Nor did I recognize you, my lord." She skittered across the room on what seemed like more than two legs hidden beneath her long gray skirts. Her white hair brushed the ground as she bowed to Eshmun and then Sam.

Sam dipped at the waist in return, but Eshmun grabbed her by the back of her dress and pulled her upright. "She has traveled from afar," he said. "Customs differ."

"I see what she requires," the woman said. She set her hands upon her bulbous stomach, thrumming her fingers. "Oh, I see, see, see."

"A proper haircut," Eshmun said.

"What?" Sam asked, realizing what the woman had been sharpening. Scissors.

"We will need to wash it first," the woman said, assessing Sam's hair.

"But—"

"Her clothing as well," Eshmun added.

"She will clean up nicely," the old woman said. "Indeed she will."

"Is this necessary?" Sam asked. "We need to get to Sidon."

"You are as filthy as a sailor's mouth," the old woman said. "Follow me. Behind here. Undress. No one can see."

"I don't care how I look!" Sam told Eshmun. "We're wasting time."

But the old woman shushed her, leading her to an enclosed changing area behind a woven screen. Grudgingly, Sam untied her rabbit-fur belt and placed the empty vial on the ground. Around the

side of the screen, the woman handed Sam a bucket of water and a lump of something black. "Wash yourself."

Sam held the lump to her nose and then thrust it away. "What *is* this?"

"Soap," the woman answered.

"That's not soap."

"Indeed it is. Made of goat's tallow and wood ashes."

"Tallow?" Sam asked.

"Fat," Eshmun's voice came from across the room.

Sam handed it back to the woman. "I'll just rinse off," she said. "Water only."

The old woman pressed it back. "I insist. You will emerge radiant, and all the others in the marketplace will desire my services."

"Fine," Sam said with a sigh.

She sloughed off her bag and dress and began to bathe. The water was freezing, and the soap didn't lather. There were black marks on the tips of her fingers on her right hand; strangely, no matter how much she scrubbed them, they wouldn't come off. Through the crack in the enclosure, she could see Eshmun step back outside. Her teeth chattered as she poured the cold water down her arms and over her head.

Moments later, the old woman thrust an arm around the screen with a robe. Sam wrapped herself in it, and then sat in the chair in the center of the room.

"Be still," the old woman instructed as she braided Sam's long bangs. The scissors were strange: two bronze blades connected at the bottom with a U-shaped handle. "Why are you trembling like a newborn? It is only hair, my beauty. I am not cutting out your heart."

"I feel like my heart is already missing," Sam said heavily. "Have you seen another girl like me in the marketplace? She's taller and younger."

"I am sorry, I have not, my child." The old woman positioned the scissors just below Sam's eyebrows, and then squeezed the curved handle at the bottom. The blades came together with a ringing sound. Several inches of Sam's bangs fell into her lap with a soft thud. Lost in thought, she thumbed the braided strands of hair, while the woman skittered around her.

"Not yet," she said, pressing Sam back down into the chair. She used another set of scissors, smaller, along with a comb, carefully snipping. Sam exhaled, blowing pieces off her lips.

"Now it is straight," the old woman said, hooking a finger under Sam's chin and twisting her head back and forth to examine her work. "A line as perfect as the horizon, where the sea meets the sky."

"Yes," Eshmun agreed as he returned to the shack. From his bag, he pulled a swath of soft, sheer fabric. "Silk," he said, handing it to the old woman. "Procured from a recent expedition to Amarna."

"It is very fine," the woman said. She turned to Sam. "Now you can see the world, and the world can see your exquisite face."

Soon, Sam's dress was returned damp but clean, and she put it on behind the screen. The woman had mended the tiny holes in the fabric where the spit of the *tannîyn* had burned through. Sam picked up her bag and once again slung it over her shoulder, the weight of it beginning to feel familiar. Eshmun thanked the old woman, and she bent low.

"The reason you did not see the lions tracking us in the Beqa," Eshmun said once they were outside, "is because they blend so perfectly." He placed a soft hat on Sam's head, its sheer veil streaming down her back to her waist. "Do you understand?"

"You're saying I don't blend."

"The finer details are lacking," he said, handing her a new pair of sandals. They roped up her legs with soft bands of leather and tied just below her knees. He then opened his palm and showed her a ring.

"Pretty," she said.

"Put it on."

Sam hesitated before sliding it onto a finger. The gold was buttery against her skin, and the stone wasn't like any she'd ever seen before; it had not been dyed and polished or cut with smooth facets. This was a raw stone, rough and green, riddled with dark gray like a tornado sky.

"An emerald," he said. "Does it fit?"

She spun the band on her finger, uneasy. "Yes," she said, considering the weight of it. Something had changed; he was being too nice, and it made her uncomfortable. What had he been quietly deciding as they'd walked through the cedar forest? Had her harsh words in the mountains gotten to him? Was he feeling remorseful? Did he feel a sense of *tyābutā*, of shame, for betraying the gift of his ancestors?

Or was he only planning more pain for her?

She almost pushed the ring back; she didn't want to owe him anything. But then again, if a ring, a veil, and a haircut would camouflage her, they would help her disappear into a crowd when the time came to run again—and it *would* come, she was sure. And she could trade the ring later for something else. Something more useful.

"Wait. This isn't about blending in," she said, another possibility dawning suddenly. "You're going to *sell* me, aren't you?"

"I could," he said. "The gods would wage a bidding war over you."

She felt a rush of dread. If she had the chance again, would she try to kill him?

"What *should* I do with you?" he asked, studying her face. "That is why we are here. To consult with the fortune-teller."

He turned, and with a flick of his wrist, he directed her toward a tent. Its flaps were closed, but he parted them and motioned for Sam to follow. She stepped inside reluctantly, remembering the psychic Mom once paid to come to the house for a private séance.

Mom had collected a few of Dad's things and spread them out on the floor. His hairbrush, a favorite flannel shirt, a baseball he'd caught at a Texas Rangers game when he was a kid.

"I feel him here," the psychic had said. She'd made her voice sound spooky, wavering with sharp notes as she called to the spirit world. Underneath her flowing black gown dotted with sequins, Sam had seen tattered blue jeans.

"You mean he's dead?" Sam had asked. "You feel his ghost?"

"Is he coming home?" Mom asked.

"What do the Marines tell you?" the fortune-teller responded.

Sam was confused by her answer, which was actually a question. "I thought the stars or spirits or whatever are supposed to tell *you*," she'd said. She'd looked down at the pile of Dad's stuff on the floor and suddenly felt the need to gather it up and put it safely away.

Now, burning incense cast a shroud of smoke in the dimly lit tent. A woman sat on a woven rug, cross-legged, back turned. Her long black hair spilled onto the ground. A snake was coiled next to her; she reached out and stroked it, her hands cloaked in gauzy fabric, and in the shadows of the candlelight her long fingernails traced the snake's curved spine.

"Greetings, my lord," she said, not turning to face them, not standing.

Eshmun pressed his palms together. "Arba`ta`esre," he said to her back.

"Your dreams have been strange of late."

"Yes."

"As have mine. I dreamed there was a dead rabbit upon my hearth," she said. "I took it as an omen. Within my dream I fell into a trance so that I might read its entrails. The heart and mind are at odds."

"Yes," Eshmun agreed.

"How will you reconcile them?" she asked.

"Tell me," Eshmun said.

"Beneath the surface of the sea," she said, "there is a flash of scales and color. What is it?"

"Tell me," Eshmun said again.

"See with your own eyes," Arba`ta`esre said. She motioned to a table to her left. On top sat a round shape, covered with a cloth. At first Sam thought it must be a crystal ball, but when Eshmun pulled the swath of fabric aside, she saw that it was a bowl of water. Inside swam a winged, iridescent creature with the head of a horse. Where its mane should have been, flowing fins streamed like a thousand miniature flags.

"Is that...a hippocampus?" Sam asked.

"A daughter of Yamm," Eshmun said. He picked up a candle and took a step closer to look. "They were hunted to extinction."

"It will grow until it is the size of a merchant vessel," the fortune-teller said. "The question is: Is there another so rare? Would you not keep this gift safe and close?"

Eshmun watched the water horse in silence. "You will release it," he said.

"Precious things must be guarded," Arba`ta`esre said. Still without turning to face them, she added, "The girl stays for a moment. Her fortune differs."

Eshmun gave Sam a solemn nod. He placed a coin on a plate before stepping back outside into the marketplace.

Sam shifted uncomfortably, not sure she wanted to be alone with this woman in the tent, not sure she wanted to know her future.

Arba`ta`esre stood and lifted the snake from the ground, draping it across her shoulders as she turned. Sam took a startled step backward. With what seemed like a trick of the candlelight and smoke, Sam realized that the woman's hair was gray, not black. How could she have mistaken it?

And though her nose was pierced with gold studs, and symbols were tattooed across her cheeks, there was no mistaking her.

"*Zayin,*" she choked.

"One vial," she cooed, "is so little to ask. And yet you willingly promised more." She'd changed her voice for Eshmun, Sam realized. Just like the psychic had done for Mom. "Do you know where the tears are yet?"

"I will," Sam said, her voice hoarse with fear. "I need more time. We're still on our way to Sidon."

The snake stretched toward Sam's face, flicking its tongue. "Ah, but no," Zayin said. "You cannot want more, because now you have less. Your sister," she said with a coy shrug. "Taken."

"How do you know that?" Sam asked, beginning to sweat. "The jackals have her."

"*Had,*" Zayin corrected. "Commodities change hands quickly in this world."

"My sister is not a commodity," Sam said.

"No? What is she worth to you?" Zayin asked. She dipped her gauze-covered fingers into her robes and pulled out a small mother-of-pearl box. She pressed it toward Sam, her long fingernails jabbing Sam's stomach.

"Where is she?" Sam asked, recoiling. "Did you...*buy* her? From the jackals? How is that possible? They were bringing her to—"

"Warships," Zayin said. "Their bows extend into sharpened points of bronze. For ramming enemy vessels." She pressed her nails deeper into Sam's skin, twisting. "I will scrape your insides out, like a rabbit's. I will read your entrails. Do you understand?"

The snake raised its head and swayed—so close—eyes glinting in the candlelight. Sam grimaced and carefully stepped back. "Yes."

"Since our last meeting, I have acquired new information," Zayin

said. "A coin of Chusor's gold may be in this world. Where would it be?"

"I don't know," Sam said, trying to steady her voice. "I don't have it. That's not our agreement, anyway."

"True. Perhaps I shall make another deal with your sister. *She* might know where it is," Zayin said, her amber eyes glowing. She reached inside her cloak and pulled out an ashen gray feather. "Here is a fallen angel's feather." She stroked it against Sam's bare arm. "I have procured the poisonous arum berries, the scorpion tails. I have memorized the incantations long ago. What I lack is a strand of Eshmun's hair, a drop of his blood." She pressed Sam's hands around the mother-of-pearl box, squeezing tight, Zayin's hands feeling bony and hard. Cold. "Get them for me."

"That's *not* our deal, Zayin."

"The price has increased, if you wish to buy back your sister."

Sam swallowed. "Why do you need Eshmun's hair and blood?"

"To make him mine," Zayin said, batting her impossibly long eyelashes, "for a hundred centuries."

"But Rima?" Sam choked. "Where is she?"

"Were you not listening?" Zayin shrugged, her voice acid. "The longer you take, the more you pay. And do not rely on Eshmun to find her—he will not. He has plans of his own, of course...."

"Continue to Sidon with him," she ordered, punctuating each word with icy precision. "Procure the items. Make haste."

The snake hissed and snapped at the air just above Sam's head.

Fumbling backward, she tucked the box beneath her belt and struggled to find the part in the flaps of the tent. Finally she burst through and hurried back into the marketplace where Eshmun stood waiting.

The sound of Zayin's venomous laughter echoed behind her.

11

Teth kept sneaking glances at Sam with her clean dress, new veil, and haircut. "I have had a feast in Sarepta, but you are one for the eyes," he finally blurted with a grin, handing her a cookie. "Sesame pastries. Still warm."

Sam took it but did not eat. Her thoughts churned.

If Rima had been traveling the entire time they'd been in Sarepta, the gap between them had widened. The hours were slippery in this world, and Sam could feel hers running out. She could only imagine how Eshmun had interpreted his own cryptic fortune. *Precious things must be guarded.*

What was the precious thing? Her? The obol? Zayin had certainly meant to manipulate him somehow, to her favor.

Sam deliberated her choices: Should she tell Eshmun what had just transpired? In the mountains, Zayin had warned her that Eshmun would never let her go, that she couldn't trust him. He had his own hidden agenda. But what if Zayin had been lying about having bought Rima? What if the jackals still had Rima, and they were still taking her to Môt?

The outskirts of the marketplace behind them, Sam felt something velvety brush her arm, rousing her from her thoughts. Before she could react, the old gray mare had stolen the pastry—right from her fingers.

"Hey!" Sam said, smiling in spite of herself. She patted the horse's side, the ribs just underneath. "It's good to see you again."

"You do not need a horse," Eshmun said, frowning. "It is a manageable walk from here."

"I have chicken wings, too," Teth added, holding up a parcel tied with a knot. "We can eat on the road!"

"I *do* need her," Sam said, as the horse chewed on her stolen treat with her big yellow teeth.

"She is not an acceptable specimen," Eshmun said. "She looks unhealthy. The finer details, you understand."

"What I understand is that you didn't heal the blisters on my feet," Sam said, "which would have been vastly more helpful than buying me a ring." She squeezed Teth's arm and motioned for him to help her up. He offered his laced hands, and Sam stepped onto them to mount the horse. Seated, she looked down at Eshmun. "A horse will get me to my sister faster."

"What did Arba`ta`esre tell you?" Eshmun asked her for the third time.

"She said we have to find Rima," Sam lied.

He narrowed his eyes at her but said nothing.

♈︎

Soon, the walled city of Sidon and the breadth of the Mediterranean Sea spread before them.

The water glimmered navy in the dusky light, the same color as Glen Lake on a summer's night. Palm trees stretched toward the cloud-streaked sky, and a few seashells littered the pathway beneath her horse's hooves. Sam could smell the tangy sweetness of salt water ahead.

They zigzagged downhill until they reached the massive city wall

made of stones, each as big as Teth. Even higher rose the watchtowers and turrets. A great wooden gate was guarded by men armed with spears and crossbows. Across the doors was a carved inscription:

𐤟𐤕𐤁 𐤉𐤉𐤁 𐤅𐤀 𐤉𐤀𐤉�28 𐤉𐤉𐤀𐤄 𐤌𐤌𐤅 𐤆𐤉𐤂𐤌𐤆𐤉 𐤒𐤈𐤂 𐤋𐤋𐤀𐤆𐤉𐤏 𐤅𐤀𐤒𐤀 𐤉𐤉𐤌𐤆𐤋 𐤕𐤂 𐤉𐤉𐤂 𐤅𐤀

"What does that say?" Sam asked.

Teth put a hand to his chest. *"We have built a temple for Eshmun, the holy prince,"* he said solemnly, *"at the purple-shell river."*

In unison, the guards above bowed to Eshmun, the joy on their faces evident. While some stayed true to their posts, others hollered to each other and pointed, edging closer for a better look. One held a giant conch shell to his lips and blew.

"Welcome home, my lord!" a gate guard said. He gave a signal, and a moment later the doors began to swing open from the inside, pulled by horses.

"Forgive the protocol," another guard said, stepping forward. He was older than the rest, his face carved with wrinkles. "You must present your hands before entering the city. We cannot be too careful. The Alchemist has been on the prowl."

"My uncle's shapeshifter?" Eshmun asked.

The guard nodded, and Teth let out a gruff breath of air. "In the name of Ba'alat Gebal," he said, shaking a finger at the sky. "We do not need more trouble! He is his foulest servant."

"It is to be expected," Eshmun said, his eyes darkening.

He held out his empty hands, and so did Teth. The guard looked at Sam, so she leaned down from the horse, holding out her bare hands as well, opening her palms.

"I don't have any weapons," she said.

The guard's gaze lingered on the stubborn black stains on her

fingertips—and then on the emerald ring—before he gave a nod. "Welcome," he said, bowing.

Once they were inside the walled city, the doors ground closed behind them. As in Baalbek, the buildings of Sidon were small, and most were made of stones piled into uneven walls. But here, some roofs were palm-thatched, and at nearly every turn, there was a stunning view of the water.

At the city's waterfront, battered seawalls dropped down to the rocky beach below. A long line of boats was moored in the harbor, inside a circular sea fort guarded by three turreted towers. There were vessels with horse-shaped prows and purple sails; others had three levels of oars and teemed with men, a hundred feet long from stem to stern. All of them, according to Teth—who kept up a running commentary—belonged to Eshmun.

"Are there many places to sail from here?" Sam asked, looking toward the horizon. Outside the walled fort, a few small fishing boats sat serenely upon the water.

"Of course!" Teth said. "We sail to Tarshish to trade our timber and dye for peacocks and silver. Tanis for gold. Akko for olive oil and livestock, Tell Kazel for pottery, Ophir for sandalwood and precious stones. We sail for spices, for tin and copper. All of Canaan is here, as it was on Earth."

And Rima's out there somewhere.

Sam sucked in a long breath, but then spat it back out.

"What is that awful stench?" she asked. She put a palm over her face and breathed between her fingers—it smelled like her bait bucket when it sat in the sun too long. "I might throw up," she said, waving a hand in front of her.

"That is the odor," Teth said, "of rotten, decomposing snails. Vats of them."

"Disgusting," Sam said, her eyes watering. She nudged the horse forward with her heel.

"Our famous purple dye comes from them," Teth laughed. "Their mucous secretions. The dye is worth its weight in gold! And the addition of sea salt alters the shades of purple. There is a fine art to achieving the desired range of colors." He nodded to the neckline of Sam's dress, to the sash around Eshmun's waist. "Purple is worn only by those who can afford its price."

Sam plugged her nose shut and, walking beside her, Eshmun let out a small chuckle. "It is a stench that could raise the dead, is it not?"

"If only!" Teth laughed. "If only that were true. You would not need your obol, my lord."

Eshmun pulled in a deep breath. "It is," he said, "for better or worse, the smell of home."

Sam looked at him and saw the wistful excitement on his face. *Home.*

She felt a stab of jealousy. She would give anything to be able to walk up her own driveway to her lopsided trailer. How many times had she taken that last turn in the road for granted, knowing her family would be there, waiting for her? What she would give to be there now.

Sam dismounted the mare, afraid of how narrow the street had become against the seawall. The old horse had already faltered once on the rough road, where a patch of loose stones had made it difficult to find sure footing.

"Is that yours?" Sam asked, pointing out to the sea, where a small castle sat in the water at the end of a stone bridge.

"Yes," Teth answered for Eshmun.

"Is that where we're going?" she asked, but the men continued on without answering.

They soon reached a wider road. Within moments, it broadened into a main thoroughfare. Women turned to look at them approaching; men pointed. Sam could hear squeals rising up from the children, who tugged on the women's dresses.

"Lord Eshmun!" someone cried out.

Doors opened and people looked eagerly outside. "Who is she?" Sam heard echoing through the commotion. "Who is the girl?"

"Relation or lover?" Teth asked Eshmun as more people began to gather. "Ally or prisoner? What is she to you?"

The horse whinnied, agitated. "I know," Sam said, patting her. "It's like the paparazzi."

She watched a flicker of panic cross Eshmun's face. He came to a halt in front of a rubble-walled building with a flat roof. "Enfeh!" Eshmun called, tipping his head upward.

A boy, about fifteen years old, looked down at them from the roof. "My lord!" he said, bowing deeply, his black curls of hair flopping into his eyes.

"Where is your father, my loyal retainer?"

"He is not far off," Enfeh said. "I expect him soon."

"Good, then," Eshmun said. "Until he returns, you are in charge of this woman. Keep her here." Eshmun motioned to a ladder for Sam to climb up onto the roof. "Hurry," he said, glancing nervously at the gathering crowd.

"What?" she asked. "No. You promised we would get word about Rima when we arrived in Sidon! I'm not going to just sit while you go off without me."

Teth leaned toward Sam's ear. "I believe my lord has realized that his attempts at making you look ordinary have failed," he whispered with a chuckle. "I could have told him it was an impossible task.

It is not safe for so many to see you when he has no ready story to explain you."

"Up," Eshmun commanded.

Teth patted the horse's side. "I will take her to someone I know," he said. "She will be well taken care of."

"We will return for you later," Eshmun said. "Go."

"You will be more comfortable," Teth added.

"On a roof?" she asked.

"Yes," Teth said. "You will understand in a moment."

Fuming, Sam handed her bag to Teth before climbing the wooden ladder. Enfeh offered a hand and she shinnied onto the rooftop.

From here, she could look down on the streets, watching as the city swarmed to greet Eshmun. Entire families spilled out of their houses. Women slapped their hands to their cheeks and knelt to kiss the ground near his feet. Men as big as Teth were crying. *Crying*. An old woman put her hands to her chest and shrieked Eshmun's name over and over again.

"He is home!" Men's voices boomed out in joy.

"Quickly!" a gray-haired man called over the din of the crowd. "Bring them drinks. A place to sit. A feast! A feast! This calls for music!"

Sam turned to find Enfeh staring at her. "Who are you?" he asked.

"Sam," she answered simply. "I'm not Eshmun's servant, and I'm not *ḫayuta*, and I'm not in the mood for questions." She motioned to the sheets of fabric spread across the rooftop, grains scattered on top of them. "What is all this?"

"Wheat. It is drying, and I must guard it against the birds." He was looking past her now, straining to see where Eshmun had gone. His face hid nothing: He looked absolutely tortured as shouts

of celebration echoed throughout Sidon. Everyone was joining the party...except Enfeh.

"It's not fair you have to miss the *'aḏ'iḏā*," Sam said slowly, a plan forming in her mind.

"They will be serving squash filled with rice and pine nuts," Enfeh said wistfully. "Kawkbā will take yesterday's bread, rip it into pieces, and crisp them in a pot of hot oil. She sprinkles them with sea salt. And there will be oysters." He sounded anguished now. "My auntie will bring sour green plums, and honeyed mulberries served over *labneh,* and rose water to sip. There will be parsley with tomatoes and wheat like you see here."

"Sounds lovely," Sam said, amused that he seemed more interested in the food than Eshmun. A girl's laughter rose above the happy shouting, and Enfeh stood up straighter at the sound.

"That is Kawkbā," he said, his voice reverent. "Her laugh is unmistakable."

"Who is she?" Sam prodded. "Your girlfriend?"

"No," Enfeh said. He stepped closer to the edge of the roof, eyes trained on the crest of the road, as if he could see over it if he tried hard enough. "Though...I would like her to be."

"Will there be dancing?" Sam asked.

"Of course."

Sam let the silence play out for a few minutes; she let him think about Kawkbā dancing with someone else.

"We walked from Baalbek," she said, sitting down. "I can hardly keep my eyes open."

"Sleep comes when he wants," he said, gazing fixedly at the crowds. "I cannot ward him off for you."

"No," she agreed. "I could sleep for eons. Nothing would wake me."

She yawned loudly and lay down, tucking her hands beneath her head. Eyes closed, she steadied and slowed her breathing. The smell of the wheat was earthy and bright, and above that, she could practically taste the food from the feast, the aromas catching on the wind.

Enfeh was already standing over her, studying her, she could sense it. She made her eyes dart beneath her eyelids and, gradually, let her mouth fall open. Should she snore?

Before she could decide, she heard the ladder creaking beneath Enfeh's weight, and then the sound of him sprinting down the street, his feet smacking against the road.

Sam guessed he would only risk being gone for a few minutes. She rose and rushed to the edge of the roof—only to find that the ladder lay flat on the ground. Enfeh had taken it down.

She considered jumping, but the ground looked unforgiving. Pacing, she looked for another way—and found a protruding beam of cedarwood under the rim of the roof, part of the house's ceiling.

She considered it for a moment. And then shook the wheat from a sheet of fabric, mumbling an apology to Enfeh. After rolling the sheet diagonally, she tied it around the beam, tightening a clove hitch—an essential boating knot—the way Dad had taught her.

Dropping to her stomach, she shinnied backward, grabbing onto her makeshift rope and sliding down.

She jumped the last few feet, the impact sending a jolt of pain up her shins. Rubbing the ache away and holding her breath, she looked left and right, but the streets were empty; everyone was at the *'aɔ'iɔā*. Above her, the birds had already begun to squawk and descend upon the wheat.

Quickly and quietly, she backtracked the way they'd come into the city, zigzagging along the stone roads until she found a route

leading down toward the shoreline. There was that small castle built upon the sea, the water lapping at its walls on every side.

Eshmun's home. A place where he might keep his tears.

A long, solid bridge was the only way out to the castle, which appeared to be two or three rooms at best, with an open terrace along the back. Men, who looked massive even from where Sam stood, held spears at their sides. They guarded the end of the bridge.

Maybe Zayin was bluffing, lying. Trusting her was a gamble, Sam knew, but she didn't doubt that her threats were real.

I will scrape your insides out, like a rabbit's.

Sam would need to play a strong hand to get Rima back. To save them both. She needed Eshmun's tears, hair, and blood.

She needed currency.

The only choice would be to swim, or to take a boat and try to climb up onto the patio. Thinking hard, she assessed her options—and spotted a small opening, a window. Below it was a pitted slab of rock.

A climbing wall, Sam thought. *Just like at Girl Scouts summer camp.* It was about a hundred feet out into the water.

Taking a breath of courage, she scrambled down to the beach, hiding behind a stony outcropping. At the next opportunity—when the guards were not looking her way, seeming to be listening to the celebration—she sprinted straight for the bridge, her heart pounding madly, and pressed herself against its side. The closest guard, above her, could not see her unless he leaned out over the edge to look directly down.

The waves slapped against the cold stone of the bridge, masking the noise she made as she waded out into the water until it reached her shoulders. She then scrabbled along, swimming and clawing as her veiled hat was swept away, filling with water and dipping below the surface like a boat with a hole in the bottom.

The strong current sucked her away from the wall and then threw her back, smashing her shoulder against the stone. Briny water rushed into her nose, and her muscles burned with fatigue.

Three more labored strokes and she found a knob of rock to hold on to, the castle's bedrock. She desperately pulled herself out of the water before it yanked her down again.

Straining to look, she saw the opening, straight up about fifteen feet over her head. She clawed her way up to the next jut, and then climbed, one handhold at a time.

The higher she went, the drier the stones became, making it easier to get a firmer grip. *You're halfway there,* she thought, pausing to catch her breath. Her legs quivered. Her arms were numb. Her bracelets scraped against the wall.

By now Enfeh might have realized she had escaped. Would Eshmun send men to hunt her down? Would those men use crossbows from the shoreline, taking her down like a bird? Or would they rain arrows down from the window above her? She thought of the old arrow Zayin's hawk still had lodged in its side. She forced herself higher, but her legs seemed to weigh a hundred pounds; her fingers felt like they might snap.

If I fall, she thought, *if I drown, I'll become a* ruḥā. *I'll be trapped here in the underworld as a ghost.*

The thought was enough to propel her. She climbed faster toward the window—now so close. Finally, she reached its lip, peered into the room, and then heaved herself inside, gasping for air and flexing the ache from her hands.

She lay on the floor for a solid minute, waiting for her heart to slow, trying to regain her strength. At last, she pushed herself to her feet and surveyed the room.

There was a bed covered with a fur blanket, and that was all.

No shelves or boxes or anything else that might hold vials of tears. She looked under the bed, just to be sure, but there was nothing there besides cobwebs.

A doorway led to the patio. Peering outside, she held her breath, listening. But she saw no one and heard nothing except for the sounds of waves and gulls, of her own hair and clothes dripping onto the floor. There was a magnificent view of the sea and the blue-streaked sky.

Quietly, hesitantly, she crept out toward the stone railing. The patio floor was also stone, irregular pieces fitted together.

Except for one spot.

Sam knelt and ran her hand across a piece of opaque glass. A panel.

Underneath, something moved. Undulated.

Maybe it was water, the sea lapping under the glass. Or maybe it was a vat full of tears. She hooked a fingertip underneath a notch in the corner and lifted the lid. In an instant she realized what was really inside:

Snakes.

Dozens of them, twining around each other. They licked the fresh air Sam had let in, and coiled to climb out. Their red eyes flashed.

She swallowed a scream before dropping the lid back in place, her entire body shaking.

She took a long trembling breath before standing up again. Still staring at the covered snake pit, she wondered why Eshmun would keep such a horrible thing in his house. Was it protecting something? It had to be. But what? Were his jugs of tears hidden beneath this writhing coven of snakes?

She decidedly couldn't dig through them to find out. Hot tears welled in her eyes as she headed back inside, still trembling as she approached another doorway. It led into a room she hadn't explored

yet. Could the tears be *there*? It was possible. They might have nothing to do with the snakes. She couldn't know unless she looked.

Steeling herself for another surprise, she took a cautious step across the threshold.

Wooden tables ran in rows. On top of some sat stone tablets carved with symbols—at least twenty, set side by side, like the pages of a book laid out to read. On top of others were colorful illustrations drawn on animal skins.

It's some sort of library, she realized.

The walls were bare, and there were no vials or jars, but anything could be hidden here. As she searched, she kept returning to one of the illustrations laid out on the tables, a hunched man chewing on a human leg. Something about it gave her the strangest sense of déjà vu, but where could she possibly have seen such a gruesome picture before?

She leaned in close, trying to understand.

A half-memory wavered ahead of her like a mirage. She could almost reach it. It had something to do with Mom, something to do with a cave. Mom's voice came to her: *Sometimes things aren't what they seem.*

And then she was suddenly jerked from her thoughts by an angry voice. "Do not move," the guard said, taking a step closer. "Or I will spear you like a fish."

12

The guard poked and prodded and cursed at Sam the entire way back to the party. "She claims she was searching for her sister," the man snarled when they found Eshmun.

Hushed murmurs swept through the crowd. Everyone turned to stare.

Sam was dripping wet, and her cheeks flushed red—though not with embarrassment. She was angry at herself. She'd been in Eshmun's house but had failed to find any tears. She should have moved faster. She should have been bolder. And now here she was, returned to him once more, as if tethered to him by some invisible thread.

Eshmun looked her up and down as she plucked her wet dress away from her stomach. "After all that effort in Sarepta," he said. "And where is your hat?"

The party had fallen silent. Sam could feel the crush of people gathering around her. She shrugged.

"I went for a swim," she said. "The hat did, too."

To her shock, Eshmun tipped back his head and laughed. It was hard to tell because of his beard, but Sam was almost sure he had dimples.

He thanked the guard and waved him off. Someone draped a blanket around Sam's shoulders and she used it to towel off her hair. Eshmun urged the onlookers to continue eating and dancing. Reluctantly, they dispersed, and the hum of the party resumed.

"You're not angry I was snooping around your house?" she asked. She thought about the snakes. *Were* the tears hidden underneath them? Should she try to go back to find out?

Eshmun shook his head. "If I am to speak honestly, I admire your persistence."

"Don't blame Enfeh."

"The odds were not in his favor," Eshmun said with a crooked smile. He seemed like a different person in Sidon. Happier. She felt another stab of jealousy. This time it plunged deeper.

"It must be nice to be home," she said as a basket of bread was passed through the crowd, along with flasks of wine. Food seemed to be coming out of every kitchen in the city: roasted chickpeas spiced with *za'atar,* braided white cheese speckled with nigella seeds, skewers of grilled vegetables with lemony sumac, dried sardines and fried squid. Sam tried a little of everything, and then she caught sight of a grinning Enfeh, who was feasting on a leg of lamb while dancing with a beautiful girl who could have only been Kawkbā.

"So do you know where Rima is?" Sam asked. "You promised you'd find out. Have your people seen anything?"

"Be patient," Eshmun said.

"How can I?" Sam asked.

A tapping on her hip made her look down. A little girl peered up at her, her long hair tied back in a ponytail. She had round cheeks and dark eyes, and wore a rose-colored dress.

"Hello," Sam said, surprised.

The girl scrunched her face. "You speak strangely."

"I do?"

The girl nodded. She thought for a moment. "You pile your words on top of each other until they tip over."

Sam smiled. "I have an accent, don't I?"

Her mind flashed to when she'd first arrived in Baalbek. She wondered now if this was why Eshmun thought she'd had the coin hidden in her mouth. She glanced at him, but he was distracted, speaking with a knot of old men.

"We want to know who you are," the girl said, still poking Sam's hip. "Where did you come from?"

"Far, far away." Sam winked at her. "You're very brave. I think most everyone else is afraid to talk to me."

The girl nodded. She tapped her fingers against Sam's bracelets. "I like your ring," she said, and trotted off.

Sam watched her ponytail bounce as she disappeared into the crowd, but now there was an old woman approaching her. Staring at her. "Forgive me," she said when Sam met her hazy eyes. Her ancient skin was the color of tea. "You look strangely familiar."

"My sister?" Sam asked, a charge running through her heart. "Have you seen her? She's two years younger than me. Maybe she came through Sidon already? Is she here?" She spun around, scanning the sea of faces.

"A girl? No," the woman said, shaking her head. She searched Sam's eyes, much the way Eshmun had done several times now. As if there was something there they couldn't quite discern. "How did you get here?" she asked. "Where is my obol?"

"*Your* obol?" Sam asked, flabbergasted.

"Are you not the one who has twice summoned me?"

Sam shook her head. "No, I...no," she managed. "Who are you?"

"I am Sbartā," the old woman said. "I am a descendant of Ba'al Saphon, the storm god."

"I'm sorry, but we've never met," Sam said. Although, now that she looked...the woman was strangely familiar to her, too. How could

that be possible? Her hair piled high and sharp on top of her head. Her cloudy eyes. Sam searched her face. *"Do* I know you?"

"No," Sbartā said slowly, hesitantly. She continued to study Sam in the same grasping way. "Forgive me for disturbing you. I am mistaken. You are not the one."

"Wait. What do you remember?" Sam pressed. "About this woman who summoned you?"

"There is a box," Sbartā said. "There is a man who holds a banner with an eagle and an anchor."

Sam fumbled for words. "I... I wish I knew what you meant."

Sbartā pressed her palms together and bowed. She hobbled away, vanishing into the crowd before Sam could say another word.

Meanwhile, a makeshift stage had formed in the middle of the road, where people now took turns singing songs or telling grim stories (all of which seemed to involve a demon or a marauding invader). Sam couldn't tell if they were invented tales, or if the people were recounting what had happened to them or their ancestors in another lifetime or another world. They began each story with the refrain, *"Kan ya ma kan, fi qadim az-zaman."*

It happened or it did not, in the oldness of time.

Sam sat on a barrel and listened, her clothes and hair drying out. A little boy sang about the rising sun and the harvest moon. A woman with hair all the way down to her ankles recited a recipe for sesame seed paste. At first Sam thought it was a love song, the way she called it out with heartfelt joy.

Sam sloughed off her blanket and had just started to look for Eshmun when someone screamed his name.

A woman cradling a small child in her arms rushed toward him, sobbing. "He is dead, my lord!" she wailed. The boy hung limp in her arms. "Is it too late?"

The interruption had diverted the crowd's attention from the stage. People turned and pressed closer to see, while others pointed toward the sky. Sam looked up and saw the boy's *ruḥā* hovering overhead, a dark kite on a string, still attached to the body by a wavering thread.

"Give him to me," Eshmun said.

The mother handed her child over to Eshmun, who then placed his hands upon his small bare chest. The boy couldn't have been more than two years old; he was just a baby.

"He is my only child!" the woman cried. "Please. He has been sick. I rocked him to sleep. I only thought he was sleeping!"

"Methlem-wā kull kibā," Eshmun murmured. "In the name of my mother, royal healer, and her father, and her grandmother before, chemists of salves and incantations, I invoke their power, which runs through my veins."

In the sky above, the boy's *ruḥā* twisted into a dark ball of thread, spooling downward. It slid into the child's mouth.

A white glow spread through his chest and into his small limbs. Sam was speechless.

As tears streamed down Eshmun's cheeks, an old woman knelt next to him with a piece of curved glass pressed to his face, which channeled his tears into a vial underneath. Sam's heart jumped.

A vial of tears.

"With ancient prayers, I beseech you," Eshmun incanted. "Focus your light within me, grant what I need. From you is born the power of life. *Etkteb qðim men."*

"Hurry," the mother said frantically. "He still does not breathe."

"Be calm," Eshmun said. He chanted a moment longer, wiping his wet eyelashes and then stroking the boy's cheeks with his fingertips.

The boy's eyelids fluttered open.

"He is well," Eshmun said, and he handed the child back to his mother.

She opened her mouth but said nothing, uncertain, frozen. Finally the boy cooed and pressed his small head into the crook of her arm. The entire crowd sighed with relief, and then erupted into joyful shouts of praise.

"Thank you," the boy's mother said, her voice trembling. "My lord, you are truly a worthy god and prince. I am forever in your debt."

Tears. Sam pressed her fingers to her side, feeling for the vial and the small box, both still secure under her soaking-wet belt. Eshmun had held his fingertips to his eyes as he was healing Rima's *tannîyn* wounds, too...and his face had been wet after he'd mended Rima's ankle, but she'd thought it was only river water. And when he healed Sam's bruised neck, he'd wiped his face, but she'd thought it was because of the ash in the air.

Whenever he healed someone, he cried.

"Pour the tears into the water jugs," Eshmun said to the woman who'd collected them. "Everyone will partake of a drop or two."

His tears *healed*.

The crowd roared with a collective cheer, and then people returned to their food and conversation. Eshmun's name rang out through the festivities with notes of celebration and reverence.

"You are staring at me, Samira," Eshmun noted.

"You...you..." Her voice trailed off. "It's one thing to heal cuts and bruises, but you...you brought that child back from the *dead*."

Sam remembered standing quietly behind Dad once, caught for a moment by the war movie he was watching on TV. The screen was green, the scene shown through the eyes of a soldier wearing thermal goggles. Ahead, there was the body of a man he'd shot, his heat leaving him. The soldier could see it through those goggles, lenses into an

invisible reality. That heat rose off the dying man like a mist, escaping into the night.

"I have my limitations," Eshmun said. "He was nearly beyond my reach. There have been maladies that outwit me, illnesses that defy me."

"My heart is racing," Sam admitted. She'd been clutching her dress. She let it go and smoothed out the damp fabric along her thighs.

"As is mine," Eshmun said, letting his eyes linger on her face. Sam looked away. *What is he* doing? *Is he* flirting *with me?*

On the stage, a group of four men with instruments had started playing. The music reigned now, and the tables were pushed aside to make a larger dance floor. Eshmun bowed and held his open hands forward, an invitation to dance.

"No." Sam shook her head.

"Do you dislike me so much?" he asked, his hands still open.

"Obviously."

But she wondered. Mom believed in Fate with a capital *F*. She believed in signs. And now Sam had begun to ask herself: Had she always been linked to Eshmun somehow? To this world? To the coin?

And Sbartā, the language, and even the gruesome illustration had stirred something deep, like memories so distant they might not be her own—as if she'd inherited them from generations long gone.

"Do you never allow yourself a moment of joy?" Eshmun asked. "I, too, know the weight of constant worry. It will crush you."

"Is that what happened to you?" she asked, narrowing her eyes. She thought of what Teth had told her in the forest. All the friends and relatives Eshmun had lost along the way. The burden of being the one who would save everyone. In all honesty, she knew how that felt. "You've had to bear too much. And that's why you're so dark."

"Some light remains."

"Do you want to know why I dislike you?" she asked.

"Please," he said. "Tell me."

"For starters—I shouldn't even have to say this—because of the way you've treated my sister and me. But there's more than that." She took a breath. "Do you not see how much people need you here? They love you. So what if you find your obol? How can you just abandon everyone? What about the *tar'ā*?"

"My coin has summoned me," he said, lifting his chin. "It is my destiny."

"You can make your own destiny," Sam said. "Leaving is a choice. When we make promises, we should keep them. It's called duty."

"Is it my duty to serve the destinies of others until the end of time?" he asked, aggravated. "How long must I wait until I am permitted to pursue my own?"

"Maybe I don't like you," Sam said, "but I *do* understand who you are."

"Oh yes?" he asked. "Who am I?"

"You're lost. As empty as a *ruḥā*. You want to be reunited with your family," she said. "Just like I do. You want everyone to be together again."

He gazed at her for a long moment. And then, surprising her, he closed his eyes and nodded solemnly.

They'd been edged closer together by the crowd dancing around them. Tambourines crashed and small flutes whistled like birdcalls, making it harder to hear. Eshmun leaned toward her ear.

"Did you hide my burial obol somewhere along the way?" he asked. "Tell me."

"What did Teth's moth say?" Sam countered. "I bet he sent it back along our route to look."

Eshmun nodded.

"And I'm sure you have other spies and confidants who have been searching Baalbek and elsewhere on your behalf. So, no, I didn't hide your obol, and you should know that by now." She stared at him, hard. *"Precious things must be guarded."* She spread her arms toward the people of Sidon. "Isn't this worth guarding?"

"Ah, the words of the seeress. Tell me, do you remember these? *Is there another so rare?"* he asked, the intensity of his gaze almost too much to bear. His keyhole pupil widened, as if inviting Sam to look inside. *"Would you not keep this gift safe and close?"*

Sam felt the heat rise in her cheeks. "I'm not a gift," she said firmly. *And Arba`ta`esre was not who she seemed.*

He took her arm and turned it over. "You have bled here."

"From the mountains," Sam said.

He wiped the scabs away with one swipe, as if clearing nothing more than flecks of dust. "Where else?" he asked, letting the tears run down his cheeks and into his beard.

She showed him the palms of her hands. The blisters from digging in her backyard.

"What has happened here?" he asked, frowning. The black marks on her fingertips had gotten bigger, spreading like an ink stain.

"I don't know," she said. "I touched a *ruḥā.*"

He blinked at her. "Why would you do such a thing?" He shook his head. "One girl, and yet enough acts of foolishness for an entire city-state."

"I wanted to talk to it."

"The dead keep their secrets. He used you. He only wanted a taste of life."

"Maybe I was being brave," she said. "Sometimes I think you confuse the two. Foolishness and courage. I have to try whatever is possible."

He held her palm to his and twined his fingers through hers. She closed her eyes as his heat swept through her, her skin tingling with an electric intensity. When he let go, the blisters were healed. But the black marks had only faded. They were still ash gray.

"Why won't they go away?" Sam asked.

Eshmun seemed confused. "Stubborn," he said. "Like you." His expression turned sober. "How long did you hold on to the *ruḥā*?"

"Not long enough, I guess. I didn't learn any secrets."

He nodded, still frowning as he studied her hand. All around them people clapped, danced, and sang, while Sam and Eshmun became an island in the middle. Drums beat a steady rhythm.

"Where else do you hurt?" he asked.

"The blisters on my feet," she said, "and the hole in my heart."

"If there is emptiness within," he said, "it is because you try to fill it with hope. It is like trying to drink fog to quench your thirst."

They weren't quite dancing, but they were being carried back and forth now by the shifting crowd around them. Sam raised her voice and stood on her toes to tell him, "Hope is all I have."

"Which kind?"

"What do you mean?" Sam asked. "Hope is hope."

"No. There are two kinds...one that heals and another that harms. Sometimes we cling to hope like a raft when in fact it is an anchor, and the weight of it will bring you down. Sometimes we think that hope is a salve, yet it only prevents a wound from healing."

"You promised you'd look for Rima. Now you're saying I should give up? No."

"Only on impossible hopes, ones that you insist on nurturing, no matter how difficult it is to keep them alive."

"I must hope. Rima is alive, and we'll find her," Sam said. The crowd spun around them and they likewise turned in circles. She

pretended to stumble forward, put her hands on him, and plucked a strand of black hair from his cloak. "Besides, why should I listen to you? You've given up on everything."

"There is no one in this world who speaks to me in this manner. With such—"

"I know," Sam said, cutting him off. "With so much insolence."

"May I finish?" he asked with a small smile. "With such *quṣtā*."

Truth. Sam pulled in a long breath. Nodded.

"As you told me in the mountains," Eshmun continued, "true words hurt. I will never forget what you said to me about my mother. No, she would not be proud." His eyes dropped.

Sam tilted her head at him. She pinched the hair tighter between her fingers. "So...you realize you've gone from calling me a liar to calling me honest?"

"The truth is this, Samira," he said, "the *ruḥā* gather like storm clouds. They are my constant shadows, reminding me of my failure to find passage. There are those who have lost faith in me. They mock me." Sam thought of the few dismissive looks they'd gotten in Sarepta, the undercurrent of disdain. "The rising voices of my people are like thunder on the horizon."

A pained look swept over his face as he pressed a hand to his heart. He opened his mouth to say more, but at the same moment, another commotion broke out in the street. Carefree voices turned instantly to ones of warning, panic. The music stopped.

"Wanderers!" a man cried out. "Strangers from beyond the city gates!"

A group of women—flanked by two of Eshmun's guards—had padded into the feast. One had scratches all over her arms and legs. Another was missing an eye, and the skin had grown over the socket

like a wrinkled tarp. They stood at the periphery of the party, five of them, in torn clothing.

"We know these nomads," one of the guards called out. "They bring news."

"Sire!" one of the Wanderers said. She looked among the throng until her gaze fell upon Eshmun. "We made our journey to warn you."

"You followed us," Teth said. He appeared out of the crowd and took his place protectively next to Eshmun. "I knew a party of five trailed behind us from Baalbek. I smelled you. Were you sent by Melqart?"

"No," she said. "And we did not intend to follow you so closely, but a *tannîyn* drove us into the mountains."

"A *tannîyn*!" someone shrieked, and then an angry chorus followed: "Shush, old man! Do not speak its name!" Next to Sam, a woman put her hands to her cheeks and moaned. A worried murmur swept through the crowd.

While anxious words were passed back and forth, Sam used the distraction to place Eshmun's strand of hair inside the little box, snapping it shut and hiding it once again under her belt. A tinge of guilt pricked her, but she reminded herself that she owed him nothing. She could *not* trust him. And if she had to pay Zayin to save Rima, so be it. *He* wasn't doing anything. He was telling her to give up.

Eshmun held up a hand and the crowd fell silent.

"Continue," he said. "Why do you seek us out here and now?"

Another nomad came forward, her neck long and slender and ridged with uneven skin. Her hips sat impossibly wide atop skinny legs. Sam thought she might be *ḥayuta*, an ostrich. "We bring news from Baalbek," she said, glancing at Teth and then turning her eyes to the ground. "I am sorry, brother."

"Ushu," Teth said with recognition. He took a step forward. "What is it?"

"There is no easy way to say this."

"Say it, then."

"It is Meem..."

Teth pulled in a breath, a low growl pooling underneath. Sam looked up at Eshmun to find his right pupil narrowed into a closed slit: The keyhole had locked tight. The crowd was silent, waiting. Sam heard a fork or skewer hit the stone road with a clatter. A dog barked in the distance.

Ushu let her long neck bow to the ground, the image of a wilted flower. "Meem...has been murdered," she said. She shifted uncomfortably on her long legs, as if she herself were feeling the worst of the crime. "They cut off her feet."

13

A musical instrument plucked out a single flat note, and then Teth slammed a fist into a table, sending food everywhere. *"No!"* he roared, his head thrown back. *"Meem!"*

He smacked his hands to his temples and pulled at his hair, wailing. Screams and gasps spread through the crowd as Eshmun took the stage, standing above everyone with raised hands.

"Stay calm," he said. "There is nothing to fear here."

But Teth's cries had turned to low, guttural moans. Sam shuddered, watching him sprout fangs, still tearing at his head as if he could rip the news away. A storm of panic was brewing. Sam could sense it all around her—the words *ḥayuta, tannîyn, murder, Kition,* and *gihannā* ran through the street like currents of electricity, charged and ready to catch fire.

Teth's shirt split along his spine and his pants ripped across his thighs as he morphed. All signs of his human shape were disappearing. His nose was a snout, his ears had shifted to the top of his head. Saliva dripped from the corners of his black lips, his canines growing longer.

The little girl with the ponytail—the one who'd admired Sam's ring—slipped her hand inside a woman's, and the two of them hurried off, the girl's rose-colored dress fading into the crowd. One by one, people turned away, trading horrified glances. Their fast footfalls made a pattering noise like rain.

Sam whispered his name—"Teth"—as if she could bring him back. But he stood on his hind legs and roared. Sam winced and covered her ears, tears streaming from her eyes. Plates and goblets crashed to the ground as he barreled away in an anguished rage. "Teth!" she cried after him.

"Stay calm!" Eshmun again shouted out to the crowd. "You are safe here in Sidon!"

The party broke up as quickly as it had come together. Tables and chairs disappeared from the street, one by one, until it was empty again. An overturned cart lay on its side like a slain beast; from its bed, cracked melons spilled, wet and full of seeds. Sam could hear doors locking, the sound of metal bars sliding into place. Even the makeshift stage had already been disassembled.

It was as if the party had never happened.

Someone handed Sam her bag with the frying pan still heavy inside. She looped it over her shoulder as she navigated around the shards of a broken bowl and a splintered chair, trying to catch up with Eshmun.

"You were close behind us," he was saying to Ushu. "When did this happen?"

"We were joined by Addir, the falcon, who flew to us and then went his own way afterward," she said. "He brought the news. The *ruḥā* of Meem haunts her parents' home. She hovers at their doorstep."

"Who has done this?" Eshmun asked.

"We know not," Ushu said. "A neighbor said she heard a man's voice demanding the shoes."

"Shoes?" Eshmun asked, bewildered.

"*Shoes*," Ushu repeated, as if Eshmun should know, as if there were only one pair of shoes she could possibly be talking about. She fanned her fingers nervously across her wide hips.

Behind Ushu, one of her travel companions, the woman with only

one eye, pulled a small clay tablet from a bag and offered it to him. "Forgive me, but perhaps my lord has not yet seen this."

"What is it?" Eshmun asked, taking it from her.

"A record of the symbols," Ushu said, "which were inscribed within the shoes. Codes, or...directions of some sort, said to point the way toward the *tar'ā*. Meem copied the symbols and sold them on papyri and clay tablets—such as the one you hold now. She then offered the shoes themselves for sale. There was to be an auction." Ushu wrung her hands together and then began fanning her fingers again, as if she could fly away. "That is, as I understand it, when the negotiations turned hostile. Buyers began threatening each other. Her price was outrageous. And so someone decided to take the shoes, along with her..."

Ushu's voice trailed off.

"I see," Eshmun said.

Sam wrapped her arms around herself. She tried to keep from imagining Meem, how her mutilated body would have looked. The blood. Severed ankles. Her small face, cold and pale.

An animal's distant keening made Sam's heart slam against her chest. She was sure it was Teth on his way back home to Meem, too late to save her.

"May you find the guilty party," Ushu said, bowing her ungainly head.

"Teth will find him first," Eshmun said grimly. He took the tablet, studied it briefly, and then tucked it inside his cloak. His fur collar, Sam noticed, looked tired and matted.

"I am sorry to be the bearer of bad tidings," Ushu said. "Of all the things we have carried back and forth across this land, this news was our heaviest load. To think, a murder so savage outside of Gadir or Kition! Baalbek *has* become darker since Ba'alat Gebal went east, but this? Meem was of a native ruling house, the merchant aristocracy!

Her great-grandfather once served on the Council of Elders. It is a brazen crime."

"Yes," Eshmun said. "Her grandfather Rabā is a loyal ally. I consider him family, an uncle. This disturbs me greatly. It is a gruesome offense. An affront." He was silent a moment in thought, and then he pointed down the street. "I imagine you are weary from your journey. There is a home at the corner with round windows and a copper cat at the door. The couple there takes boarders for a fee, but I will arrange to pay it myself."

At this Ushu smiled. "Your reputation for kindness is well deserved," she said. "Thank you."

"Wait, please!" Sam said, taking a step forward. "Please, before you go, could you tell me if you saw anyone unusual along the way? I'm looking for my sister." She cast an angry glance at Eshmun; he should have asked.

Ushu's head dipped again, making the mottled skin along her neck dimple. "We *have* heard talk of a strange girl being taken by boat to Kition. Perhaps to the dark marketplace...or even as an offering to the god of death himself."

"When?" Sam demanded.

"I am sorry, but I have no other information," Ushu said as her travel companions fell in behind her. The one-eyed woman hobbled as they made their way down the road.

"Thank you," Sam whispered, watching them go.

I'm a concubine and Rima is cargo, she thought. She pressed her palms to her eyes, despair casting shadows over her thoughts. An *offering.*

Back inside that candlelit marketplace tent, Zayin *had* lied to her about having Rima. Or she'd soon after sold her off.

The price would have been high. A *commodity.*

Sam looked up at Eshmun.

"I need to get to Kition," she said, her voice dripping with acid. "Where is it? When can we leave?"

"Pe of Arwad," Eshmun said, talking to himself. "Glassmaker. Bayt, builder of homes. Mengebet, captain of the sea."

Sam lunged at him and grabbed him by the arm. "You're listing names again! Stop! Where is your uncle? I want to go there, right now!"

"I had hoped it was not true, but it sounds as though she indeed has been taken to him," Eshmun said, incredulous, disgusted. "He was to stay in Gadir."

Sam looked down at her feet, at her new sandals. "Meem was murdered for my shoes," she said. Sam remembered the way Meem had examined every item of her clothing with fascination. The zipper in her pants; her bra, the way the stitching was sewn.

"She was ordered to burn your belongings," he said. His eyes flashed. "She disobeyed."

Meem had wanted money. *If Teth had more wealth,* she'd said. She'd been trying to make him into a suitable match. So they could marry. Sam's heart lurched for Teth, for both of them, and the wedding they would never have.

"Does Meem's death mean you'll turn back for Baalbek to find the murderer? Teth will," she pressed, "won't he? He's already on his way. I'll go alone to Kition, then. Tell me how to get there."

"Come," Eshmun said, leading Sam along the street where a group of men stood huddled, talking and smoking, sending blooms of smoke over their heads. "You will sleep while I attend to business. One cannot stroll into Kition. We will need men. And we will need to sail—I must ready a crew." He pulled out the clay tablet the Wanderer had given him and tilted it toward Sam. "Can you decipher this?"

NE WEST.

She ran her finger over the letters. "Northeast west, maybe?"

It didn't make sense—but then she read the rest of the etched letters: MADE IN CHINA US 8M. It was from the inside of her shoes. NINE WEST, they had once said, but the *N* and the *I* had long ago worn off.

"This is written in English," Sam said. "My language, from my world. It's not some magical message about finding passage. There are no instructions. It's just my shoe size and where they were made." She looked at Eshmun, feeling her heart stutter. Meem had not been entirely kind to Sam, but she did not deserve such cruelty. No one did. "Meem is dead because of me."

"No," Eshmun said. "That is not true. If she had burned the shoes as she had been ordered, this would not have happened." He raked his fingers through his beard. "If I had allowed you to wear your own shoes, this would not have happened."

"If you hadn't brought us here to this world," Sam said.

He frowned at her, a sad twist of his mouth. "It is exactly as Zayin said back in the temple in Baalbek: I cast my blame in the wrong direction." He tossed the tablet onto the ground, where it cracked in half.

Sam felt broken, too. Who was to blame for all of this? Rima was missing because of Eshmun. Meem was dead. Sam was the one who'd touched the coin in the first place. Maybe she should blame Jiddo for sending her the ancient jug.

She stopped walking. *If someone would murder Meem to have my shoes,* she thought, *what would they do to have* me? She thought of the *tannîyn* and the jackal-women. She suddenly registered all the stares she'd gotten at the feast just now, the men who seemed to be studying her, the women afraid to come too close. She looked over her shoulder, certain she was being watched. "Where are you taking me?" she asked.

"To someone I believe you already know," he said, "but have never met. She has a soft pillow, a place for you to lay your head. Your eyes

are so dark and your skin so pale, one might think death is beginning to take you. You are exhausted."

"Yes," she said. "I am. But I can sleep on the boat."

"What boat? No boat is ready," he said. "My men are not yet assembled. I have not yet given the orders. In the meantime, there is nothing you can do."

"Then when are we leaving?" she pressed.

"Enough. Come."

He tossed his head sideways for her to follow. They walked between two long buildings, passing doors on either side. Along the narrow alley, the occasional oil lamp flickered by their heads, small green fires housed in jars of opaque glass. Dark shapes danced along the walls behind the flames: shadows of insects or smoke. Eshmun licked his fingertips and extinguished them, one by one.

Finally, they slowed and approached a door on their right. Eshmun tapped several times, and when no one came, he cleared his throat.

"Helena!" he hissed, pressing his mouth close to the door. "It is Eshmun."

Almost at once, a latch clicked and the door swung open. A woman stepped forward.

While most everyone else they'd met along the way had seemed cowed by Eshmun, afraid to touch him, Helena did not hesitate to embrace him. A smile blossomed across his face as she cupped his cheeks against her palms.

"Where have you been?" she asked sternly. "I was beginning to think you'd gone after Ba'alat Gebal, and we had been abandoned. A *tannîyn*, Eshmun! My neighbor has just left here after sharing the news from the feast. A murderer who takes the feet of his victim! A hellfire in the cedar forest! What can all this mean?"

"It is good to see you as well," he said as she clucked at him. "And

please do not mention the beast by its name. We do not wish to summon it."

Helena pulled back and Sam now had a clear view of her face.

Her face.

"Mom?" she choked, though of course it couldn't be her mother. Mom was in Michigan. This woman lived here, in this stone building. She didn't look *exactly* like Mom, but the resemblance was uncanny: She had the same narrow nose, the same light brown eyes flecked with lines of olive green. She wore a simple dress and no shoes.

Sam reached out for Eshmun's arm, feeling like the world was tipping beneath her. "Wh-who are . . . ?"

"Eshmun?" Helena asked. She seemed just as flustered. "Who is this girl?"

"Samira." Eshmun sighed heavily. "When I see you together, all uncertainty vanishes. The similarities are undeniable."

"Do I know you?" Helena's eyebrows came together. She stepped toward Sam for a better look. Sam fumbled for words, and Helena seemed equally distressed. They stood staring at each other, nearly like looking in a mirror.

"Come," Eshmun said finally. He ushered them inside the small apartment, cozy and warm with a fire crackling. A metal grate sat inside the fireplace; on top of the grate a wooden-handled pan bubbled with dark liquid.

"Would you like *ahweh*?" Helena asked. "Do you know what that is?"

"Coffee," Sam said, breathing in the smell. "I would love some."

Eshmun declined and sat on a chair, watching while Helena poured the liquid over a piece of fabric and into a cup, filtering out the beans. "It is spiced with cardamom," she told Sam.

Sam took the cup and peered into the steaming brew. She sipped slowly, knowing it would be strong.

"Goat's milk?" Helena asked.

"No, thank you." It was perfect the way it was. Bitter and fragrant. She shed her bag and sat at a small round table across from Helena.

"Ah! Qamar," Helena suddenly cooed as a long-legged cat emerged from the back room. The cat was tawny with black spots, too big to be an ordinary housecat.

"That's a serval," Sam said with certainty, déjà vu stirring in her once again.

"An Egyptian breed," Helena said. "She was just a kitten, a baby, when Eshmun gave her to me as a gift."

"Hello, Qamar," Eshmun said, and at his voice the cat erupted into a purr so fierce Sam could feel the vibration in the air. Qamar darted across the room and launched herself into Eshmun's arms. He smiled and rubbed his face against hers, scratching behind her ears.

"Let the fire die, now, Helena," he said, setting the cat on the floor, his face turning serious again, "so that it might not become possessed."

She gave him a startled look. "Of course," she said. *"Allahu al mustaan."*

Sam cocked her head at Helena. She had just spoken Arabic. *God help us.* It was something Mom said every once in a while, one of the few phrases Sam recognized.

Ahweh. Another Arabic word Sam knew. She looked into the dark liquid, as if it might hold answers.

"Who are you?" she asked Helena. "How do you know Arabic? Why do you look so much like my mother?" Helena's hair was the identical color and texture; she even tucked it over her ear the same way.

"Who is your mother?" Helena asked.

"Helena," Eshmun interrupted before Sam could answer, "please

tell Samira how you came into this world. That is the place to begin the story."

Helena furrowed her brow, perplexed.

"Tell her," Eshmun said.

"If I must?" she asked. A dark look had settled in her eyes. She seemed to shake off a chill, pulling her arms around herself.

"Please," Eshmun urged.

"It was so long ago, and yet I remember it like yesterday."

"As do I."

"It was the year 1903 on Earth." Helena blew on her cup of coffee to cool it and then sipped. "Not that the years matter much here." She looked at Samira. "On one of my many walks, I found a jug. I thought I'd uncovered every trinket around my mountain village, but there it was, a perfect artifact." She smiled. "I remember being thrilled. It had been sitting sideways, just inside the cusp of a cave, one I'd explored before. I'd gone inside to get out of the sun for a moment."

"The sun," Sam repeated wistfully. On the wall behind her, a mosaic of pottery shards and bits of glass had been artfully arranged into a golden circle with outreaching beams, floor to ceiling. "Did you make that?"

Helena glanced at her work. "Yes," she said. "Of all the things I miss most, it is the sun. Sometimes I dream of it. I am able to reach over the horizon and pull it back up by the scruff of its neck. It is just there over the edge, so close." She reached an arm out across the table toward Sam, showing her how it was done. "All it takes is the tips of my fingers to pinch it."

"It's a beautiful mural," Sam said.

"It warms my home," Helena said, "in its own way."

"The jug, Helena," Eshmun urged. "Go on."

She nodded, took another sip of coffee. "I carried the amphora home and set it aside. I was busy with my tasks: picking grape leaves

and sweeping the porch, making cookies for the church. It wasn't until later, by the light of the moon, that I discovered what was inside. A coin! I was sure it would be worth something."

"A coin," Sam said, setting her coffee down with a clatter. It sloshed onto the table as she shot a look at Eshmun. He nodded, as though confirming the connection she was making.

"It was odd," Helena said, her voice far away as she remembered. "I knew it from the moment I saw it. I picked it up. I had it between my fingers and then..."

"The ground opened up," Sam said.

Helena nodded, putting a hand to her chest as if she were feeling physical pain, deep inside. "I dropped the coin back inside the jug, but it was too late to stop what had started."

"There was a funnel," Sam said quietly.

"You know about coffee," Helena said. "They had not heard of coffee here before I arrived. Imagine. I could not live without it, so Eshmun brings me beans when he finds them in his travels. I have not yet figured out a way to grind them properly. A mortar and pestle are a difficult way to do the work. I have spoken with the blacksmith and carpenter about the old grinder I had in the village, but they cannot get the crank just right. My diagrams are terrible, I know."

"I cannot understand this obsession," Eshmun said. "It is like drinking soot."

"You know about coffee." Helena kept her eyes on Sam. "And you know about funnels opening up at the touch of a coin."

"Yes," Sam said. She turned to Eshmun. "Where is my letter? The one Meem took when she searched me."

Eshmun already had it in his hand; he must have known this was coming. He unfolded the thin paper and held it out to Helena.

"Will you please read this for me?" Sam asked. "It's from my

great-grandfather. He sent it along with an old jug that was filled with coins."

Helena's eyes widened.

"One of the coins brought me here...through a funnel," Sam said quietly.

Helena cried out. "What are you telling me?" she asked.

"Read the letter," Eshmun said.

Helena could not keep her hands steady, so she set the paper down on the table next to Sam. *"My dearest Samira,"* she began. *"Beloved daughter of my beloved granddaughter. My only living kin and the last direct descendants of my bloodline are your mother, your sister, and you. By all accounts you are the most responsible, Samira. Therefore I send you my dearest possession. I send you this amphora, which my own mother discovered in a cave in Lebanon."*

Sam pulled her hands into her lap and tried to steady them. She'd broken what he called his dearest possession. It lay in pieces in her yard back in Michigan. "It was *your* jug?" Sam asked, but Helena continued shakily reading the letter.

"I have made wishes my entire life, but the genie refused to come again. And therefore, upon my death, I bestow it to you. My only regret in my living life is that I never met you, my great-granddaughter, nor your sister, my flesh and blood. My eyes."

"My eyes?" Sam asked.

Helena nodded. *"Einee.* The Arabic word is *einee.* It's like saying *my heart.* He writes at the end, *'May all your wishes come true.'"* She tapped a finger to the page. "This is his signature, the name I gave him when he was born." Looking up, she wiped a tear from her cheek. "His handwriting is so beautiful, isn't it? This...this was written by my son. Eshmun, is this true?"

Eshmun was silent, his head bowed. Qamar twined between his ankles, still purring.

Sam was trying to understand. "You're the genie," she said to Eshmun. "Jiddo thought you came out of the jug, so he tried to bring you back, along with his mother...Helena. He spent his whole life making a wish that could never come true. The coin was at the bottom of the jug, and he never knew it was there, or what it would do if he touched it. He thought he had to rub the jug like a genie jar." She paused, thinking. "He must have added his own coins over the years, maybe hoping it would work like a wishing well." How many times had Mom given her and Rima lucky pennies to toss into fountains? *Don't tell me your wish, or it won't come true.*

"Oh." Helena let out a trembling breath. She looked up at Sam with tears. "I missed his whole life. What did he do? Where did he live? Who did he marry? He was just a child when I was taken from him."

"Like he said in his letter, I never met him," Sam admitted. "He only had one child, late. I think he was about fifty when he finally got married, and he stayed in the village his whole life. He would be a very, very old man now." She hesitated. He'd sent her the jug because he was dying. She reached out and touched Helena's arm. "I'm so sorry."

In the few photos Mom kept framed on her bedroom walls, Jiddo smoked hand-rolled cigarettes, his olive skin deeply lined, his nose hooked. In one picture, he had a plate of figs and olives on the table in front of him. In another he posed with Sam's grandmother, still vigorous and healthy, in front of some ancient ruins at sunset.

Ruins at sunset. *Baalbek.*

Sam knew she'd seen that word before, written in blue ink: Her great-grandfather's precise and ornate handwriting on the back of a photo, along with a long-ago date.

"So I *am* in Lebanon," she said, confirming what she already knew.

"Syria," Helena said, seemingly confused by Sam's assessment. "A part of the Ottoman Empire. At least that was what it was when I left.

As you have probably surmised, we were both brought by the coin to another world—that of the Phoenicians."

"We are Canaanites," Eshmun said, adding his own correction.

"Yes, yes, that is what they call themselves. *Phoenician* is a word that would come later." She leaned toward Sam and searched her face. "And you are the daughter...of the granddaughter...of my son," she said, piecing it together.

Sam gripped the edge of the table. The very same coin had brought them both here, Sam and Helena, more than a century apart.

Helena reached out and squeezed Sam's hands. "This is a gift," she said. "It is almost like having him back, in some way. A part of him."

Arba`ta`esre's words came back to Sam once again, though being called a gift by Helena felt different. It felt right. "My mother says I have his hands," Sam offered. "Long fingers."

They sat looking at each other, wiping away their tears before they spilled into their coffee, while Sam told her about Rima, about the jackal-women, about the journey from Baalbek. Eshmun finally spoke. "I must go," he said, stooping to give Qamar one last scratch behind her ears. "I have a boat and a crew to ready."

Helena stood suddenly and thrust a finger at him. "Shame on you."

Eshmun grimaced. He put his palms in the air. "When my obol calls me, I—"

Helena held up her own hand to stop him. "Not once, but twice you have pulled my family apart."

Eshmun seemed to shrink. "I am overtaken by a force I cannot fight," he mumbled.

"The damage you have inflicted," Helena admonished, wagging a finger at him. "The hurt you have caused. *Tyābutā*." She raised her voice. "Her sister—my great-great-granddaughter—is in grave danger!"

"I will find her," Eshmun said.

"*Yallah!*" Helena said. *Hurry!* Eshmun stepped back, seeming to cower in the shadow of her fury. "I will not allow my family to suffer. *Again.*"

"It has been so long since you have recounted your story," Eshmun said quietly, "I had nearly forgotten about your son."

"Of course you did," Sam chimed in. "But you think about *your* past, and being reunited with *your* family. So much, actually, that it blinds you."

Eshmun pulled himself to his full height. He would tolerate Helena berating him, but Sam knew he would accuse her of being *insolent*. She braced herself, ready to argue, but instead he nodded.

"I will set things right." He turned toward Sam. "I promise."

"And *tyābutā*, for not healing this poor girl's feet!" Helena cried. She pointed at Sam's toenails. "They are green. There is something wrong with them!"

Eshmun's face shifted. He let out a loud, deep laugh, and this time Sam couldn't help but react with a small laugh of her own.

Palm up, he curled his fingers toward himself, beckoning Helena closer. Still huffing with indignation, she rummaged on a shelf, and then came to him with the same type of channeled glass the woman at the party had used. She pressed it to his cheek so his tears ran through it and into a vial she held underneath.

And while he finally repaired her blistered feet, and his healing tears were bottled, Sam looked out the window and wondered how far it was to Kition.

She wondered if Rima was still alive.

14

"I have a thousand questions," Sam said to Helena after Eshmun had gone, "but I'm too exhausted to ask them all."

Eshmun's healing earlier had given her a wave of strength, but now she ached to lie down. Helena set the vial of tears on a windowsill next to a potted mint plant and three other vials.

"Start with one question," Helena said, draping a blanket across Sam's legs where she sat at the table.

Qamar twisted around Sam's calves, purring, and she reached down to let her fingers run through the silken fur. She felt oddly at home. Helena was already treating her like her own, doting on her and offering every possible comfort. Even though Sam had stuffed herself at the marketplace in Sarepta, and had eaten again at the feast, she could not resist a bowl of lentils seasoned with garlic and drizzled with olive oil. A pillow with brown feathers poking out of its seams was nestled behind her back, too, after Helena insisted the chair was too hard.

Sam had already told her as much as she could: how she'd gotten the package in the mail from Jiddo; about Rima and the *tannîyn* and jackal *ḥayuta*; the journey through the mountains; the cedar forest; Sarepta.

"Helena, do you have a map?" Sam asked. "Of this world?"

"I do," Helena said. "I drew it myself." She pulled a basket from underneath another small table. Within it there were several white rolls, tied with bits of twine. She unknotted one. "Here it is."

Sam spread it across the table. "It's so soft," she said, running her fingers across the mountains and sea and the dots of the coastal cities.

"Lambskin," Helena said, placing her coffee on one corner and Sam's cup on another to keep the map from curling up.

"Kition is just off the coast?" Sam asked, pointing to an island. "And we're here." She tapped a star on the mainland's shoreline.

"That is correct."

"I can't read your Arabic," Sam said. "Is this Baalbek, over here?"

"Yes."

Sam judged the distance from Baalbek to Sidon, the route she'd already traveled. And then she calculated how far it would be to Kition from where she stood now. It seemed to be roughly the same distance. "What about everything beyond the boundaries of this map?" she asked. "What's there?"

"Nothing," Helena said. "Darkness as black as a moonless night. Some say that the border is made by an innumerable legion of *ruḥā*. They stand shoulder to shoulder. They will slowly press toward us, shrinking this world until it is engulfed in final darkness."

Sam swallowed, staring at the map. "Can you tell me the story of Eshmun and the prophecy?" she asked. "It's been mentioned more than a few times now."

Helena went back to her basket and plucked out another rolled skin. She flattened it across the table, covering the map underneath and securing it again with the cups. She ran her fingers down the page, across the Arabic script.

"Did you write this?" Sam asked. The handwriting was beautiful and precise, just like Jiddo's had been.

"Yes," Helena said. She tucked a strand of hair behind her ear. "I wrote it as I have heard it recited so many times." She pointed to a

place on the skin and read, *"And then a mortal—a human of otherworldly beauty—shall wed the beloved, a godly match."*

"Okay, so a mortal married a god. There are more than a few gods here, right?" Sam asked. "I've lost count."

Helena held up a hand for Sam to be patient and listen. "This mortal was Eshmun's mother, a princess from the city of Tyre. Eshmun's father is the god Melqart, who is currently residing in Baalbek."

"Yeah, I saw Melqart in the temple," Sam said, recalling the shirtless man with the tusked mask. She remembered his chest puffed out with pride, the sleek leather gloves on his hands. "Surrounded by beautiful women."

"That would be him, yes." Helena said wryly. "You see, back when the Phoenicians reigned on Earth and ruled the Mediterranean, their gods often lived among them. Sometimes they fell in love with mortals. Melqart has had countless lovers, but only one child. Some say it is because he only truly loved one woman—Eshmun's mother."

"She was a princess," Sam said. "A mortal. Teth told me a little about her. She's gone now?"

"Yes," Helena said. "She died in childbirth."

"Oh," Sam said. "How sad." She thought for a moment. "Does Melqart blame Eshmun for her death, then?" It would be unreasonable and unfair, but possible. "Is that why they hate each other?"

"Perhaps, but the reverse is true as well. Eshmun blames Melqart for the death of his mother. He wasn't there while she labored, and he might have saved her. But, alas, Melqart was too busy...elsewhere." She gave Sam a pointed look. "He will never have his fill of women, that god."

Outside, there were shouts, an argument. The voices faded, and Helena, who had paused to look toward the windows, shrugged. "I imagine there will be some unrest now."

She shifted in her chair. Sam offered her the pillow, but Helena waved it off. "According to the prophecy, spoken by Ēl, the supreme deity, the father of all gods," she continued, "the offspring of that union was to liberate the trapped souls of the underworld. So Eshmun searches for a rift, but he cannot find a way.

"And there's more. Legend has it that there are secret passageways to Earth, but the knowledge of their locations has been lost. You see, as the Phoenicians fled Earth, the storm god, Ba'al Saphon, remained to fight. He roiled the sea and threw invading ships upon the rocks. He shook the earth and sky, causing earthquakes, wind, and lightning. But the enemy could not be routed, and finally, he vanished. Ba'al Saphon has never been seen again.

"It was he who sealed the boundaries between worlds so the Phoenicians' enemies could not follow them into the underworld, and it was he, they say, who left well-hidden rifts, should they ever wish to return."

The knowledge of their locations has been lost.

But Zayin had promised she would help Sam get home, if she was paid in tears. Was it a lie? Did *no one* know where these gateways were? Not even someone like Zayin, the consort of a god?

If only Sam could be sure. Who could really help her?

"How did everyone end up here?" Sam asked. Maybe understanding better how the Phoenicians had originally gotten into the underworld would give her a clue as to how, or where, to get out. "Like, how exactly did that work? Teth told me a little, but..."

Helena raised an eyebrow. "Môt invited Ba'alat Gebal—goddess of fertility, beauty, and love—to shelter here. She was an impossible desire, but he saw the opportunity, and he begged her to join him in the underworld for safe haven. As the war raged, and as the Phoenician people on Earth were being slaughtered and taken as slaves, the

goddess accepted on one condition. A considerable one." Helena raised a finger. "She would join him if all others could escape with her as well. And so the underworld was flooded with refugees—including gods.

"Ah, look, I had forgotten this one." Helena unrolled another scroll and smoothed it out. "An ancient fairy tale about the magical sword, guarded by a *ghūl* named Marid."

Sam sat up straight, suddenly breathless with the memory. "And a riddle," she added.

"You know this tale?" Helena asked.

"I...," Sam said, grasping for the details. She thought of the gruesome illustration in Eshmun's library. It had seemed so familiar. And then her mother's voice came to her once more. *Sometimes things aren't what they seem.* "I remember...I remember my mother used to tell us a story about a cave...and a monster that lived there. I remember it scared Rima. The monster eats the dead."

Helena nodded. "Most likely the same story I was told as a child. I then told my son, who then told your mother. The cave is real," she explained, "and Marid, the *ghūl*, is real. They exist here in this realm. But no one has been able to retrieve the sword." She held a finger in the air again. "It is the only weapon that can kill a god."

Sam could feel her eyes widen. She leaned over the scroll, searching the words even though she couldn't read them.

"Do not even think of it," Helena warned, watching her closely. "A thousand men have died in that cave."

"But what if I need it?" Sam asked. "What if I have to fight a god to rescue Rima? Or to get out of the underworld?"

"Cast every last shred of the thought out of your head. You cannot fight the god of death," Helena said sternly. "Understand: He owns the gateway from the underworld to *gihannā*—no matter where he treads, beneath him is a ready doorway. Phoenician hell is an endless sea with

no ports and no wind." She gripped Sam's wrist. "It is a mariner's worst nightmare. The damned float on rotten flotsam among other evil souls for all eternity. Would *you* wish to be banished there? Doomed forever?"

"But Eshmun's uncle might already have Rima!" Sam said, eyeing the dying embers in Helena's fireplace. *The god of death.* She thought of the hellfire and Môt's powerful voice, of his plumes of flaming flies. She shivered with dread. "Rima is being taken to Kition. I'm running out of time to save her."

"You will not go with Eshmun," Helena said suddenly, smacking a palm against the table. "You will stay here. Let him sail with his men!"

"I *have* to go."

A silence fell between them.

Sam sat back. She took another sip of her coffee. Her eyelids were heavy, but she needed more answers.

"I wish I'd never touched Eshmun's coin," she said quietly. Her lashes grew hot with sudden tears.

"As do I," Helena said. "If I could go back, I would never lay my hand on that jug." She was quiet for a moment, then refilled Sam's cup of coffee and nudged a plate of dried fruit toward her. "You can tell me the truth."

"Tell you…?" Sam asked, confused.

"Where it is. Eshmun's obol."

"I dropped it in my garden back home. Or Rima might have it," Sam added, remembering her lie.

"Hmm," Helena said. She didn't press further. "You may ask me one more question," she said, patting Sam's hand. "And then you must sleep."

Sam already knew what her last question would be. "Tell me how Eshmun would unlock the *tar'ā*."

"It might have something to do with this," Helena said, pointing to one of the unrolled lambskins on the table. She ran her finger down its text. *"The blessing of Ba'alat Gebal...,"* she mumbled, skimming ahead. *"The prophecy of the sun*...ah, yes, here it is. This passage speaks of a dagger tipped with a golden key. *The key forged from Chusor's gold,* it says."

Sam studied the indecipherable words beneath Helena's finger. She thought of how she'd wanted to stab Eshmun straight through the eye. Sam looked up at her great-great-grandmother and flushed. She would be outraged if she knew Sam had wanted to kill Eshmun—and that she still intended to draw his blood, when she had the chance.

What other lead for escape did she have? Zayin no longer had Rima—maybe she never did—but the coveted items obviously held great value, and her threats still haunted Sam. She would be back to collect, sooner or later.

Would Zayin uphold her end of the bargain? To tell Sam what she knew about a portal home? Could Sam sell Eshmun's tears, hair, and blood—*commodities*—to someone else for the same, or better, information?

"So Eshmun is not only supposed to find the doorway, he needs a special golden key to unlock it?" Sam asked. "Where is he supposed to get that from?"

"It is unknown. Chusor did not escape to the underworld when the Phoenician civilization fell," Helena said. "Nor did his coffers of sacred gold."

"What if it's all a fairy tale, then?" Sam asked. "Obols and passages and golden keys."

"Why do you doubt?" Helena asked with a laugh. "Look where you are! And how you arrived here. Do you not believe that Eshmun's obol has power? That Chusor's gold can unlock another world?"

Helena leaned toward Sam, lowered her voice to a whisper: "Aren't you afraid?" She pressed a finger to Sam's chest, to her heart.

"Of what?"

"Death."

Sam swallowed. "Of course I am."

"And so," Helena continued, "what if you had a coin that you *knew* would take you to paradise, to heaven, the hereafter, to *šmayyà*... whatever you choose to call it? At the time of your death, the obol is placed beneath your tongue, and then its magic takes you to your family and friends who have gone before you."

Beneath your tongue. So *that* was why Eshmun thought she'd hidden the obol in her mouth.

"I would want to find my coin," Sam said, thinking of the fine line between life and death. The heart beats and then it doesn't. A plane disappears from the radar. We take a breath, and then we don't. Tenuous. Fragile. The lines between worlds were thin.

"Everyone would."

"Or another sure way. A route from one world to the next. Passage."

She imagined what it would look like. A funnel, maybe, like the one that had brought her here. But this one would be lined with soft blue skies and flecks of sparkling light. It would smell sweet. It would be warm. Inside, there would be the sound of laughter and music.

"The son of a god and a mortal... foretold to be a salve," Helena said reverently. "From the day he was born, he was destined to come to the underworld. To heal this land. To lead the lost to our afterlives, so we may rejoin our long-deceased loved ones."

"But he hasn't delivered."

"And so there is doubt brewing," Helena said, nodding. "There

has been for quite a long while. When I arrived, there was even talk that the prophecy needed to be reinterpreted."

"Read another way?" Sam asked. "Why?"

"Think." Helena raised an eyebrow. "Could the god mentioned in the prophecy mean *Eshmun* instead of Melqart?"

"Eshmun," Sam mused. "*He* would be the father," she said, making sure she was following correctly. "And *he* would have the mortal wife."

Helena nodded. "He has not yet been married. And so there were those who believed *I* was the mortal. A young woman delivered into his arms by fate and gold—a bride from another world. They urged Eshmun to marry me, so that we could have a child. *That* child would be the one to fulfill the prophecy."

"The child of Eshmun and a mortal woman," Sam said, understanding.

"But I was already married!" Helena said, again slapping a hand against the table and making her coffee cup jump. "I'd already had a son! The prophecy is specific in that regard—the woman is a virgin, and there shall only be one male child born to her. That is why none of the gods had much interest in me. I was already..." She swept a hand toward a copper tray on the table. It had turned greenish, and was pitted with dark spots. "...tarnished, so to speak."

Sam mulled all this over.

"Besides," Helena said, "I did not love Eshmun. I hated him! He had brought me to this world, had taken me from my family. How could I be his wife? Even now, after all this time, I wake up sometimes and think I am home. It takes me a moment to remember where I am."

"How could you ever forgive him?" Sam asked. "I'm so angry, I could just..." She glanced at Helena, biting her lip. "This is his fault."

Helena leaned down and scooped Qamar into her lap, stroking her head as she spoke. "Soon after I arrived in this world, Eshmun

overheard me talking about a serval cat I once had. A wedding gift."
She smiled. "Oh, how I adored that cat. She brought me such comfort.
She would disappear for days at a time, as a wild cat should, but one
day my heart told me she'd been gone too long."

Helena sucked in a breath. "I found her, shot by the roadside. The
horrible men who sometimes raided our village had killed her—that
happened in those days, you see. I buried her and prayed on her grave
until the day I was brought here."

"Eshmun got Qamar for you," Sam guessed.

Helena nodded. "She was an orphan, like me. No family."
She reached across the table, once again squeezing Sam's hands.
"Until now."

Sam squeezed back. "You forgave Eshmun then?" she asked.

"Oh no," Helena said. "It has taken many more acts of kindness on
his part. A century of good deeds."

"A hundred years," Sam said in disbelief. She motioned to Helena's mural on the wall. "How do you even keep track of time? The sun
never rises or sets."

"It is an imperfect art," Helena said, nodding to a few plants
growing on her windowsill. "Thanks be to Ba'al Hammon, the god of
agriculture, we know by the seasons of crops, the gestation periods
of the animals, the blooms on flowers. There are clues." Sam smelled
the outside air coming through the windows, balmy and fragrant from
blossoming orange trees.

"I wondered how anything could grow without the sun," Sam
said, thinking of her backyard garden, the tomatoes. The green pepper plant Mom had bought with her casino winnings. "Ba'al Hammon.
He's another god here in the underworld?"

"Yes." Helena leaned into Sam, close. She studied her face. "Now
I see it."

"See what?" Sam asked.

"You have the eyes of my husband!" Helena said something else in Arabic, a reprimand. "How could I have forgotten?"

Sam smiled. "Your eyes are just like my mother's," she said. "Exactly. And they remind me of how my sister's are like our father's."

"It is a strange thing, isn't it?" Helena asked. "How traits can skip a generation or two, and then they are reborn again?"

"You really don't hate Eshmun anymore?"

"No. Though I am angry with him once again. He has reopened an old wound."

Sam nodded. Helena had told her she could ask one more question, but that had been at least a dozen questions ago. She stifled a yawn.

"It is a strange life here, but not a terrible one," Helena said comfortingly. "You will become accustomed to it, as did I. Qamar and I have hardly aged, thanks to the vials of tears Eshmun gives me every now and again. He takes care of this city and its people. There is much love in Sidon."

"The tears give you eternal youth?" Sam asked, though she was already sure of the answer.

No wonder Zayin wanted them. *Make haste,* she'd told Sam in the mountains. *I do not care to grow any older waiting.*

"They do not grant *eternal* youth," Helena said. "Death waits patiently for all of us. But the tears are quite curative, as you can see."

Helena turned her hands over: They were rugged and worn, but her beautiful face was only creased at the corners of her eyes. Sam would have guessed her age to be forty.

"We tell no one of these vials of tears," Helena said, nodding to them in their row by the plants. "Do you understand? No one. Otherwise I would have thieves at my doorstep—and much worse."

"I understand," Sam said.

"I can still see my son's face," Helena said. "A child's face. In my mind, *he* is forever young."

Sam let the silence that followed hang over them. Finally Helena took a breath and went on.

"We work hard for our food here," she said, still examining her hands. "I sweep the floor. I wash and mend clothing. I bake bread. In all honesty, my life has not changed much." She smiled. "It is not so bad."

"I'll take you back home with me," Sam said earnestly. "First I need to find Rima, and then we'll figure out a way."

Helena shook her head. "What would be there for me? What is that world like after all these years?" she asked. "No. Eshmun will find your sister and bring her here. I will look after you both. After all, you are family. You have the eyes of my husband and the hands of my son." She tipped her chin at the fireplace, the mural of the sun, a stack of terra-cotta plates, her oblong windows that let in the dusky light. "This is where I live. I have animals to tend, friends who make me laugh. Even if I could, I would not go back now."

"But we don't belong in this world," Sam insisted. "I'll find a way." The more she said it out loud, the more possible it seemed.

"So very long ago," Helena said, "when the Phoenicians fled from Earth, they were refugees of war. They were the displaced, the homeless. They struggled. The *ruḥā* frightened them, as did the absence of the sun. To them it was a cursed bargain—they were saved from the sufferings of conquest, and yet this was no paradise. Trapped here, they of course only wanted to go home.

"But later, for those generations who came after, for those born here, this was all they knew. It is home. We have food and beds, songs and poetry, work and dreams. Going back now would make no sense.

"Death will come for me eventually, and I will become *ruḥā*," Helena continued. "But I keep hope that a gateway will open for us all someday. Just as Eshmun recites the names of his lost friends and family, I try to keep close the names and faces of those I will see again in *ǰmayyà*."

The coffee had grown cold and sleep was impossible to fight. Sam put her hands to her chest, her heart aching. Helena looked so much like her mother it hurt.

"You've been here since 1903," she said. Helena had missed two world wars. She would not know what a microwave was, or a computer or a cell phone. Men had walked on the moon.

"Yes, my love," she said. She pressed her palms against Samira's cheeks, gently cupping her face. "Do you understand what I am saying to you?"

Sam nodded and forced the lump in her throat to recede. "But did you look for a way?" she pushed. "Did you search?"

"I did."

She led Sam to the back room, where there was a cot waiting. Judging by the layer of cat fur on the pillow, Qamar must have slept there often. Helena helped Sam settle in, pulling the blanket to her chin and kissing her forehead tenderly.

"You are so brave," Helena said. "Braver than I ever was. But I cannot let you go. Eshmun will take his best boat with his fiercest crew. You will stay here. If need be, I will put a hundred locks on the door to keep you safe inside." She ruffled Sam's hair, her newly cut bangs. "Eshmun will agree."

Sam didn't have the energy to protest; now that she was lying down, she struggled to keep her eyes open. "Your cat's name was Shams," she said. "I remember now. When we were little, my mother told us stories about a serval cat." She smiled at Helena. "She wasn't forgotten."

"Sleep, my great-great-granddaughter." Helena let out a small laugh. "It never ceases to amaze me."

"What?" Sam managed to ask as she began to drift into a dream. Sleep was taking her so quickly.

"Life," Helena said simply. "Life."

15

Keep an eye on your mom while I'm gone.

Dad's voice woke her. She sat up and looked around the room as if she might find him sitting quietly in a chair, watching her sleep. But of course he wasn't there. He was only in her dreams.

The curtains glowed with an amber cast, like bronze on fire. She smelled coffee and spices and burning firewood, and she remembered where she was. Dad wasn't in this world, and he probably wasn't in the world back home, either. He wasn't anywhere, except in her memory.

Sam closed her eyes again and summoned up an old favorite. It was a sun-kissed day out on the lake, and he was teaching her how to cast the line. "Flick your wrist," he said, cupping his big hands over hers. It was the same advice he'd given her about throwing knives. "Like this." Dad's soft stubble—blondish red—brushed against her cheek as he leaned over her.

"You're tickling me!" she remembered squealing.

Dad had thrown his hands up in mock disgust. "You're scarin' the fish off," he'd said. "Stop laughing." But he was laughing, too.

I'll keep my promise, she vowed as she ran her fingers across her face, trying to trace the faint spray of freckles that hugged her own cheekbones. Rima had more of them, but nowhere near the number Dad had.

Another memory suddenly sprang to life, and Sam stood up with it. There she was, just like yesterday, nestled on Dad's lap and trying to

count his *face confetti.* That was what she used to call his freckles. She'd forgotten that. *Nineteen, eleven-teen, fifteen, twenty.* She must have been three years old. Mom used to say he was the only adult she knew with so much face confetti. Dad would say, "It's 'cause I'm still a little boy inside."

Helena's apartment was quiet; through the windows, distant terse voices trickled in from the streets. Sam rubbed her face, and the emerald ring from Eshmun bumped across the bridge of her nose.

The ring from Eshmun.

No.

All at once, she was filled with certainty and dread. Why hadn't she put it together sooner, after what Helena had said about the prophecy?

There were those who believed I was the mortal woman.

A young woman delivered into his arms by fate and gold.

They urged Eshmun to marry me, so that we could have a child.

Sam pressed her hands to her chest, as if she could calm her stuttering heart.

She knew what Eshmun intended to do with her now. It was clear why he'd dressed her up, confided in her, healed her. If she didn't have his obol, then Sam would be his bride, a mortal wife who would bear him a son.

The son who might finally fulfill the prophecy and find a passage to heaven.

A swirl of fear and anger carried her back and forth across the apartment. She stopped to lace up her sandals as her questions turned darker: What if Eshmun believed that *Meem* had stolen the coin from Sam and Rima? By some bird or butterfly, a *ḥayuta* messenger, he could have sent word back to Baalbek to have her questioned...or worse. Anything was possible.

Why should I trust you? she had asked Eshmun.

You should not, he'd answered.

He used his healing powers to manipulate, to make people feel grateful and warm, and the realization made her cold inside.

And now she shuddered with another thought:

Helena's apartment would become her prison if she didn't leave.

"She must be guarded," Helena would tell Eshmun. *"I will keep her safe for now."* Eshmun would thank her for her wisdom. He would believe this was the fortune Arba`ta`esre had divined.

Sam's mind raced. Could this all possibly be part of Zayin's plan? She'd wanted Sam to stay close to Eshmun, forever? So Sam could eternally deliver vials of tears to her, whenever she demanded, meanwhile doling out false hopes and clues about the way back to Earth? Had Zayin and Eshmun actually been working together, for some purpose she couldn't quite put together yet? Had Zayin and Môt been communicating?

Teth's voice came back to her:

This world was set with traps before, but now you must calculate every step.

Helena slept soundly on an oxhide mat next to the fireplace while Sam quietly repacked her bag with one of Helena's wool blankets, Zayin's empty vial and mother-of-pearl box, a bowl, and a few items of food and water from Helena's baskets. From Helena's scrolls, she took the map; from Helena's sewing supplies, she took a needle; from Helena's peg, she took an old cloak. She left the heavy copper frying pan on the table in exchange for a knife.

The row of vials lined the windowsill. All were empty except the one Helena had just filled with Eshmun's tears. Sam took it, silently apologizing. Helena would understand if she knew.

At the door, she paused to look at her great-great-grandmother's beautiful face, so peaceful and quiet as she slept with Qamar curled into the crook of her arm. She looked happy.

With a silent goodbye, Sam let herself out, into the dusk, alone.

She headed west, winding through the maze of streets, until she found the first stone pathway that led down toward the sea. Below, the water was dotted with rocks, and an anchored fleet of boats went on and on, one after another. Carved figureheads looked over the harbor—horses with nostrils flared, ready to gallop across the waves. At each stern a wooden tail curled up.

From her hiding spot, she watched the buzzing activity on the largest boat. It had purple sails and three galleys of oars, one above the other—a *trireme*, Helena had called it last night. She'd told Sam that Eshmun had sailed into every cove and port, looking for a gateway to another world. This particular trireme must have required a crew of hundreds.

Sam ducked her head and pulled the cloak's hood tighter, worried that this was the very ship that Eshmun was readying.

There was no way she could steal a boat from the guarded harbor. Sailors milled all around; there were the turreted watchtowers. But then she remembered the few fishing boats she had seen at the fringes of the city. Those would be easier.

She backtracked until she found a stone stairway curving down to the beach, and it was there that she found the perfect boat. It was banana-shaped, hollowed out like a bathtub. Not quite a canoe and not quite a dinghy, either, but manageable. With a single sail and tiller, she could man it alone.

She unrolled Helena's map and oriented it along the shoreline, and then dipped the bowl into the seawater, filling it halfway. Next, she magnetized one end of the sewing needle by rubbing it against an orange-colored rock she'd found. A mint leaf she'd plucked from the pot on Helena's windowsill would make a little raft for the needle. She

carefully punctured the leaf, poking a hole at the top and bottom, and left the needle to span the leaf lengthwise.

"Work," she commanded, setting the needle and leaf to float in the bowl of water. She thought of her room, of how she'd retacked her old Girl Scout sash to the wall. Her CAMPER badge, right in the middle. She'd slept in a tent, made basic survival compasses, had 'smores with her troop. That day in the woods felt like a million years ago.

The needle spun and settled, pointing due north.

She looked at Helena's map and gauged the direction of Kition. It would be a long sail, a full day or more depending on the wind. She could only hope it was less than a hundred miles—and that she could average five per hour.

She untied her sandals, slipped them off, and tossed them along with her bag into the hull of the boat, where a pair of cedar oars sat at the bottom. She nestled the homemade compass against her belongings and then gave the stern a shove toward the water, pushing until the cool sea lapped against her calves. As she climbed aboard, she hiked up her dress and cloak to keep them dry. It only took a few oar strokes and she was clear of the shallow bottom.

Soon, she found the wind. She pulled the oars back into the hull and set them down. An adjustment of the sail sent her across the water, slowly but steadily.

I'm coming, Rima.

Eshmun's fleet receded behind her and the wind dried her legs. She took a long breath: She was on a boat, sailing on open water. If she closed her eyes, she could almost believe she was home, out on Glen Lake with an evening of fishing ahead. She'd eaten well in Sidon and slept for what felt like a full night. Eshmun had cured all of her wounds. She felt good; she felt ready.

No more Eshmun.

No more detours.

There was no telling what was ahead, and there was no looking back now. Whatever stood in her way of Rima...she would have to face it, outsmart it, run from it, or thrust a knife into it when the time came.

If she could navigate her family through the rough terrain of their daily lives, if she could nurse the open wound of Dad's absence, if she could survive rivers, mountains, and forests, then she could handle this, too.

She plunged her oars into the water whenever the wind disappeared, but it was never long before the small sail filled again and sent her flying toward Kition.

ᗐᗏᗕ

Hour after hour slid past. Gradually, her worries mounted. When would she be able to see the island on the horizon? How would she find Rima once she was ashore? Where would she hide her boat? How would she enter the city?

She looked down at her fine clothing. Even with her dress dirty and wrinkled again, she still looked as if she were going to a party. She should have done more than take one old cloak for a disguise. Cut off the rest of her hair. Worn one of Helena's plain dresses.

She adjusted the tiller and squinted to find the shoreline behind her, but it had long since vanished. Without city lights, and with the clouds pretending to be mountains along the horizon, she could no longer tell if she had any land within sight at all. The sky and the sea were the same color in places.

She carefully stood and scanned every direction, but she'd lost her bearings.

Sitting back down, she found her orange stone, remagnetized her

compass needle, and set it to work. With the boat rocking, the needle leaped back and forth. She swore, trying to steady it.

"Come on," she said, holding the bowl between her knees.

But the needle dipped and sank—and suddenly, small waves began to lap over the gunwales of the boat.

Sam's head snapped up, and she felt fear rising. Was the boat *sinking*? How? Since when? She had no life vest.

Worse, when she set the bowl down, she gasped with horror at the sight of her own skin. Her fingertips had turned black again. Frantically, she checked all the other wounds Eshmun had cured—the blisters, the scrapes, the bruises on her throat—but they were all still healed. Only the place where she'd touched the *ruḥā* persisted. And it was spreading, dark as blood in water. Lines ran down her fingers, tracing a course toward her palm. She flexed her hand. It didn't hurt; it was progressing silently like a cancer.

A puddle of water sloshed through the hull. Her bag was drenched, and she cursed—she didn't have to look to know that the food she'd brought from Helena's was ruined. An imperceptible hole, an invisible crack was letting the sea into her boat, little by little.

Using the bowl, she threw the water out, one small scoop at a time, peering into the sea below her. She was certain there were monsters hiding in the depths—they were everywhere else, after all. She could turn back for Sidon, but which way was that? She thought it might be behind her, but the wind had shifted several times and now she would have to fight it with her oars, and without the compass working. She would just spin herself in circles.

The waves were getting bigger. She bent with the bowl to scoop out more water from the bottom of the boat.

Needles of fear prickled through her.

Dad is dead. Rima is doomed. You are trapped here forever.

Another wave smacked the boat sideways, tilting it onto its side, and in a blink it disappeared from underneath her. She'd been thrown out of the boat and into the sea.

Dark, cold water bubbled across her vision. Funnels and mountain cliffs and hopelessness. All of it wanted her to descend, to fall, to fail.

The bottom of the boat thudded against her head, knocking her down deeper. Her lungs burned and blood rose toward the surface, turning the water ruddy. The metallic taste. She saw torches lighting a hallway, a blackened waterfall. Her own hair, or seaweed, or an eel lashed against her cheek.

It would be so easy...It would only take one breath of seawater and she could forget everything.

And then her vision narrowed into focus and she was suddenly looking through a lock in a door, her eye pressed tight against the keyhole. She saw vignettes of her life: the persistent Easter lilies blooming back home; Mom's book of Kahlil Gibran poetry highlighted with green marker and exclamation points; Rima's soccer cleats, her rainbow of nail polishes. A locked velvet box, the one Mom kept hidden in the back of her closet. It opened, revealing its contents: gold bangles, turquoise charms, wishbones, and a few old coins. She could hear Mom's voice. *Don't you ever touch this box, do you hear me? I have things in here from Lebanon. Sam and Rima, I mean it. Never ever.*

And then she could see Rima's face, her hazel eyes. She led Sam by the hand. *Don't worry, Sam! We're not lost forever! We're fine! Dad won't leave without us!* They'd thrown darts at balloons and ridden the teacups. They'd circled the carousel again, searching for Dad. *This way. This way quick.*

Sam kicked, and Rima was gone. The water seemed thinner, brighter.

Breaking through the surface, she choked down air and vomited seawater. She slapped her way toward the listing boat and struggled back inside. It was flooded with a foot of water. The bowl was gone.

Shivering, she sat for a long time, coughing. Sobbing. Drenched. Cupping her hands together, she threw the sea overboard, one useless handful at a time. The water level rose. It was only a matter of time.

A bank of clouds spooled across the horizon, and a large black dot moved through them. The thud of Sam's heart seemed to make the entire boat lurch.

She knew what that dot was.

She grabbed her bag, slung it over her shoulder, and then closed her eyes. She pushed all the air out of her chest, calming herself. Then she breathed back in and raised her arms over her head.

There was only one thing to do.

"*Tannîyn!*" she screamed.

It was too far away. She called for it again and again until she was hoarse. "*Tannîyn,*" she wheezed, dropping to her knees. The water was up to her elbows. She scanned the horizon for one of Eshmun's great boats, but there was nothing. There was no one.

The air above her moved.

The *shush-shush* of flapping wings.

Without looking, she knew the *tannîyn* was hovering over her. She didn't want to see its crocodilian face, its black talons. She closed her eyes and braced herself.

"Take me to my sister," she whispered.

16

They were locked inside Mom's minuscule closet, piles of shoes and clothes all around them, along with the smell of unwashed laundry. Sam could hardly breathe. She was young, still afraid of the dark. Only slivers of light found their way through the slats in the door. She'd gone into the closet to play dress-up, and Rima had followed, her little shadow. Sam wanted to try on Mom's shoes, but they were still too big for her.

I can't do it, Dad. I can't take care of everyone.

"Go get your sister, will you?" he said through the door, sounding impatient. "She should have been home by now."

"She's right here," Sam said, but when she turned to face Rima, she was gone. *Gone!* Sam pressed her small fingers through the slats, and from the other side, he touched her fingertips. "Dad!" she cried. "Please! I can't get out!"

Mom's forbidden velvet box shook in the corner, as if something alive were trapped inside it. It rattled and skittered toward her. She backed into the darkness of the closet, and then she felt the pain in her shoulders. There was something wrong with them. She touched one and her fingers came away wet. She looked left and then right. Wire hangers were threaded through them. Someone had hung her up in the closet like a garment, ripped and torn.

There is a box, she heard Sbartā's voice, echoing. *There is a man who holds a banner with an eagle and an anchor.*

The closet door suddenly opened, and Sam was thrust out into twilight.

There was nothing underneath her feet. She was in midair. Flying.

The *tannîyn*'s razor talons dug into her. She could feel the blood running hot down her chest and stomach until it dripped from her toes. Below, there was land. A shoreline ahead.

She struggled to reach into her bag, fingers probing until she found Helena's kitchen knife. Closing her eyes, she searched inside herself, desperate to find one last buried shard of strength. It was there, somewhere, she knew it.

Rima, she thought, and with a swift arcing motion she thrust the knife into the *tannîyn*'s leg, screaming at the pain in her shoulders as the *tannîyn*'s shrieks ripped through her eardrums. She twisted the knife.

The *tannîyn* let go.

ᴠᴠᴠ

Copper rocks, the color of bloodstained teeth.

A bird called out bitterly and the sea slapped against her feet. Sam crawled and turned to lie on her back. Everything inside her was broken. A veil of fog hung over her like a shroud.

"Dad?" she breathed. *I'm lost, Dad. I'm so lost.*

She turned sideways, the bones in her neck crackling. Her bag. So far away. She stretched her fingers toward it and hooked it with a finger. She pulled. Inside she felt the blanket, the vial of tears. The cork was too tight. She gripped it between her teeth and pulled.

And then she drank every drop. It tasted like salted honey.

Sleep took her for what felt like a thousand years. But when she finally awoke, she could stand up.

Helena's cloak was gone, her dress stained with dried blood. She pulled the torn fabric aside at the shoulders and rubbed her fingers

across healed skin. Helena's knife was gone, too. She was barefooted and she remembered that her sandals were in the bottom of the boat. The vial of tears was empty.

What have I done? For a moment, she brimmed with regret, but she knew she'd had no choice but to drink it. Otherwise she would have lain down on those rocks to die.

Rima, she reminded herself. *I'm here to find Rima.*

She unpacked the damp wool blanket and pulled it around her shoulders, leaving the empty vial and her bag on the ground, her fingertips still stained gray. Inside the mother-of-pearl box, Eshmun's small black hair remained. Sam snapped the box shut and tucked it beneath her belt once again.

The farther she went, the thinner the fog became. The land was stony and barren. Walking inland, she soon found a narrow footpath. Ahead, an old woman with gnarled hands begged for money, and Sam smelled something acrid in the air. There was a fork in the road.

"Is this the pathway to Kition?" Sam asked the woman, pointing right.

"Doorstep to hell." The woman nodded, peering closely at her. "You seek the girl."

"The girl?" Sam repeated.

"The girl, the girl, the strange, foreign girl," the woman chanted. She grinned, showing her swollen gums and her few yellow teeth. "In the dungeons, of course. Through the marketplace. Follow the lonely road." She shrugged. "There, Môt will kill you."

And then she pointed down the other fork in the road. Left.

"What's that way?" Sam asked, following her finger.

The woman leaned forward and narrowed her eyes. "You seek the weapon?" she asked. She spread her arms wide and cackled. "You?" She pointed. "You!"

"The weapon," Sam said. Somehow she already knew, but she asked anyway. "Is the cave of Marid that way?"

The woman nodded eagerly. "He will eat your corpse." She leaned back and brushed her hands together like two dry leaves, as if indicating the end of something. Done.

Sam stood at the crossroads, weighing her choices. She felt like the old gray mare, waiting for a signal, a heel in her side.

She could go straight to Kition to find the dungeons of Môt's temple. Without a weapon. With no way to fight. Or she could try to arm herself. Either way felt like a deathtrap.

She gripped her blanket tightly around her shoulders. How did it come to this? How did she end up here? She ground her teeth. She had always felt trapped, even before she fell into this world. No matter how hard she ran, she always looped back to the same place, over and over again. Nothing would ever change.

Unless she forced it to.

She drew in a long breath and chose the left path.

She followed it for some time. It descended, and eventually she could see the entrance to the cave, a hole in the rocks, an open mouth. She could still turn around. She could change her mind and take the other path, to Kition.

She stopped and closed her eyes for a moment, and she was suddenly ten years old and in bed as Mom told the story of the ghoul who ate those who failed. His monstrous appetite for dead flesh would be forever satisfied, because men were full of hubris: Every one of them thought he could outwit the cave and solve the riddle. *You know what the moral of the story is?* Mom would ask as Rima hid underneath her blankets. *Don't go chasing after crazy-big goals. You don't need to be a smarty-pants. There is nothing wrong with being average.* To Sam, it never seemed like the right ending to the story. Where was the hero? Where was the reward

for bravery and perseverance? And so she once asked, *It's okay to give up before you even try?* Mom had nodded deeply. *Bingo,* she said.

Sam slowed her pace as she approached the cave entrance. Her heartbeat was so fierce it made her temples throb. She could hardly believe what she was seeing.

There he was, as if lifted from the pages of a book. Alive. Just inside the lip of the cave sat the monster of her childhood fairy tales, his spine so curved that his body resembled a question mark. Thick horns curled from his forehead. He wore a cloak made of skin, a patched garment bound by threads of human tendon. His earrings were small bones, his necklace a braid of hair.

That's how the story went, Sam remembered. He clothed himself with the dead.

Her throat had gone dry. She struggled to swallow; her breath felt sharp and jagged. From inside the cave, there was the steady drip of liquid hitting water, like blood falling and pooling. The air was as cold as the breath of a corpse.

"Are you Marid?" she asked, her voice shaking.

The ghoul turned to her and nodded. "Come, come," he said, standing. "I will not harm you. Only your choices will." His breath smelled like rotten flesh, but Sam willed herself to step forward. His skin was the color of a scab. "Please. Welcome. You are free to search the cave."

It seemed too easy. Behind him was a boat, smaller than the one she'd taken from Sidon. It was black and shiny as a beetle's shell, a single oar inside. Marid motioned to it, and Sam realized that within the cave was a lake.

"Go, then. The weapon that kills a god awaits," he said. "*Rugzā* is in plain view. Will you find it?"

She blinked at him. The sword was named *Wrath,* and it was in

plain sight. This was the riddle. How could she find something that wasn't even hidden?

Sam nodded and climbed into the boat, leaving her blanket behind on the rocks.

Marid handed her a bucket and she accepted it, looking inside. It was empty. The boat's bottom was dry. "Will I have to bail out water?" she asked. "Is there a leak?"

The horned ghoul said nothing. He only pushed her out onto the water, which was as turquoise and bright as a well-lit swimming pool. Stalagmites rose from the floor and stalactites dripped from above, making ghostly fingers, drapes, and cages. The lattice of a bridge was suspended from the ceiling of the cave.

Sam paddled on. The lake became a waterway, winding deeply and silently into the cave, until finally a grand archway of stalactites — almost like marble pillars carved by human hands—opened onto a lagoon ending in a crescent-shaped shoreline. It was as though she were crossing a boundary, entering an unholy kingdom.

She stroked to the middle of the lagoon, dipped her oar into the water, and looked down—

—and then she saw it.

Just as Marid had claimed, it lay in plain view: a golden sword gleaming with a rainbow of gemstones along its guard. It was in the clutches of a dead man. His eyes were missing, his white face still contorted with panic, his beard moving with the underwater current. Sam would have to pry *Rugzā* from his fingers.

For Rima, she reminded herself. Her pulse pounded down to her bones. *I'll kill Môt or Eshmun or whatever godly or ungodly thing might get in the way of my sister.*

Easing herself over the side of the boat, she plunged into the frigid water to dive down to the dead man.

For a moment, she wondered what his name had been. Did he have a family? Had they given up searching for him, wondering if he would ever come home? How long had he been here?

At the cold bottom of the pool, she steeled herself, reached out, and grabbed his wrist. She pulled, trying to loosen his grip on the sword. But to her horror, his arm separated from his hand, unleashing a chunk of decaying flesh into the water. His hand stayed firmly attached to the sword's grip.

Sam nearly screamed underwater, her mouth bubbling. She kicked back up to the surface and sucked in a long breath, coughing and gagging, the water clouded with the dead man's flesh.

I can't do this.

She desperately wanted to climb back into the boat, to paddle away.

I have to do this.

I will.

Even if it meant she would have to take the dead hand along with the sword. Inhaling as deeply as she could, she dove. This time, she pulled the wrist loose . . . only to reveal another underneath.

Grimacing and aching for air, she felt her heart jolt with the realization that there were layers upon layers of other bones under the man's. Thumbs. Knuckles. Grips of desperation, of determination. Hands that were bound to the sword, but detached from their bodies.

She let go again and swam to the surface. Sucking in a breath, she wailed it back out, her cry echoing and disappearing into the depths of the cavern.

A gray stew of skin and tissue floated around her as she thrashed back to the boat, pulling herself inside to lie empty-handed in the hull, staring up at the bulbous ceiling of the cave.

How many men had died trying to carry this sword to shore? Big,

strong men, who each thought they would be the one heroic enough to finish the task? One after another had pried a dead man's hand away—maybe carried the sword forward a bit themselves—before sinking and suffering the same fate.

She sat shivering, her teeth chattering. What had Marid said when he gave her the boat? He said she'd have a choice.

But there was only one magical sword, one *Rugzā*. So how could that be?

She sat up and paddled the boat farther across the lagoon, gazing into the water, looking.

There were more bodies. Each was pinned to the bottom beneath a magnificent sword, similar to the one she'd just fought for. Each twinkled up at her, winking and beckoning.

In plain sight, she thought. *A choice.*

She navigated toward the crescent shoreline and stepped out to wade through the shallow water, pulling the boat onto a mound of stalagmite-covered rocks. Once it was secure, she stepped ahead and squinted into the darkness past the lagoon, but what was beyond was impossible to see. The cave could have extended ten feet deep or a thousand.

She took a few more steps before looking down at herself, still dripping with water. Her dress glowed. The droplets of water that clung to the ends of her hair looked like lightning bugs.

The water, she realized. *The water gives off light!* She hurried back to the boat and pulled the bucket from the hull. Maybe this was what it was for. She filled it with lagoon water and held it ahead of her as she ventured into the darkness. It was like a lantern, providing a small circle of light around her.

She wasn't sure how long she walked. But eventually, rows beyond rows of stone pedestals rose around her, maybe a hundred of

them. Sam walked faster, her heart catching as she realized what they held.

On top of each rectangular pedestal was a sword.

Sword after sword after sword after sword.

She put a hand on one, icy and damp to the touch. Which was the right one? Some were gorgeously decorated, others plain. The biggest extended far beyond the edges of its pedestal; it was black from tip to hilt, glimmering like liquid tar.

But which could kill a god?

Mom's voice came to her once again: *Sometimes things aren't what they seem.*

Not what they seem. She bit her lip, thinking, passing up any sword that was studded with rubies, sapphires, or amethysts, any encrusted with gold. Instead she stopped in front of the smallest, the most innocuous-looking blade. It was the size of a kitchen knife.

"Is it you?" she asked.

How could such a sword yield any kind of wrath? But then she thought of Teth, transforming into a bear. It was true: *Sometimes things aren't what they seem.* Tears could be medicine. A coin could open a gateway.

Still full of doubt, she picked up the dull, rusted sword and tucked it into her rabbit belt. At least it wouldn't take her to the bottom of the lagoon to drown.

Am I completely stupid? she wondered, continuing deeper into the cave, hardly paying attention to her feet until she nearly stepped over an edge and into sheer nothingness. A drop-off into the bowels of the earth. Her heart pounded inside her ears so loudly it seemed to echo across the chasm.

She turned around, gasping for breath and holding the bucket farther ahead of her, her hands shaking so badly the water sloshed over the

sides. She retraced her steps back the way she'd come through the pedestals, tempted again by what might be better choices—a sword made of sharpened wood, another with a femur for the grip. But there was none smaller than the one she'd chosen. None more rusted and dull. She was torn with indecision, but she kept walking, and before she knew it, she had reached the shoreline, where she cried out with dismay.

The boat was gone.

Her legs went weak with panic. She spun back and forth, searching, but there was no sign of it anywhere.

"No," she moaned. There was only one way to go: out into the luminous waters, back toward the entrance and Marid. She would have to swim, even though she was exhausted. She set down the bucket and waded out into the bone-chilling water. Soon it was too deep for her to touch the bottom, but there were small stalagmite islands, and she swam from one to the next, holding on to their slick sides before swimming again. From the bottom of the lagoon, the dead bodies watched.

Ahead, there was a daunting gap from one island to the next. She took a long breath before striking out. The glimmering water roiled beneath her with each kick, and then it suddenly darkened. A shadow.

She gasped, pulling in a mouthful of water and then choking it out. Something was circling beneath her.

Wheezing for air, she swam faster, but not before looking over her shoulder. She was halfway between islands. It would do no good to turn back now. The creature passed close below her. It was long, eel-like. Sam held in a scream and kicked hard and fast, the island still so far away. The creature brushed against her feet and knees as it swept by. She shrieked and floundered, her voice echoing through the chamber.

"Go away, go away!" she pleaded, but a moment later it emerged from the water just ahead of her, blocking her way.

Slowly it rose higher and higher, its flat head jutting forward.

Blank white eyes sat near its mouth, where sharp whiskers protruded from either side. A torrent of water dripped down its blotchy gray sides.

Sam held up the rusty little sword, the only weapon she had. "Get back!" she screamed.

The thing opened and closed its gaping maw. Rows of small sharp teeth shone blue from the glow of the lagoon.

Sam splashed backward. "I'll...I'll kill you!" she spluttered. As she looked up, she saw the lattice of stalactites, the gnarled bridge suspended from the ceiling. Frantically, she scanned the edges of the lagoon for some sort of ladder or wall she could climb. But there was nothing.

And then, as slowly as the thing had risen, it lowered itself and slid beneath the surface once more. It would grab her by the feet. Pull her under.

But instead it only kept circling as she struggled forward, hardly making any headway, before it pulled itself up again, rising slowly to its full height and then dropping down, only to circle once more beneath the surface.

With a sickening wave of realization, Sam understood: It would wear her out. Soon she would be too tired to hold her head above the surface. The creature was a bottom-feeder, and it was waiting for her to sink. Its eyes were low and wide-set, just above its mouth.

She looked up at the bridge once more, pulled in a deep, long breath, and dove, holding the sword ahead of her.

As the thing wormed past, she grabbed onto its neck, clinging to it as it slowly reared out of the water once more, twisting with agitation as Sam dug in her heels. Higher and higher it rose, shaking its head— once, twice—but Sam held on, grimacing at the feel of its spongy skin against her cheek. Finally, when it steadied at its full height, Sam put the sword in her mouth. She scrambled onto the top of its head and

stood, reaching for the slats of the bridge. With a grunt, she caught one with one hand and then the other.

The creature descended, and she dangled, her arms aching, her lungs bursting. The water was almost a hundred feet below. If she fell now, she would die. There would be no second chance.

I'm not dying, she thought. *I have to save my sister.*

With her last ounce of resolve, she swung a foot up to the stalactite structure, and painfully squeezed between the open slats of the bridge.

She lay sobbing on her stomach for a long time, gripping the small sword and praying it was the right one. That it had been worth all this.

Finally, she stood and walked, still shaking. She stepped over gaps in the bridge, gripping the wet stalactite railing. Slowly, it led her downward, ending near the entrance, where Marid still stood, his spine curved like a scythe.

He was hunched over a waterlogged corpse, eating the flesh from its torso, making an awful ripping sound like a torn promise. *Marid likes his death old and rotten,* she remembered from the fairy tale.

Sam hid the sword behind her back, edging past Marid. He sniffed the air and turned to face her, chuckling.

"The child emerges unscathed," he said, tipping his head sideways. "Tell me. Did you find anything interesting?"

She almost showed him. She almost asked: *Is this the right one? Did I choose correctly?*

"No," she said, swallowing down the lie. "Nothing."

If Sam had the one *Rugzā*, then no one would come to look for it again. If no one came into the cave again, Marid would have nothing to eat. She backed away, keeping her eyes on the monster as he edged closer.

"Giving up so soon?" he asked. "If you did not find what you

wanted, you should try again." He swept his arm toward the cave once more. There was another boat waiting. Another bucket. "Go on."

"Tell me, Marid," she said, crouching to grab Helena's wool blanket from the ground where she'd left it. "What would someone want with a drop of blood, a strand of hair, and a fallen angel's feather?"

He wiped the drool from his death-stained mouth. "Why forge a dark obol, my child?" he asked. "It will bear no power to carry a soul to heaven. It will only hold the victim in living limbo." He strummed his fingernails across his braided necklace of hair. "Is that what you desire? A soulless slave?"

"Why would I want that?" she asked.

"The body provides," he said. "Without the conscience objecting." He shuffled toward her. "The hearts of men are made of gold, malleable when the fire burns hot. So easily molded and corrupted."

To make him mine, Sam thought. *For a hundred centuries.* That was what Zayin had said. Did she intend to trap Eshmun somehow, body and soul, with a false obol? His tears would be hers, whenever she desired.

Sam inched away from Marid as he slunk closer, still carefully hiding the sword, and then she turned and fled as fast as she could into the dusk light.

〰〰〰

At the fork in the road, the old woman was no longer there, but Sam recognized the junction. She turned and headed toward Kition and its dungeons.

Through the marketplace. Follow the lonely road, the old woman had said, and soon Sam saw two towers rising up, marking the city entrance, a knot of dread tightening in her chest. The towers were made of skulls. Hundreds, piled on top of each other, reaching

toward the dusk-muddled sky. Vacant eye sockets. Cracked jawbones clicking—*whispering*—as she approached.

Hinnē! Ġalmatu maġayat.

Look! The maiden has arrived.

Horrified, she rushed past the chattering skulls, nervously looking around her. No one was nearby. No one had heard their announcement. Shaking, she pulled Helena's wool blanket over her head to substitute for the lost cloak, tucking her wet hair inside.

Soon, she found herself on the outskirts of another *šuqā*, a street lined with vendors. Tents and lean-tos displayed goods for sale. Men haggled and argued over prices. She slowed her pace, second-guessing her decision to come this way.

"Hello," a man said, stepping toward her. His cloak was covered in black bird feathers, shoulders to ankles. He lifted a lip at her, showing his gray teeth. "You are new here."

Sam avoided his bloodshot eyes and walked on.

Kition was a dark carnival version of Sarepta. Instead of linen scarves and fragrant herbs for sale, here there were skulls and bones. The more booths she walked past, the faster her heartbeat. Sculptures of distorted faces peered out at her. Vials of dark liquids bubbled. The air carried a sulfurous odor like rotten eggs. Every instinct told her to leave this place. Her temples throbbed with adrenaline. *Run. Hide.* Suspicion and malice flashed on every face she passed; she was certain everyone was looking for an opportunity, predators watching for prey. Behind a group of women, *ruḥā* trailed. They hung on to the women like black wedding veils, following no matter which way they turned.

"A coin?" a voice asked behind her. "Is that what you seek?"

Sam's heart lurched and she turned warily. It was a familiar voice. One she knew, but had almost forgotten.

One she loved, deeply.

A blond man with reddish stubble on his chin stood behind her. He wore a flannel shirt—his favorite. The tips of cowboy boots poked out from underneath his blue jeans. They were the boots he'd bought in Texas, before Sam was born, and he'd taken them with him when he'd been deployed.

"I've been looking all over creation for you, kid." He spoke perfect English with a slight twang. "I knew I'd find you sooner or later." He smiled at her.

In that instant, every hope she'd been harboring, every dust-covered artifact of belief turned new and bright again. It was as if an entire fleet of sailboats suddenly caught their breath all at once, full sails leaping up, waking from a long, stagnant slumber.

Alive. He's alive.

"Daddy," she choked, heart racing. His grin made his eyes crinkle at the edges. "What are you doing here? Why..."

"Sammy," he said. He took a step closer. "Whatcha say we go get an ice cream at Dairy Queen? Don't tell your momma, okay?" He winked.

Inside, she felt like a kid again, small and full of joy. She wanted to brush her fingertips across his cheeks to count his face confetti. *Nineteen, eleven-teen, fifteen, twenty.*

"Okay," she said helplessly. She inched closer, so much of her wanting to hug him. She kept Helena's blanket tight around her. "How did you get here, though? How..."

Her voice trailed off.

It was his hands. They were all wrong. Bony and old, worn raw at the knuckles. They weren't Dad's hands, strong and young.

"Who are you?" she asked, backing away, hope waning.

He tucked his hands into his pockets and shrugged. "Don't you

recognize me?" He twisted his mouth with disappointment. "I guess I've been gone too long. Hands got all tore up. Street battle. Docs patched me up best they could."

"No," Sam said. "You can't be...You're not my father. Who are you?"

For a split second, the façade fell, and Sam saw that his eyes were the wrong color. They were icy blue. "Anyone you want."

"Stop it," Sam said, her heart in her throat. Without realizing it, she'd been backed toward a doorway. Was that what this creature wanted? To force her somewhere private? She sidestepped and spun back out into the marketplace.

"Where you goin'?" he asked. She walked faster, but his voice persistently followed. "Your rent is overdue!"

Sam glanced over her shoulder. He was Mr. Koplow now, down to the thinning hair and ill-fitting pants. But the terrible hands were the same.

"Go away," Sam said. But Mr. Koplow had already overtaken her, and now he walked backward ahead of her, blocking her path, darting left and right each time she tried to pass. She spun and walked in the opposite direction, and he followed. She stopped and said, as firmly as she could, "Leave me alone."

"Alone?" The Mr. Koplow look-alike sneered. "You can't do this alone. That's your trouble, see? You can't admit you need a little help. You can't do it all by yourself. You're not supposed to." With each sentence, he took a step closer. She could smell his cigarette breath. "Let a man take care of you. Sooner or later your mom will. She's this close." The look-alike pinched two fingers together, a sliver of space between. "So close to paying rent the way I want it."

Sam's stomach churned. He knew enough about her and her life

to turn into Dad and Mr. Koplow. Maybe he knew about Rima, too. "Where's my sister?" she demanded. "Have you seen her? Is she here?"

She blinked and he was Eshmun now, his keyhole pupil flaring. He wore his fur-trimmed cloak, and underneath it his hard chest was bare and glistening with sweat. His voice was a comfort. "Marry me and I will tell you how to get home."

"Stop it," Sam said, her heart pounding so hard she thought she might faint. "You're not Eshmun. You're some sort of shapeshifter."

He laughed and then tipped his head sideways, his eyelashes extending into long wisps and his skin turning gray. "Where are the tears? Where is my vial? Have you filled it yet?"

"I—" Sam fumbled for words. "You're not Zayin, either. Your hands stay the same, no matter who you pretend to be."

"Ah," Not-Zayin said with a pout. "The stains of alchemy. The substances burn deeply. Wounds born from dark magic cannot be masked."

Was this why the guards at Sidon had asked to see their hands? They weren't looking for weapons. They'd wanted to know if they were who they appeared to be. They'd been looking out for Môt's alchemist—his shapeshifter. His gnarled hands.

Sam's thoughts shifted to Zayin's beautifully smooth skin. Her flawless hands and elegant fingers. But then Sam remembered how she'd carefully concealed them with gauzy fabric while in the tent in Sarepta. How the fortune-teller had so seamlessly transformed from Arba`ta`esre to Zayin. It hadn't been a trick of the candlelight.

"You're Arba`ta`esre," Sam said.

"Sometimes."

"Zayin wants the tears to stay young," Sam said. "But you...you want the hair and the blood to make something terrible. Don't you?"

"Did you get them for me?" the shapeshifter asked.

Sam swallowed, looking left and right for an escape route. She still had Eshmun's hair in the small box, but she'd never give it to this vile creature.

Her hesitation cost her. The shapeshifter thrust out a hand and took her by the throat, clenching tight. Sam felt the world close in on her, like a door slamming shut. The business of the marketplace went on around them as if nothing were happening. No one cared.

There was suddenly the sound of whistles and shouts, and the shapeshifter turned to glance at a group of half-transformed *ḥayuta* who stood on the street corner. They bleated at the shapeshifter, beckoning. Sam clawed at her neck and pulled in a whistle of air, watching as one of the *ḥayuta* stood upright on hooved feet, showing her belly dotted with eight swollen nipples.

"You have been summoned!" she said.

The shapeshifter morphed into a gray-haired man with clenched, even teeth, his sharp green eyes still locked on Sam's. "I cannot go to her in the dungeons without rousing suspicion," he hissed at her, "but you can." His handsome face still didn't match his bony hands. *Another false identity*, Sam thought. "Above all, I want the gold of Chusor. I know your sister has it. Bring it to me, or die."

Sam's vision turned cloudy. There was a hammering inside her skull. She pulled in small gulps of air, hardly able to stay on her feet.

"You must go to Môt!" the *ḥayuta* insisted from her street corner, tutting at the shapeshifter. "Do you dare keep our master waiting?"

With that the shapeshifter released Sam as suddenly as he had grabbed her. As he turned his attention toward the *ḥayuta*, Sam steadied herself, and ran.

A tent hid her, and then another, and then she ran again. Gasping for a breath, she dodged a huge rooster with beady, watchful eyes

as she pulled herself behind a crumbling wall, just catching a word behind her: *Dungeons*. She froze.

"This leg of lamb," a man said, wearing what looked like a uniform, a badge on his sleeve, "if you take my shift in the dungeons." A leather whip was curled through his belt. "You might get a look at that foreign girl."

Foreign girl.

Sam held her breath, her hands sweaty as she gripped her blanket even tighter around her face. If these men worked in the dungeons, they might lead her there. She could follow them in.

"Leg of lamb? There is not a shred of meat left on that bone," the man's companion snarled. "A full flask of wine and another man's wife are waiting for me. I will not take your shift. A *look* at a girl. Does no good for these loins." He spat on the ground as a final gesture, then turned and stalked away.

The first man sucked on his bone, ripping at dark, greasy tendons with his teeth. As Sam moved closer, she caught a whiff of his foul hair and clothes, or maybe of his food. She could not imagine eating anything here. The marketplace had an underlying scent of sewage, and the vendors' hands were creased with filth.

"Crocodile hides!" a hawker cried out. "From an expedition to Naukratis! What do you offer?"

"Trireme in the hidden harbor!" someone else shouted with a cackle. "They think they're sneaking in! Who wants to kill some men and steal their cargo?"

"Vipers for sale!" another man shouted into the marketplace. "Scorpion tails! Come now, make a trade!"

Finally, the guard tossed his bone onto the ground. He picked up a caged rabbit that sat next to him, and then walked alone at a slow, uneven pace, in no apparent hurry. Sam followed at a careful distance,

stepping around a man sitting cross-legged on the ground, surrounded by caged monkeys. They screeched at her, making a racket like an alarm. She flinched and quickened her pace, passing three sulking men with thick gray wings on their backs. As they glared at her, she could only imagine they might be fallen angels.

A ship in the harbor, she thought as she walked. A merchant ship? Pirates? Or could it be Eshmun's? If it was, would his ship be attacked, driven out to sea, sunk? Had they sent only one ship as a decoy, while the rest of his fleet made landfall in another port?

Ahead, the guard sang to himself and stumbled back and forth across a dirt alley, the cage banging against his leg, the din of the marketplace fading behind them. The city ended, and fields of crops began to rise out of the land. It seemed, all at once, too quiet. Sam became aware of the sound of her own breathing. If the guard glanced back, he would see her following him. Meanwhile, she kept looking over her own shoulder, making sure the shapeshifter hadn't followed her.

But the road was empty behind her, and above, the sky was darker than usual, a dull gray without any wisps of pastel colors. Nightfall seemed imminent.

Nearby, a farmer was sowing his seeds over tilled earth. Mist rose off the field like a tattered bedsheet, and as the road took Sam closer, she saw that this was no ordinary crop the farmer was tending. It was not like the garden of summer vegetables she was planting in her own backyard. There was something odd here—something evil.

The prison guard wobbled ahead slowly, allowing Sam a moment to pause. She watched as the farmer fetched and pushed a cart. Inside its wooden bed was a small *tannîyn.* Dead. Its lifeless toad-face grimacing with what must have been its last moments of pain. Flies lifted away from its scaled skin.

The farmer lifted pliers. *What in God's name is he doing?*

She held her breath and watched as the man leaned into the dead *tannîyn's* mouth and clamped the pliers around a fanged tooth. There was a sickening ripping sound as he extracted one tooth after another, twisting and yanking, dropping them into a nearby bucket. Sam's stomach lurched, and she clapped a hand over her mouth. The farmer set the pliers down on the cart and walked into the rows of the field, scooping out a small hole for each tooth. He tamped the soil back in place with his foot.

He was planting *tannîyn* teeth. *Why?*

Sam's heart pounded as she hurried on, her nerves making her tremble with each step, but the answer came soon enough. In the next field, dark roots sprang from the soil like bird legs—rows and rows of clawed feet.

They're growing tannîyn in the soil. They're harvesting a whole crop of them.

Her vision blurred with tears, but she wiped them away to keep sight of the prison guard through the mist.

The road curved and rose and then ended at a wall encrusted with lichen. Sam crouched behind some craggy ruins, watching closely as the guard approached a gate in the wall. Why did it seem to be moving? She crept closer, not understanding at first.

Goose bumps erupted along the back of her neck when she finally saw: The gate was made of dry vines with thorns the size of her thumb. The vines twined around each other, shifting, tightening, as if they sensed that someone was near.

The prison guard warily eyed them, approaching a face carved into the stone. The sculpture's lower lip extended to make a bowl. While its eyes glittered with inset jewels, its tongue didn't seem to be made of stone; instead it had a wet, soft quality.

The guard set down the cage he'd been carrying, pulled out the rabbit, and placed it inside the bowl.

"An offering for the god of death," he murmured over the noise of the rabbit struggling.

The guard fidgeted, shifting from foot to foot, waiting as the vines began to untwine: pulling back, unknotting, vanishing into crevices. With a hurried step, he walked through an opening they'd revealed, and a moment later the vines creaked back into place, curling around each other, thorns clicking like locks.

Heart thrumming, Sam pulled in a breath for courage. She could smell the contents of the offering bowl—death and decay, the metallic tang of blood. She stood and went to it. Inside was a stew of bones and skins. The rabbit was an empty carcass, as if it had been consumed from the inside out.

"In the name of the gods," she said sadly.

She took a long breath and looked at the gate of vines. What could she do to make it open? What did she have to offer? She had a blanket, and the weapon from Marid's cave. She had a strand of Eshmun's hair. She could cut herself. Her blood might be enough of a sacrifice. She could try.

Blade against the palm of her hand, steeling herself, she angled the tip. She would let her blood drip onto the mealy tongue.

But instead she hesitated, the metal sharp against her skin. *Why?* she thought. *Why should I give Môt any part of myself?*

If anything, she wanted to spit on the stone face, right in its cold, jeweled eyes. Slipping the weapon underneath her belt again, she secured the blanket around her shoulders and stepped up onto the lip of the bowl. The nose and brow made solid footholds until she'd clambered onto the head of the sculpture and stood. From there, she swung a leg over the wall.

Straddling it, she looked down onto the head of another sculpture, directly below, a mirror image, probably to open the gate from

the opposite side. Shinnying onto her stomach, she lowered herself onto its head, and then jumped to the ground.

It had been too easy. Maybe no one had ever dared to try something so sacrilegious. So much was driven by fear and superstition here. She looked ahead, expecting to see a building—turreted prison walls lined with armed guards.

But there was nothing but a gaping hole in the ground.

She ran to it and dropped to her knees. Leaning over the edge, she could hear the guard's off-key singing and see a spiral staircase leading deep into the earth. If the sun had been shining overhead, she might have been able to see the bottom, but it was impossible to discern anything beyond the first curve of stairs, which were lit by a torch.

Dizzy with fear, she pulled the torch out of its ring. She could carry it ahead of her down the stairway, but then again, it might give her away.

Sam was still deliberating when she felt the crush of a bony hand around her ankle. "No!" she gasped. She spun to look, but it wasn't the shapeshifter—it was a vine that had unwound itself from the gate and slithered for her.

She struggled to free herself, yelping with pain as it tightened its grip, a thorn grazing her calf. It dragged her backward toward the gate, which was now twisting like a nest of snakes. Maybe they would strangle her. Maybe they would rip her apart and put her, piece by piece, into the offering bowl.

She waved the torch uselessly at the vine as it pulled her across the hard ground. The flame was too small. With a grunt, she brought it back toward her face and whispered one word:

"Môt."

The flames turned green. Their heat felt chemical, smelled like burning acid.

She sat up and grabbed the vine—narrowly avoiding thorns—and stabbed the fire into it, sending sparks worming into its dry, stringy pith. Green flames crackling and tearing through it, the vine withered and loosened its grip. She desperately kicked it away and hobbled to her feet, bleeding from the wound the thorn had left. Then she threw the torch at the gate—flicked it like a knife—and it struck: an angry stinger in the center of the brambles.

The gate erupted with hellfire.

She turned, the wicked heat of the fire on her back, and ran to the hole in the ground, wavering at the top. *Was* Rima down there? She knew she was.

But *what else* was down there?

"I'm coming," she whispered breathlessly, her voice cracked and splintered.

She glanced back one last time at the fire sending black smoke into the air, then put her foot on the first step, slippery with moss.

She gripped the cold stone railing—which was broken in spots, leaving dangerous, unguarded sections—and began to go down. One false step and she could fall straight to the bottom. As she descended deeper and deeper into the pit, the smell made her gag; it was as if the walls themselves were exhaling a wet stale breath.

The guard's singing had long faded away, but other sounds began to filter up to her. A scream. The clanking of metal. A grinding noise, like a rusted gate closing. She was blind in the dark. The air clung damply to her skin. And the stairway seemed endless, spiraling, down, down.

Finally, at the bottom of the staircase, she was greeted by a large black bird sitting on a perch, lit by torchlight. The upper half of its beak was missing. It gaped at her, adjusting its wings. *"Bișā,"* it squawked. *Evil. "Dḥeltā." Fear.*

Sam made a wide circle around it, hunching her shoulders so she wouldn't brush against the walls. She was in a low, columned passage, and there were crude cages everywhere. Inside them, lions paced with listless eyes, ribs showing through thin fur. Gruff voices rang through the dripping dark, and though Sam moved quietly, every footfall rebounded. Her breath came short and fast. Underneath her bare feet were puddles of dark liquid. Little bones.

"We will sacrifice her to the ancient god, Ba'al Shamem, Lord of the Heavens," a voice said. Sam jumped and pressed herself against a column. The echo made it impossible to know which direction the voice came from. How close it was.

"Yes, she will be a *debḥā*," another said.

"Fool! The great god only accepts infant sacrifices!"

"She is young enough, and pure. She will do."

"You mule! We shall ship her to Melqart."

"Yes. He would pay for *ḥayuta* such as this."

"Melqart!" another said. "Have you not heard? He is nothing but a prisoner now, humming the notes of his own dirge. And so we shall kill her, and we shall eat her."

A din of voices roared in agreement.

Sam peeked around the column and caught sight of a child, maybe eight or nine years old, lying on the ground and curled into a ball. Shackled by rusted metal chains, she was surrounded by five men—creatures—who nudged her with bare toes, their nails thick and purple. Eyes wild and white with no pupils. Tangled greasy locks of hair, bare scalps shining underneath. The girl visibly trembled, whimpering.

"Keep your filthiness away from her!" the largest of the creatures cried, swatting the others back. His entire mouth seemed to be full of canines.

A scrawny one with a lump on his back was pacing in circles, frothing at the mouth. He punched the largest creature in the chest.

"She is mine!"

"Get away from her!"

"I found her first!"

"We must give her to the Lord of Death!"

All at once they went into a frenzy, tearing at each other and cursing. Meanwhile, their prisoner tried to wrench her little wrists through the handcuffs. Sam could feel the dull, rusty sword from Marid's cave hiding underneath her belt. Anguish lodged itself in her throat. She couldn't fight five creatures with it. They would eat her, too.

But she had to do something.

"Here," Sam hissed at the child. She made herself seen for only a second, and then ducked back behind the column. A moment later she looked again to find the girl's eyes lit with surprise.

No, the girl mouthed back. She shook her head fiercely at Sam. *Go.* She had one hand out of the shackles, but the other was still trapped inside a rusted ring of metal.

The men fought like wild animals, clawing and gashing each other as they rolled across the floor.

"The Lord of Death will know nothing if we murder you!" one screamed.

They were completely distracted, savaging each other in a pool of torchlight. It was Sam's only chance, so she took it, crawling to the girl across the cold, wet floor where she cowered in the dark. Sam put a finger to her lips and took the cuff in her hands. With a small grunt, she pried the band apart, forcing it open just enough for the girl to slide her hand out. With a look of pained triumph, she offered Sam a weak smile. Blood streaked her wrist. She cradled her hand to her chest.

"Slice him to pieces!"

"That would be a favor to me!" the hunchbacked creature said, his white eyes wild with fury. "Make me *ruḥā*. It could be no worse than this tainted life!"

"A demented lunatic such as yourself does not stay to haunt and roam the underworld!"

"No," the largest one said. He pressed a filthy fingertip into the hunchback's neck. "You will descend to swim in the muddy pool of the lowest level. Hell awaits."

"Kill him!"

"*You* will rot in *gihannā*, you murderers, all of you!" the hunchback cried. "But you shall not see me there! I will become a *ruḥā* shadow and cling to your backs for the rest of your putrid days. I will follow you like a cloud of flatulence!"

Sam took the girl by the hand, and they dashed into the shadows and behind a wall. Sam faced the child and felt her heart break a little. She was so young, so pretty. She might have been someone's little sister.

"This time you will escape," the girl said to her.

"What do you mean?" Sam whispered. She shook her head. The men would hear them. "Go while you can."

"Come with me," the girl pled.

"I can't. I have to find someone first."

The girl looked confused. Sam wiped the tears from her soft cheeks, then threw her blanket around the girl's shoulders and gave her a gentle nudge. She watched the child sprint in the direction of the staircase, nimble and lithe. For a moment, Sam wondered how they'd ever captured her in the first place, she was so light on her feet. She had to have been some kind of cat.

"Good luck," she murmured, and then she turned back to find her way toward Rima.

"*No!*" A scream rang through the dungeons, echoing off the cold, hard walls.

Sam put her hands to her ears. *No, no, no.* They'd done it. They'd murdered that man. She could hear him gurgling on his own blood. The others had gone silent, and his last gasps seemed to be right in Sam's ears.

Her own breath came hard and fast. What was she doing down here? They would see her. They would kill her next.

She edged away and soon found a hallway, but it turned pitch-black after several steps. She turned back and ran straight into a guard—the one she'd followed from the marketplace.

"Again?" he asked. He cackled and sank his fingers around her forearm.

"No," she whispered, struggling to pull away. "Don't touch me!"

"The stupid girl with the fine white teeth and the strange accent." She strained to reach the sword in her belt, but his grip was brutally tight. "Next time I ought to feed you to the lions," he whispered into her ear. "You would be digested and forgotten."

17

The guard bound Sam's wrists behind her back. He shoved her down another hallway, this one narrow and lit by torches held in sconces of human bones, their sickly green flames lapping at her hungrily as she passed. She stumbled by one cell after another until she lost count, their metal bars clenched tight as teeth.

"Again with you! You cannot escape. If you flee to the marketplace," he said, as he flicked his whip across the backs of Sam's thighs, "someone will bring you back for a reward, but only after they have corrupted you in a thousand ways." Sam looked over her shoulder at him as he grinned at the thought, his teeth as narrow as pins.

Although the cells all seemed empty, Sam swore she heard breathing coming from dark corners, prisoners pressed against the walls.

The guard shoved again, his palm hard against her spine. She wished she could reach up and grab a torch and burn him with it, but even if her hands had been free, the torches here were chained in place. He continued to force her through a maze of passageways, one turn and then another, until they reached the end of a dank corridor.

"We are on an island," he said, taking her by the shoulder, "and you cannot swim to the nearest shore." He yanked her close to his face. His breath smelled like tobacco and the greasy leg of lamb he'd been sucking on. "If Môt did not forbid it, I would have you right now."

He released Sam's arm, and she felt the blood coming back in a hard rush. Then he pushed her over the threshold and into the cell,

locking the door before he left. The sound of his cackling rattled through the hallways until all grew quiet again.

The cell reeked of urine. An animal made a keening noise. A damp cough resonated through the passageway, and then a howl. Sam's own breathing was short and hard.

And then, from the far, dark corner of her cell, she saw a pair of eyes.

"Who's there?" she asked, her heart in her throat.

A shape emerged from the shadows, and then a voice.

"It was the cream cheese," it said.

"Oh!" she cried. *"Rima!"* She nearly fell to her knees at the sight of her sister.

"I'm telling you. It was that stupid caramel-flavored cream cheese. It poisoned our brains." Rima was trying to smile, but it came out crooked and pained. "You have bangs," she said.

"Oh my God!" Sam said, rushing toward her. "Quick, untie my hands!"

The moment her wrists were free, she grabbed Rima's trembling hands in hers and turned them over. Yes, they were Rima's and not the shapeshifter's. Young and smooth, although most of her knuckles were cut, and her normally perfect fingernails were chipped and rimmed with grime.

"It's you. It's really you." Sam dropped her hands and grabbed Rima madly around the waist, pulling her into a bone-crushing hug. "You're alive."

"So are you." Rima was shaking. She was wearing a dirty white dress—similar to Sam's, but without the finer embellishments. "I was so worried...I didn't know if I'd ever"—she took in a long, tattered breath—"if I'd ever...see you again."

"You're *alive*," Sam repeated, sniffling against Rima's limp hair.

"Alive, dead, in between. It's all screwed up here, isn't it?" Rima pulled back and wiped a hand across her face, smearing her tears into dirty smudges. She forced a small laugh, and then gripped Sam by the shoulders and shook her. "Where have you been?"

"Looking for you," Sam said. "From the second you disappeared in the mountains."

Rima nodded and hiked up her dress to wipe her nose. "The dog-ladies took me in a cart. I was blindfolded, and then I was on a boat." She let out a sob, and Sam took her into her arms again. "I'm so hungry."

"Are you okay?" Sam asked. "I mean, did they…hurt you?"

"No," Rima said. "At least there's that. They're apparently saving me for some death god. Which is great, you know? Because I hear he's the Underworld's Boyfriend of the Year. According to the friendly creeper-guards," Rima said, "he likes to keep women in the dungeons until they break a little. You know, lose their will to fight." She took Sam by the hand. "There's a bench here. We can sit down. Super comfy."

The bench was sticky, and Sam thought she saw something worming through the wood. She sat anyway, moving closer to Rima until their thighs were touching.

"But you're not broken," Sam said.

"No." Rima paused a beat too long. "Not yet, anyway. Maybe a little." She sniffed. "Now that I see you again, I feel better." She nudged Sam with an elbow, then looked her up and down. "So what about you? A ring?"

"Eshmun," Sam said, and then told her about the cedar forest, Sarepta, and Sidon. She told her about Helena, and how she thought Eshmun might intend to marry her. How Môt must have gotten the same idea.

"It's that *stupid* prophecy everyone keeps talking about," Rima said.

Sam nodded. "Apparently we fit the description."

"Getting married and having a kid was not on my underworld bingo card," Rima said. "Eaten by a flying crocodile, sure. Honeymoon, no." She squinted at Sam. "Is your neck bruised?"

"Yeah," Sam said. "For the second time, actually. I'm okay, though." She sifted through her thoughts for a moment. "I think that guard thought I was you. Did you manage to get out, but they found you?"

"Twice." Rima nodded weakly. "When these assholes come to bring disgusting food, I hide way back in the corner so they leave me alone. There's one who can't get the lock right—he always leaves the door unbolted. The first time I thought he made a mistake. The second time I thought he was doing it on purpose." She shrugged. "But then he wasn't there to help me find my way out, so I don't know."

Sam stood and tried the door, but it wouldn't budge. Flakes of rust clung to her fingers as she pushed and pulled until her hands were slick with sweat.

"There must be another way out," she said, looking up at the ceiling. There was always more than one way, wasn't there? "Besides the spiral stairs."

"Maybe. All I've found is one dead end after another. How do we get home, Sam?" Rima asked. Her eyes were swollen from crying; her cheeks looked sunken. Sam put a hand to her sister's forehead, what Mom used to do when she checked for a fever. "Even if we get out of this prison, which way is Michigan?"

"I don't know."

"Oh," Rima said. She sounded confused, disappointed.

"Do you remember that time we got lost at that county fair?" Sam

asked, sitting beside Rima on the bench again. "We went on the Ferris wheel. We could see clear across the whole world—at least that's what it felt like."

"I was scared."

"You were?" Sam asked. "That's not how I remember it. You didn't seem scared."

"I was. And this is no county fair. I haven't seen a corn dog stand anywhere, have you?"

"I'm just saying," Sam said, "we've been lost before. Maybe we've been lost all along. Ever since Dad left."

Rima fell silent. "Dad was the one who found us," she finally said. "At the fair. But he can't find us here."

"I saw him," Sam said. A chill shook her, hard, as if someone had suddenly grabbed her by the shoulders. "I saw Dad *here*. I mean, it wasn't really him, but for a minute I thought it was. It was awful and amazing all at the same time."

"It's this place," Rima said. "It makes you think about dead people."

"You think Dad's...dead?" Sam asked.

"Of course he is," Rima replied.

Sam was silent. Rima hadn't even hesitated with her answer. A grinding metallic sound rang through the hallways, followed by a scream. She pulled her sister closer.

"I promised him I would try to keep things together," Sam said, her voice faltering. *Try hard, kiddo. I love you.* The last words he'd ever spoken to her. "I'm starting to wonder if it was fair of him. I've taken that promise pretty damn seriously, you know? I was only twelve years old. A kid. What was I supposed to do? And now look at this mess we're in. How am I supposed to make things right?"

"You will. Because you always do. That's why Dad trusted you."

Rima looked down at their intertwined hands. "Your fingernails look like hell, sister."

Sam let out a small laugh, but the sight of her own blackened fingertips startled her; the *ruḥā* stains were spreading. She tucked her right hand behind her, where Rima couldn't see the trickle of black down her palm.

"When we get back," Rima said, "we're going to blow some of Mom's big casino winnings on a mani-pedi day. I've decided."

"Remember how Dad used to pick us up from school?" Sam asked. "He had that old red truck, and the windows were always stuck? Country music blaring. We'd go to Dairy Queen. He made us swear we wouldn't tell Mom."

"Sure," Rima said. "And I remember the epic fights they had because we were so stuffed from Peanut Buster Parfaits we couldn't eat dinner."

"Epic fights?" Sam repeated.

"Yeah. They argued a lot." She raised an eyebrow at Sam. "Let me know where you buy your rose-colored glasses because I want a pair."

"What are you talking about?" Sam asked. The only time she remembered her parents fighting was when Dad bought her a fishing pole and wouldn't tell Mom how much it cost.

"You've got things all rearranged in your head, that's all," Rima said. "It got a lot more peaceful after he left."

"Don't say that," Sam said. "Please, Rima. I like the way I remember him."

"Okay," Rima said. "He was amazing. I'm just saying. You've always had blind spots with our parents." She let out a weary breath. "I guess it doesn't matter now anyway. How long have we been here? What day do you think it is?"

Sam shrugged. "Friday maybe? I was supposed to present my business plan in Ms. Bishop's class today."

"Hooked," Rima said. "Fishing Gear for Women."

Sam had created a mock-up website, along with T-shirt slogans: FLY GIRL and REEL TALK. She'd designed a product called Bait Bling: lures that looked like jewelry.

"It was a good business plan," Rima said quietly, her voice dropping off. *Was.*

The minutes dragged on, and Sam felt the cold sinking into her bones. Her heart was sinking, too. "So this is what you've been doing?" she finally asked, her voice breaking the silence. Her back crackled as she twisted her torso to stretch. "Listening to water drip and people scream occasionally?"

"I'm not sure it's water," Rima said. She tipped her head toward a wailing sound. "And I'm not sure those are people."

"I can't stand it." Sam took a long breath and inhaled the stench of urine again. She put a hand over her face. "We have to do something. They think there's only one of us, right? A stupid girl with white teeth and a strange accent."

"Yeah," Rima said. "So how does that work to our advantage?"

"I'm not sure," Sam said. "But it should, somehow." She pulled out the sword from Marid's cave. "Maybe this will help us. That idiot didn't search me. Must've thought I didn't have anything, being you."

"What's that?" Rima asked. "A sword for killing mice?"

"Probably," Sam said. "Or maybe to kill a god. I'm not sure which."

Rima made an uncertain noise. She took the weapon from Sam and held it in her hand. "Um, okay?"

"So, also, there was this woman I met," Sam said. "I can't stop

thinking about her. It's just so weird—I felt like there was some connection between her and us, somehow, but how is that possible? She said I summoned her. Me. And she said I had her obol, just like Eshmun." Sam paused. "She looked so familiar. She had this crazy, wiry hair pulled up into a tall, pointy bun. Her eyes were all white and clouded over."

"That's the witch," Rima said instantly.

"The witch?"

"From the stories Mom used to tell us when we were kids. The witch who would rise up out of the ground."

"I don't remember that one," Sam said. "She rose up out of the ground, like from the underworld? The way Eshmun did in our backyard?"

"You think Mom has another coin?" Rima asked.

Sam's eyes widened. "In that velvet box in her closet...It's possible. She could have touched it and summoned Sbartā. If Sbartā really is 'the witch.'"

"I don't know how that helps us, either way," Rima said, "and I'm too tired to figure it out."

Sam chewed on her lip. "Even if we're right about the coin, there's no way for us to tell Mom."

"Nope," Rima said. "We're stuck in this cell, Sam. We're not going anywhere. I need to sleep a little, okay? I've been too afraid to close my eyes."

"Go ahead," Sam said, her mind scrambling. They couldn't be stuck. She needed to form some sort of plan. *Attack the next guard that delivers food? Make a run for the spiral staircase?* But the way those guards had killed their comrade...they were like bloodthirsty animals, feral, frenzied. If she started a fight with one, could she really win, or protect Rima?

Rima stretched herself out and put her head on Sam's lap. "I love you," Sam whispered, looking down at her sister's face. Within minutes, Rima was asleep, still gripping the sword in her hand. Sam stroked her forehead and added, "More than anything."

She tipped her head back to rest on the wall behind her, and it shifted a little.

"Oh," she gasped.

Gently, she moved Rima onto the bench so she could slide out from underneath her, and then she pushed against the wall. The stones behind the bench barely budged, but there *was* weakness in the wall. She began a systematic check of every row along each wall. She pressed and palmed, finding some slightly tremulous, until she reached a corner in the back where the stones half-crumbled with a single push.

"Come on," she whispered as she wrestled decayed stones out of their places. She pawed at them, digging, until there was a hole almost big enough to crawl through. She lay flat against the ground, trying to see what was on the other side, but all she could discern was a dim light. Another room? A hallway?

On her knees again, she wriggled another wet rock free, inching it out of the way and making the opening wider. All the while she kept an eye on the cell door, wondering when one of the guards would show up.

Suddenly there were scratching sounds in the hallway. Sam stood and went to the front of the cell to peer through the bars. Down the dark corridor, a pair of eyes glowed greenish yellow. Then another pair of eyes. Three sets, and then five.

Sam stifled a scream.

The eyes came closer. Then Sam saw fur—black and glossy, as if coated with mucus—or blood. One of the animals raised its nose and

sniffed the air, whiskers twitching. It stood fully upright and Sam's heart slammed so loudly she thought the sound of it might give her away. A rat creature...the size of a small child.

Abruptly, they all scattered at once. Sam turned and saw, with a shock, that the same guard from before had reappeared soundlessly, peering in at her with a smug look on his filthy face. With him were three others. She jerked back from the bars.

Rima was still sleeping quietly in the shadows. Sam felt dizzy with fear. "What do you want?" she asked.

He tapped a finger to his ear. "You hear that, love?"

"What?" Sam asked. It was quiet, other than the sound of the men's wheezy laughter. Could they hear Rima's steady breathing behind her? She stepped forward to block their view.

"You do not hear that?" the guard asked, his face blooming with glee.

"What?"

He leaned closer, his breath assaulting her. "I hear wedding bells," he hissed, rattling the key into the lock.

She wrapped her arms around herself and felt the bile rise in her throat. Sensing a slight motion behind her, she realized that Rima had sat up.

"Let's go, then!" she said quickly, before the guard noticed Rima in the corner. "I'm sick of this cell. I've been here so long."

Stay quiet. Don't lift the sword. We can't win.

I'll protect you.

The guard let out a laugh, surprised by her reaction. "So eager," he said, "to get to your marriage bed." He swept out an arm, beckoning her to exit the open cell.

She hesitated. "Will all the guards be coming to the wedding?" she asked. "Is everyone invited?"

"Of course," he snarled. "My lord wants it to be a spectacle."

"Lead me, then," she said. The guard gave her a searching look, but she kept her eyes straight ahead. She wanted to call out instructions in English, tell Rima to escape through the hole she'd made, but she was afraid it would make the guards suspicious.

She'd come to save Rima, and maybe she'd just done it. Tears streaked silently down her cheeks. *You can run away now,* she wanted to shout. *You have the sword. They won't be looking for you. You have a window of time. Hurry before the rats come back. Every guard will be at this wedding.* My wedding.

The guard pulled up the back of Sam's dress and patted her. His rough, icy skin made her turn rigid with disgust. "Oh, how I cannot wait to witness this," he said.

Sam spun and swatted his hand away. "I will tell him," she threatened, tugging her dress back down. "The god of death is the only one who can have me."

The guard laughed. "So, so eager." He pushed her hard, thwacking the small of her back with the whip he carried. The other men laughed, whooping like a pack of hyenas. "I cannot wait to see."

18

Sam was shoved into a room where two women poured water onto hot rocks, filling the room with steam. They wore rows of beaded neck rings all the way up to their chins, and their dark eyes were lined with white paint. Their bare arms and legs seemed to be made of pure muscle.

"Clothes off," one said over her shoulder at Sam. The guard lingered in the doorway. "Get out! *Puq!*" she screamed at him, and then crossed the room to slam the door in his face.

Sam stripped and crossed her arms over her body, but the women pushed them out and away, yanking and twisting her so they could mercilessly coat her with gritty soap.

"What is that?" Sam asked, alarmed: One had retreated into a corner of the room and opened a box, retrieving a long, curved metal blade from it. Sam eyed a second doorway, but how could she run away like this? Naked and defenseless?

"Vacant girl," the woman said, smiling at Sam's fear. "See?" She pulled the blade across her own arm. "It cleans you."

Sam closed her eyes as they scraped her skin, desperately willing herself to be elsewhere. She tried imagining home, school, work, but it was impossible to pretend she was anywhere but here.

She glanced around again. If there had only been one woman, and if they both hadn't been so much bigger than her, she might have chanced a fight.

"What is this?" the taller one asked. She turned Sam's right hand upward, where the blackness had leached even darker and deeper, running down her palm, through her life line and fate line, mildew-like.

"I touched a *ruḥā*," Sam said.

"What of it?" she said. "Many have touched the dead. Never have I seen this before."

"I have," the other said. "It happened to my own brother. He embraced the *ruḥā* of his dead wife. He held on too long and looked inside her. He saw into her world. He waded into the pool of death, and then he could not dry himself of its waters."

Sam looked down at her hand. "What happened to him?" she asked.

"Slowly, he turned into a pillar of empty skin," she said. "He became stale and brittle from the inside out. And then the wind took him." She blew into Sam's eyes.

"You are cursed," the other said, and they both laughed. "The ancients say the only cure is the sun, but alas, there is no such light in this realm."

Sam felt sick. Eshmun's healing powers had at least been able to push the blackness down. How long would it take for her to turn to ash? How much time did she have left?

"You will not live long as the bride of Môt anyway," the taller one said, as if answering Sam's unspoken questions. "He will use you and dispose of you."

Sam hugged herself.

Her skin became pink and raw from being scrubbed so mercilessly. After she'd been washed and slathered with fragrant oil and had her hair brushed with ivory combs, she was handed an elaborate purple gown, richly embroidered at the hem with golden thread.

If Teth had thought the outfit Meem had given her was too fine, he would have been astounded by this dress. It must have been silk, it was so supple and weightless.

Once she was dressed, they hung dark purple flowers around her neck and placed rings of bells around her ankles. She was given a new belt of fur. "Give me my bracelets back," Sam insisted. They were her last items from home, and she felt a pang of finality. Without them, she would have nothing left of her old life.

"Is this your engagement ring?" the woman asked, tapping a finger against the emerald. They'd already taken the small box, not noticing the strand of Eshmun's hair inside, and decided it was worthless.

"I suppose," Sam said miserably, realizing she'd been doomed from the moment she set foot in the underworld to wed one of the gods. The prophecy.

"Hmm," the first woman said, still considering the gold ring.

The second woman threw her head back and laughed. "Take it," she said ruefully. "I should like to see what he does with you as punishment for such a theft. If the Lord of Death gave it to this girl, it is worth your life and then some. Take it!"

"This way," the first woman said, leaving the ring on Sam's finger.

Sam followed once again, leaving the room. This was not the dungeons or anything close to it anymore—this was a temple. The dark floor, which had been polished until it looked wet, was cold against her bare feet. Her ankle bells rang as she walked, making a rhythm of her march.

"The show is about to begin," the first woman said. She adjusted Sam's bracelets on her own wrist with a smirk, and then led her through a final maze of fine stone hallways attended by liveried guards. Sam's thighs burned as they walked up an incline, and she felt herself shaking as the hallway widened and led into a strangely open

area. The woman pointed for Sam to continue, and then she retreated, disappearing back down into the den of torchlit hallways, the flames' green light casting bruised shadows.

Sam looked over her shoulder and then took a few steps forward, her heart thudding. The open air filled her with a sour and sickening dread as she realized where she was:

On a stage in an amphitheater.

Rows of stone benches sat empty, waiting for spectators. At the center of the stage was a majestic bed, carved from wood and decorated with jewels, and topped with a thick mattress and embroidered pillows.

Dark ovals littered the stage, and at first Sam thought they were insects. Cockroaches. She jumped when she felt one under her bare feet, but they were only flower petals strewn everywhere. An unseen musician played mournful music, which floated through the amphitheater like a foreboding fog. Above her the sky was slate gray.

She shivered in her thin gown and looked out across the benches as prison guards filed in, taking their seats in the front row. She recognized a few faces from the marketplace, too: There were the naked *ḥayuta* women with their matted fur, and there was the man who was selling caged monkeys. They spoke to each other, but their eyes were on Sam. All the people of Kition were assembling here, it seemed.

She shrank back toward the passageway she'd come out of, but then the growing crowd fell silent. From the opposite side of the stage, Eshmun emerged.

He'd been captured.

He was a prisoner, too.

The boat in the harbor... it *was* his. He must have been ambushed. But where were the rest of his men? Had they been thrown in the dungeons? Were they dead?

"Eshmun," she whispered.

His eyes swept over Sam's hair and gown; the flowers around her neck, the bells she wore around her ankles. He was naked except for a small skirt of fabric around his waist. He had been whipped: His chest and stomach were torn apart and he was bleeding. Three guards stood a few feet behind him, their arms folded across their meaty chests. She saw now that Eshmun's hands were bound behind his back. The crowd grew noisy again, shouting insults at him.

"Half-god! Empty promises!" The stone benches had filled with more and more wedding guests. "To hell with him!"

Sam felt an angry swell of protectiveness. This wasn't right. Eshmun was always in charge, always strong and regal. She was glad to see that his posture was still proud, his eyes lit with their usual fire.

Then a trumpet-like blast interrupted, and Sam turned to find a man blowing into a long, curled horn. His cheeks swelled with each note, the sound somber and deep.

"Oh!" she gasped as an elephant walked onto the stage. It was draped with streamers of lavish fabric, which billowed with each step. Jewels dotted its face. The elephant stopped just short of the edge of the stage. Strapped to its back was a square platform with an ivory railing.

Sam looked up at the man who stood atop that platform. He pounded his chest and spread his arms wide at his audience, who cheered with thunderous applause.

"Môt!" she heard Eshmun growl.

Sam strained to take in Eshmun's uncle, who stood some fifteen feet above them. He was bare-chested, and he wore a gold skirt and a tremendously tall hat—also gold—with a flat circular top. His arms were unnaturally long, and his tapered torso was nearly the same width as his neck.

"*Lêpa`né Môti hbur!*" he cried. *At the feet of Môt bow down!*

At once the audience dropped to its knees.

"Welcome, nephew!" Môt called down to Eshmun. The elephant shifted its weight and Sam backed away from its long tusks, which were sharpened to points. "I see you have enjoyed your stay so far." He nodded to one of the guards, who cracked his whip and sent a fresh stream of blood down Eshmun's arm. Eshmun winced, his jaw clenched. "And I appreciate the speech you gave in the marketplace earlier, pledging your allegiance to me."

"I did no such thing," Eshmun declared.

Môt let a smile play on his lips. His skin had an odd green cast to it, like copper that had accumulated a patina. Strangely enough, there was something magnetic about him: He had Eshmun's cheekbones and finely sculpted muscles, his bare abdomen stone hard. Sam felt herself staring, taking in every detail, unable to look away. His presence was powerful.

"Ah, but you did," Môt insisted.

He motioned toward a man standing at the back of the stage. Sam felt her vision blur with adrenaline. It was the shapeshifter. He strode forward and, with a shake of his shoulders, morphed into Eshmun.

"Citizens of Kition, hear me! I am but a meager half-god," the shapeshifter shouted in Eshmun's voice, stroking his fur collar with his bony hands. "I concede that I must submit to Môt, the true and rightful king of the underworld. The only king."

The crowd applauded such a convincing performance, and the shapeshifter took a bow. With a step backward, he changed again into the gray-haired man with the green eyes and even teeth. He smiled at Sam, a wolf's smile.

"Shall we proceed with the ceremony?" he asked.

"Yes, yes, of course." Môt gazed across the rows of benches

toward the back of the arena and flicked his fingers, beckoning an entrance. On his cue, a swarm of the giant rat creatures raced down the aisles, the slick, black things Sam had seen in the dungeons. There must have been fifty of them.

They scurried onto the stage and Sam cringed as they wove greasily around her legs. The elephant reared and Môt gripped the platform's railing. "Away!" he commanded. "Away from the elephant!" The rats obediently receded into the shadows. Others hid under the massive bed.

"What are these rodent abominations?" Eshmun demanded.

"My faithful spies and thieves," Môt said. "Are they not lovely?" The rats tittered and squeaked, smoothing their whiskers away from their faces, chewing their nails. Their eyes were flat and dead. "Among other things, they let me know you were coming. They see everything, my precious rats."

"You should not be here," Eshmun said. "You were given charge of Gadir. You were to stay there."

"Gadir was acceptable until my darling Ba'alat Gebal left me," Môt snapped. "I have been here in Kition for some time now, and I have brought my people with me. My plans have been—how shall I put this?—*expanding.*

"Indeed," Môt continued, nodding, agreeing with himself, "I found Gadir to be far too removed." He looked out at his crowd and made a face. "You see, the other gods felt that I needed to be kept at arm's length." The crowd murmured and he put up a hand to calm them. "Yes, yes, I know. Have they forgotten whose domain this is, and who has allowed them to be here?" His face twitched as he put on a false, dramatic smile. "But I have missed them all, dearly and truly, in my exile. I feel that the time has come to become reacquainted. To bring them to me." He pressed both hands to his heart.

"I feel the time has come—how shall I put this?—to *crush them*. So that I may finally rule once more." He thrust a fist in the air and peered down at Eshmun. "You really should stay in better touch with your dear uncle. These things would not come as such a surprise to you."

"Shall we proceed with the ceremony?" the shapeshifter asked again, more insistently. The crowd responded with a growling cheer. "Take her to bed!" a guard in the front row screamed. The one she'd followed from the marketplace. The one from the dungeons, the one who'd lifted her dress and snapped his whip at her.

"Yes, yes," Môt said. He climbed down a rope ladder from the elephant's platform and jumped to the stage with theatrical flair. Again, the crowd went wild. "Let us proceed!"

He stalked across the stage and smacked Eshmun on the shoulder as if they were old friends. His eyes were fixed on Sam, taking her in from head to toe.

"I hope it takes some time to impregnate my bride," he said, approaching. He circled Sam and let his hand slide along her arm. "I should like to work at it for a long while." Sam recoiled, her skin bristling with goose bumps.

She curled her hands into fists, wishing she had *Rugzā* again. Her fingers itched for it. She could have been sinking the blade into the hollow of Môt's neck.

"Do not touch her," Eshmun warned.

"Oh, I will," Môt said, and the crowd whistled. "Every inch of her!"

"Take her now!" the guard in the front row screamed. Sam inhaled—deep, deep, deep—and closed her eyes. *Please,* she thought. *Let lightning strike. Let Eshmun have some other magical powers. Make me disappear.*

"And what of Ba'alat Gebal?" Eshmun asked. "Your goddess of love. Do you not still hope for reconciliation?"

Môt's face sank into a hateful grimace. "There will be no forgiveness," he said. "Always in Byblos on some pretense of checking on her precious city-state. She has lovers there, of course. And then, as if I could not reach so far east, she ran to Baalbek with my own brother."

"And you, Uncle?" Eshmun asked. "You were always faithful?"

"I am faithful to myself!" Môt spat. "It is over, especially for her. Though I am still considering how exactly I'll deliver her to hell. There must be some sort of show, a grand event." He spread his arms wide, and the crowd erupted with cheers upon his cue.

"My father was right about you," Eshmun snarled at Môt. "You were not to be trusted. We should have never given you an inch of the underworld. Not even Gadir."

"The underworld was *mine*!" Môt roared. "All mine, until you cowards fled from Earth! The time has come for me to remind you that it is *still* mine. And your father!" He laughed. "The handsome one, the gregarious one. Always so popular. Where is he now? Ah! Here he is."

Môt motioned once again to the shapeshifter, who strode toward Eshmun, morphing into the likeness of Melqart as he walked. His bare chest was thrust forward with pride, and he wore a mask of bright feathers. "Son," he said, raising a goblet to his lips. "Where is the passage, Eshmun? The *tarʿā*? Where is it?"

The rat creatures tittered. A roar of laughter lifted from the crowd. Sam watched helplessly, feeling like a trapped animal. She was sweating through her gown.

"Still, after all this time, you have not found it? Eshmun, my son, are you *blind*?" the shapeshifter asked. "And now you believe that if you cannot find the way, your child will? All these centuries, and you have not impregnated a single soul. You are powerless. *Impotent*. Really, you have been such a disappointment to me."

"You impregnated only one," Eshmun said angrily, "and then you let her die." He shook his head. "No. I will not have an argument with this ancient *shapeshifter*. You are not Melqart." He turned to his uncle. "And Samira is not yours to marry. You cannot have her. You will not." He said it simply, an indisputable fact.

Môt laughed wickedly. "You *delivered* her to me, did you not? Whether intentionally or by your own stupidity, I cannot say, but does it matter? You brought her here. You brought her into this world, into *my* domain. *My* underworld. She is my property. As are you all."

Môt hooked a finger under Sam's chin. His breath smelled like the stone walls of the prison: cold and dank. She cringed and turned away. "Is this the one the jackals captured?" he asked the three guards who stood behind Eshmun. "Where is the other? The one who wandered through the marketplace like a fly into a spider's web?"

"No," Sam choked, feeling like the air was suddenly too thin to breathe. He knew there were two of them. That meant—

Rima was shoved onto the stage, looking terrified. She was still filthy from the dungeons, wearing the same stained dress, but her hair had been pulled back into a messy, low bun.

"We assumed you drowned at sea in your tiny little boat," Môt said, confusing the two of them. "You must have been very determined to reach me. Sisters, yes? I wonder which of you the prophecy means."

Rima looked him up and down before her eyes went to the rats hiding in the corners. She screamed.

Sam flashed a desperate look at Eshmun. *We have to do something.* She could see that he was pulling at the rope that bound him. But the arena was packed with spectators; the rat creatures paced and skittered along the edges of the stage and through the aisles; burly guards flanked Eshmun. The elephant shifted nervously on its feet, its tusks scraping the stage. There was nowhere to go.

And now, behind Rima, one of the women who had scrubbed and scraped Sam stepped forward. She held a pillow. It was small and elegant, the kind that would normally hold wedding bands. But instead, on top of the pillow were Sam's old shoes, the ones Meem had been murdered for. Sam slapped a hand to her mouth, but not before blurting out a cry of disbelief.

"Whose shoes are they?" Môt called out to the rapt audience. "We shall see!"

The woman first took the shoes to Rima, but Sam already knew what would happen. Even though she was taller than Sam, her feet were smaller, so the shoes would slide right off. Rima shook and was as pale as death as she put the shoes on. Sam ached to reach out to her.

"Walk!" the woman barked at Rima. Rima took one trembling step after another, the shoes flapping at her heels as she crossed the stage.

"The other, then!" Môt said.

Rima took the shoes off and handed them to Sam, her eyes filled with despair. Sam put on the shoes, bloodstained and stiff with Meem's murder, and walked.

"Ah, then they *are* yours!" Môt followed gleefully, gripping his greenish fingers around Sam's arm and whispering in her ear. "You *did* come through the gateway! You will tell me what they say. And you will tell me about your passage to this world. I will be the master of every border."

"I'll tell you nothing," Sam croaked.

There was a long, pregnant pause, and then Môt smacked his slim stomach, forcing an overacted laugh. "She thinks she has a choice!" The audience roared with laughter as he stalked across the stage, pumping his fists and working the crowd into a frenzy.

"The prophecy means that I myself am the god who is the father,"

Môt continued from center stage. He thwacked his chest. "Forget Melqart and his Tyrian princess. Forget this half-breed nephew of mine. Here are *my* otherworldly mortal brides. *My* child will be the one, the one with the gift of finding passage, and so I will own every gateway that might be revealed. In the meantime, I will *rule* this underworld. I will no longer share it with any other god. I will not be sent to far-flung cities. This is my domain and I mean to reclaim it!"

He walked back and forth, enjoying his soliloquy.

"I have always despised children," he continued from across the stage. "I have been very careful not to have any of my own. But now is the time! Fate has decreed it! I will plant myself inside these beautiful girls, whose father was a noble warrior, a hero of war. My seed will make a true prophet, and as my son, I will rule him."

As Môt spoke, Sam inched toward Rima. *Do you still have the sword?* She was desperate to ask, but Rima's terrified eyes were on the rat creatures hiding in the corners.

"What did you do with Ba'alat Gebal?" Eshmun asked after the roar of the crowd had subsided. "Where is she?"

Môt raised his eyebrows at the interruption. He turned slowly to address Eshmun. "Oh, how we all hold her up as if she were the light of this world, the sun," he said bitterly. "Let me tell you: Where there is sun, there are shadows, long and dark. She is not blameless. She is vain."

"If she turned to despair," Eshmun said, "it was because of you. She withered in the depths of Gadir. Tell me. Where is she now?"

"Ba'alat Gebal is with your father," Môt said with a sneer.

"In Baalbek?"

Môt made a face laden with false concern. "You are so confused. He is here." He swept his hand toward the shapeshifter who still looked like Melqart, sipping wine from his goblet.

With a condescending sigh, Môt told the audience, "Oh, Eshmun. You were never good at finding anything, were you? No sense of direction." He spun back to face him. "Do not worry. I will take you to Ba'alat Gebal and Melqart, and soon I will have Ba'al Hammon as well, and all his crops will wither, and his precious fields of lavender will die. And then, in a grand show of celebration, I will torture every one of you and throw you into the depths of hell, and thereby reclaim my kingdom once and for all. Have you forgotten who I am?"

Hands on his hips, he spread his legs into a wide stance and mumbled something—a prayer, a curse. One of his guards knelt before him and handed him a torch, green fire leaping from its tip. Môt opened his mouth, tipped back his head, and pushed the flame deep into his throat. The guard fumbled to his feet and drew away as Môt's eyes rolled back into his head.

A moment later, at the death god's feet, the floor opened into a gaping hole.

Moans of suffering rose up and out of it like a mist rising from a dark swamp. It made Sam dizzy. She closed her eyes and suddenly she was in a boat—her boat—wobbling across a midnight lake. But the water smelled sulfurous and stale. It was full of dead fish. They bobbed around her, lifeless eyes trained upward, seeing nothing.

Môt clapped his hands and the pit disappeared. The stage was solid again underneath his feet. Sam blinked the images away, though she could still smell death. The audience had fallen completely silent.

Môt nodded solemnly. "Yes," he said. "A reminder."

By now, Sam was close enough to Rima to hold her hand. Rima's fingers were as cold as marble, her posture rigid with fear. But before Sam could speak to her, she felt a bony hand on her shoulder and spun to find the shapeshifter lurking behind them.

"Give me the obol," he breathed, tangling his fingers into her hair.

She tried to wriggle away, her heart jolting. She looked at Rima and saw the tiny handle of the sword peeking out of her hair. Rima had used it—hidden it—by threading it into her bun.

"Come, Alchemist! Let the wedding ceremony begin!" the god of death cried, snapping his fingers at him.

The shapeshifter bowed and, with a shake of his shoulders, he became a young man dressed in a long white robe, a red stole folded over his shoulder and a square turban on his head. Two musicians came onto the stage, playing small flutes, a sad and slow melody like a funeral march.

"Do you take this god to be your master and husband?" the shapeshifter asked Rima as he yanked her away from Sam. "To obey, worship, submit to, and pleasure until the end of time?"

Rima shook her head. "No."

Stab him, Sam thought. *Pull the sword out and strike!*

The shapeshifter fluttered his arms and in an instant, he was Rima in a purple wedding dress and bare feet with bells around his ankles. He sidled up to Môt. "I do," the shapeshifter said, batting his eyelashes and clasping his terrible hands over his heart. Sam felt her stomach churning. He looked just like Rima; his voice was hers.

"She does not," Sam whispered, shifting in her bloodied shoes, clenching her teeth.

"And you," Môt said, turning to Sam with a cold smile. "Yes, you. I will wed you *both*. We shall see who is the first to birth a son." He clapped his hands. "It will be a race! A grand competition." He narrowed his eyes at the girls. "Who will win?"

Sam shuddered and turned to Eshmun, but he was looking upward with the oddest expression on his face. Sam suddenly felt dizzy as she followed his eyes to a nascent swirl above his head. It was a small tornado cloud, an eye at the center. Slowly, it descended, a blanket of gray pressing down on them.

A funnel!

"I cannot believe it," Eshmun whispered. "It summons me once more."

"What is this?" Môt screamed at the thick, opaque fog. "Whose sorcery is this?" He stood at a distance, his knees bent and an arm shielding his head.

Sam's heart pounded. Tears flooded her eyes.

The crowd had fallen silent once again. The prison guards cowered away from the stage. The cloud hung above Eshmun's head like a black halo, and his eyes turned toward a distant place. At his feet sat the rope that had bound his hands; he was free, and the three men who had been guarding him backed away into the corners along with the rats.

With Môt's attention diverted, Sam lunged for Rima and yanked her close. "Grab onto him!" she cried, kicking a rat to get to Eshmun and pressing Rima against him as the cloud slid over his head.

"Seriously?" Rima screamed, kicking at the air. "He's all slippery and bloody!"

"Just hold on! We're going back!"

A moment later, the funnel began to lift the three of them up, twisting them in midair. Sam felt her toes leaving the ground below.

They rose and spun, Sam closing her eyes against the dizziness. She wrapped her arm around Rima's waist, locking her close as they ascended with increasing speed. She ran her fingers through the back of her sister's hair, grabbing onto the small sword and extracting it, but then Rima started thrashing wildly.

"What are you doing?" Sam screamed. "Hold tight! We're going to lose you!"

"Rat!" Rima shrieked. Sam could see the black shape as it clawed up Rima's leg. Rima frantically tried to shake it off, making herself

slide downward with the effort. Sam was losing her grip on her sister, holding the sword in one hand and Rima's arm with the other. The rat was too far away to stab.

"Rima!" Sam screamed. And then her heart leaped into her throat.

Môt's green face was there, below them. He was holding on to Rima's ankle, and he looked up at Sam with a sneer of triumph.

Rima was there one moment and gone the next, falling back down into the underworld.

19

"No!" Sam screamed. "No!"

She heard the sound of her sister, along with Môt, hitting the stage with a *whump*, and the roar of the audience. And then Sam's ears filled with a dense and muffled hum. The black clouds around her turned grainy as soil, and she was suddenly facedown in her backyard garden. There were Mom's plastic pots turned on their sides, the abandoned gardening spade and gloves.

And Mr. Koplow was there.

He held a coin in front of him, gape-mouthed, hand shaking. "What the hell?" he asked, his eyes wild, his face an awkward grimace. "Is this a joke?" he asked, his words slurred and thick.

Sam rolled away from the edge of the funnel and looked at her lopsided house, which to her had never looked so perfect and so beautiful. She wanted to run inside, but there was Eshmun standing larger than life in her backyard, half naked and bleeding; the lower half of his body was a swirl of smoke. Mr. Koplow went pale and tripped backward.

"Mine," Eshmun said. "Give me my obol."

Mr. Koplow palmed the coin and turned to run, but Eshmun caught him by the wrist and he cried out. "Help," he choked. His hand was frozen closed, Sam knew. It would be almost impossible to let go of the coin.

The inky ground beneath Eshmun's feet roiled and then changed

direction, pulling downward rather than up. Sam felt it tugging on her feet and she skittered away from the growing edge.

But she felt ripped in half.

Stay here!

Go back for Rima!

How could she live with herself if she stayed? How could she willingly return to the underworld? Abandon Rima, or Mom? She knew this moment would haunt her, no matter what she chose.

She looked at her house again. Inside was her bed, her clothes, her fishing gear, her homework. Her entire life was here, waiting for her return. *Home. I'm home!*

Eshmun still had Mr. Koplow by the wrist. Mr. Koplow gave Sam a pleading look as if she could help him, but she had already wrapped her arms around Eshmun, pressing her face against his bloodied back. Would she ever get the chance to come home again?

At the last moment, Mom opened the back door.

Sam's heart slammed into her throat at the sight of her. Mom's hair looked unbrushed and her skin pink from crying. She probably hadn't slept since they'd disappeared.

"Sam!" Mom screamed, thrusting her hands forward. But Sam squeezed her eyes closed. "Sam, my sweet baby Sam!"

"I'm sorry," Sam whispered through her tears. "I'm so sorry."

With one last glance at Mom, she let herself fall away, hearing the sound of her name being called over and over again, her mother shrieking for her to come home, to come back.

20

Sam crashed down onto a hard surface, gasping for air. She could hear muffled voices. There was no sign of Eshmun or Mr. Koplow or anyone else.

Standing slowly, she rubbed a throbbing elbow and moaned. The inside of her mouth tasted like potting soil. Her ribs were tender. When she touched her face and drew her fingers away, she found them sticky with blood—it must have been Eshmun's, from pressing her cheek against his bare back. The funnel had made her dizzy, but she felt even sicker about what had just happened. Mom had been twenty feet away.

She'd been home.

Môt's voice oozed through the walls, and in an instant, Sam realized where she'd landed. She was backstage. *Rugzā* lay at her feet, and she picked it up and tucked it under her belt. Following Môt's voice, she walked through a damp hallway until it ended, and she was able to peer around a wall to see onstage. To her right, a ladder went up and out of the amphitheater—a ladder to freedom. She was tempted to climb it, but she needed to get Rima first.

"Come now." Môt was beckoning to Rima. He turned to the audience and held out his arms. "I should like to get to the kiss!"

The audience was wilder than ever. "There was a passage!" a woman screamed. "Eshmun found a doorway!" Meanwhile, a man jumped onto the stage and thrust his hips back and forth, humping the air, his tongue lapping. A guard shoved him off the stage back into

the crowd, where several men were chanting loudly, "Take her, take her, take her!" For a moment, Sam thought that the dusky sky above was finally turning black, that nightfall was coming on. But then she realized it was only her; she needed to breathe or she would pass out. Little stars orbited through her vision.

She'd been *home*!

She blinked and steadied herself.

Rima stood with her shoulders slumped in defeat, her terrified face wet with tears. Sam gripped the sword. Like she always did with Dad's Swiss Army knife, she held it up to her lips and kissed it for good luck.

"Can you kill a god?" she asked. "Are you *Wrath*? If you are, it's time."

Before her eyes, the blade suddenly extended and widened, shimmering like liquid mercury. Gasping for a breath, Sam held it away from her, the weight of it almost too much to bear. It slipped to the ground, nearly stabbing her foot as she stifled a scream. Heart pounding, she took it by the hilt, struggling to hold it at hip level.

She looked out onto the stage once more. There was the shape-shifter in his white robe, ready to declare Rima the wife of Môt. Sam's eyes went to his gnarly hands, and then she saw him react to something unseen: He flinched, sidestepping away from Rima and Môt. The slightest shadow of fear crossed his face, and in an instant he deftly morphed from young man to rat creature, shedding his robe and turban and scurrying toward Sam. For a heart-jolting moment, she thought he'd seen her. But then he suddenly stopped and clawed at the floor; a trapdoor opened and he was gone, vanished into some sort of underground crawlway.

It all happened so fast. While her eyes had been on his escape, a roar had risen from the audience. Sam took a small step forward to

see what was happening—and gasped as a huge shape stalked onto the stage.

Teth!

He pounded toward Môt, hurtling at him with a look of sheer hatred. In his huge hands he wielded a massive black sword made of stone rather than metal. Its polished blade flashed as he raised it high over his head. The entire audience was on its feet, pointing, but Môt mistook their bellowing and screaming for applause. He bowed.

Finally he must have felt Teth upon him. He spun to face him, pulling his own weapon from its sheath. It was too late.

"Revenge!" Teth thundered.

Teth's sword met with Môt's body, but the blade instantly turned green with fire. It burned like a match and fell to the stage in a pile of ash, while Teth was left holding nothing but the hilt.

Môt laughed wickedly and then, like a dragon, he breathed a stream of flame at Teth. Teth's beard caught fire and he fumbled backward to his knees, pawing at his face. Môt exhaled again, which ignited Teth's sleeve.

"Teth!" Sam screamed.

She summoned every ounce of strength she had and ran onto the stage, carrying the sword ahead of her. Teth's face bloomed with astonishment; Môt's darkened with fear. She pointed the blade at him clumsily, struggling to wield the enormous weapon.

But *Rugzā* seemed to know its target. It lightened, lifting in Sam's hands. She swung at Môt and the blade made an airy, beautiful whistling sound, even as it split Môt's torso cleanly in two.

His body fell in half onto the stage, Rima let out a bloodcurdling scream, and all hell broke loose.

The elephant crashed off the stage and charged through the amphitheater, trumpeting, crushing benches into rubble under its feet,

and spearing men with its tusks. The crowd screamed and wailed. Sam stood, holding the sword in both hands, frozen with shock at what she'd done. Behind Teth, an army of Sidonians in their long tunics, along with many *ḥayuta*, rushed into the fray, pouring down the aisles. Three gray-skinned men stampeded across the stage, sprouting rhinoceros horns as they went.

Sam frantically looked for Rima. *She was right here a second ago!*

"You will suffer," Teth growled at the dying Môt, "as she did!" He took *Rugzā* from Sam, raised the blade, and sliced through Môt's ankles, leaving his feet detached on the stage.

"Eshmun," Môt sputtered, blood spilling out of him. He looked down at his severed lower half. His voice was a gravelly whisper. "Where are you, my nephew? Put your...hands on me. Mend me."

"You ordered the murder of Meem," Teth said. His hair was burned, his beady eyes charged with fury. He turned to slice through a dozen panicked rat creatures with one swing of *Rugzā*, sending their flesh in splatters across the wedding bed. He triumphantly thrust a fist to his chest, his bear canines long and sharp. "There will be no healing."

Where is Rima?

Daggers flashed and women screamed. Rats screeched and men bellowed. Sam scanned the stage and finally found her sister in the clutches of the guard with the whip. He was clawing at her, tearing at her dress.

"No!" Sam shrieked.

She didn't think. The next moment Môt's abandoned weapon was in her hands. And then she was driving the sword between the guard's shoulder blades.

He reeled around to face her, and she kicked him in the groin. He sank to his knees, cursing. "You little whore."

Sam leaned over to whisper in his ear. "Go to hell." And then she kicked his chest, making him topple backward onto the ground.

"Sam!" Rima cried. "You're here? But…you went up in the tornado!"

"I'm back," Sam said.

"I think you just…" Rima looked at the crumpled guard. "You killed him!"

"Had to," Sam said, her chest exploding with adrenaline. She felt like she might throw up. "He would've…" She didn't want to finish the sentence. "We have to get out of here." She grabbed Rima's arm while a groundswell of shouting erupted near the back row of benches. Across the amphitheater, she saw them coming in, one after another.

Lions.

Ribs showing through their patchy fur, teeth bared, they could only have been the caged lions Sam had seen when she'd descended the spiral staircase. Someone had released them. And like Teth, they seemed to have one thing on their minds: *revenge*. They darted past Teth's crew of Sidonian men and *ḥayuta*, intent only on the prison guards. Sam threw her hands over her face as a lion leaped and took a guard by his shoulder, the man's white eyes globes of terror. When she looked again, the man's arm was on the ground next to him as the lion dragged him by the feet.

"This way!" Sam screamed, but Rima couldn't get past Môt, who was still gurgling. "Let's go," Sam urged, but Rima stood frozen, her mouth open.

Môt's contorted face looked greener than ever, his eyes turning slowly from side to side. His tall golden hat lay at his side. Dark blood had made a puddle all around him.

"Rima!" Sam said. "Come on! *Rhaṭ!*"

She pulled her sister by the arm until she found the stone ladder, camouflaged so well it was nearly invisible. "There!" she cried. Rima

climbed first and Sam followed. She gripped rung after rung, kicking a rat creature as it clawed at her feet. It tore her ankle bells away, and then her old shoes. Her bare toes curled on the stone as she climbed, wiry whiskers on her heels. "Hurry!" She pushed on Rima's thighs, terrified that the rat would sink its teeth into her. With a grunt, she kicked as hard as she could, catching the creature across its snout and sending it into the air. It plummeted to the stage below, where a lion eagerly scooped it up.

"One of Teth's men must have let the lions out," Sam said when they finally got to the top. Below on the wedding bed, a lion was making a feast of two guards, gnawing their limp bodies.

"It must have been her," Rima said. She pointed toward the rear of the arena, where the stone benches had been crushed to pieces by the elephant. Sam squinted to see.

There was the girl she had helped rescue earlier in the dungeons. The sweet-faced *ḥayuta*, who Sam thought might have been a cat. With a raised fist, she rode the back of a lion, seemingly directing their charge. She was still wearing the blanket Sam had given her.

"They're only going after the prison guards," Sam noted. "The people who caged them."

"Maybe those lions are her family," Rima offered.

Teth was still wielding *Rugzā*, his roars lifting as dozens of *ruḥā* began ascending, floating up from the amphitheater like a flock of crows. At Môt's severed feet, a swirling green abyss had formed, bubbling like a cauldron. Hell was opening up.

"Look," Sam said. The guard she'd stabbed was turning dark, and for a moment she thought his *ruḥā* was separating from his body. But instead his corpse twisted and broke into tiny pieces, which rose up off the ground, a swarm.

"What is that?" Rima asked.

"I think...they're flies," Sam said. "Thousands of flies."

They buzzed toward the seething hellhole and dove down into it, the sound of screaming and suffering rising up. It was deafening, the shrieks of heartbreak, wickedness, agony, despair. Sam pressed her ears closed, felt her mind turn cold. She saw herself falling. She wanted to. One step and she could throw herself over the edge, to break open, to see how hollow she was.

She opened her fist. The black lines had spread down her palm and into the veins in her wrist. Darkness was pushing its way into her blood. It would pump all the way to her heart.

Snap out of it! Look away!

Sam tore the necklace of dark flowers from her neck and hurled it over the edge. She hooked an arm around Rima and shook her. "Get back," she said. "It's reeling us in."

Rima nodded, hard, and closed her eyes.

When Sam turned to stand, she found Eshmun just behind her. "You're here!" she gasped. "Where's Mr. Koplow?"

"Who?" He shook his head. No time for questions. "Quickly."

Sam grabbed Rima's hand and they followed, hurrying past the opening in the earth that held the spiral staircase; through the vine gate that had burned to ashes; and beyond the fields of *tannîyn,* where the ground was stirring.

The ground was stirring.

"Eshmun!" Sam cried, wanting him to stop so she could show him. She slowed and stared. Rootlike claws were flexing open and closed. They began to push up toward the sky, freeing scaly bodies from the soil. The farmer was nowhere to be seen.

Eshmun and Rima were sprinting ahead toward the marketplace. Sam ran to catch up, finding when she reached town that the caged

monkeys had been released and were running wild, leaping from head to head, tearing at hair and ears and noses.

Sam grabbed Rima's hand again as they struggled to keep pace with Eshmun, who darted through a pack of glassy-eyed men who were looting the tents. They stuffed food into their mouths and pockets, smashed pots and vials of stinking liquids. The marketplace smelled like a chemical spill and Sam's lungs burned with every breath.

"Eshmun," she gasped, losing sight of him. She tripped over a skull, her bare toes meeting bone. A crippling wave of pain made her falter and then fall to her knees. But Rima was still running, so she forced herself to stand and sprint to catch up. From the corner of her eye, she could see a band of rat creatures scurrying across the tops of the tents and lean-tos, making the roofs pitch and sway.

A wall came crashing down behind them, Sam shoving Rima out of the way. Kition was collapsing. They had to find their way to Teth's or Eshmun's boat, to any boat moored in the harbor.

"It's coming for me again," Rima said, cupping her hands over her ears. It was unmistakable: the telltale shrieking. "Sam!"

Trembling, Sam looked up. The clouds were an ominous shade of green. There was not just one *tannîyn*—there were many, circling, assessing their targets. Six of them. *Six*. Two were small, as though freshly hatched from the earth, but the others were as large as the one that had followed them into the mountains. Sam pressed her hands to her ears as they shrieked again, their voices like a hundred knives being sharpened upon stones.

Teth's men answered with a roar of their own. Sam spun to find two dozen of them, wearing metal helmets and breastplates. They knelt with bows and arrows, about to fire.

Sam caught sight of Eshmun ahead, where he'd halted, waiting,

to wave her toward him. But then he disappeared again behind a cart full of hides and hooves.

"Eshmun!" she yelled, just as the first *tannîyn* descended.

Sam hooked her arm through Rima's and they dove under a tipped lean-to, peering out as the *tannîyn* careened through the marketplace. It shredded rooftops with its talons, upending a wagon full of wooden statues, sending them skittering through the street like frightened animals.

To Sam's right, an abandoned bow and a single arrow of Kition make lay on the ground. She grabbed them and knelt to take aim, sweat half blinding her. She nocked. She sighted. She drew a breath.

A moment later, Rima screamed at the sky. "They shot it! It's falling!"

There was a horrific boom and then a cloud of dust. And then it was silent.

Sam held her breath for a very long minute, until Rima finally tugged on her dress, staring at her. "*You* shot it?"

"I think that was my arrow, yeah," Sam said with an astonished grin, still holding on to the bow. "Girl Scouts. Archery badge. Plus a few lessons from Dad."

The massive *tannîyn* lay crookedly across the road; its body had flattened everything underneath it. Its tail still twitched, threatening anyone who came too close. Sam glanced up at the other *tannîyn*, still silently circling above. Waiting.

Eshmun leaned over the injured *tannîyn*, which had taken Sam's well-placed arrow to the neck, and put his hands on it.

"Is he crazy? What is he *doing*?" Rima asked, her voice strident.

"I don't know," Sam said, but a moment later she did.

The wound diminished under Eshmun's touch. Blood stopped coursing out of the *tannîyn*'s neck. It fluttered its wings, sending another marketplace tent to the ground. The arrow slipped out, falling

benignly at Eshmun's feet. He kept his hands steady, his eyes closed in concentration. Radiating beneath his fingertips, a glow spread across the *tannîyn*'s body, turning it from reptilian green to bright gold, shimmering as Eshmun's magic spread. A gasp rippled through the small crowd that had gathered.

Sam eyed the sickly sky and the remaining five *tannîyn* assessing their next strike. One had dropped below the others. "Hurry, Eshmun," she whispered as he pulled his hands away. The beast was now pure white. Its face was placid, benign; the evil flash in its eyes was gone.

"Get on," Eshmun said, turning to face them. His face was soaked with tears.

"What?" Sam asked.

"Mount it," he said.

"Are you kidding me?" Rima shrieked. "It has"—she glared at Eshmun and pointed—"scales and teeth. It has wings!"

"Exactly," Eshmun said. He wiped the tears from his face and ran his hands across the wounds on his chest, making them disappear.

Sam glanced up. Another *tannîyn* had dropped to a lower altitude and had tightened its circle of flight. The two of them were homing in. An abandoned quiver full of black-fletched arrows lay on the ground. Sam slung it across her back.

"Sit in the middle," Sam said to Rima. Teth's men had reloaded their bows and were aiming them skyward. "Hurry."

"You want me to ride a dragon?" Rima asked, her voice cracking. "With the dick who brought us here in the first place?"

"Yes," Sam said, though her own voice was quavering. She flashed Rima a weak smile. "It's our only choice."

Eshmun had already straddled the white *tannîyn*'s back, and Rima reluctantly climbed on, clutching his waist. Sam sat behind her sister and reached across her to hug Eshmun's waist as well, pressing

Rima tight in-between them. She wasn't about to lose her grip on her sister, not again. The *tannîyn*'s scales were firm and sticky, softer than Sam imagined. She squeezed her thighs tight against its warm body and took a breath.

"Ready?" Eshmun asked.

"No!" Rima screamed.

The white *tannîyn* took three long strides and with one powerful flap of its wings, they were airborne. Rima howled. "I hate this place!"

In a matter of seconds, they'd left Kition's shoreline behind and were soaring over the sea. Sam let out a surprised laugh. "In the name of the gods!" she cried out.

Gliding close to the surface of the water, the *tannîyn* flew steady and strong. Sam felt as if she could stretch out her bare toes and touch the water, the way she sometimes let her fingers trail along Glen Lake when she was fishing.

She looked over her shoulder at the island's profile fading behind her, and her heart jolted. "Three *tannîyn*!" she screamed.

They were in pursuit, their faces drawn into evil grins. Soon, one of them pulled in front, gaining on them—it flew as if it had been shot from a cannon, it was so much faster than the others. It raced underneath their white *tannîyn* and then doubled back, speeding toward them head-on.

"It's going to crash into us!" Rima screamed.

It was using itself as a missile. Sam pulled an arrow from her quiver and aimed for its head. But their white *tannîyn* jerked higher and then lower, making Sam's shot sail wildly off target.

She pulled another arrow taut, squeezed her legs achingly hard to keep her balance, sighted the other *tannîyn* as it sped over the waves, and let the arrow go.

The shot flew straight and fast and nipped the *tannîyn*'s right

wing, making it flap crookedly. It began to drop, passing just below them. Then the beast flipped sideways, falling into the sea with a crash of white waves.

Still, the other two *tannîyn* were close behind.

Ahead, Sam spotted a ship with purple sails, its hundreds of oars striking the water in rhythm, heading toward Kition. It must have been coming to help. The water around the boat roiled like boiling tea as the sailors pounded the surface and propelled the ship with astonishing speed.

Eshmun seemed to be directing the white *tannîyn* straight for the ship. He leaned forward and spoke commands into its ear. Sam glanced over her shoulder at the other *tannîyn* trailing them like rockets, tightening her grip on Rima until she yelped.

"Eshmun?" Sam called. *What are you doing?*

At the last second, he barked a word at the white *tannîyn* and it suddenly lifted upward. Sam's stomach fell and she gulped back a wave of nausea; Rima screamed.

A hundred arrows shot upward from the deck of Eshmun's ship, sinking into the evil *tannîyn's* bellies. A wing smacked the mainsail of the boat and the vessel tipped precariously.

"No!" Sam cried, turning to look back.

One of the *tannîyn* skipped across the surface of the water like a stone, and then it crashed and sank, its head straining to stay above the waterline. With a final, garbled shriek, it vanished into the depths.

"They got one!" Sam shouted to Eshmun. The boat had righted itself and was rowing away into calmer waters. The second *tannîyn* screeched at them like a bullet. "The other one is still coming for us!"

"Then let it keep pace if it can!" he shouted back.

A long chase began. Sam's legs went numb as the minutes and then hours stretched on and on. The *tannîyn* neither gained on them

nor fell behind as they flew for what felt like an eternity. She could feel Rima's heart beating through her own chest as she pressed her close. The sea swept beneath them like an endless gray highway. They glided over a small coastal city and then the blackened forest of cedar trees. Her arms quivered from holding on for so long.

Ahead were the mountains with their steep and narrow passageways. Eshmun leaned forward and spoke again into the *tannîyn's* ear, and the white beast suddenly ascended, making Rima scream all over again. Sam squeezed her eyes shut, her stomach lurching from the quick ascent.

The air grew thin and cold. Their *tannîyn* soared straight for a snow-capped mountain peak and came to a landing.

Eshmun jumped off. "Lie flat," he told Sam and Rima.

Sam slid off the *tannîyn's* back and collapsed into the snowpack. "No problem," she said. She couldn't have stood up straight if she'd tried.

Sloughing off her bow and quiver to lie down next to Rima, she closed her eyes and thought of home, long ago. The two of them dressed in winter coats, making snow angels in the backyard while Dad stood on the back porch watching. His breath coming in white clouds and the steam from his coffee swirling up into the frigid air.

The white *tannîyn* stood over them and spread its wings, making a canopy of itself, camouflaging them with its brilliant white hide. Sam heard the evil *tannîyn* shrieking, the volume rising and then falling, piercing her ears and then fading away. She shivered so badly her teeth chattered, and she almost worried the sound was loud enough to give them away. This would be another way to die, she thought, frozen to the core, lying in a bed of snow. She held Rima's icy fingers in hers.

"Is it gone?" Rima whispered finally.

"I think so," Sam said.

Still, they waited a long time, a very long time. Sam was sure she could feel her heart slowing, hardly beating at all anymore. She exhaled and looked for the cloud of breath above her face, but there was none.

Eventually, their white *tannîyn* sat back on its haunches, retracting its wings. Its long tongue curled out of its mouth as it panted. Bright-eyed, it considered its passengers.

Sam reached out and stiffly patted its leg. "Th-th-thanks for the r-ride."

"Sit up," Eshmun said, and he put one hand on Rima's back and the other on Sam's.

Warmth poured through her, making her feel strong and awake. A tingling sensation spread along her spine. Pain dissipated like a fine mist rising off a lake and burning away in the heat of the sun.

She chanced a glance at her hand. The dark lines had receded into her palm, but they were still there. Her fingertips were as black as a moonless night. She would show Eshmun later. She didn't want to scare Rima.

Eshmun cupped Rima's chin in his hand and looked her in the eye. "Give me my coin," he said.

"She doesn't have it," Sam said. "You know that. Our landlord picked it up in our backyard. He has it now."

"Actually...," Rima said, opening her fist. A small parcel of fabric lay in the center of her palm. She peeled the corners back and Sam gasped.

There was the coin.

21

Eshmun's hands trembled as he took his obol from Rima. He stifled a sob and looked up at the sky. "Mother," he said, his voice cracking, shoulders shaking. He pressed his hands to his face, and when he took them away, tears streamed down his cheeks.

"I found it on the amphitheater floor," Rima said. "I saw it falling from the sky."

Eshmun held the coin to his chest and began reciting his list of names again, his friends and family who waited for him.

"Wait," Sam said to Eshmun. "This means you're going to... die now? Helena said you have to be dead for the obol to take you to *ʒmayyà.*" She gripped his arm and he put his hand on top of hers. Would he place the coin underneath his tongue and walk right off the side of the mountain? "You can't leave the underworld yet. You have to say goodbye to Teth and Helena. You have to find the way out for everyone. You have to find out what Môt did with Ba'alat Gebal."

"I am not leaving. Not yet," he reassured her.

Rima cleared her throat. "Sorry to interrupt," she said, "but can we get off this fucking freezing mountaintop?"

Eshmun nodded. "We turn back for Sidon now that the *tannîyn* searches ahead."

Since she was out of arrows, Sam left the bow and quiver behind. They mounted the white *tannîyn* and flew again, soaring away from the mountains and above the scorched cedar forest until Sam could see

the outline of Sarepta and its marketplace. Past that lay the sea, and finally the rocky beaches of Sidon itself. Eshmun's fleet of ships sat in port, their purple sails like a field of lavender across the shoreline.

After a gentle landing, they slid off the *tannîyn*'s back and Sam patted its side. "Thank you," she said. A moment later it took flight and disappeared over the twinkling sea.

Eshmun was already walking toward the stone bridge, arching over the water, that led to his home. He waved them along, straight through into the center of the fortress, out to where the patio opened up toward the sea and the indigo sky. There were no guards this time. All of Eshmun's men must have been on the boats to Kition.

Rima sat on the stone floor, pressing her back against a wall, while Eshmun paced along the railing, looking out at the water. Sam eyed the covered pit of snakes, then went and slid down next to her sister.

"Are you okay?" she asked.

"I'm tired," Rima said, resting her head on Sam's shoulder. "Very, very tired."

Sam nodded. She closed her eyes, too. "So how does California sound? After you graduate high school. There's a lake Dad and I picked out as a fishing spot. Road trip, and then spend the summer? Maybe I could get a job at a tackle shop."

"Maybe you could open your own tackle shop."

Sam smiled. "Maybe."

Rima's voice was hollow. "I know we're stuck here," she said. "I know we're never going home."

"Don't say that." Sam heard footsteps and opened her eyes, looking up at Eshmun as he walked toward them. "She needs to sleep, and then we both need food."

"This way," Eshmun said.

Sam helped Rima to her feet and they followed him into the small

bedroom. Rima settled underneath the fur blanket, and Sam nestled next to her. Eshmun excused himself.

"You don't seriously *like* him, do you?" Rima asked once he was gone.

"Eshmun?" Sam asked.

Rima rolled her eyes. "No, the big bear man." She sat up and frowned at Sam. "He's a prick, you know that."

"Yeah, maybe," Sam said. "I don't know. Is he?"

"He tied us up," Rima said. "He kidnapped us. I don't care how hot he is, or mysterious, or that he's a half-god prince, or whatever. He's an ass. Seriously, Sam. You're going to end up like Mom."

Sam threw her hands in the air. "What is *that* supposed to mean?"

"You deserve better."

"Stop, okay? A lot happened after you disappeared," Sam said. "And why are we fighting right now? I'm not in love with him. We just understand each other at this point. That's all."

"Sorry," Rima said quietly. She squinted at Sam, chewing her lower lip. She sighed. "Maybe I'm afraid *I'm* going to end up like Mom.

"You know, because I've had some time to think here. About what I would change," she continued. "I made some serious promises to higher beings. If we could get home, I would hit the reset button and fly straight. No more crazy parties or shoplifting. I swore on it. Maybe I could even get a soccer scholarship somewhere. I guess it doesn't matter now."

"It matters," Sam said quietly.

Rima put her head down. Sam ran her fingers through her hair, pushing it away from her face, until Rima suddenly caught her by the wrist. "What's wrong with your hand?" she asked.

"Nothing," Sam lied. "I...burned it on a torch. Eshmun will fix it." She saw the worry in Rima's eyes and tucked her hand under the blankets. "So I wonder how Mr. Koplow is doing," she said, trying to change the subject. "He's here, somewhere."

"He probably likes it just fine," Rima said. "This place is right up his alley. He can be a sleazy slumlord."

Sam laughed. "You're probably right. Now go to sleep, will you?"

"Shut up so I *can* sleep."

Sam smiled and patted Rima's hand. Within minutes, Rima's eyelids fluttered closed and her breathing fell into a peaceful rhythm. Sam was nearly asleep, too, when Eshmun came back into the room.

"Come with me," he said, hooking his finger at her.

She quietly slipped out of bed, and they returned to the patio. Sam stepped over the hole in the floor covered by the layer of opaque glass. A constant motion still churned underneath, just as it had when Sam had climbed into Eshmun's house from the sea.

"Why do you keep snakes in there?" she asked. When Eshmun responded with raised eyebrows, she added, "I looked when I broke in. I know it's snakes." She shrugged innocently.

"Of course you did," he said, giving her an admonishing smile. They leaned against the stone railing under a sky that had turned pink and violet. The air was rich and humid with the smell of salt water. "Their venom can be quite useful for curing certain ailments. It seems counterintuitive, does it not? That poison can be curative? How we so often need the very thing that can kill us."

"For life and death are one," Sam said. *"Even as the river and the sea are one."* She paused. She could practically see the green highlighter on the page. "That's from my mother's favorite book of poetry."

Eshmun nodded. He gazed out at the water. "They captured me in Kition because the Alchemist took on your appearance. I ran into his open arms without thinking."

Sam opened her arms now and wrapped them around his waist. "Thank you for sailing to save my sister. And thank you for getting us out of Kition," she said. When she pulled away, he took her hands into

his and studied the dark stain that spilled from her fingertips down into her palm, pressing its way into the veins in her wrist.

"Can you heal it again?" she asked.

"Of course," he said. He mumbled an incantation and pressed Sam's hand between both of his. When he withdrew, the blackness was still there.

Sam choked back a whimper of fear.

"*Wāy!*" Eshmun cried. "What is this darkness, this *ḥešukā*?"

"It's getting worse," Sam said. A stone of dread lodged itself in her chest. How long would the *ḥešukā* take to kill her? She couldn't die here. She couldn't leave Rima here alone.

"I have cleansed the marks of *ruḥā* before," he said. "But this is something deeper." Eshmun raked his fingers through his beard. "If only I could confer with my mother and my ancestors who healed before me."

"You could," Sam said. "You have your obol. You could go to your ancestors to talk to them."

"But then how would I return to you here?" he asked.

"I don't know," she admitted.

He turned away and was silent, his eyes scanning the horizon as if all the answers could be out there somewhere. Sam looked at her hand again; she flexed her fingers. "I have my great-grandfather's hands. Helena's son's hands."

"Strong," Eshmun said.

Sam thought of the old photos they had of Jiddo, sitting on his stone porch, smoking hand-rolled cigarettes. "He's the reason I'm here," Sam said. "In more ways than one."

"I thank him for that," Eshmun said softly. "I saw the way you protected your sister, how you fought for her. Your love of family runs strong within you. You chose to come back into this world. You could have stayed home."

"Yes," Sam said. "I..." Her voice broke off. Had she seen her mother for the last time? "I can still hear my mom screaming my name. The way she was reaching..."

"She is here." He pressed a hand to his chest, to his heart. "I will find a way to help you," he said. "There is an ancient remedy I can try to distill."

Try. Sam could read the doubt on his face.

She turned her head toward the sea. "I know why it won't go away." She held up her hand. "This. This is what happens when you cling to the dead."

"You held the *ruḥā* too long."

"Yes. I've been holding on too long," she said quietly. "I need to accept that he's gone. That my father is gone, and he's not coming back." She pulled in a ragged breath.

"Perhaps I have been grasping at an illusion as well," Eshmun said. He furrowed his brow. His keyhole pupil swirled.

"What do you mean?" Sam asked.

"Now that I have my obol," he said, "instead of feeling fulfilled and charged with courage, I only feel...confused. The coin called to me with such force, but now that I have it, it is silent."

"It's not time for you to go yet," Sam said.

He took her hands again and twisted them to look. His fingers lingered on the small white scar across her left wrist.

"It's not what you think it is," she said.

"Will you tell me now?" he asked. "How it happened?"

She nodded. "I got this...crazy...stupid idea. That if I took some of my father's things outside under a full moon, and if I dripped my own blood across them, somehow it would bring him back."

"Did it work?" he asked.

She squinted at him. "Of course not. I was a kid, and my

mother went through this woo-woo stage, and then there was this old *Scooby-Doo!* episode." She looked up at Eshmun's perplexed face. "Never mind." At the time it was a very big idea. It felt ceremonial and magical. She *did* think it might work.

"It was practice, was it not?" Eshmun asked with an eyebrow cocked. "You wanted to know if it would be difficult."

"No." She pulled her hands away.

"You were testing the possibility."

"No," Sam said. "I wasn't. I was just trying to get him back. I would have done anything to get him back."

Eshmun nodded and took her hands again. He wrapped his fingers around her wrist and closed his eyes. The warmth started as a small flame and then it spread.

She yanked away. "No," she said. "Stop."

"Why?"

"I don't want you to erase that scar. It's a part of me. It's a reminder of my father and how hard I was willing to try to have him home again."

Home.

She was supposed to be graduating from high school. She was supposed to be taking entrepreneurship classes, starting the rest of her life. She didn't belong here. She wanted her future, and not one that was spent waiting for her father to come home, or for her mother to act like an actual adult. *You make your own destiny,* Sam had told Eshmun. *Leaving is a choice.*

But now that Eshmun's obol was here in the underworld, there was no chance of anyone else back home summoning him. His obol would not pull him—or her—back to Michigan...ever again.

Her mind raced. Couldn't there be other obols on Earth, waiting

to be touched? In museums. In ancient tombs or other buried jugs. In coin collections...

...or in locked velvet boxes full of good-luck crystals and trinkets.

She sucked in a breath and put both hands on Eshmun's face. She held him close. "There was an old woman in Sidon who thought I had her obol. She thought I'd summoned her before. Her hair is pulled up into a tall point. She has white eyes. She looks absolutely ancient."

"Sbartā," Eshmun said. "She is a descendant of Ba'al Saphon, and she is one of the few who has been called to Earth."

"Yes!" Sam's heart thumped inside her, the idea pounding its way forward.

"What of her?"

"Whoever touched her coin...whoever summoned her looks just like me," Sam said. "It could be my mother. Sbartā said she saw a box, maybe my mother's velvet box. And she said she saw a man with an eagle and an anchor. I'm sure of it now—that's the Marine insignia. She saw a photo of my father, holding a flag. I *know* that photo."

Eshmun's eyebrows came together. She'd had to switch to English for the words *Marine* and *photo*.

"What are you telling me?" he asked.

"What if I'm right? What if my mother has Sbartā's obol?" she asked. "When I first arrived, you asked if I'd ever seen a *ruḥā* on Earth. Teth said they can cross the boundary to haunt people in their dreams."

"That is true," Eshmun said. "Yes."

"It's not safe here for us," Sam said. "Another god will come after Rima, or me. Your father, maybe. The brother of Môt."

"Perhaps."

"Then I want to die now," she said. "I need to die."

22

She would become a *ruḥā*.

She would slip through the boundary like water through a sieve. She would reach Mom with her message. Eshmun would heal her and bring her back to life, and Rima would never know. She would sleep through the entire thing.

"You want to go to Earth to haunt your mother?" Eshmun asked, incredulous. "To speak to her?"

"Yes," Sam said. "To tell her to touch the obol she has. I have to try. It's my only chance."

"Samira," Eshmun chided.

"Stop," she said firmly. "No lectures. This could work and you know it."

"And that is why I hesitate," he said. "You will leave me."

"I'm *dying*!" Sam shrieked, holding up her hand. "And you can't heal me."

Eshmun looked away, his expression wracked with anguish.

"Besides, you have your obol, and sooner or later you'll use it to leave. Now give me *my* chance, please." She grabbed Eshmun's hands. Her voice broke. "I have to hope. I have to try."

"All that time Teth was pressing me to decide what you were to me. Cousin or confidante, slave or ally. I know now. You are my truth," he said. "My *quštā*. You shine a light into my darkest corners."

"You're welcome," she said.

She was terrified of what she was about to do. It could go horribly wrong. She pushed him away because otherwise she would start to cry, and there was no time for tears. "Now go find Sbartā. And tell Helena. If this works...if she wants to come back with me, this could be her only chance."

But Eshmun didn't move. He looked into ʿSam's eyes. "What if you venture beyond my reach?—Too deep into death to return?"

"I won't," she said, trying to convince herself as well. "I'm coming back. This isn't goodbye. Not yet, not like this." Trembling, she swiped a tear from her cheek. "Go. Now!"

Eshmun nodded. "I will prepare the poison," he said. "It will be painless." He kissed her forehead, then pulled away and searched her face.

"Samira. My light," he said before sadly turning away. She watched as he walked out onto the stone bridge that led back to the mainland and the city.

As soon as she lost sight of him, she went back to the small bedroom to check on Rima, who was still sleeping soundly, even as Sam kissed her cheek. "I'll be right back," she said quietly into her ear. "I won't be gone long."

"Ah, but where are you going?" Zayin suddenly appeared, stepping away from the stone walls where she'd been camouflaged.

Sam's heart jolted with panic. Her mouth turned dry.

"*Šlama 'lekh,*" she choked, backing toward the doorway, curling her hands into fists.

"You owe me something." Zayin extended a gloved hand. "The vial of tears. The full supply, actually."

"I had a vial," Sam said, "but...I had to use it. I can get you another." She glanced at Rima, who was stirring in her sleep.

Zayin's eyes narrowed. "You used it? Did you drink it yourself?" she hissed.

Before Sam could answer, Zayin grabbed her by the hair and clamped a hand over her mouth, dragging her out onto the patio. "Let me tell you a story," she said into Sam's ear. "Once there was another *ḥayuta* like me. Her skin was nearly purple. Melqart adored her because her skin was the color of the royal dye. He would arrange grapes and flowers across her stomach and we all watched with jealous eyes as he devoured her." She pulled Sam's hair with a vicious jerk. "Do you know what happened to her?"

Sam tried to shake her head. She could hardly breathe.

"She grew older," Zayin hissed, "and Melqart's desire for her went cold. He turned his attention toward me. I became the favorite, the queen of his court. So what do you think will happen to me if I grow old?" She shoved Sam to the stone floor, where she hit her head. "I will not allow it. I will not be forgotten."

Sam's lips were against the floor as she spoke. "That might be true. That might be Zayin's story," she said, turning over, trying to pull herself up against the dizziness. "But you aren't Zayin, are you? Why bother with this charade? Show your true self. Take off your gloves."

"True self? There is no such thing," Zayin snarled. "We are all simply potential."

"I know who you are," Sam said.

Zayin cackled, and then shook her shoulders to shed her appearance. She became a withered, weathered old man. Sparse, wiry hair. Loose, mottled skin. Knobbed, bony hands.

"I am the Alchemist!" he cried. "I am chemistry. I am fluid. I am an epoch of knowledge: every ancient text, recipe, and concoction. I render dark magic unseen. While Eshmun was a prisoner of Môt, I took his blood and hair myself." He squatted to lean close to Sam's face, his uneven yellow teeth bared. "Because you failed to serve me."

Sam's head still swarmed with stars. "I serve no one."

"If you wish to redeem yourself, tell me where his obol is."

"No," Sam said. "I won't tell you."

"I wonder. What could I make with the blood of a god-slayer and prophesied queen?" The shapeshifter considered her. "I would like to experiment. I would like to know. What could I do with your heart? What is your potential?"

Sam saw the flash of the knife. And then she felt it.

"No," she wheezed. The pain was searing, a fire made of glass shards and *tannîyn* talons. Her hands went to her stomach, where she was bleeding. It was just like Rima's recurring nightmare, the one where Sam was leaving to fight in a war instead of Dad. She wore a uniform that was too big for her. Her hands were covered in blood. It was warm and sticky.

"You die alone," the shapeshifter said. "For dishonoring our agreement. I will slice the throat of your sister next, but I will take her to Eshmun to heal, and he will give me the tears you owe me. And then I will take *all* of his blood and hair, every last drop, and every strand."

Sam felt herself separate, torn in half like a sheet of paper.

Her body below.

Her *ruḥā* hovering above.

She was dead.

23

Eshmun. Hurry.

There was a rift in the sky and she slid through it like a shadow. Ahead was a dark waterfall, a thin sheet of water, too black to see through. *I'm dead*, Sam thought. *So fast.* Behind her trailed a thin line of smoke still connecting her to the world of the living, to Eshmun and Rima.

Death was loud. There were so many voices, a hive, a constant buzzing.

Mom? Sam cried out. *Where are you?*

She touched the waterfall and it parted around her finger, which was now a black twig of bone. She gasped at the sight of her reflection in the spectral water, a skeleton draped with tendrils of shadows. A curtain hung upon a midnight window.

She had no breath to hold as she floated through the frigid waterfall and beyond. Behind her, the line of smoke remained. Voices flooded over her. *Mom! Is that you?*

It was like tuning Dad's old radio to his country station. Sam trained her attention back and forth, nudging it a fraction of an inch.

And then suddenly she was in a restaurant. A diner with red-checkered tablecloths. There was a glass case full of pies, and no one in the restaurant except for her mother.

Mom sat alone in a booth, twirling a spoon in her mug of coffee. At her feet, a brown dog panted happily. His name was Kibbee,

Mom's dog before she met Dad. Sam knew all this, even though Mom had never told her.

Mom. It's me. It's Sam.

Sam. Sam! Her mother leaped up from the booth and hugged her. *I have been looking everywhere for you! Where have you been?* She pulled back and screamed. *You're dead! Look at you... you're...* She backed away, horrified, and then turned and ran through the doors and out into the street.

Wait! Sam followed. Outside was New York City. Or maybe it was Paris. There were huge buildings with massive carved columns. Buses and taxis lined the curbs. The air smelled like smog. *Stop!* she cried, catching up with Mom and taking her by the arm.

No, no, no. I need to wake up from this dream. Which way gets me out? Mom's eyes went to a subway entrance ahead and she ran toward it, but Sam blocked her way.

Please, Mom! I need your help! Sam clasped her dark hands together. *If it's too hard to look at me, just close your eyes and listen.*

No. Let me wake up. Mom was intent on getting to the subway entrance. Sam stayed ahead of her.

Listen to me. Do you have a coin somewhere? A magic coin?

Suddenly, all around them, the streets disappeared and the buses changed into elephants. Above, a man walked on a high wire, and Mom had popcorn in her hand. A clown walked past holding a bouquet of giant white balloons, floating like bubbles through the air.

Mom! Listen to me. You have to go touch the coin. The coin from Lebanon. Do you have one? One that's special? Maybe it's hidden somewhere with your tarot cards and crystals. In that special box you keep hidden in the closet. The locked box with the gold bracelets and the wishbones inside. Mom!

Mom turned. Held out her hand and unfurled her fingers. In her palm was a square piece of fabric. Black silk. She unfolded it and a coin sat in the middle. *This one,* she said, not a question.

Yes! That's the one. I need you to wake up and go get it. Go touch it. When you're awake. I know you might be afraid of it, but it will bring Rima home. She can come home if you touch it. Do you understand? I'm sending you a sign. This is your sign, Mom.

Mom looked at her, searching her face where her eyes should have been. Sam knew she would only see pits of nothingness. *You said it will bring Rima home. What about you?*

Sam looked over her shoulder at the black thread that was still connecting her to life. It was so thin. Unraveling, fading.

She sobbed, making a horrible rattling noise, December ice cracking the surface of a lake. It was too late. Eshmun hadn't found her yet. She couldn't go back to him, either. There was no way to retrace her steps to the living. No compass would work, no map would guide her. She was nowhere and never. A threshold had been crossed. A boundary. She was in her mother's dreams.

Behind Mom, an acrobat flipped through the air. A child squealed with delight.

Mom repeated her question, more urgently: *You said the coin will bring Rima home. What about you?*

She wanted to hug her mother but knew it would only terrify her to be embraced by death. Instead she wrapped her brittle arms around herself: the empty cage she'd become.

I'll come to you in your dreams again, okay? I'll see you here again at the circus, the diner, or wherever you want. Soon.

Mom nodded. Tears streamed down her cheeks, and Sam ached to brush them away.

Goodbye, Mom. I love you. Please. Save Rima. I love you. Goodbye.

24

S am pressed her fingers into the waterfall. She could go back to the underworld as a *ruḥā*. Or she could stay here on this side and haunt her old life. She could go to prom, if it hadn't already passed. Instead of wearing that new dress Mom had promised with her casino winnings, she would wear her shredded garment of death. She'd float across Glen Lake, watching the fish dart below the turquoise surface, and she'd lie in Mom's bed to sleep next to her at night.

Maybe she could even find Dad. She turned toward the chorus of voices again, trying to sort through them for his. Was he here somewhere? If she called his name, would he hear her?

And then a voice asked: *Sam? Is that you?*

No. Another *ruḥā* floated toward her. *No! What are you doing here? You're dead! You cannot be dead!*

Sam hugged it tight, the two of them clacking against each other like broken wind chimes. It was Rima.

I came to rescue you, you idiot. Eshmun's going to pull me back to life, and you're coming with me.

It's too late for me. I've been dead too long.

Shut up. I'm not letting you stay here. Hold on to me. We have to try.

Sam nodded. She gripped her sister's ghost and pressed her head against her cold, sharp spine. The cord of black that tethered Rima to her body—to life—tightened and pulled.

Do not let go of me.

I never have.

The icy waterfall clattered like a curtain of teeth as they passed through it, and then the wind cut straight through her, whistling, like a sail full of holes.

And as suddenly as Sam had found herself at the circus with Mom, she was back at Eshmun's castle by the sea.

Below her lay her body in a puddle of blood. It spread around her, soaking Rima's dress. They were dead, side by side, but she could see that she was still linked to her body by a single, wavering thread, like the last strand of a spider's web.

From above she watched as Eshmun knelt between their bodies, a hand on each. Her gold-and-emerald ring shone like a watchful eye. She could hear him mumbling and chanting his incantations—

—and then Sam felt life pushing its way into her again.

First it was a slight movement, like flower petals unfolding. And then an entire universe winked inside her and the stardust swirled into a wave, carrying her back to her body. There was the pain of the knife wound, and the warmth of Eshmun's hand. Prisms of light flashed. Her head ached with a rushing pulse. She opened her eyes and looked up at the indigo sky and then Eshmun's worried face.

He cupped her head in his hands. "I thought it was too late," he said gently.

She smiled weakly. "But you didn't lose hope." Her voice was hoarse, as if she'd been screaming the entire time she was on the other side.

"As you told me," Eshmun said, "one must try whatever is possible."

Thick tears streamed down his cheeks and into his beard. She reached up and gathered the drops on her cursed fingertips and put them into her mouth, tasting the salt and honey. But the *ruḥā* stains

were still as black as tar. Persistent, patient. Death was waiting for her, still so near.

"I don't want to die again," she said. She sat up and looked at Eshmun. "I don't want to go back to that place."

"You will not," Eshmun said. He pressed a jar against his face as he continued healing Rima, who moaned and gasped for breath. The glass lip hugged his cheekbone and his tears ran into it, filling it to the top. Sam watched Rima's chest rise and fall more and more evenly, the blue in her lips and the gray in her cheeks fading. Sam held her hand, whispering Rima's name until she finally opened her eyes and blinked up at her.

"We made it," Sam breathed. "You got us back."

Eshmun stood and set the jar of tears on the stone railing. "Leave it," he said. "I am creating an elixir for your hand. I need to gather silphium, bedolach, myrrh, herbs, and bird bones, among other things. I will return as quickly as possible." He hurried through the center of the fortress, and Sam watched him cross the arched stone bridge.

She squeezed Rima's hand. "You okay?" she asked.

"Would you stop asking me that?" Rima replied. She motioned to her bloody dress. "Of course I'm not okay. We were just dead." She sat up and rubbed her neck. "Stupid caramel-flavored cream cheese."

Sam's mouth was dry. Her head still throbbed. "What happened to you?" she asked. "Did you get stabbed, too?"

"No, not stabbed." Rima squinted like she was trying to see something in the distance. She swallowed. "I woke up because I heard something, a scuffle, maybe a scream. So I came out onto the patio, and I found you." Her voice broke. "You were bleeding like crazy. I completely freaked out, and then out of nowhere this gray lady had me in a choke hold."

"Zayin," Sam said. "Actually, probably not. The shapeshifter."

"Regardless, psycho," Rima said. "Eshmun scared her off. Or him?"

"I'm not sure. He can take on any form, I think. So he killed you?"

"No, I stuck my hand in the snake pit," Rima said, "so I could go get you. Eshmun had poison for me to drink, but I was afraid it would take too long." She nodded to a green vial on the railing. It sat next to Eshmun's jar of newly collected tears.

"The snakes," Sam said, wide-eyed. "You let them bite you." She glanced over at the pit, her stomach churning at the thought: their venomous, sharp fangs sinking into Rima's hand.

"I didn't think about it. You would have done it for me." Rima looked into Sam's eyes. "So what was it like? On the flip side. You were back there a while."

"I saw Mom," Sam said. "I tried to get her a message."

She explained the obol Mom might have, and how she'd told her to touch it. How they had to hope that Mom remembered her dream, and that she would act on it. Sam flexed her hand; it was starting to go numb.

"It looks worse," Rima said, standing and then helping Sam to her feet.

Sam nodded. The skin on her hand was drying out. It was cracking.

"You need to drink those tears," Rima said, just as there was a whoosh of air above them. A flash of wings.

Sam's heart slammed with panic. Another *tannîyn* had come for them.

No. It was Zayin—or the shapeshifter—on her hawk, swooping over their heads.

The hawk landed, its talons clattering against the stone. Zayin slid off and stalked toward Sam and Rima. She held her knife, still

stained with blood. Her hands were gloved. "Give me that fresh vial of tears," she demanded. The hawk cocked its head, angling its pointed beak.

Sam and Rima stepped backward until they were trapped against the railing. The vial of poison and the jar of tears sat just behind them. Zayin snarled and pointed the knife toward them.

"Take it!" Sam said suddenly, yanking Rima sideways. She reached behind her. "Just take the tears and go!" she cried, thrusting the green vial at Zayin.

Zayin grinned and licked her lips before snatching the vial away from Sam. She was tipping it back toward her open mouth when a voice cried out.

"Fool! It is poison!"

It was Zayin. Another Zayin. This one was dressed the same as the one Sam had met in the mountains. Thigh-high leather boots, and a necklace made of teeth. "Ah, and here we have the spy from Gadir, the messenger from Ugarit." Her kohl-blackened eyes turned and swept over Sam, coming to rest on her new ring. "Pretty bauble," she said. Her bare hands were flawlessly young.

"Hello again," Sam said.

The shapeshifter lowered the vial of poison. "Thank you for the warning," she cooed.

But the real Zayin drew closer to her mirror image with a fast, purposeful stride. Before Sam could understand what was happening, she pulled a dagger from her belt and leaped onto the shapeshifter, stabbing her in the chest and twisting. She pulled out the bloody blade with a grunt.

The shapeshifter wheezed and pressed her hands to her wound as she slumped to the ground. Her face twisted into a grimace. She coughed, spraying blood across the patio. And then she morphed. She

was Mom dying, her lush hair spilling across the stone patio like a silken scarf. Dad dying, his flannel shirt soaked with blood. "Sam," he said, reaching out for her. "Don't let me go. You wouldn't do that to your old man, would you?" Rima dying. Her long legs thrashed uselessly. And then Eshmun. Dead. His face as pale as a tombstone.

"Stop it!" Sam cried.

Slowly, the shapeshifter's gray skin darkened and wrinkled. He shrank and shriveled into the shape of an old man, paper-thin flesh hanging from his bones. His eyes were sunken, his head too small for his bony shoulders. Finally, the gnarled hands matched the rest of the body.

"How dare you impersonate me," Zayin said to the shapeshifter, kicking his face with the crack of a breaking nose. "And my master, Melqart. To think I shared my bed with you, you foul demon!"

The shapeshifter's blood ran across the stone patio, pooling black. "Have mercy," the Alchemist croaked. "I cannot grow old and die. I will not allow it. I will not be forgotten. I am the next ruler of the underworld. I have been waiting for the death of Môt..." He paused to cough again, blood burbling across his lips. "Have mercy....Give me...tears..."

"Mercy?" Zayin laughed. "After you put your lizard tongue in my mouth? After you stole my hawk? My beautiful face? I shall tie you to a post in Baalbek and let the vultures eat you."

She tipped her chin toward Sam and Rima, batting her long eyelashes. "Do give Eshmun my regards."

With that she took the fresh vial of tears from the railing, heaved the bleeding shapeshifter onto the hawk, and then mounted it as well. Its wings beat the air with a *whump-whump*. As they lifted away, a feather swirled to the ground, and Sam reached down to pick it up.

Instead she gasped and stumbled backward.

Rima grabbed her by the wrist. "What the hell?" she cried.

Sam wrenched her arm away. The *ruḥā* stain had suddenly crept past her elbow. The black lines were like lightning bolts, zigzags of cracking ice. Sam looked at her sister; she could feel tears stinging her eyes. "It's moving faster. I think it's in my veins."

"We shouldn't have let Zayin take those tears!" Rima said. "You need them!"

Sam felt the patio tip sideways underneath her. "I'm dizzy. I need to lie down."

Rima draped Sam's arm across her shoulder and helped her back to the bedroom where Rima had slept earlier. "Where is Eshmun?" Rima asked, tucking Sam under the fur blankets.

"I am here," he said, rushing into the room. His eyes widened when he saw Sam's arm. *"Wāy,"* he whispered.

"You can fix it, right?" Rima asked. Sam flinched at the sound of Rima's voice, high and desperate. "You can make it go away."

"We cannot let it reach her heart." Eshmun sat on the edge of the bed and pressed a wooden goblet to Sam's lips. She choked down the liquid, which was thick and tasted metallic. "Where are the tears?" he asked.

"Zayin took them," Rima said.

He growled as he opened a jar and a smell wafted through the room. Mint and alcohol. It was a gritty lotion, and he rubbed it into Sam's arm, pressing deeply with his thumbs. *"L-kun w-netiheb ǰal,"* he murmured.

"Does it hurt?" Rima asked.

"No," Sam said. She looked at Rima. "Did you know that birds have hollow bones? That's what it feels like. Hollow." The room was foggy. She felt like clouds were rising up from underneath her. They would carry her off. "I'm a bird. I could fly away."

Sam saw Rima give Eshmun a hard look, and then she raked her own fingernails down her arm, drawing blood. Eshmun nodded. He put his hands on Rima's scrapes and tilted his head to let the tears fall into Sam's mouth.

But the blackness did not fade or recede. Sam's heart pounded out a slow beat, counting time, the moments she had left. The *ruḥā*'s touch would reach her heart and then death would be pumped throughout her body, reaching every vein and vessel. She would turn to ash.

"It doesn't hurt," Sam told Rima again.

"Eshmun, I'm going to stab myself," Rima said. "We need a bigger wound for you to heal. More tears. Give me a knife."

"No," Eshmun said. "If you die, I cannot bring you back a second time. I have had my turn. Death will take his."

"It's not so bad," Sam said. "It's not terrible."

"No!" Rima sobbed. "You can't leave me!"

"You have Helena. That's her there," Sam said, lifting her good hand and pointing to a woman who was walking into the room. "That's Jiddo's mother. I told you about her. Our great-great grandmother."

"This must be the sister Samira so valiantly fought to find," Helena said. She turned to Sam with a sad smile. "My sweet Samira," she said, sitting next to her on the bed. "What has happened to you?"

"I didn't know when...to let go," Sam said. Her voice rattled. It was getting hard to breathe. "I...I held on too long."

"Keep holding on," Helena said. She made a fist. "Fight it."

"Where is...Sbartā?" Sam asked. "Is she coming?"

"She is on her way," Helena said, nodding.

What if Mom forgot her dream? What if she'd been drinking, and her memory had been too blurred to keep Sam's message safe? But then again, this was *Mom*. Believer in ghosts and cosmic energy, crystals and horoscopes. She would cling to any sign the universe gave her.

"I want to go outside," Sam wheezed. "I want to see the sky."

Eshmun nodded. He carried her to the patio and kept his hands on her, chanting and cursing, trying a hundred prayers. The blackness crept on: Sam looked down at her chest and saw its inky fingers reaching, invading. She closed her eyes and remembered what the attendant in Môt's dungeons had told her:

You are cursed.

She gripped Rima's hand. "I want you to scatter my ashes over the sea," she said. "That's probably..." Her voice failed her. She could hardly breathe. "Probably where Dad is. At the bottom..."

"Shut up," Rima said, sobbing. She pressed her wet cheek against Sam's. "Just shut up."

Beyond Rima, Sam could see through the center of the castle. Sbartā was running across the bridge. She was screaming. "It calls to me! It summons me!"

"There!" Helena suddenly said, pointing skyward.

Sam turned her head to look. A low, circular cloud moved toward them. "Is it?" she asked.

"Yes!" Rima said, tugging on her arm. "Come on, Sam, stand up. Stand up! You have to rally one last time. We'll get you home. We'll get you to a hospital."

"Your mother heard your wish," Helena cried. "She heard you, *einee!*"

"Come," Sam said, her voice hardly a whisper. She drew in another shallow breath. "With us."

"No," Helena said with a kind smile. "This is my home, here in Sidon." She hooked an arm underneath Sam and helped lift her. "I will be staying."

Sam nodded. *I understand.*

"May you have a safe journey home," Helena said. "I am so happy

to have met both of you, the daughters of the granddaughter of my son." She kissed Sam's forehead and then Rima's. "I will never forget you."

"Go on," Rima said to Sam. "Kiss your prince goodbye. Hurry."

Sam folded herself into Eshmun's arms. "Thank...you," she breathed, looking up at him, his keyhole pupil ablaze. She put her hand on his chest, over his heart. He rubbed a finger across the emerald-and-gold ring she still wore.

"No matter how long...you will lead them...to *šmayyà*," she wheezed. "You are the door...the gate...the *tarʾā*."

"Stay with me," he said. "Marry me."

Sam searched his face. "Can't," she said.

And I can't bring my father back, and I can't save my mother from herself. And you shouldn't leave this world, not yet. She looked over her shoulder at Rima. *It's time to go home.*

Eshmun pulled Sam tight against him, and for a moment she was afraid he wouldn't let her go. He stroked her jaw with his thumb, kissed her lightly on the cheek, and then allowed her to pull away. She nodded at him.

And as she stepped toward the funnel with Rima, she raised her blackened hand and managed to whisper, "Goodbye. Goodbye."

EPILOGUE

The bells on the bait shop door jingled as Sam stepped through. She felt the stares of a few customers, but most of all, it was Chase at the cash register. "Hey," he said, dropping a stack of receipts and coming around the counter. For a second she thought he was going to hug her. "You're back," he said. His green eyes were bright.

"Yeah," Sam said. "I'm back."

"And you're okay," he said.

"Yeah," she said. "I'm okay."

He was the one who occasionally gave her supplies for free, though she always paid him back. The owner probably never knew. For all the favors he'd done for her, they'd never exchanged more than a few words. She knew he was a year older, taking college classes online. Once or twice she'd seen him out on the lake, fishing.

"The aliens released you," he said.

"Huh?"

"That was one of the rumors going around town." He pushed the hair out of his face. It was longer than she remembered, blonder. Maybe the summer sun was making it lighter. "You were aboard the mother ship."

She laughed. "That's not what people thought," she said.

"Yeah," he said. "I swear." He pulled in a breath. "People ... well, *I*

thought . . . the worst. Everyone was worried." He cleared his throat. "I was really worried. So . . . where were you?"

"Um," she fumbled.

She reached inside her shirt and thumbed her new pendant. The sun, *Jemʃā*. It was $59.99 at a nice jewelry store at the mall, worth every penny. *The ancients say the only cure is the sun*, the women in Môt's dungeons had told her. And when the funnel pulled her up and into her backyard, the heat of high noon had kissed her. The sunlight poured into her. Her skin drank the light. She opened her mouth and swallowed it. She breathed it in, and the stains of death faded from her chest, her arm, and then finally down to the last of her fingertips.

Sam pointed to the sign behind Chase's head. "I need a cup of worms and some ice for my cooler."

"Sure, yeah," he said. "Sorry. It's none of my business."

Sam had an official story, but she didn't like telling it: She and Rima decided to do a cross-country fishing trip that Sam and Dad had once planned. They'd shown the cops a map with bright orange star stickers marking each of the destinations. They didn't tell Mom anything about the trip because they knew she'd say no. They'd stolen the cash from her casino winnings. They'd taken buses and rideshares, and then walked the rest of the way to Bull Shoals Lake, where they fished and camped. And then they got on a bus toward Florida when they realized they were running out of money. They'd gotten off and turned around and taken a bus home. Sam had looked up Greyhound routes and schedules, and some campsites on the internet to make their story sound true. She said they didn't sleep well along the way. They shouldn't have gone. It was a bad idea and they were very sorry. No one believed them, she could tell. But they were home and not dead, so their lies were good enough for the necessary paperwork.

"So how about some cherry pie?" Chase asked.

"What?" Sam asked.

"I mean...," Chase said. "I, uh, I promised myself that if I ever saw you again I wouldn't chicken out." He paused. "So." He took a deep breath. "Do you like cherry pie?"

"Of course," Sam said. "It's required if you live here, right?"

"The tree in our backyard is loaded with them right now. A little early this year. Cherries." He ran a hand through his hair again, brushing it away from his face. "So, is that a yes or a no?"

"Wait. Are you asking me out?" Sam asked.

"Yeah," he said. "Will you have pie with me?" He shook his head. "This all sounded so much smoother in my head."

Sam smiled. "I'll have pie with you."

"Yeah? Okay?" he asked, grinning. He put a hand to his chest. "Okay. Um... Tonight?"

"Sorry, I can't. I'm meeting my sister for ice cream," she said. "We've kind of been obsessively craving Dairy Queen lately. I promised her."

"Tomorrow?" he asked, undeterred.

"She's got a soccer game," she said. His face clouded, so she hurriedly added, "But I'm free Saturday."

"Awesome!" he said. He cleared his throat, adjusted his voice back to a normal volume. Tossed a shoulder up with a nonchalant shrug. "Okay, yeah. I can do that. Pie."

Sam stifled a laugh. He was adorable. Why hadn't she noticed before?

"So... I'm gonna go fishing now," Sam said, hooking a thumb over her shoulder toward the lake. "I'll catch up with you in a couple hours. Will you still be here?"

"I'll wait for you."

On the boat, out on the lake, she thought of Eshmun. Her

gold-and-emerald ring was home, safely hidden. She would probably keep it, no matter how much it might be worth if she sold it. He still felt close, so nearby, like she could reach through a crease in the sky and find him. She wanted to tell him. Late at night in her bunk bed, staring up at the mattress where Rima slept, she'd seen it, imagined it.

She understood now. She knew where the gateway was.

The prophecy of the sun. The key Helena had mentioned, the key that would unlock paradise for all the trapped souls in the underworld. It was to be made of Chusor's gold, but not a gram of it existed in the underworld.

Not until now. Because Eshmun's obol was made of it.

His obol *was* the key.

All he had to do was take it to the blacksmith in Sarepta, to Mhaymnā, who had divine blood and could turn a ring into a necklace over a fire. He could certainly turn an obol into a golden key. The key would be melded to the tip of *Rugzā*, and it would go into Eshmun's keyhole pupil.

It had to.

There had been so many little signs. She could see them now, fitting together like puzzle pieces. The knife sliding into the *tannîyn's* eye, the way it seemed to fit, like it was meant to be there. The animal urge she'd had to stab Eshmun through his pupil while he slept in the mountains. Even the letter from Jiddo. He'd written the Arabic word *einee,* my eyes. Eshmun had been looking for a door, when he was the door himself.

But what was Sam supposed to do? Spend months or years or a lifetime searching through museums or caves in Lebanon until she found another Phoenician obol so she could go back? Sbartā had claimed hers from Mom, and there weren't any more in her collection of charms and coins. Sam had looked.

No. She shook her head at herself. Saving the underworld was *not* her job, and the plan was in place. *Her* plan, for herself. She would stick around another two years until Rima graduated high school. She would save money and take business classes. Then she and Rima would move together, somewhere sunny where her fishing venture could run all year long. Clear Lake in California looked good.

The future was hers. There was no looking back. Though the conversation she'd had with Mom hadn't been easy.

"I've sort of realized. Other people will make you feel like you're supposed to *be* something or *do* something," Sam told Mom. They were in the backyard again, working on the garden. "But I don't want to stay here. It's not my..." She'd faltered. She wanted to say *It's not my responsibility to take care of you anymore. It never really was.* But she was afraid of hurting Mom's feelings. "It's not my dream," she said. "I need to think about what I want from life."

Mom had wiped a tear from Sam's face, sending a streak of gardening dirt across her skin. She smiled. "I'm proud of you," she'd said as she hugged Sam close.

The promise she'd made her father had been too big.

And so was the burden of saving the underworld. It didn't rest on her shoulders, either. It wasn't her quest; it was Eshmun's, and his alone. She didn't owe him anything, she reminded herself. She was right to leave. She would have died there in his arms.

And yet, she would never forget him. She never wanted to. Whenever the sun warmed her cheeks, she could almost imagine his laugh or his healing hands. Whenever she felt hope, she could hear his voice, calling her name.

Sam paddled toward the center of the lake, thrusting herself forward. Out in the fresh air with the sun shining above, she threaded a worm through her hook and tossed her line into the water. She thought

about her date with Chase and cherry pie served with fresh whipped cream.

It was hard to tell from this distance, but she could see something standing on the opposite shoreline. Her heart pounded a little faster. From where Sam sat, it looked like a rat.

A big one—glossy and black—standing on its hind legs. She paddled closer until she could see that its eyes were flat and dead. It gnawed on its nails as it stared directly at Sam as if to say *I see you.*

AUTHOR'S NOTE
❖❖❖

Growing up, every Sunday, we went to my grandparents' house for dinner. It was a standing invitation, an expectation. A usual gathering meant about twenty of us, a small group by Lebanese standards. My grandfather was one of ten; my grandmother was one of thirteen. All told, my father had seventy-four first cousins. Some still lived in Lebanon, others had emigrated to Australia, while many were near enough to make our gatherings swell to fifty, a hundred, or more. (There were six hundred guests at a recent family wedding, where we danced the *dabke* and feasted on twenty-five hundred grape leaves, which our family hand-rolled.)

I grew up watching my grandfather play *shesh-besh*, learning how to pinch dough around dumplings for *shish-barak* with yogurt broth, and listening to Arabic (a familiar song to my ears, and yet regrettably, I've learned very little). Over the dinner table, stories were often shared about "the old country":

How my grandfather hurled stones at wolves or jackals when they came too close to the flocks of goats and sheep.

How a few village girls went to the mountain spring for water too early one morning, before daybreak, only to be greeted by a pack of hyenas. They scared them off by sparking stones together, or so the story goes.

How locusts left a swath of dead trees and crops.

And perhaps the most heartbreaking…how my grandfather backtracked home in the dead of night so he could tuck in his younger siblings one last time before setting off for America. On his way out of the house, he scooped a layer of fresh *labneh* from a pot on the stove, to leave a sign that he had been there. A final goodbye.

The stash of coins is based on a real collection my great-grandfather Assad found in his mountain village, Karm El Mohr, in about the year 1954. The coins may have been in a cave, but others say they were unearthed while someone was digging in a garden, and yet another version claims the coins were discovered when the family was building the foundation for a home. All three of these versions might be true; the coin collection may have accumulated over a period of time, and not all at once. My brother, who extensively researched the collection, speculates that the coins were buried about AD 260 by Roman soldiers or traders. There might have been an urn at one time. The coins were said to have been divided among whoever was present when the urn finally came out of the ground nearly two thousand years later. We still have what eventually became my grandfather's portion. Of those fourteen coins, all are Roman except for the oldest, which was minted approximately between 121 BCE and 96 BCE, which my brother finally, painstakingly identified as Greek. But since it remained a mystery for the longest time...I, of course, imagined it was a magical Phoenician coin.

My father loved to talk about Middle Eastern politics, history, and the Phoenicians. After he passed away in 2008, I inherited one of his books, *Peoples of the Past: The Phoenicians* by Glenn Markoe, which I have now read from cover to cover, more than once. The Phoenician civilization existed from approximately 3200 BCE until 332 BCE, when Alexander the Great conquered the city of Tyre and the region fell to the Greeks.

The Phoenicians were famous for their purple dye, their mastery of the sea, and their trade in majestic cedar trees. Ironically, even though the Phoenicians are generally given credit as the inventors of the modern alphabet, nearly none of their literary records survived the ravages of war, weather, and time. The inscription in chapter

eleven, one of the precious few examples we have of Phoenician script, was taken from an Egyptian-made sarcophagus of Eshmunazar II. Unearthed in 1855 near Sidon, it is now on display at the Louvre.

Historians and archaeologists have surmised that the Phoenicians lived in independent city-states, and for each, there was a god or goddess. Ba'alat Gebal's name means "Lady of Byblos." Eshmun, the god of healing, was associated with Sidon. Melqart was the god of the island city Tyre. Chusor was a craftsman god, Ba'al Hammon was the god of plants and agriculture, Ba'al Saphon was a storm god, Ba'al Shamem was the lord of the heavens, Ēl was the supreme deity and father of all gods, and, last but not least, Môt was the god of death.

I did my best to stay true to the materials the Phoenicians would have used; the food and animals they might have had; and the scope of their region, which is modern-day Lebanon with some exceptions, such as Cyprus and Carthage, and other far-flung trading colonies. I drew from many sources of inspiration, including the story of Prince Cadmus, who planted dragon teeth. The quest through Marid's cave was written after learning about the Jeita Grotto, which is a breathtaking labyrinth of underground caves and water; archaeologists believe it was the location of an ancient foundry where swords were made. Despite the countless hours of research I did, there are undoubtedly details that an expert might question. I also took some liberties with Lebanese geography and topography, so if you plan on walking from Baalbek to Sidon, or sailing from Sidon to Cyprus, please don't use my book as your map.

The Phoenician language in this novel is one I invented for my characters. It's an uneven mash-up of Classical Syriac, Ancient Ugaritic, Aramaic, and a little Arabic thrown in for good measure. If you are an expert in ancient Middle Eastern languages, you have my sincerest apologies.

Helena is based on a real person (by the same name) who was a friend of my grandparents. She was abducted from her Lebanese mountain village (then Syria and a part of the Ottoman Empire). Even though she was already married, Helena was forced to wed her captor, and she had two children by him. One day she saw the opportunity to escape and did so, leaving her children behind. She made her way, despite hyenas, wolves, and difficult terrain, back to her native village. Once home, she found that a friend was about to leave for the United States, and he was able to smuggle her as a stowaway. When Helena's abductor came looking for her, the villagers accused the man of a ruse, saying he must have killed her. Finally, after years apart, she was happily reunited with her first husband, who had come earlier to the United States. Helena grieved her whole life for the two children she had left behind.

FOOD FROM THE BOOK

✦✦✦

These recipes represent over a hundred years of Bishara family history. Generations of Bishara women have cooked the cuisine of Lebanon and passed on their traditions, customs, and recipes. Each recipe is taken from the family cookbook.

BAKLAVA

2 lb fillo (strudel) leaves

2 lb butter (half can be margarine)

4 cups ground walnuts

1 cup sugar

Syrup (Attar):

Makes enough for 3 pans of baklava

5 lb sugar

7 cups water

Juice of 1 lemon

Directions

Make the syrup by boiling the sugar and water over low heat for about 1 hour or until candy thermometer reads 220°. Then add the lemon juice and let cool thoroughly before using.

Render (clarify) the butter and keep warm but not hot. Discard the solids. Brush the clarified butter generously in a cookie pan with sides, 18 ½ to 19 inch x 15 inch x 1 ¾ inch deep. Lay a leaf of dough on the pan and brush a taplespoon of butter as evenly as possible over the dough. Continue in this manner until there are 25 layers of buttered dough. Keep the dough from drying out while you work with it by

covering the unused leaves with a damp dish towel and by working as quickly as possible.

Combine the ground nuts and sugar and spread evenly over the top of the 25 layers. Gently press down the nut mixture to compact it a bit. Then place a leaf over the nut mixture, butter it, and continue with layers until there are 20 buttered layers. Cut into diamond shapes with a sharp knife. Put more clarified butter in the areas that look dry, like around the edges of the pan. Cover with aluminum foil and bake in a preheated oven at 325° for about 45 minutes. Then uncover and bake another 15 minutes or until golden brown. Gently lift up a corner to make sure the bottom crust is lightly browned. Remove from the oven and cool. Then drizzle 3 cups of the syrup over the baklava. Later, if the baklava is still a little dry, add more syrup. Leftover syrup can be stored in a jar for several months. To serve, cut through the baklava diamonds in the pan and place each one in paper pastry cups.

KHUBZ (LEBANESE PITA BREAD)

12 cups flour

2 tbsp. salt

2 tbsp. sugar

4 cups warm water

⅔ cup milk

2 tbsp. oil

2 env. dry yeast or ½ cake yeast

Directions

In a large plastic mixing bowl, make a well of the flour, salt, and sugar. Dissolve yeast in warm water; add milk and oil. Pour into well and mix well. Then knead until dough comes off hands and sides of bowl. Do not overknead or the dough will be tough. Form into a large ball

and make the traditional "sign of the cross" in the dough. Oil the top of the dough lightly and cover with clean plastic wrap and clean dish towels. Place in a warm area and let rise for approximately 2 hours.

When dough has risen, punch down and separate the dough evenly into 8 balls about the size of a large orange. Place on clean tablecloth on the table and cover again with clean dish towels and plastic wrap to rest for about ½ hour to 45 minutes. Then pat down a ball of dough, using a rolling pin to roll out evenly and form a flat, even circle about 10 inches in diameter. Place back on the tablecloth and cover while you roll out the remaining dough balls.

Preheat the oven to 450° and bake on the middle rack, 1 loaf at a time. Lightly brown 1 side. The bread will puff up like a pillow. Do not puncture. This is what makes the pocket. Do not brown too much. Turn over and brown the other side. When cold, place in plastic bag and freeze.

LEBANESE LAMB STEW

Serves 4–6

1 ½ lb lamb (leg of lamb), trimmed and cubed

4–5 medium potatoes

1 medium onion, chopped

2–3 cups water

1 tbp. salt

½ tsp. pepper

½ tsp. cumin

6 tbsp. butter (do not substitute margarine)

Directions

In a stainless steel pan (4–6 quart size), brown lamb meat (diced into ¾-inch pieces) in butter. Add onion to lamb meat while browning. Add peeled

and quartered potatoes to meat; add salt and spices. Cover with water and bring to a boil. Taste and adjust seasonings. Reduce to medium heat and cover. Cook approximately 10–15 minutes until potatoes are cooked. Enjoy with fresh Lebanese bread. Delicious on a cold winter day.

CUSA-IB-LABAN

Makes 20 cusas

Use small cusa about 6 inches long. (Small, smooth-skinned light green squash, similar to zucchini.) Wash, dry, and trim off end of stem. Hollow the cusa with a special tool used for this purpose. Can be bought at Middle Eastern specialty stores.

Stuffing mix:

2 cups long-grain rice, washed and drained

3 lb chopped lamb or lean ground beef (preferably lamb)

1 tbsp. salt

½ tsp. black pepper

½ tsp. cumin

½ tsp. garlic powder or 1 medium clove fresh garlic, chopped

Wash rice and squeeze out excess water; place in large mixing bowl. Add chopped meat, salt, pepper, cumin, and garlic. In a small saucepot, lightly brown ½ cup pine nuts in ¼ lb butter or margarine (stir often while browning to avoid burning pine nuts). Add butter and pine nuts to the rice, meat, and spices. Mix thoroughly. Add more seasoning if desired. Stuff each cusa to within ½ inch of lip. Cook in laban sauce.

Laban sauce:

2 qt. laban (plain yogurt)

3 tbsp. flour

1 egg, beaten

1 tbsp. salt

1 ½ qt. cold water

In a large 8-quart saucepot, mix laban, flour, egg, and salt. Beat well with electric beater until creamy. Add cold water and beat well. Place on stove to boil, stirring often. Mix will curdle if this is not done. When it boils, drop the stuffed cusas in and cook over low flame for at least 25 to 30 minutes. This is a favorite meal—well worth the effort—and serves 7 to 8.

LAHAM MISHWEE

Use leg of lamb which has been boned, trimmed of excess fat, and cubed into 1-inch to 1 ½-inch cubes. Do not use shank portion because it has too much muscle and gristle. Thread onto skewer (either stainless steel or bamboo skewers will do). Salt well and cook over hot charcoal or gas grill. Cook until medium or well done, according to taste.

Variations: Onion pieces, tomato, and quartered pieces of pepper may be used between meat for a very good flavor. Soften the pepper and onion before putting on skewer by pouring boiling water over or microwaving about 1 minute. They will not break if you soften.

LEBANESE STUFFED GRAPE LEAVES

1 cup rice

1 ½ lb lamb (leg of lamb), trimmed and chopped fine

(Lamb meat can be ground on large chopper, in grinder, or cut finely)

½ tsp. cumin (ground)

½ tsp. ground black pepper

½ cup pine nuts

½ cup butter or margarine

½ tsp. garlic powder

1 tsp. salt (to taste)

2 medium garlic cloves (chopped)

3–4 sprigs mint leaves

1 green onion

¼ cup lemon juice (or lemon juice from 2 lemons)

75 grape leaves (approx.)

Directions

Wash rice and squeeze out excess water; place in large mixing bowl. Add chopped meat, salt, pepper, cumin, and garlic powder. In a small saucepot, lightly brown the pine nuts in the butter or margarine (stir often while browning to avoid burning pine nuts) and add butter and pine nuts to the rice, meat, and spices. Mix thoroughly with your fingers.

Spread grape leaves flat with stem facing you and smooth side facing down. Place approximately 1 teaspoon mixture (more or less according to size of leaf) width-wise across widest part of grape leaf. Roll leaf away from you after firming mixture into a roll and tuck in each side of grape leaf and continue to roll. Squeeze rolled grape leaf gently to help firm the filling and distribute it evenly. Line a large 6-quart stainless steel pot with aluminum foil and layer rolled leaves in alternate directions for each layer to facilitate even cooking. Fill pot with rolled grape leaves, place whole green onions, mint leaves, and chopped garlic on top of leaves; cover with water and a heavy dinner plate. Bring to a boil and lower heat to medium and simmer for 20 minutes. Add lemon juice and cook for additional 15 minutes.

MY FAMILY IN PHOTOGRAPHS

✦✦✦

My great-grandfather, Assad, who unearthed an ancient coin collection in his village of Karm El Mohr, Lebanon

My great-grandfather, Assad

My great-uncle Bashir

My great-uncle Hanna
and his wife, Adra

My great-aunt Mamie (l.);
grandfather, Norman (c.);
and Hanna Jabbour (r.),
taken circa 1926

My great-uncle Hanna

My grandfather, Norman
Bishara (l.), with Hanna
Marroun, taken circa 1926

My cousin Georgette Dib; my great-uncle
Hanna; and my father, John Bishara

ACKNOWLEDGMENTS

✦✦✦

First of all, thank you, reader, for choosing this book. If you've come this far, you've followed Sam's epic journey to the very end. Years ago, when I started jotting down a few little story ideas, I had no idea where this labyrinth of a plotline—a hero's journey—would lead. But what I truly didn't expect was the depth of my own journey, which came from researching my Lebanese heritage. Like Samira and Rima, I'm half Lebanese, but it's a very big half. A treasure trove of precious memories and details of my family are nestled in the lines of this story. (My grandfather used to crack walnuts with his bare hands, like Teth, for example; and writing about the food brought back the intensely redolent aromas of my grandmother's kitchen.) I hope you enjoyed being immersed in this rich and beautiful world as much as I did.

My goodness.... I asked so many questions! Thank you to the legions of generous and wonderful people who patiently fielded them. To my family! Big hugs to every aunt and cousin who filled in details about our family's village in the Lebanon Mountains, the story of Helena, and our family's ancient coin collection. Thanks to my brother, Matthew Bishara, who was a captain in the U.S. Army and was twice deployed to Iraq, for helping me with the details of Sam's dad's military life. My brother also researched the coins, one of the original points of inspiration for this book. It took an intercontinental team of Assad's grandchildren and great-grandchildren to locate and reproduce his portrait photo shown above, which is hanging on the wall of a family home in the mountains of North Lebanon. Endless gratitude to Pierre Bechara, Mary Tannous, Violette Tannous, and George Tannous in Australia; Edy Bechara and Joseph Sukhun in Lebanon; and Chuck Bishara, Dolores Bishara, and Liz Yazbek Paris

in the United States. Even more thanks to my aunt, Dolores Bishara, for helping me hunt down additional old family photos, and for taking the prologue to Sister Madeleine Iskandar at the Antonine Village in Youngstown, Ohio, for her to read and check my Arabic. Also thanks to Lina Fraifer, Charbel Dib, Roula Saab, and Marsha Elias for their help with Arabic and/or answering questions about Lebanon. And thank you to my mother, Judy Bishara, a skilled genealogist and our official family historian, who is always happy to research the most obscure bits of information.

Did you read a draft of this story along the way? Thank you! Especially Trish Doller, who read the entire manuscript at least twice, and who's met me for many writing and brainstorming sessions (er, beers) over the years. Extra-enthusiastic hugs to Annie Gaughen, who generously dove in and sent margin notes (!), and who challenged me with a crucial question at one of our Florida beach writing retreats: "What's the worst thing that could happen to your main character?" I jokingly replied, "I could kill her." So—uh—I did. Also: Wendy Mills; Miranda Kenneally; Lorin Oberweger; Judy Bishara; and Karyn Fischer, who either read pages or patiently listened as I rambled on about character arcs, pacing, world-building, or plot threads. Sometimes the smallest nudge in the right direction was all I needed to keep going.

If anyone has read this story as many times as I have—which is to say, approximately a million—it's my literary agent, Minju Chang. I owe her as many thanks—a million, and then some. Her generous insights, thoughtful notes, gentle prodding, and intuitive suggestions along the way made every draft stronger. Thank you for sticking with this story. You told me early on, when I had maybe 15,000 words written, that you thought this story was "special."

Vial of Tears might literally not exist—it could still be a Word

document on my laptop—without my editor at Holiday House, Mora Couch. Thank you for believing in this story and world, seeing its potential when it was still rough, for your unflagging enthusiasm, and your vision, which is both eagle-eyed and expansive. I am so very lucky to have you in my corner. Also at Holiday House, my gratitude to designers Kerry Martin and Chelsea Hunter for their creative expertise. Thank you to Emily Mannon, Sara DiSalvo, and Michelle Montague, enthusiastic promoters in marketing and publicity; Della Farrell in editorial, who helped keep so many moving parts on track; and copy editor Barbara Perris, for her commitment to small but important details. And finally, a heartfelt thank you to Syd Mills, an artist with awe-inspiring and unbounded talent. Even the earliest comp of the cover made me gasp, and the final product...just...wow.

And finally, a shout-out to anyone and everyone who helped entertain, feed, or chauffer my children in order to help me score some extra writing time, including Kathy Igo, Patty Hadgkiss, Judy Bishara, and, of course, my super-husband extraordinaire, Terry Igo. Many thanks to my aunt and uncle Linda and Lloyd Yazbek and my uncle and aunt Chuck and Linda Bishara, for letting me use their beautiful, peaceful Florida condos for writing retreats.

It took a village to make this book.